For Humanity

William Dafoe

Canadian ISBN Agency

ISBN: 978-0-9918652-1-5

Cover design by Tamian Wood, www.BeyondDesignInternational.com

eBook conversion by eB Format, www.ebformat.com

Chapter 1 – Day 365

Fifty-one years old, but maybe I'm fifty-four! That's all part of the story. They say truth is stranger than fiction, maybe this was just a dream? I really don't think so, and if the Secretary General doesn't stop banging his gavel I may put it where the sun doesn't shine.

I guess the best place to start is at the beginning and how I became the lead character in a story that ended with the disappearance of a number of countries and the elimination of millions of people; bringing peace, health and prosperity to an entire planet – earth, not to mention that I became engaged in the middle of it all.

A little background is probably necessary, although I am sure you will find it will be quite boring. My career is in international sales and marketing, I had sold to governments, government institutions and industries in more than sixty countries. I had spent the better part of my thirty year working career on airplanes and in hotels. Most of my friends thought that my job was exciting, seeing all those foreign cities, I only wish! When your travel plans are a day or two in any one place, all the cities become a big blur. My life was one big line up. Line up to get on an airplane, line up to get off the plane, line up at the baggage carousel, line up to go through immigration and then customs, line-up to get a taxi, line up at the hotel reservation counter to check-in and then to the room, where I would try to figure out what time it was and how long it would take to get from my hotel to the customers I would be meeting. With a little luck they might speak some English, but in many cases I spoke through an interpreter, who, in many cases, seemed to translate a lot more or a lot less than what I said!

The important point, as far as the story goes, to all of this meaningless background information is that I had hundreds of government and business acquaintances all over the world. While many would use the word friends, I always considered them acquaintances rather than friends, when you are conducting business with someone; you always have to be on your guard and careful about what you say and how you act. I had made some friends, but in most cases those were people who had left the employment of their respective governments or businesses and we continued to stay in-touch, basically I had nothing to sell them anymore so I could be myself – whoever that was.

I hadn't been inside the United Nations complex in New York before all of this started and although I had sold products and services too many UN agencies, most of them based in Geneva, Switzerland, I found this to be an awesome facility and even though it is located within the boundaries of New York City, it's an international zone, with its own fire department, security force and post office. In operations it reminded me of the Vatican, a country within a country.

For those of you who have not seen the inside of the General Assembly meeting hall of the United Nations I will provide you with a brief description. Picture an amphitheater with a stage and rows of seats on an upward incline from the bottom of the stage. The primary difference between the General Assembly and a live theater is that the seats have been replaced with rows of tables and chairs.

Finally, silence in the room, the 1,800 plus delegates representing the 193 member nations of the UN had finally quieted down and come to order. This was a special and quite unusual meeting of the UN General Assembly, and only the second meeting that I was attending. Special because it was the meeting that culminated 365 days of diplomacy at its highest level and a lot of hard work by a small group of very dedicated individuals. Unique because it was called for 5:00 p.m. on December 31st and would continue for approximately twenty hours.

The Secretary General, Chitundu Owusu rose from his chair that looked much more like a throne and called the meeting to order and thanked the member nations for attending.

He then introduced the Right Honorable William Harmon, Prime Minister of Canada, a career politician and an excellent speaker. It was Canada that held the presidency of the 15 member nations of the UN

Security Council at this time.

It had been determined, by the members of the Security Council, many years ago that its leadership would rotate on a monthly basis and would be designated to a country rather than a specific individual. The designated country chooses who will represent them on the Security Council. In most cases the Ambassador to the United Nations, of the country that is chosen, is the individual that will represent the country in all affairs pertaining to the United Nations, however because of this crisis and what it would mean to humanity as we know it now, a few changes were made to the normal protocols and procedures. First and foremost, because of the overall impact of the circumstances surrounding this situation, the Security Council voted to temporarily suspend the standard monthly rotation, allowing Canada, who held the presidency when the Security Council was first made aware of the crisis, to hold the presidency until the situation was completely resolved and secondarily, the presidency was undertaken by the Prime Minister of Canada rather than Canada's Ambassador to the UN.

As Prime Minister Harmon stood up and walked towards the podium I thought about my own public speaking abilities which at best were relatively poor when faced with a large audience especially of the stature of the individuals here. My abilities as a salesman and speaker were much better attuned to meetings that where one-on-one or small groups of less than ten people. In those circumstances I felt confident that I could control my audience and deliver my message so that everyone was pulling in the same direction. But put me in front of hundreds of people in an auditorium or theater environment and I would talk to fast, fidget, sweat and feel extremely uncomfortable.

I looked out over the delegates, Presidents, Prime Ministers, Chancellors. Most of the world's leaders were in this room, most had their headphones on so that they could hear the speech in their native tongues. The UN headquarters employed a group of simultaneous translators so that all delegates, no matter what their language, would get a very accurate translation of the information being disseminated and although a few were talking amongst themselves most were glued to the Prime Minister as he walked confidently towards the podium.

Once at the podium Prime Minister Harmon slowly scanned the delegates from left to right, then he went through the lengthy salutation that started most speeches at the UN.

"This year has seen dramatic changes to our civilization; positive changes in our attitudes towards others; our hostilities and our compassions. Global militaries have been dramatically reduced, our humanitarian efforts dramatically increased. Thousands of miles of borders between countries are now unguarded. We are close to eradicating a number of diseases. Our planet is no longer under the threat of having a nuclear meltdown. We have an abundance of inexpensive electrical energy and the ability to forecast earthquakes and volcanic eruptions, potentially savings tens of thousands of lives.

"In a few hours, we will have a clean atmosphere, our oceans, lakes and rivers will be toxin free, our ozone layer will be thickened and we will see an end to all weapons of mass destruction.

"We are all aware that there is one man who is the key driving force behind these monumental changes to our global society; Mr. William Dafoe."

The Prime Minister, for the second time, had broken with protocol. Instead of returning the floor to the Secretary General who would then have introduced me, he skipped that step.

"Mr. Dafoe the podium is yours!"

As I stood up and walked towards the podium my mind wondered back to how I became the "chosen one" in the first place.

You should understand that I wasn't present during the initial UN Security Council meetings. The information on what happened at those meeting is strictly hearsay and I personally question how accurate it is. I relate it to you as some background information; take it for what it's worth, the details, if sometimes fuzzy or even nonsensical don't have any real effect on the outcome of the story.

The details will be made evident further along, but suffice to say that a message was received by five radio telescopes in different geographic locations around the globe at preciously the same instant. The substance of the message was that the entire population of earth was going to be annihilated by a faction called the Group of Inhabited Planets. The only hope of salvation was to send an emissary to meet with them and present a rebuttal to their reasoning and ultimate decision. The leaders of the five countries that had received the messages contacted each other and the other members of the Security Council and set up an emergency meeting for the next day. Time was of the essence, and even though many of the Security Council members were on vacation there was no time to wait for their official return.

The meeting took place via a conference call initiated by the

President of the Russian Federation, Viktor Masmekhov.

It's my understanding that during telephone calls, prior to the official meeting, many of the leaders of the countries making up the Security Council believed that the message must have originated from some terrestrial location and that it was nothing more than an elaborate prank or hoax. However, the President of the United States pointed out that the message was heard in the first language of anyone that listened to it. Apparently the fact that it was heard in the first language was found out only by accident when the message was first played to the President's cabinet. Three of the individuals on the President's cabinet did not have English as a first language. There was an individual with Spanish another with Italian and yet another with Navajo. The cabinet member that spoke Navajo as his first language remarked that he thought it was unbelievably strange that the message would be sent in the Navajo language. This immediately brought out statements that it was in English, Spanish and Italian. I can just imagine the bewilderment that occurred!

It was also difficult to explain, if indeed it was a prank, how had the message had been delivered precisely at the same instant to different parts of the world. Even a satellite broadcast would have shown small micro or nanosecond delays.

Once the members of the Security Council had agreed to take the message seriously, although some still had severe reservations as to its authenticity, the problem of choosing an individual to meet with the Group of Inhabited Plants became the next major hurdle that the group had to overcome.

Apparently the discussions over who to send were quite heated and it was finally decided that each country would produce a list of ten people that they felt would be able to represent earth and defend its long term existence. The group also agreed that human nature would have each member country create a list of ten people that were from their country, which would mean that they would be no closer to agreeing on an emissary. In order to avoid this hurdle, it was agreed that only three people could be from the country creating the list. It was hoped that by forcing the countries to suggest individuals that were from different countries a name may appear that was at least acceptable to more than one country and would be a starting point for the selection process.

Each country was given a maximum of eight hours to prepare the list, if they could generate the list quicker, than all the better. It was also agreed that the message would not be released to the public nor would it be released to any of the other members of the United Nations. Any scientists or other individuals given access to the message would be sequestered from the news media and public in general, and they would be sworn to keep the information highly confidential to the point of "Secret". Any individual who released the information would be charged with treason.

I can only assume that each Leader went into meetings with their colleagues in order to develop a list of ten candidates. Everyone then emailed or faxed their list to each of the other members.

I have never seen the original lists or copies of them, but I was told that of the fifteen lists that were circulated all but one country had placed their head of foreign affairs or secretary of state as the first name on the list. But more importantly, I guess, my name appeared on lists created by three of the permanent members; Russian Federation, United States and United Kingdom. Apparently the fact that I was acceptable to the Russian Federation and the United States was significant even at this early stage.

For those of you who may not be aware of the inner workings of the United Nations' Security Council, I will give you a brief overview. The Security Council is made up of five permanent nations that include; the People's Republic of China, France, Russian Federation, United Kingdom and United States, and ten non-permanent members who are chosen from UN member countries and become part of the Security Council for a period of two years.

It was then decided that the countries would take one hour to look at each other's lists and determine from the names that others had chosen if they would like to change or modify their selection. Five names were held in play, as they said, in other words five names could not be changed, mine was one of them.

When the new lists were created and exchanged amongst the members of the Security Council, my name now appeared on six of the lists and one of those was People's Republic of China. This meant that I was now on the lists of four of the five permanent members of the Security Council and two of the non-permanent members.

Although it had little meaning at this time, it turned out to be very significant later on. I was told that France did not submit a second list and in fact from that point on refused to join into the conference calls.

A conference call was held and it was pointed out that my name appeared six times on the lists, the next individual who was on multiple lists was only on three and all three were from non-permanent members. I have no idea as to what took place but by the end of the conference call it was decided that the President of the United States would ask me to represent earth in a meeting with the extraterrestrials.

Chapter 2 – Day 2

Picture this if you can. I am sitting at my desk; I have little to do as the first couple of weeks of January are not what you would call the best time for international sales efforts. It's one of the few periods in the year when nobody really wants to talk to you. Some of the Asian countries were still doing business, but they also had a case of North American New Year's mentality even if they didn't use the Gregorian calendar.

My desk phone rings and this very attractive voice said "I'm trying to reach Mr. William Defoe".

"Speaking"

"I have a call for you from the President of the United States. Please hold while I transfer the call".

Now, the first thing that goes through my mind is which one of my friends or business associates is going to be at the other end of the phone. It definitely isn't going to be the President of the United States, it may however be the President of one of the companies I do business with, who thinks that this will be funny and if he is a good account, someone I am planning on doing a lot of business with in the future, trust me, it will be hilarious!

I hear a click and then; "Mr. Defoe, this is President Wycliffe. I hope I have not caught you at a bad time. Do you have time to talk?"

I didn't recognize the voice, but on the other hand I was sure it wasn't the President of the United States, so I responded with; "Mr. President, how is Mrs. President and all the little Presidents?" I thought that the question might give me some insight into who I was speaking to.

There was a momentary pause in the conversation while the person on the other end of the line decided how to respond. The response was quite unexpected.

"Mr. Dafoe, I can understand your apprehension, but I am President Wycliffe and I, actually the world, needs your help to diffuse a very serious situation. There is a US military aircraft on route to Toronto to pick you up and bring you back to Washington so that I may discuss the situation with you in person. I am transferring the phone to Major Stewart Arnold who will give you the logistical details of the flight. Thank you. I look forward to meeting with you in a few hours."

Although not much was actually said I was having a hard time absorbing it, my mind was having a great deal of difficulty accepting that I had just been speaking to the President of the United States and that somehow I had the ability to help diffuse a very serious global situation. Dah, I'm a salesman, a damn good one, but help diffuse a global crisis seemed to be stretching my salesmanship abilities way beyond their capabilities.

Secondarily, I'm a Canadian and very proud of it. Whenever I travel outside of Canada I always wear a Canadian flag lapel pin to make sure that no one ever makes the mistake of thinking that I am an American. I have little respect for US ideologies, especially the belief that everyone in the world would prefer to be an American and live in the United States or at least live in a duplicate of the US form of civilization.

There was another click on the phone.

"Mr. Dafoe, this is Major Arnold, further to your conversations with President Wycliffe, there is a US Military Learjet on route to Toronto's Lester B Person Airport. It's scheduled to touch down at 11:17 a.m."

I glanced at the clock at the bottom right hand side of my computer, it was 9:57 a.m. this was all happening a lot faster than I liked.

Major Arnold continued; "A priority flight path and clearance has been arranged through our contacts in the Canadian Government. It will park at the Flyservice facility on Midfield Road in Mississauga. Mr. Dafoe, are you familiar with the FlyService facility?"

I knew where the Flyservice facility was as I had used their charter services a few times over the years.

"Yes."

"Will you be there at 11:17?"

I paused for a second. My brain was in major turmoil. "Do I need to pack a suitcase and if so for how long?"

Major Arnold thought for a moment. "We will provide you with anything you may need, time is of the essence and I don't see any value in delaying your arrival while you return home to pack."

He was going to continue, but I interrupted him. "I will leave the office as soon as we are finished. That should allow me enough time to arrive at the FlyService facility by 11:17, pending traffic of course".

"The captain of the Learjet will be informed to wait for your arrival once he lands;" he blurted back. He continued; "Do you have any other questions?"

"I'm good"

"Thank you," he said, another click and then the line went dead.

I leaned back in my chair to try and absorb what had just occurred. I realized that I didn't get an answer to my "how long will I need to pack for question". I had no idea how long I would be gone, but I thought, it's a meeting with the President of the United States, that can't last longer than ten to fifteen minutes and I am sure that the whole thing, whatever it may be, has been blown way out of proportion and I will be home for dinner. The crisis situation will probably be resolved before I even get to Washington. Little did I know, at that time, that my life would be changed forever.

I picked up the phone and called my daughter's cell phone, she was in her second year at university, with a major in anthropology, funny how lives can become interrelated. She lived on campus at one of the dorms. My daughter was used to my calling and telling her that I would be travelling, not next week, not tomorrow, but right now! I have been a widower for about two and a half years. I had been married for twenty-six years and I was on the road for most of them. I ended up talking to my daughter's voice mail, I left a message telling her that I was off to Washington and would probably be back later this evening, but I would call her and let her know as soon as I knew. There was little sense in telling her that I was going to have a meeting with the President of the United States as that would only bring up questions that I didn't have answers too and she probably would have thought that I was joking with her anyway.

My boss had taken the week off, but I left a message on his voice mail in the unlikely event he was looking for me. All I said was that I was taking the rest of the day off and would be back at work tomorrow morning. That very brief message in itself would confuse him if he ever heard it. My life was my work and my daughter and I seldom took any time off.

I took one last gulp of cold coffee. Closed my laptop, put it in its carrying case along with its power supply, my cigarettes and lighter, a pad of paper and a couple of pens. I never went anywhere without my laptop, a pad of paper and pens or my cigarettes. I checked to ensure that my passport was in the side pocket of the laptop case. Put my coat on; it was a blistery 25°F outside, although the sun was shining and it felt somewhat warmer than that. Toronto hadn't had any major snow falls as of yet this winter.

I hadn't bothered to put a suit and tie on this morning because there would be few people in the office and I didn't have any meetings. I was dressed in a pair of light brown Khaki pants and a plaid shirt. Not quite the dress code for meeting the President of the United States. For a moment I considered going home to change, but my home was twenty minutes in the opposite direction of the airport. The airport was 45 minutes from my home, obviously that would make me late for the arrival of the Learjet.

I glanced down at myself and thought, to hell with it, he said it's urgent and time is of the essence. If he doesn't like the way I am dressed he can refuse to talk to me and send me home.

They say that time flies when you're having fun. Was I having fun? Not really but time was flying. I looked at the clock on the dashboard of the car and it was already 10:46.

I sat in the car pondering the best route to the FlyService facility. I could drive to the commercial terminals of the airport with my eyes closed, actually I believe that the car could go there without my assistance. However, the FlyService facility was not close to the commercial terminals it was on the west side of the airport complex and although I could get to the FlyService facility by taking my normal airport route it was actually out of the way as it would require that I drive all around the airport. Now I found that I was blabbering to myself.

I should have printed a Yahoo map while I was still in the office; well I'm not going back in I said to myself.

I decided that I would take the route around the airport because I was sure I knew how to get there and trying to find a shorter route had the potential that I would get lost. With everything that was swirling around in my head, choosing an unknown short cut was just not in the cards.

I pulled into the FlyService parking lot at 11:12 according to my dashboard clock. I decided to park the car off to one side of the parking lot considering that I had no idea how long it would be parked there. I went inside the terminal and reported in at the customer service counter. I gave them the make, model and license plate number of the car and told them where I had parked. They asked me how long I would be gone and I said that I wasn't really sure, but it was highly likely that I would be back in Toronto this evening. I've been wrong about return dates from business trips in the past. I get hung up with meetings at customer facilities and a one day trip turns into a two day trip. In one instance, on a sales trip in Russia, a four day trip turned into seventeen days as one person suggested that I speak to another person and so on and so on.

In this case, although I didn't know it at the time, I didn't have any inclination that it would be more than three months before I returned to Toronto.

Another thought entered my brain. Would they send me home on a commercial airline? That would be a royal pain in the butt, as there is no convenient method of getting from the commercial terminals to the FlyService parking lot other than a taxi cab. I decided that I would confront that problem when and if it arose and filed it in the back of my mind for future consideration.

You can't see the tarmac area from the front of the FlyService terminal so I couldn't see if the Learjet had arrived and was impatiently waiting for me.

With my laptop case in hand I walked towards the back end of the terminal that faced the tarmac where the private and charter planes were parked. I glanced at my watch and it was 11:19, two minutes after the scheduled arrival. As a frequent flyer I know that the term arrival time is somewhat confusing to those not familiar with it, as it is the time that the wheels of the aircraft touch down on the airport runway, not the time when the aircraft arrives at the gate. In the same manner departure time is when the airplane backs away from the gate, not when it takes off from the runway. At some airports, depending on their layout and how many runways they have it can take ten to fifteen minutes from touchdown to actually arriving at any specific gate.

I wasn't surprised that the Learjet was not sitting on the tarmac behind the terminal waiting for me. I was actually comforted by this. I would much prefer to be waiting for people than have people waiting for me. I am always early for appointments and if necessary I would wait out of view until it was time for the meeting.

I stood at the window studying the different aircraft parked on FlyService lot. There was everything from single engine Cessna aircraft to a Boeing 737. Many of the planes were tied down, one was being refueled by a tanker truck and a few were undergoing service and maintenance.

While I was watching a twin engine aircraft having its nose wheel changed, an aircraft jockeyed into position in front of me. A United States Air Force Learjet, how could I tell? It said United States Air Force across the upper front of the fuselage, had the standard US Air Force insignia on the engine and I was familiar with the outward appearance of a Learjet.

My private bus has arrived, I thought to myself.

The aircraft parked and shut down its engines. A few seconds later the door opened and the stairs were lowered into position by a girl in a blue US Air Force uniform. She backed out of the doorway and a very well dressed lady, descended the steps and walked quickly towards the terminal doors. She was wearing a tan Cashmere double breasted coat that fell just below her waist, dark brown leather gloves, a dark blue skirt and knee high brown leather boots that matched the gloves perfectly; between the tops of the boots and the bottom of the skirt I could see a shapely pair of legs encased in fine silk stockings. This lady had class I thought to myself. I caught her eye as she walked and I made my way over to the doors that exited onto the tarmac. I opened the terminal door just as she arrived. She looked at me; "Mr. Dafoe?"

"Yes."

"My name is Elizabeth Montgomery. It's a pleasure to meet you. Shall we board?" She extended her gloved hand and I shook it. She didn't wait for an answer. She turned and started to walk back to the Learjet. I followed.

As soon as I had cleared the interior area of the aircraft door, the Air Force girl raised the steps and locked the door into the closed position.

Once inside the Learjet Ms. Montgomery motioned me to a

specific seat. Following her lead I removed my coat and placed it on the seat directly opposite where I was going to sit. I was facing the front of the aircraft. Ms. Montgomery took a seat in front of me facing the back of the aircraft. There was a table between us. The inside of the aircraft was not opulent but the seats were first quality, similar to those in business class on most commercial airliners. They were covered in US Air Force blue leather. The interior of the aircraft was in keeping with a private industry business jet.

There were only the three of us inside the cabin of the aircraft; me, Ms. Montgomery and the Air Force girl.

Ms. Montgomery nodded to the girl who then picked up an intercom phone and informed the captain of the aircraft that he could depart.

Ms. Montgomery looked at me, her eyes were very sincere; "On behalf of the United Nations Security Council and the President of the United States I would like to thank you for meeting with us. I am sure you have a lot of questions and I will do my best to answer as many of them as I can."

That was the first time that the United Nations Security Council had been mentioned and it just added to the overall mystery. A weird thought entered my mind. Defoe is not an uncommon name, maybe there's another Dafoe that would be much more suited to whatever is going on. They're talking to the wrong guy - wouldn't that be the chuckle of the century?

The sound of the jet engines starting broke my train of thought. A train that was definitely on the verge of derailment!

As the plane began to move a voice came over the intercom. This is the captain, we are going to have a very bumpy assent to our cruising altitude, please make sure your seat belts are tightly fastened. Once at cruising altitude it should be a smooth flight.

I pulled back on the buckle strap of my seat belt ensuring that it was snug.

Ms. Montgomery looked at me and smiled. "Let's wait until the plane has reached cruising altitude before I try to brief you on the situation at hand".

She was an extremely attractive woman and I had to keep reminding myself not to stare at her. Staring at or ogling beautiful women was a serious bad habit that I had developed years earlier and I was always on my guard.

Looking out the window of the aircraft I could see the normal long line up of aircraft waiting to takeoff. Welcome to the Lester B. Pearson International aircraft parking lot, I thought, we won't be off the ground for at least a half an hour. Wrong again! The captain maneuvered the Learjet to the front of the line of waiting commercial jets. I am reasonably sure that I saw the captain of an American Airlines jumbo 747 give us the finger as we took his spot for takeoff. Seconds later we were racing down the runway and lifting off. Someone has a lot of clout, I thought to myself.

I was waiting for the bumpy ride that the captain had promised us, but the assent was quite smooth, maybe it would have been considered bumpy for unseasoned travelers, for me it was a walk in the park. I looked out the window and watched everything becoming smaller and smaller. It struck me that the aircraft had not been met by the Canadian Border Agency, no customs or immigration officials. It would have taken a lot of influence to stop that from occurring. In recent years the Canadian Border Agency had become a powerhouse even to the point of arming its agents. More guns, will we ever learn?

Once we had reached cruising altitude I loosened my seat belt slightly.

Ms. Montgomery spoke; "The President had originally considered coming to get you himself, but having the President travel internationally on very short notice is a logistics nightmare. There is security to consider and the media would want to know why they weren't invited. He wishes to apologize to you for sending me as his envoy. He will speak with you directly when we arrive at the Whitehouse".

"There is no need to apologize. I am sure that I am much more comfortable talking with you than I would be with the President of the United States." I briefly paused trying to think of which question I wanted an answer to first.

One of the first rules of sales, know the authority level of the person you are talking to. Ms. Montgomery may I ask what your position is within the US government?"

"My official title is Counselor to the President. I am a member of President Wycliffe's cabinet and I undertake special assignments that do not fall under the prevue of anyone else in the cabinet and I would like you to call me Liz;"

Hmmm, call her Liz, I thought that was awfully chummy and

possibly a bit uncomfortable for me, but the customer is always right so Liz it shall be. It was obvious that Liz was very polished when it came to dealing with people, which is nothing more than a good salesperson. I would have to be on my guard.

"Liz"; I said in an acknowledgement to her goodwill gesture. "Please call me Will."

Liz smiled and didn't seem to have any problem addressing me by my first name. "Will, before I reveal the crisis situation with you I would like you to be aware of the protocol with regard to your visit to the Whitehouse. Besides the President you will be meeting Ambassadors from three of the other four permanent members of the United Nations Security Council, possibly a number of members of the President's cabinet, other government officials and bureaucrats. I will be with you at all times to ensure you can find your way through the mazes of hallways and rooms and to be available to answer any questions you may have. Always feel free to ask me anything, if I do not know the answer I will do my best to find an answer for you. The only time I will leave your side is if you ask me too, your sole prerogative at any time. In other words, if you wish to speak to someone without me present, just say so, I will not take any offence and will wait for you on the other side of the door. If anyone with the exception of the President asks to have a private meeting with you it will be up to you as to whether I stay or go, not the individual you are meeting with."

Liz paused for a moment; "Are you okay with that?"

"Sounds perfect to me" Confusion reigned supreme in my mind.

"Would you like something to drink or eat?"

Before I could respond Liz pressed a button on the console beside the seat and out of nowhere the Air Force girl appeared. Liz asked the girl if there was any food on board and the girl told her that there were some egg salad, roast beef and tuna sandwiches and an assortment of beverages. She asked me if I wanted anything, but other than some water, my stomach was too tied up in knots for me to eat. I told Liz to have something if she wanted and not to worry about me, I told her that I generally didn't eat lunch, which was true. Liz asked for an egg salad sandwich and an ice tea if she had one. In less than a minute my water and Liz's food and ice tea arrived. The Air Force girl then disappeared again.

Liz took two bites of her sandwich and put the rest to the side of the table. It didn't look overly appetizing.

Liz looked at me her eyes were foreboding. "I guess it's time for me to brief you on what's going on. I think it's best if I give you an overview and then let you ask questions". She didn't wait for a response, and carried on speaking. Her voice changed dramatically, from someone who was completely confident in what they were saying to someone with a high level of trepidation in their speech.

I immediately pulled out the pad of paper from my laptop case and a pen and loosening the seatbelt even more, positioned myself at the table to take notes.

"We have received a message from a group of extraterrestrials advising us that they are going to annihilate the human race in three months!"

Now I consider myself to be a good salesman, and two of the traits of a good salesman are never to be at a loss for words and never appear to be caught off guard. Guess what, I was at a loss for words and this truly did catch me off guard. Annihilation of the human race in three months, what does one say in response to that statement? Have a pleasant day.

"That being said, the extraterrestrials have given us one chance to avoid what I am calling dooms day. We can send one emissary to meet with their leaders to plead our case for continued existence. It has been suggested that you are the person to send."

When I get very nervous my brain goes into joke mode and I can get very sarcastic.

"You want me to sell them something?" I responded without any thought. I immediately realized what a stupid statement that was, especially under the circumstances. "I apologize for that remark."

Liz looked at me as if to say, I think we may have chosen the wrong person to represent us.

"I didn't choose you, but I would have if it had been my decision."

It made me uncomfortable that I had misread Liz's facial expression. I chalked it up to my brain being in overdrive and slightly screwed up.

Why would they pick me, rather than a known diplomat, someone who had faced negotiations with leaders' hell bent on war and destruction? Surely there were hundreds of people much more qualified to plead our case than I was. 'Please don't call me Shirley' spun in my brain. I felt like I was losing it, and fought to regain my composure. My immediate feeling was to tell Liz to have the plane turn around and take me back home.

"Liz, I need a few minutes to let all this sink in."

I stared out the window of the plane, my stomach was churning and my heart rate had climbed. My little grey cells, as Hercule Poirot would say, needed time to absorb and focus on the information supplied to this point.

"Liz, I would kill for a cigarette right now."

She looked at me and smiled, reached over to her purse and pulled out a package of cigarettes and offered me one. I reached into my laptop computer bag and pulled out my own.

"A woman after my own heart! Is it okay to smoke here? I don't want to create any problems for you or anyone else."

Liz didn't respond other than to pull a lighter out of her purse and light a cigarette. We both leaned back in our seats and enjoyed that first drag and the taste of the tobacco smoke. Liz moved her ice tea bottle to the center of the table and we used that as an ashtray. I wondered if the Air Force girl would come out and say something, she was nowhere to be found. I'm guessing that because of Liz's position in the government, she was after all a member of President Wycliffe's cabinet she had some sort of immunity when it came to breaking small rules such as No Smoking and considering that the world was about to come to an end, smoking aboard a government aircraft seemed very trivial indeed.

The intercom clicked. "We've just crossed into US air space;" came the unidentified voice.

I glanced out the window, I'm not sure why. Did I expect to see a different air space than the one we had when we took off? The air space wasn't different, but we had company. There was a fully armed F-16 flying a hundred yards or so off our wing tip. Now that was spooky! I quickly decided not to make any comment to Liz.

We finished our cigarettes. I had a million questions, but the one that was haunting me was; why me?

"Liz; Why me?"

"Without getting into the nitty-gritty of the process, the members of the Security Council were requested to suggest individuals who they thought could be the emissary. Your name was on more of the lists than any other."

"That really doesn't mean that I am the best choice."

Liz paused for a moment. It was obvious she was trying to come up with a plausible explanation or at best an explanation that made some sense.

"I don't want to hurt your feelings, but it's important that you understand the politics that were involved in the selection criteria. The decision on who too send as our emissary is covered by two completely different criteria. The first is that the individual must have better than average, proven capabilities when it comes to presenting a point of view and negotiating. They must be able to sell the extraterrestrials on the value of not destroying humanity and who better than a good salesman to get them to buy into something that would go against their current judgment and a decision which has apparently already been made and ratified.

I know that you have been successful selling to all types of individuals and entities and the people you sell to still like you after the sale. Your selling abilities seem to cover all races, religions, gender and ages. You are used to dealing through an interpreter which may or may not be an advantage in this situation.

The second criteria relates to the acceptance of the individual by all the members of the Security Council. You are a Canadian and at this moment Canada holds the Presidency of the Security Council. There is worldwide respect for Canadians and Canada in general. Canada doesn't have an arsenal of nuclear warheads mounted on missiles and to our knowledge doesn't have chemical or biological weapons. Your name appeared on six of the lists generated by the members of the Security Council and four of those lists came from the permanent members. In fact, no country on the Security Council voiced an objection to you or vetoed your name, whereas there was at least one objection or veto to every other candidate presented.

With such a very tight time frame, which I realize I haven't disclosed to you yet, it was imperative that the members of the Security Council gave their go ahead for discussions to take place with an individual and you are the one they chose.

"Does that answer your question?"

I could feel my eyes roll back. "Yes, what about the time frame?

"It's very tight. We have to have our emissary at a specific set of coordinates at noon tomorrow and before you ask, I am not privy to the location."

"What is going to or supposed to take place at the location? Is that where the meeting with the extraterrestrials will be held?"

I could tell that I was getting into some areas that were uncomfortable for Liz. But after some contemplation she said; "The emissary will be transported to a location somewhere in outer space to meet with the Council of Inhabited Planets. That is what they call themselves."

"Transported!" I said under my breath but loud enough for Liz to hear.

"Yes!" she said firmly, "Transported."

"Did they say how or what they meant by transported?"

Her reply scared the hell out of me. "No!"

"Did they indicate how long this trip would take and if they had plans on returning the emissary, hopefully in one piece?"

She smiled and actually chuckled. "They said you would be returned to the same spot as the departure point in exactly 93 days. They didn't say anything about how many pieces they would be returning."

I wrote a big 93 on my pad, as if I might forget. I also picked up on the fact that Liz wasn't using the term emissary anymore; she was specifically referring to me. But her chuckle impressed me and she had some wit about her.

So much for being home for dinner, and I don't have a change of underwear, something I could really use right now! My mind was getting sarcastic again, focus, focus, I kept repeating to myself.

Being physically separated from my daughter for 90 plus days would not be anything new for us. There had been numerous times that we had been apart. I spent three months in the Netherlands, seven months in Dallas, a year in Florida and three months in Las Vegas. The big difference would be that previously when I was away we spoke by phone at least once a day and I was able to bring her to me or go back home for a couple of days every few weeks. It was my guess that I wouldn't have any contact with her during this 93 day period. The cell phone roaming charges would be out of this world, no pun intended.

Focus, focus, focus.

"Did they happen to say why they wanted to annihilate the human race?"

"According to the message and I am paraphrasing somewhat, they said that because we had developed the technology to explore outer space, our war like nature and continuous development of weapons of mass destruction meant that we were an unacceptable threat to the trillions of sentient beings that lived in the galaxy."

Maybe surprisingly, it made a lot of sense to me. I wondered how one could argue that the premise was incorrect. Looking at the world as it was at this moment; more and more countries getting atomic weapons; hidden biological and chemical weapon plants, more and more countries sending objects into space and planning to explore the galaxy and at least one war or civil uprising going on at any one time. It would be easier to defend their point of view then it would be to change it.

After a pause Liz continued. "You will be able to listen to the message in its entirety when we arrive at the Whitehouse. I am sure that it will create more questions for you than it answers. We know very little about their thought process or anything else about them for that matter. Obviously the extraterrestrials are very technically advanced."

It was definitely time for another cigarette. I took the package out of my laptop case and Liz, seeing what I had planned, reached for her cigarettes as well. I remembered to be a gentleman, basic instincts and lit Liz's cigarette for her. She gave me a smile that made me melt. Neither one of us said anything. My mind was still in turmoil. I had to relax so that I could think things through, but it wasn't going to be easy.

Finally I broke the silence. "Liz, what if I decide not to go? What is the Security Council's fall back plan? Is the President talking with anyone else?"

"To My knowledge there is no backup plan and I am not aware of any other candidates. If you decide not to undertake this assignment there won't be time to select and brief another candidate. The world will face dooms day. Those relatively few people who preached that there would be an Armageddon an apocalypse, will have been proven right, however they will not be around to brag about it."

All of a sudden my mind cleared and I realized that the only thing I really needed to consider was whether or not I could change the minds of the extraterrestrials. If I thought that I could indeed change their minds, I had to go. If I felt that I couldn't change their minds then I should choose to spend the last three months with my daughter.

Without actually hearing the message all I had to go on was Liz's paraphrasing as she put it. Although it's probably a long shot, there may be something subtle in the message that would help me decide the potential of selling them on the concept that they should not annihilate the civilization on earth.

There were two different sales strategies that I could take. The first would be to sell them on all the good and positive things that were part of our civilization and hence make a case that we should be saved. That would be a real hard sell. The second would be to accept their premise and try to negotiate a compromise that would not involve the total annihilation of all of mankind. This sales strategy may have possibilities. I really needed to hear the actual message.

My mind shifted to my daughter. What would I tell her? Hi darling. I'll be gone for about three months. I won't be able to contact you. I have to go visit some extraterrestrials and save our planet from annihilation. Don't worry about me, I'll be fine, take care of yourself, I'll miss you. Bye for now, see you in three months. It was going to be a very interesting conversation. My daughter had always supported anything I wanted to do, but I really wasn't sure how she would react to this.

Joking aside, if I do decide to go, I would want to ensure that my daughter is taken care of. What if I went and something happened and I did not return and the extraterrestrials didn't annihilate the planet. It was a real possibility. I must make sure that she is secure, both physically and financially. I thought about that for a few minutes.

What if my going ended up being leaked to the press? Would her life be in danger? There are a lot of loons out there.

I picked up my pen and scrawled a note below the big 93 that I had written on the pad. Physical and financial security for Barbara!

I would also ask for a commitment that if my daughter needed anything that she would have someone assigned to help her or answer any questions as best they could.

I wrote another note. Barbara must have a primary contact person – possibly Liz. I couldn't really explain it, but I was becoming enthralled by this very attractive lady sitting across from me. It could have just been my male hormones; it had been a long time since I had been with a woman.

I wouldn't say anything to Liz about the possibility of her being a primary contact person for my daughter at this time. I may choose not to go and then the requirement of a contact person would have no meaning.

I knew in the back of mind that not going was really not much of an alternative, but I didn't mind kidding myself for the moment.

My train of thought was interrupted by the captain. "Please ensure that your seatbelts are fastened we are starting our decent to Andrews".

I glanced out the window and saw the F-16 make a sharp bank to the left and disappear into some low clouds.

With my thousands of flights over the years I had never flown into Andrews Air Force Base in Maryland. Andrews is well known as the base of operations for the President's two Boeing 747 aircraft – the call sign being Air Force One.

"We will be taking a marine core helicopter from Andrews to the Whitehouse;" Liz said.

I nodded in reply.

The landing was very smooth. The Learjet quickly moved off the runway and taxied towards a parked Lockheed Martin VH-71 marine helicopter. As soon as the engines were shut down, the Air Force girl opened the door and released the steps. Unbuckling her seat belt, Liz rose from her seat, grabbed her purse and coat which she tossed over her arm. I unbuckled my seat belt, put my cigarettes, pad of paper and my pen in the laptop case, picked up my coat and followed Liz through the doorway of the Learjet and down the steps.

The sun was shining when we landed and it was a very comfortable 65°F.

Liz led the way as we walked briskly towards the waiting VH-71 helicopter. We approached the helicopter from the front. There were two pilots in the cockpit and a marine in full dress uniform standing by the helicopter's open door. I continued to follow Liz as she climbed the helicopter's steps. Once we were inside, the door was closed. We sat down and buckled ourselves in. Liz adjusted herself in her seat and her leg and thigh came to rest against mine. I expected her to quickly move it as anyone would if you accidentally brush someone's leg on a crowded bus, airplane or in theater seating, but she didn't. I figured she didn't realize it was up against mine. Hell, I wasn't going to move my leg!

I could hear and feel the massive engine start-up and could see the rotor blades beginning to turn, very slowly at first, and then faster until their rotation was nothing more than a blur.

I had only been on a helicopter a few of times in the past. I used the shuttle helicopter from the rooftop of what was the PanAm building in New York to JFK Airport twice and I had taken the helicopter sightseeing tour out of Las Vegas over the Hoover dam.

Liz looked at me. "It's a very short flight to the Whitehouse."

Liz wasn't lying, before I had a chance to get my thinking cap back on, I looked out the window and could see the Whitehouse. Probably could have walked I thought to myself.

The helicopter started its decent and we landed on the south lawn of the Whitehouse, Liz's leg and thigh still firmly against mine. The engine was shutdown and the rotor blades began to slow. Once the blades stopped spinning the helicopter door was opened by a marine, in full dress uniform, from the outside of the helicopter.

Liz went first and I followed, like a puppy dog would follow their beloved master.

As I exited the helicopter I noticed a large group of people, a reception party? Liz, without hesitation, went up to one of the people, I was close behind.

I prided myself on being a very observant individual and the first thing that I observed was that everyone was dressed very formally in business suits, shirts and ties for the men and business suits with skirts for the ladies. I began to feel uncomfortable standing there in casual clothes.

"Mr. President;" Liz said. "I would like to introduce Mr. William Defoe". In the same breath she looked at me and said; "Mr. Dafoe, the President of the United States."

The President immediately put out his hand and I shook it. It was a very firm handshake. "Welcome to the Whitehouse, Mr. Dafoe, I am very pleased to meet you. I hope you had an uneventful trip".

"The pleasure is all mine Mr. President." Yes, the salesman came out in me; sometimes I do tell white lies. "The trip was fine."

The President glanced to his immediate right: "I would like to introduce you to Ambassador Vladimir Balabanov, the Russian Federation representative at the United Nations."

Pleasure to meet you Mr. Ambassador;" we shook hands.

As I shook the Ambassador's hand, I realized that he looked very familiar to me. As a salesman I had one very large fault, I couldn't remember names. I compensated for it by never forgetting a face. I was sure that I met Ambassador Balabanov somewhere before, but I couldn't place him. I knew it would drive me crazy until I figured it out.

The President continued. "Standing next to Ambassador

Balabanov, is Ambassador Zhang Wei. Ambassador Zhang Wei is the United Nations representative from the People's Republic of China;"

I smiled and looked at Zhang Wei. "It's a pleasure to see you again. How are you and your family? Is your daughter still playing the violin?"

I had met Zhang Wei on a sales trip to People's Republic of China about five years ago. At that time he was the head of the Chinese Ministry of Science. He had invited me to his home, a great honor in China.

Zhang Wei extended his hand. "We are all well. My daughter has earned the second violin position with the China National Symphony Orchestra."

I shook Zhang Wei's hand as if we were very close friends. "I am so pleased for you. It's a great honor that you're daughter was chosen to play with the symphony. I hope someday that I will have the honor of hearing her play. Please give my best wishes to your entire family for me".

The honor would be ours. Zhang Wei nodded as we broke the grip on our handshake.

The President smiled at me, I think he was somewhat impressed that I knew Zhang Wei and was able to have a personal conversation, although very short, with him. He then glanced to his immediate left, "William, I would like to introduce the Ambassador for the United Nations representing the United Kingdom, Heather Middleton."

"A pleasure to meet you Ms. Ambassador;" we shook hands.

President Wycliffe was a gifted diplomat, his expressions and mannerisms made me feel very comfortable; "I am sure that Elizabeth has told you that time is of the essence and although I am sure you would like a few minutes to relax, if you are up to it we would like to meet with you right now."

I prided myself in the fact that I paid attention to small details. I always felt that it was part of my success as a salesman. That made me wonder why Ms. Montgomery had asked me to call her Liz when the President addressed her as Elizabeth. I would file that in the back of my mind.

"I would actually prefer that we get down to it. I believe that we may have a lot to cover and as you and Ms. Montgomery have stated many times, time is on the essence." I'm not sure why I used Liz's surname, it just rolled out of my mouth that way.

There were at least ten other people standing behind the President and the Ambassadors and I wasn't introduced to any of them. A few were obviously secret service as they had small white plastic cords from communication devices coming out of one ear. I had no idea who the others were, and I must admit I was a little curious. The salesman in me was coming out. Always know who the people are that are involved in the negotiations, I thought to myself.

All together the group turned and started walking towards the Whitehouse. A couple of unknown individuals led, the President and Ambassadors walked together, I followed with Liz on my right. We walked along a walkway where two men held open a set of French doors and we all proceeded inside. I love a parade, I thought to myself.

We proceeded down a hallway where another two men held open a set of doors. A meeting room, the décor was definitely my style – wood, a dark oak - floors and walls! None of the grandiose leather chairs at the table were taken but there were a number of people seated on much less expensive chairs lined up against the walls of the room. Everyone rose as the President and the Ambassadors entered the room. I'm reasonably confident that they didn't rise because I entered the room.

As we entered the room Liz nudged my arm and in so doing directed me to a leather chair positioned at the center of a classic wood table. Liz stood by the chair next to me. We remained standing as the President and the Ambassadors walked around to the other side of the table. The President stood beside a chair directly opposite me. Zhang Wei, the Ambassador for People's Republic of China stood to his right. On his left was the Ambassador for the Russian Federation and next to him was Ambassador Middleton of the UK. The President sat down, and everyone else including Liz and I followed suit.

The President spoke. "William, I would like to thank you again for attending this meeting on such short notice. The Ambassadors and I represent four of the five permanent seats of the United Nations Security Council. The seat not represented here today belongs to France. Seated around the room are some of the Ambassadors' support staff, some members of my cabinet, some senior administration officials and the Chairman of the Joint Chiefs of Staff. I am confident that Elizabeth has outlined the current situation. I would also imagine that you have a number of questions and we will answer them as best we can. How would you like to proceed?"

"I would like to hear the original message and I would like to have a verbatim transcript of the message, if that's possible?"

The President looked towards an individual with a military uniform seated on one of the chairs and said; "General Adams would you please play the message for Mr. Dafoe."

As he spoke a young lady handed me a file folder. I opened the folder to find one sheet of paper. Secret had been stamped in red ink in big bold letters at the top and bottom of the page. The title of the document was: *Extraterrestrial Message – January 1st, - Transcription.*

There wasn't a sound in the room, as General Adams pushed the play button on a small CD player:

"To the people of the planet they call earth. This notification comes to you from the Council of Inhabited Planets – the governing body representing fifty seven inhabited planets and over ten trillion sentient beings.

You are hereby advised that due to your technical capabilities of sending objects into space to explore the galaxy, combined with your history and psychological mind-set towards war, power, greed, corruption and the genocide of groups of individuals who do not hold to your ideologies, compounded with your continuous development of weapons of mass destruction; it has been deemed necessary to take immediate action and a motion has been unanimously approved; All human life on the planet earth must be sacrificed to protect the lives of all sentient beings in the galaxy. This motion shall be carried out in precisely one hundred days.

Under the governing rules of the Council of Inhabited Planets you have the right to present a defense and argument with respect to this motion. To present a defense and argument, the Council has agreed to sanction one human from the planet earth an audience in front of the entire Council. Your chosen emissary must be at coordinates of 40.7675573972 latitude and -73.9456279843 longitude at preciously 12:00 p.m. on January 3rd. He or she will be transported by a shuttle craft to our planet. Your emissary will be returned to the same location at 12:00 p.m. on April 5th; a trip duration of precisely ninety-three of your days. If you do not send an emissary the motion will be implemented without further notice."

I looked at the President, his face showed signs of fatigue.

"Without getting into the actual technical details of the message are you sure this is not some sort of elaborate practical joke. There are some very sophisticated groups of hackers and technical gurus having a lot of fun showing off?"

The President looked directly at me. "That was definitely our first inclination. However, we have had the best technical and scientific minds, in all four of the countries represented here today, study the message and its transmission and have definitely determined that without a doubt it is of extraterrestrial origin. Would you like me to have the reasoning explained?

"No, that's not necessary, as long as everyone here is a one hundred percent confident of its authenticity I am prepared to proceed on that basis. I would like to take a moment to read the message if I may?"

The President nodded; "Take your time"

I looked at the message and read it over a few times. The extraterrestrials weren't mincing words when they detailed why they were concerned about our exploration into the galaxy. There was nothing that I could identify in that statement that was untrue.

I remembered reading an article that said more than 175 million people had been murdered by democide since 1900. I had to look up the word democide as it does not seem to exist in any dictionaries. According to the Internet the definition of democide is any murder by individuals who are acting under the authority of a government. Of course a lot of people would dispute that number. They would remove any deaths that occurred during the world wars and similar conflicts, as those weren't murders they were casualties. The word democide may not be an actual word, but it does change the numbers.

I had to wonder if the extraterrestrials were aware of this number, how aware were they of what was happening on planet earth? There was no one in this room that could possibly answer any of those questions or even give me some insight into the alien thought process.

It was becoming more obvious that the best way to approach the extraterrestrials was with a plan of compromise. Basically we change our ways and they drop the notion of annihilation. If they were highly civilized the thought of destroying all of the intelligent life on a planet must be an extremely difficult decision to make and maybe they would be open to an alternative. Of course, getting us to change our ways was not going to be an easy task, we had honed them over thousands of years. They were so right when they said that the human race had a mind-set towards war, power, greed, corruption and the genocide of groups of individuals who do not hold to similar ideologies. Within some groups, I thought to myself, it is not similar ideologies it is identical ideologies.

I looked across the table at the President and the Ambassadors. "There is little if any value in questioning the integrity of the message or taking any specific word or group of words and trying to guess if there is a hidden meaning." I paused for a moment and made eye contact with the President and each of the Ambassadors. Then I continued; "If I accept this assignment, what authority do I have?

The President and the Ambassadors seemed to be caught off guard with my question. The President turned his head to the right and then to the left as if he was hoping someone else would give me a response to the question. There was silence, finally he said; "I'm not sure what you mean Mr. Dafoe."

"Let me explain. I do not envision any plausible outright defense of their motion. Therefore, I think that it will be a negotiation, a compromise entailing a group of commitments by humanity. In other words we commit to certain things and they agree not to annihilate us. If I commit to a group of compromises, will they be accepted and implemented by the nations involved?"

From someone sitting on one of the chairs against the wall and behind me I heard; "not likely!"

I am sure the President heard the comment, but he ignored it. "I must say that I really didn't consider a compromise situation." The President responded.

"Compromise is, in my opinion, the only plausible scenario. May I ask what you would say Mr. President, if you faced the aliens? Hey, we really are a nice group of people and we wouldn't harm anyone."

Liz reached down and squeezed my thigh. She could tell that the tone of my voice was becoming confrontational. Surprisingly, she left her hand resting on my thigh. She's preparing to keep me under control I thought to myself. Having the hand of a very attractive lady resting on my thigh provided me with no physical discomfort, there may have been a margin of mental stress but I was more than prepared to accept that.

"I apologize for the tone of my voice, Mr. President; Ambassadors."

Zhang Wei spoke. "Mr. President if I may interject." Without waiting for a response he continued. I think that it is fair to say that if you negotiate some sort of compromise solution to this problem, then part of the terms of the compromise would be that if we don't perform in the manner that was negotiated and agreed to, the aliens will revert to their original motion of annihilation. I would also like to state that the People's Republic of China has authorized me to accept any compromise that is offered in order to save humanity."

"Excellent point and I am pleased to know that the People's Republic of China will support a compromise. I can also state that the United States will accept a compromise solution" The President responded.

Ambassador Middleton spoke; "I can also commit to the acceptance of a compromise solution on behalf of the United Kingdom."

"Although I do not have the official authority to commit to a compromise without further discussions with the Russian Federation leaders, I believe, based on my conversations with them prior to this meeting, that a compromise would be more than acceptable;" responded Ambassador Balabanov.

Where did I know him from? Damn, it was really bugging me.

President Wycliffe glanced at the Ambassadors and then at the people seated around the room. "Would anyone like to make any other comments?" He asked.

No one responded to the President's offer to comment.

There was a pause no one seemed to know what else to say.

"Mr. President; Ambassadors, I realize that we have not had much time together and you really don't know me, but as time is of the essence, I must formally ask, do you want me to be the emissary that will face and negotiate with the extraterrestrials? I should advise you now that I will have a few conditions that pertain to the security of my daughter."

"I would like to have a few minutes alone with the Ambassadors." The President said.

"Not a problem." I realized as soon as the response left my mouth that it was far too casual, but I couldn't go back in time to correct it. I would have to try to be more formal in the future.

With that, I stood up, Liz rose as well, I grabbed my laptop case – force of habit, Liz grabbed her purse and together we left the room.

There were a few chairs lining the hallway outside of the meeting room; Liz and I sat down. She looked at me with a mischievous smile and then nudged her shoulder against mine, in a very soft voice, "cigarette break?"

I nodded.

We stood up and Liz motioned me towards a set of French doors. We were now on a patio with a small garden in front of it. I followed Liz to the back edge of the garden where there were a bunch of bushes and a couple of wooden Adirondack chairs. We sat and quickly pulled out our nicotine sticks. I managed to get my lighter out quick enough to light Liz's cigarette before she did.

Liz took a big drag on her cigarette and held the smoke in her lungs for a few seconds before exhaling a cloud; "I doubt if we will be out here very long.

Will, I want you to know that you are a very impressive and special individual. You are taking on the most difficult assignment of all time. But, it's not only that, it is the way you are taking it on. Your only concern is your daughter; you have shown a great deal of love and caring for her and I really respect that, more than you can imagine. You can be witty under the most trying of circumstances. You're forceful yet sincere and you're not full of yourself like most people in Washington are. Everyone I know would only be thinking of themselves, I am at a loss of words to express how I feel. You have asked for nothing in return, for yourself, in order to accept the assignment.

She paused for a couple of seconds and took another long puff on the cigarette.

"I wish I had met you under different circumstances; circumstances that would have allowed us the possibly of developing a relationship."

I had always enjoyed what I had considered to be harmless flirting. When I was married I would flirt with the receptionists or secretaries that I'd meet in offices. I especially enjoyed it when they would flirt back, a little harmless repartee between a male and female, it was fun, kept my mind sharp while I was waiting for a client and satisfied a loneliness that came with travelling. There was a secondary reason. I found that if the receptionists and secretaries, especially in the Eastern European countries, liked you it went a long way in being put in the front of the line, so to say, and ensuring that I would receive RFQ's from the companies they worked for. In one case I actually received a heads-up that my price was a little too high, and if I wanted I could resubmit my bid and the secretary would throw this one in the trash can.

Only once did I almost end up in a jackpot because of my flirting. I had been flirting with a receptionist at a company in the Ukraine while waiting for the client to bring out an RFQ for me to respond to. After waiting for over an hour, the client came out and informed me that the translated version was being held up in their legal department. He apologized and said he would have it delivered to my hotel this evening. Guess who delivered it to my room? Yep, you guessed right the receptionist that I had been flirting with. I made the mistake of asking her to join me for dinner, I hated eating alone. To make a long story short, she was looking for someone to get her and her son out of the Ukraine and I seemed like a more than willing candidate. She implied that she would do anything for a better life including being my mistress, wife or concubine. I didn't want a sexual partner or a new wife, I was more than happy with the one I had and I didn't believe in having a little on the side. After dinner I ran back to my room and hid under the bed.

You might think that an experience such as I related would have stopped me from flirting. But I continued unabashed until my wife became ill and after her passing I didn't start up again. Maybe because the flirting seemed to have a planned outcome after her death, an outcome I wasn't really interested in. However this lady had gotten a grip on me. Liz had started the flirting and I wasn't going to let her have the last word. I knew it was just harmless fun.

"Liz, I do want something for myself and myself alone for taking on this assignment, it is the greed in me. I want an undertaking from you. I want you to pledge that you will not, under any circumstances, make any commitment to any other man during my absence. Do you so pledge?"

Liz was beaming ear to ear, her eyes had moistened. "I swear and do so pledge that I Elizabeth Montgomery from this time forward will not make commitments to any man other than William Dafoe."

I put my hand out and she placed her hand in mine. She held it as if she was trying to meld our hands into a single unit.

Whoops! She is either very good at flirting or maybe I have gotten a bit of a grip on her. Couldn't be possible, this was a classy lady and quite attractive, actually beautiful. She can have any guy she wants. I'm sure that this is flirting.

I glanced at my watch. It was 4:15 give or take. If I was going to be the chosen one, I needed to do some preparation. I hope this didn't drag out. Part of me was hoping that they would tell me that I wasn't the person they wanted, however due to time constraints I thought that was highly unlikely.

Liz's cell phone rang and she quickly answered it.

"They're ready for us."

We put out our cigarettes in the garden earth and walked back to the meeting room. Liz and I sat down in the chairs we had previously occupied.

The President spoke. "William, I want you to know that no one had an objection or any negative comments about you or what you have said. We all unanimously agree that you are an excellent choice to represent the people of earth to be humanities emissary. Are you prepared to undertake this assignment?"

"Mr. President; Ambassadors, "With all due respect; I am not at all. . . prepared"—I paused to make sure that they understood the emphasis I was placing on the word prepared, no one could possibly be prepared to do what had to be done, to undertake this assignment. "I am however willing to accept the assignment under a couple of conditions." I paused again and then continued. "As I mentioned before I left the meeting, I have a couple of concerns that relate to my daughter Barbara. There are a few scenarios with respect to the undertaking of this assignment that could dramatically affect my daughter and her future. My first concern is that the world finds out that I am off consorting with aliens in order to save humanity. I want to make sure that my daughter will have all the security necessary to keep her out of harm's way in the event her safety in any manner whatsoever is in jeopardy and that includes being assailed by the press.

Should I not return and humanity is not annihilated for whatever reason, I want to ensure that my daughter is physical secure as previously mentioned and financially secure. In that regard I want a commitment that in the event that I do not return that my daughter will receive a payment from the US government in the amount of five thousand dollars per month, indexed to inflation and that she will obtain reimbursement for any and all medical costs including dental and vision that she should incur for as long as she is in school and for twelve months after leaving school. As well, she will have all her university or any other institute of higher learning tuition and other costs of attending paid for, anywhere in the world and she may continue her education for as long as she wants.

As this pertains to my daughter I would like her to have at least one person who she can contact from the moment I leave, should she need any assistance in any manner whatsoever and you will commit to providing such assistance without hesitation and promptly. I suggest Ms. Montgomery be the contact person.

My last request is that when I return my daughter will be provided with security if in my judgment I deem it necessary.

If you find those conditions acceptable, then I will undertake this assignment. I would appreciate it if you would arrange to have some legal beagle put that into legalese and provide it to me so that I can send it to my daughter before I leave."

Legal beagle, what a dumb thing to say to the President of the United States, I thought to myself.

The President didn't flinch or hesitate. "Accepted!" He pronounced to everyone in the room. He looked over at his Chief of Staff, Barry Fitzwater; "Please have a document drawn up for my signature acknowledging William's requests?" The Chief of Staff nodded his concurrence.

The President looked over at me; "Is there anything else?"

I smiled and said; "Just one other small matter Mr. President, where is the departure point?"

General Adams stood; "Mr. President if I may?" The President nodded and General Adams continued; "The designated latitude and longitude converge at a location in the Ecological Park on Roosevelt Island in New York, which is basically across from the United Nations building. Homeland security in conjunction with one hundred and fifty US marines have cordoned off and taken control of the park to supposedly conduct counter terrorism exercises. Four coast guard vessels are also in the water around the island.

Two teams, one from the Marines and one from the Army Core of Engineers have independently identified and marked the exact location."

"Mr. President, with all due respect, you have placed far too much military presence on and around the island. There is little doubt in my mind that we are unable to defend ourselves against an alien attack, having a big military presence at the landing spot only reinforces the aliens feelings about us. May I respectfully request that you downsize the military presence. The island should be secured only to a point where the public will not be harmed inadvertently.

"William your point is well taken. I will have the military presence removed and replace it with perimeter security for the park."

"Thank you Mr. President."

I looked at my watch and it was now 5:05, getting late, it was time to get this show underway.

"I have two questions Mr. President. "Should I read anything into the absence of France, who if I am not mistaken is the fifth permanent member of the United Nations Security Council?"

Ambassador Middleton responded without hesitation; "The French, at this time, don't appear to believe that the message is real. Since being informing of the message, they have refused to respond to any communications we have sent. At this time we and you must just accept their attitude, it may change, it may not, but it doesn't make a difference as to how we are going to respond, which is to send you as our emissary to hopefully negotiate the survival of the human race."

Leave it to the French to be contrary to the prevailing point of view, I thought; "Thank you Ambassador; is there any possibility that the French might try and send an emissary of their own?"

President Wycliffe responded quickly; "With the French anything is possible! However, we have had the area under tight security since early yesterday evening and there have been no attempts to breach the island. It would be difficult for the French to identify the exact departure point without sending in a high level survey team. I think we should consider it highly unlikely that the French would attempt to send an emissary of their own."

"My final question relates to why this is not all over the media, how have you managed to keep it secret, bearing in mind that I haven't been watching or listening to the news or read any newspapers." I usually get my news from the Internet, but it was New Year's Day and I spent it with Barbara and this morning I hadn't gotten around to checking the news on my computer.

The President gave me a questioning look; "We have been quite lucky actually. There was a volcanic eruption in Italy that consumed the media. When they did hear about the message all of the countries on the Security Council issued statements that it was a hoax implemented by a group of hackers in China. The Chinese government actually arrested three men and a girl, government agents, saying that they had caught the perpetrators and that they would be punished. The media bought into it and haven't revisited the story. Everyone involved in receiving the message has been sequestered.

"Thank you Mr. President

I have some preparation work and things to purchase before I leave. I would also like to stay in New York this evening if that's okay?"

The President had a very sincere look and tone to his voice; "Whatever is best for you William, Elizabeth is at your disposal and I am sure she will be able to take care of all your needs. With that resolved, I call this meeting adjourned".

Everyone stood up. I shook the President's hand and the hands of each of the Ambassadors. Ambassador Balabanov held his grip a little longer than the others, he looked at me straight in the eyes; "good luck". It was very genuine, but from the tone it didn't sound as if he was overly hopeful that I would be successful.

Bingo!

"Ambassador Balabanov may I ask you a question?"

He nodded.

"Were you formally the Deputy Director of Sudo Import when the Soviet Union existed?"

"Yes! How did you know?" He said with a grin on his face.

Everyone was starring at us and listening to the conversation.

"We have met previously; it must be at least twenty years ago. I was selling sophisticated oceanographic equipment. You were kind enough to get me a ticket for the ballet at the Bolshoi Theater. During my visit we went out a few times together for dinner as part of a larger group."

"Yes, now I remember you, I also remember how difficult, even as a Deputy Director it was to get you that ticket. That performance was not for the public, it had been organized weeks in advance for President Gorbachev and foreign Ambassadors only."

"It's good to see you again. When I return, maybe we can spend a few minutes together reminiscing over old times."

"I'd like that."

I never forget a face. I was proud of myself.

I looked at Liz and asked if there was an office or other room with some privacy that we could use, preferably somewhere where I could smoke. Liz thought for a second, picked up her cell phone, and called someone and said she needed access to one of the guest bedrooms.

Liz tapped my on the arm; "Come with me."

We walked around a few corridors, up a small flight of steps. At the top of the steps there was, what I am guessing to be, a secret service agent, he did have the noticeable white plastic cord exiting his ear. We followed him to a door, a plaque on the wall said Lincoln Bedroom.

I placed my laptop case and coat on a chair and sat down on the edge of the bed.

"Liz! I am going to need some items."

She pulled out a small notebook from her purse. "Your wish is my command oh chosen one." She paused, "sorry but it just came out."

"No problem. I will need a digital camera, nothing fancy, just point and click, with a lot of extra memory cards. I would also like to have a hand held voice recorder with a lot of memory and extra memory cards if you can find it. Keep it simple.

"I also need some clothes. Talk about flying in the dark, I will be away for ninety days and have no idea if the aliens have a laundry service and if so do they use a fabric softener provide a pants pressing service – so many questions with no answers. I may be losing my mind, put one mind on your list of things I need."

Liz started to laugh.

I continued over Liz's laughter. "I need four pair of semi-casual pants, preferably two brown and two black, four relatively light shirts, short sleeve, three long sleeve shirts, seven pairs of underwear, seven pairs of socks and a track suit." I usually sleep in the raw, but it struck me that it may not be appropriate with the aliens. "The pants should have a thirty-six inch waist and as short a leg as possible. Liz I will need to get them shortened somewhere." I was five feet, seven inches tall or short depending on your point of view and over the years I had learned that they didn't make pants with a leg length that actually fit me.

Liz interjected. "There is a seamstress on staff." Liz picked up her cell phone again and told someone to make sure that Jenny Stevens didn't go home before checking in with her.

"Toiletries!, Toothpaste – Colgate Total, tooth brush - medium, shaving cream – sensitive skin, razor – preferably Gillette Fusion ProGlide, nail clippers, a tube of skin cream for dry skin and a comb. I will also need a small suitcase, just large enough to hold the clothes, toiletries, camera and my laptop case, tell whomever that it should be as light weight as possible. Oh! One more thing, no bright colors for the shirts or the suitcase, especially no red or orange."

I was involved in a study many years ago that involved what colors were best in a working environment. The results of the study had stuck in my mind as there was no doubt that some colors increased the onset of fatigue while other colors created an aura of aggression. Pastel green was the best color as it related to both fatigue and aggression and red was the worst.

"Let me get started on these items, ponder if you want anything else." She said.

I looked at my watch it was after six and I hadn't called my daughter or my boss. "Can I use this phone to call home?"

Liz nodded a yes. "I'll give you some privacy, I'll make some phone calls out in the hall, come and get me when you are ready – no rush."

This was definitely a cigarette phone call. I lit the cigarette and dialed. I had this horrible feeling that my daughter would direct the call to her voice mail. She had a tendency to do that if she was studying. On the fourth ring my daughter picked up. After the standard set of greetings; "Barbara, there is a situation which is going to take me away for at least three months, and I won't be able to have any contact with you."

"What's going on?"

"I wish I could tell you darling, but I can't – just don't worry! You will have to take care of paying the bills."

After my wife had passed away I had spent time with Barbara explaining our finances, budgeting, our savings and investments. I wanted to make sure that if anything happened to me she would be able to take care of herself. I was confident that she knew how to handle the finances.

"Barbara, do you have a pen and paper?"

"Yes."

"Write down this name and telephone number. Elizabeth Montgomery, 202-555-3738. If you need anything at all or have any questions, do not hesitate to call her. Okay?"

"Dad is everything okay?"

My voice was choking up a bit, and I could feel my eyes getting moist.

"Everything is fine darling, I have to go now. I love you very much."

"I love you too Dad! Please take care of yourself. Bye for now." I could sense a high level of trepidation in her voice.

"Bye darling." I hung up the phone. I didn't want to give her any time to say anything else as I wasn't sure if I could respond without her hearing a very high level of anxiety in my voice.

Tears were rolling down my cheeks. I would miss not speaking to Barbara more than anything else. Was that the last time I would ever speak to my daughter? I had to wipe that thought from my mind right away.

I wiped the tears from eyes and cheeks and decided that I must leave another message for my Boss. I stopped for a second and considered what I would say. I knew that I wouldn't be speaking directly to him; it would only be his voice mail.

I dialed my boss's private number and it immediately went to his voice mail. After listening to his greeting which explained that he wasn't there, where he was on vacation, what to do in case of an emergency and that he would be back on January 9th. I was beginning to think I would be back from the assignment before the greeting was finished. After what seemed to be an eternity it finally allowed me to leave a message.

My boss is a great guy and a good speaker, but like many of us older types, leaving a recorded greeting on a phone seemed to create a level of complexity far beyond the intention of the message. I had suggested a number of times that he should ask his secretary to record the greeting. However that was to no avail.

"Steve this is Will, I'm facing a very serious personal situation and I need a three to four month leave of absence. I'm truly sorry that this is such short notice, but I have no alternatives. I will not be reachable. I will contact you as soon as I am able. Adam and Elli are quite capable of taking over for me during my absence. Speak to you as soon as I can. Take care."

I hung up.

I had no idea what Steve would think or how he would react. I might lose my job, but I had much bigger things to be concerned about. What would be would be.

Adam has been my lead salesman for a little over three years; he is an aggressive salesman and knew how to close orders, the only problem I had with him was his level of disorganization and his paperwork or lack thereof. Elli had been my Executive Assistant since I started with the company, that would be eight years now. Elli was not a secretary with a flashy title. She looked after the marketing side of my overall responsibilities. She was very creative and extremely well organized. Between the two of them they were more than competent to carry on in my absence. They worked very well together.

Adam and Elli had both taken an extra day off for the New Year's holiday, but I knew they both would be in tomorrow morning. I left messages on both their voice mails telling them about my leave of absence and instructed them to carry on with their responsibilities. They were to work together, Adam was to have the final say in sales matters and Elli was to have the final say in marketing matters. I told them to check my calendar for appointments and to either take the appointments on my behalf or cancel them as they saw fit. I remembered that I had an eye doctor's appointment in February and asked Elli to do me a personal favor and call and cancel it. I would rebook it on my return. I took one shot at Adam and told him that he reported to Elli when it came to completing paperwork! I didn't relate that to Elli.

Was there anyone else I needed to call? I sat back for a second, lit another cigarette and pondered.

Damn! I thought to myself. Daniel and Joël! Daniel had been my best friend for the last twenty-five years and Joël was a close friend for at least fifteen years. Daniel lived in the UK and although we didn't see each other very much we spoke on the phone every couple of weeks. Daniel presented a real problem. If I called and told him that I was going to be away for three months and completely out of contact, but I couldn't tell him why, he would be offended. Joël lived in Switzerland and although we only spoke to each other every four or five weeks, he would be very concerned if I didn't return one of his phone calls. I was really at a loss on how to deal with this dilemma.

I glanced at my watch it was 6:45. It was too late to call Daniel or Joël. It was almost midnight in the UK and 1:00 am in Switzerland. Emails, I thought to myself.

I grabbed my laptop and drafted an email.

Hi Daniel,

Family crisis! I will be out of touch for at least 3 months. Barbara and I are both fine.

Take care. I'll call you as soon as I am able.

Best regards to the family,

Will

I thought about what I had written. Daniel would definitely be wondering what was going on, but because he couldn't ask, I didn't think he would be offended. It was the best I could do under the circumstances.

I created another email and copied and pasted the message to Daniel and then changed the salutation to; Hi Joël.

I realized that I didn't have an Internet connection. No Wi-Fi at in the Whitehouse, I guess with overall security and paranoia that made sense I thought. I considered the situation and then I realized we would be in a hotel in a few hours and in this day and age every hotel room has an Internet connection. I would send the emails from the hotel room.

I went to the door and motioned Liz to come in from the hallway. She was on the phone talking to someone about the voice recorder I wanted.

When she finished the call, I handed her a list of prescription medication that I was taking for the usual old age problems of high blood pressure, high cholesterol and eye drops for my glaucoma. She glanced at the list, made a call on her cell phone and casually told someone that she needed some prescriptions filled. I need a 100 day supply and read off the names of the medications.

Liz gave me a questioning look; "Anything else you can think of"

"Nothing at the moment, but I'm sure something will come to mind."

"The helicopter is on standby and so is the Learjet to take us to New York. I have booked us a suite at the Century UN Plaza Hotel and made arrangements for a limo to take us from the airport to the hotel. The Century UN Plaza Hotel is only a fifteen minute drive to the position of the departure point on Roosevelt Island. Your pants should be here in the next ten minutes or so and our seamstress will do a fitting and any alterations that are necessary. All your other items will be delivered to the hotel before 9:00 am tomorrow."

As I said earlier I pay attention to details. "I have booked us a suite" hit me instantly. Then I thought a two bedroom suite, she would be readily available if I needed something. That actually made a lot of sense.

I looked at Liz; "You're fantastic! I'm getting hungry; are you? Can I take you for dinner somewhere?"

"I've got a better idea. What would you order?"

I had a big grin on my face. I had been in Washington many times and the quality of the seafood, especially shell fish, in this city surpasses any, anywhere else in the world, maybe with the exception of Tokyo; "What I really feel like is a big bowl of jumbo shrimps on ice and a couple of dozen raw oysters with some seafood sauce and a bottle of German Riesling wine, Gran Cru of course".

Liz picked up the phone in the room, pushed two of the number buttons and said; "Is this Donny? Donny this is Elizabeth Montgomery I need to place an order for the Lincoln Room. This is for two. I want two bowls of jumbo shrimps, four dozen raw oysters and seafood sauce. I also want two bottles of German Riesling wine – Gran Cru, lightly chilled and three bottles of Piper-Heidsieck Black Cancan Champagne; the vintage I would like is 2000."

Liz looked at me with a big grin. "I don't think we should overdue the wine before our flights, but we will take the Champagne with us to New York. I'm stressed out and I can't imagine how you must feel, I don't think either one of us will get much sleep tonight."

I thought I detected a slight innuendo in her voice, but it was probably only my wishful thinking. She was right about not getting much sleep, I was physically tired but my brain was in overdrive.

There was a knock at the door, Liz went over and opened it. An older woman was standing at the door with some pants over her arm and a small sewing basket.

"Come in Jenny;" Liz said. "Jenny this is Mr. Dafoe, the pants are for him. While Jenny is fitting your pants, I will run down to my office and get my always packed overnight bag".

I tried on a pair of the pants and Jenny pinned the bottom of the pant leg to the right height. As all the pants were identical, except for color, she only needed to measure one pair. Jenney said she would work on them as fast as she could, she thought it would be less than forty-five minutes. I thanked her and she left the room.

It was almost 7:00 p.m. when Liz returned and she was followed into the room by a man with a chef's outfit on pushing a hotel style room service cart with a nylon bag over his shoulder. The service cart had four platters of oysters on the half shell, two bowls of jumbo shrimp, a bowl of seafood sauce, a plate of lemon wedges, a wire bowl with bread, a small plate with butter, two plates, knives and forks and a rose in a china vase. He parked the cart and reached underneath and pulled out a leaf on each side. He then spread out the items to make them look neat. He then took two of the room chairs and placed one on each side of the table. He removed the bag from his shoulder and opened it on the desk. Inside was our wine and wine glasses. He uncorked one bottle of the Riesling and half filled two glasses. He placed the cork screw on the open bag. He looked at Liz and made sure everything was to her satisfaction.

"Bon appétit;" he said, as he shut the door to the room.

I walked around the table to where Liz was standing and pulled her chair out for her. Once she was properly seated I took the napkin off her side plate and with a flick, I opened it and laid it across her lap. I then reached over and took the rose out of the vase and handed it to her. She responded with a very warm smile as she looked directly into my eyes. She laid the rose down very gently next to her side plate.

I raised my glass, Liz raised hers, as they touched I said; "To new friendships!"

"Very long relationships"

I didn't realize how hungry I was, the oysters were unbelievably delectable, I cannot think of a description that would come close to doing them justice, only to say, I finished the first six without a break. I started in on the jumbo shrimps it was like eating potato chips, just one more and one more and one more!

Liz was no slouch when it came to eating the seafood, although she handled herself like the true lady she was, she was eating very well.

From the moment that I had received the phone call from the President up until now, my little grey cells had definitely been working at one hundred and fifty percent capacity. Finally having the dreaded conversation with my daughter had definitely taken a substantial load of my mind, at least for the moment. This was the first time that I had actually relaxed a bit. There wasn't much more for my mind to consider. I had made the decision to go, and although I was still pondering what I would say to the extraterrestrials, I couldn't really have a game plan until I met them.

With everything else clogging my brain I really hadn't taken the time to really think about Liz. I leaned back in the chair a bit, and took a sip of the Riesling, I must say it was an excellent wine, I did like my wines! I seldom drank hard spirits and had no taste for beer, which had created some difficult situations when I was selling in the UK and Germany. I had developed a taste for wine in my early twenties. I belonged to two wine clubs and had a wine cellar with more than 1,000 bottles of nectar from the gods.

Liz was definitely a lady, I had always distinguished the words female and woman from the word lady. The words female and woman defined a gender where as the word lady defined someone within the female gender. In my opinion, very few women are actually ladies. A lady presents an image of dignity, sophistication, class and grace. I don't have a check list of what specific traits actually define a lady, but a lady is not difficult to spot. They stand out in any situation, whether it's a crowd of people in the lobby of a concert hall, a dinner party, or walking down the street. It's the way they talk, they way they look at you, the way they walk, the way they carry their heads. You can always recognize which woman if any is a lady! For me the classiest lady of all times was Audrey Hepburn.

Two things attracted me to any specific female. They must exude the lady quality and they must have an attractive face. Most males fall into a category. They are leg men, chest men or butt men. They could be attracted to a specific female figure. Well, in my case, I am a face man.

Liz reminded me of Catherine Zeta-Jones when she played in the movie Intolerable Cruelty

Liz was definitely a very attractive lady! She had big brown eyes which she had highlighted with just the right amount of eye liner, her eyebrows were sculptured perfectly. She was a brunette and her straight hair hung down past her shoulders. She had a soft and very clear complexion; her facial makeup did not appear to be put-on with a putty knife and her lips were not to full. Her neck was a bit longer than most women and it suited her extremely well. I was never good at guessing ages of men or women, but I thought she looked as if she was in her early to mid thirties. She was obviously well educated and very intelligent - I abhor stupid people, not those that are uneducated, there is a difference. A person can be very well educated and still be extremely stupid and in the opposite, can be poorly educated and be very intelligent.

I am an impulsive individual and I generally make important decisions very quickly, it's the trivial things that I generally ponder for hours, even days. Many years ago I was sitting at an office desk when this attractive woman walked in the door I immediately knew that she would be my wife. We were living together a few months later and married not long after that. I was receiving the same brain vibes about Liz. But I realized that she was far too beautiful and intelligent to want to be with an old fart like me. This lady could have any man she wanted and I was sure that she had a hundred men vying for her attention and companionship. I wouldn't stand a snowballs chance in hell.

Liz looked up and caught me staring at her. My bad habit had reared its ugly head.

"Everything okay?"

"Far beyond okay!" I responded with a smile and took another sip of wine without breaking eye contact.

Liz gave me a big smile and blushed.

I refilled the wine glasses a couple of times until the bottle was empty. I went over to the bag and took out the second bottle of Riesling; there were no objections from Liz.

"This was a brilliant idea Will; I'm surprised though. I would have pegged you as a meat and potatoes man."

"Well into my late twenties I was a meat and potatoes man, but over the years I was exposed to some of the world's finest culinary delights. I am an amateur chef; I enjoy cooking, especially French cuisine."

We had devoured well over three quarters of the seafood when I said; "I think that's it for me, as I reached for one more shrimp. The wine that remained in our glasses had emptied the second bottle of Riesling and I was beginning to feel a little light headed, the wine had definitely taken the edge of me.

Liz looked at me from across the table; her eyes had a deep sadness about them. I could tell she wanted to say something to me and either didn't know if she should or didn't know how to say it. It felt like we had sat there for hours, but it was less than a minute. Liz finally put together the will power to speak; "Will, I want to talk to you."

I didn't want to break into her thought so I didn't respond.

"Can we go over there and sit together?" Liz was pointing at a settee in front of a window.

We both got up at the same time. I allowed her to walk towards the settee and I followed. She sat down and I sat beside her. The settee was built for two, but it was small, our bodies touched as I sat down. Liz took one of my hands in hers and put her other hand on top. She wasn't looking at my face but at our hands. "Will, I am not an open person, most people say I'm a cold fish, or a closed book." I actually thought she was choking up a bit. Liz squeezed my hand in between hers. She paused for a moment but didn't lift her gaze from our hands. Will, we have known each other for less than a day and at noon tomorrow I may never see you again." She paused. "This is so difficult for me." I squeezed her hand. "Will, you are the most wonderful man I have ever known. I know that sounds silly, but you are so caring, the way you speak about your daughter, your love for her. You are willing to put your life on the line for humanity and you have asked for nothing in return. But it's even more than that; it's the confidence in your voice, the way you look at people; the way you look at me. Oh Will, I know I'm babbling and I don't make any sense and what I'm about to say is totally irrational." She paused and tried to get some composure. "Will Dafoe, I'm falling in love with you." Liz started to cry. I put my arms around her and held her against me. "Do you think I'm crazy, stupid, am I a fool?"

Damn, I thought, my brain vibes weren't wrong after all. I put my hand under her chin and raised her head so that she would be looking at me. "I have deep feelings for you to Liz!" Tears were pouring out of her eyes and down her cheeks. I kissed her cheeks to absorb the tears, she had a warm smile in her eyes and then I kissed her on the mouth, very tenderly, soft and long. She kissed me back. I sat there and held her in my arms.

There was a knock at the door, Liz rose from the settee, grabbed a tissue from a box and went to answer the door. It was Jenny with my pants. Liz took the pants, thanked her and closed the door. I'm sure Jenny must have noticed that Liz had been crying but didn't acknowledge it in any manner. I supposed that Jenny had seen and heard it all working at the Whitehouse and knew when to be a shadow rather than a person. I have read that people who have service staff aren't aware of their presence in a room and that they carry on with their lives as if no one else is present.

"I think I have enough room in my overnight bag for your pants;" and with that she opened her bag, moved a couple of items around and neatly put the pants in. She continued to adjust the contents in her overnight bag in order to create a small indent in the clothes at the top. She turned, walked over to the table and picked up the rose which she had placed beside her side plate. She gently wrapped it in a linen napkin, walked back to her bag and carefully placed it in the indent that she had made. She zipped up the bag; "shall we head off to New York?"

"I think it's time;"

Liz dialed a number on her cell phone and said; "We'll be on our way to the helicopter in about five minutes".

Liz unzipped a side compartment on her overnight case and took out a small make-up bag.

"I just need a few minutes to make myself look presentable;"

"If you look anymore presentable I may not be able to control myself;"

She walked past me on her way to the washroom and intentionally bumped into me and smiled.

Liz was only in the washroom for a few minutes. I didn't even have time to finish the cigarette I had lit. With all the wine I had consumed I thought it would be wise for me to relieve the pressures of life.

On exiting the washroom I grabbed by coat, laptop bag and the nylon bag containing the three bottles of Champagne. Liz had her coat over her arm, her overnight bag and purse. We both did our final seasoned traveler glance around the room to ensure that we had not left anything behind and headed for the door.

Although we were walking side by side, Liz was leading the way, in a few minutes we were outside. I could see the helicopter about one hundred and fifty yards away and we aimed directly for it. The sun had set a long time ago, but the area was very well lit and we had no problem walking the path to the helicopter.

As soon as the helicopter took to the air, Liz placed her hand in mine and gave me a smile that made me melt.

It only took a few minutes and we were down on the tarmac at Andrews Air Force Base. The helicopter had landed about twenty-five yards away from our Learjet. We grabbed our coats and bags and briskly walked towards the aircraft.

There was a girl in an Air Force blue uniform standing at the bottom of the steps. Liz went first and I followed her into the aircraft. This was not the same aircraft that we had flown from Toronto. The interior configuration was completely different. The aircraft that we had flown from Toronto had seats from the front to the back. This aircraft only had one rows of seats and then another bulkhead with a door that was closed.

Liz placed her bags and coat on a seat and then sat in the seat on the opposite side next to the aisle. I put my things next to hers and sat down at the window seat next to her.

We both fastened our seat belts. The Air Force girl had already raised the steps and closed the door.

The engines started up and we began taxing, this time there was no communication from the flight deck. In a few minutes we were in the air. Liz undid her seatbelt, and looked at me, her face had a devious expression on it; "Come with me".

She swung out of her seat and basically reached for the door knob on the bulkhead door in one motion. I was right behind her.

The door opened outward. Liz put her hand on my back and pushed me inside. She followed, closed the door and flipped a small latch to lock it.

The light was very subdued and my eyes needed a moment to adjust, it was a bedroom!

Liz looked at me her voice was low and sexy; "I'm tired of talking and actions are much more significant than words. We have a little more than an hour before we land in New York; let's use it to get to know each other better."

She flung her arms around me and pulled me tight up against her. Her lips felt warm and moist as they merged against mine. Her mouth opened slightly and I could feel her breath, our tongues met, ever so gently at first then into a frenzy trying to tangle together.

She unfastened her lips for a moment and looked directly into my eyes. Her voice had a very sultry sound and she had a big grin on her face. "I want you to know that what we are about to do is absolutely not a part of my assignment of providing you with whatever you need."

Without hesitation she fastened her lips against mine again. I hadn't had a woman in my arms like this in quite some time. My wife had been very ill for more than six months before she passed away and there had been no one since. I had a few opportunities. My friends had started inviting me over for dinners and I wasn't surprised to learn that there would be another guest, usually a female friend of the wife who was recently divorced. Although some were reasonably attractive, none of them were ladies. I always went home alone.

There was no doubt that I wanted Liz. I wanted to hold her tight against me and I wanted to make passionate love to her.

In our hot embrace, trying to get closer to each other than is physically possible, we lost our balance and fell onto the bed. Lying beside each other, Liz was unbuttoning my shirt, I was unbuttoning her blouse; it wasn't easy our arms kept getting entangled.

Liz pulled away from me, stood up from the bed and finished unbuttoning her blouse, undid the button on her skirt which dropped to the floor, she slid her white lace panties down over her silk stockings and kicked them off. She pushed her blouse off her shoulders, reached around to her back and unclasped her bra and let it fall to the floor. I watched her as she worked to remove her clothing. She stood there for a few seconds completely naked except for the silk stockings. She had an extremely good figure, slim waste, firm breasts, at least a C cup, a suitably sized pair of hips and very nice legs. There was minimal fat on her tummy.

She kneeled on the bed and reached for my belt buckle, she pulled it apart, undid the button on my pants and slid the zipper down. She didn't have to wonder if I was excited, it was extremely obvious. I grabbed the edges of my pants and underwear and pushed them off my hips and legs, down to my feet where they fell on the floor. The buckle made what I considered to be a loud noise as it hit the floor. I wondered if the Air Force girl on the other side of the bulkhead door knew what was going on. Who cared I thought. Liz unbuttoned the rest of my shirt and pulled it off me. I reached around her and pulled her hard against me, our lips melted together again.

Her nipples were hard as diamonds as they pushed against my chest. It was evident that I wasn't the only one that was excited.

I think I said earlier that I wanted to make love to Liz and that was no lie. But we weren't going to make love, something that in my mind at least, requires a lot of tenderness and foreplay. We were going to have unbridled sex. I'm not complaining, not in the least.

We couldn't get enough of each other. We couldn't get close enough to each other no matter how hard we tried. It wasn't easy to control my passion, but I didn't want to be the one to climax first.

Finally every muscle in Liz's body tightened, she let out a small shriek as she exploded. Her tightening muscles caused me to release at the exact same instant.

Although our bodies had become limp, I wasn't going to release Liz from my arms. I lay beside her, kissed her lips tenderly and directed her head to rest on my shoulder. I could feel her heart throbbing quite hard and fast against my chest. She had laid her arm across my chest. My arm had looped around her and my hand was on her tummy. We lay that way for awhile feeling our naked bodies against each other, not speaking. The noise of the two Learjet engines in the background, generally annoying, seemed to be creating euphoria.

I was looking at her as we lay there, and she turned her head to look up at me, her face seemed to be glowing. "That was unbelievable Mr. Dafoe;" she said with a big smile on her face as she tightened her arm around my chest.

"Ms. Montgomery with all due respect, the word unbelievable does not quite do it justice, I am leaning more towards, incredible, amazing, astonishing and mind blowing!"

With that she raised her head and kissed me full on the lips, a tender but powerful statement of her pleasure.

Liz released the kiss and looked at me wantonly but very seriously. "I would kill for a cigarette." Not being able to keep a straight face under the circumstances she laughed out loud.

"Your every wish is my command, my lady!" I jumped out of bed, put my pants and shirt on, I hadn't had a chance to take my socks off, tried to flatten and comb my hair with my hand and fingers; opened the bulkhead door and looked around. I honestly expected to see the Air Force girl standing on the other side of the door wagging her finger at me, "naughty, naughty!" to my relief she wasn't anywhere to be seen. I quickly grabbed Liz's purse, overnight bag and my laptop bag and returned to the room closing and locking the door behind me.

The lights were off and the blinds were drawn over the plane windows, but there was just enough ambient light that I could see Liz was sitting upright in the bed, with the covers draped over her legs ending just below the shadows of her naked breasts. Damn, she was beautiful!

I passed her the purse and reached into the laptop case for my cigarettes. I went into the washroom to see if there was anything I could fill with some water to use as an ashtray. A small plastic cup stood by the wash basin, I put a little water in the bottom of the cup and brought it back into the room. I sat on the edge of the bed and lit up a cigarette. I couldn't take my eyes of Liz.

Liz had reached over and was holding my hand as it rested on the bed. She looked over at the clock; "I better get dressed and fix my makeup." With that she pulled the covers back and got out of bed. Liz caught me staring at her naked body.

She had a big smile on her face. "Like what you see?"

I was blushing, and I don't do that often. I felt like a twelve year old who was just caught looking at his first naked picture in a Playboy magazine.

"Very much!"

Liz walked around the bed, and stood directly in front of me.

"I've never felt like this before. I hate it when men ogle me and I get very angry when I catch a man undressing me with his eyes, but for some reason, I really like the sensation of your eyes analyzing my body."

She stood there for a minute or so and my mind photographed every square inch of her, from her toes to the top of her head. She knew what I was doing and she turned around so that I could mentally absorb her backside. I pulled her towards me and gave her perfectly shaped butt a kiss.

Liz turned around, bent over and kissed me and then went to the end of the bed and put her clothes back on. She took the makeup bag from her overnight case and went into the bathroom.

In a few minutes she came out.

"Do I look okay?" she asked.

"No! You look phenomenal".

Liz smiled, opened the bulkhead door and we went back to our seats in the cabin.

I had just fastened my seatbelt when the Captain spoke over the intercom. "We are on our final decent into New York, La Guardia Airport."

"Perfect timing!" I said.

"Unbelievable timing;" Liz responded with a smirk on her face, she paused. "Oh, you mean that we just made it into the cabin. Yes, that was good timing too."

I laughed. Liz was no slouch at delivering wit. She had a quick mind and I truly appreciated that trait.

The descent and landing were uneventful. Liz and I didn't speak, but she had placed her hand on my leg just above my knee, every now and then she would give it a squeeze.

We taxied to a location near some hangers and as the engines of the Learjet were shutdown, a stretch limo pulled up next to the aircraft. A young woman got out of the limo and stood by the open back door. The driver had opened the truck and was waiting next to her.

When Liz saw the young woman standing by the car, she squeezed my leg; "that's my executive assistant, she's not aware of the crisis, please don't say anything."

I nodded and with that Liz and I grabbed our coats and bags and exited the aircraft and went directly towards the limo. As we reached the open back door, the driver took our bags and placed them gently in the trunk.

"Good evening Ms. Montgomery;" the young woman said.

"Hi Cheryl;"

Cheryl was a very tall girl, I would have guessed six feet, four inches but I glanced down and noticed she was wearing a pair of shoes with stiletto heels; maybe six foot one in her bare feet. Why would a tall girl want to make herself look even taller, I thought? She had the figure of a runway model, very thin and lanky, a nonexistent chest and no derrière. Now I'm not a tush man, but I do like a rounded backside on a woman, nothing looks worse than a girl on a beach in a bikini with a butt that doesn't fill the bottom portion of the swimsuit. Cheryl had straight blonde hair that ended just above her shoulders. Her face had strong features and she didn't seem to be wearing any make-up, she wasn't attractive, but she wasn't ugly, at least in my eyes.

Liz climbed into the limo and I followed, sitting next to her and facing front. Cheryl followed and sat across from Liz facing the back of the limo.

The limo driver started the car and we were off.

Liz looked at me. "This is Cheryl my administrative assistant. She is the one who was out gathering up all the items you required." Liz then turned to look at Cheryl; "This is Mr. Dafoe;" Liz said.

"Nice to meet you Sir;" she glanced over at Liz and continued. "Ms. Montgomery everything that was requested is in a small suitcase in the trunk. There are few things that you should be aware of. The camera and voice recorder I purchased use the identical batteries and memory cards. Although you didn't request extra batteries I purchased twelve packages of four, a total of forty-eight fresh batteries."

I had forgotten to request extra batteries. "Thank you. I had forgotten the batteries, I'm very grateful that you caught my error."

Cheryl glanced at me, smiled, nodded her head and continued. "I also purchased fifty – sixty-four gigabyte memory cards." Cheryl paused to see if there were any comments and then continued. "When you said that the prescription medications were for a one hundred days I doubled up on the toothpaste and bought three tins of shaving cream. I also bought two small containers of Gillette aftershave for sensitive skin." Cheryl paused again. "I added three items that I thought might have been forgotten, a comb, small sewing kit and a small first aid kit. I figured if you didn't require the extras you could always toss them. I know that Jenny received the pants and tailored them for Mr. Dafoe."

"Was there anything else?" Cheryl asked.

"What color Lamborghini did you get me?" I enquired with a chuckle.

Cheryl glanced over at Liz as if to say, you never mentioned a Lamborghini, then she realized that I was joking with her and she looked at me without a smile and said with a surprising firmness; "its red, it's in the hotel room, it was a real challenge getting it in the elevator and up to the 27th floor."

I laughed.

Cheryl looked over at Liz. "Here are the keycards for the hotel suite – room 2716, the Piedmont suite, it's a smoking room. I registered it in your name. I took the liberty of booking myself a room, just in case you needed something, a last minute thought, I'm in room 1723, I wrote the number on the back of the keycard envelope."

"Excellent work as usual!" Liz responded.

"Thank you Cheryl for your excellent and extremely thoughtful efforts, I truly appreciate it." I said.

"You're more than welcome;" her face lit up with a big smile. "Can I have the Lamborghini when you're finished with it?"

I smiled back. "I'll leave it right where I find it. It's all yours, and don't ever say I didn't give you anything."

I had been concentrating intensely on what Cheryl was saying and hadn't noticed that we had a police escort, two motorcycle officers in front and two behind the limo. They were stopping cross traffic at all the intersections and we were proceeding through red lights. We were almost at the hotel.

Cheryl broke the silence. "I hope the flight from Washington was okay;"

Before Liz could say anything I spoke. "Cheryl; I have travelled on hundreds if not thousands of airplanes. I can say, without a shadow of a doubt, that the hospitality aboard that Learjet far surpassed anything that I had ever experienced before and I can only hope that I will be able to experience the exact same hospitality in the future. The flight itself seemed to bounce a lot and the temperature in the cabin made me sweat quite a bit, this is not a complaint as I truly enjoyed every minute of the flight."

"Mr. Dafoe;" Liz interjected. "There is no doubt in my mind that you will experience very similar forms of hospitality many times in the future."

Cheryl looked at us as if we had lost our minds, but said nothing more.

We pulled up in front of the Century hotel and the doorman efficiently opened the door of the limo for us. The driver opened the trunk, we exited the limo. The doorman had placed all of the bags on a luggage cart and wheeled them into the hotel behind us.

Cheryl tipped the doorman, and told him that we had already checked in and would make our way to the rooms without any additional assistance. We quickly grabbed our bags from the luggage cart and headed towards the elevators. Cheryl pushed numbers "27" and "17". The door opened on the 17th floor and Cheryl got out wishing us a good night. A few moments later we arrived on the 27th floor. We walked down a corridor past a couple of rooms until we came to a room with a plaque on the wall identifying it as the Piedmont Suite and a number on the door that said 2716.

Liz removed a keycard from its paper pouch, slid it into the lock slot below the handle, a small green light came on, we heard a slight click and I reached for the handle and opened the door. Liz dropped her purse and overnight bag on the floor inside the room, and hung up her coat in the coat closet that was just on the inside left of the door. I gently put the nylon bag holding the Champagne on the floor and hung up my coat beside Liz's.

"What would you like to do now?" Liz asked with a grin on her face.

"There is a big difference between what I would like to do and what I need to do;" I went over to her, put my arms around her and kissed her, she kissed me back. "What I would like to do first and foremost is make love to you;" still holding her in my arms. "But I need to do a couple of things first and we need to talk about a couple of things. Then when there is nothing more I can do that relates to the assignment I can put one hundred percent of my concentration where it belongs – YOU!"

Liz had a big smile on her face, she gave me a kiss; "Well make it quick;"

"First, I am going to get some ice to chill the Champagne." I grabbed the ice bucket and headed down the hall, filled it at the ice station and returned. Liz was standing there holding one of the bottles of Champagne. I put the ice bucket down on the desk and she dug a hole in the ice and planted the Champagne in it.

"What's next?" She asked.

"It's not that I don't trust Cheryl, but I want to check the items in the suitcase." I grabbed the suitcase and Liz's overnight bag and went into the bedroom. Liz followed. I opened the suitcase and laid everything out on the bed. Cheryl had purchased a small nylon bag and had placed all my toiletries and medications in it. I opened it as well and added the items to the top of the bed spread. I asked Liz to remove my pants from her overnight bag and place them with the other items on the bed. She did that and removed the rose from its linen napkin wrapper and placed it on the night table beside the bed.

I looked at the collection of clothes and other items. I picked up the camera box and removed it from its packaging and tossed the packaging in the waste paper basket next to the bed. The camera looked simple enough. I opened the camera and inserted four batteries. There was a memory card already in the slot. I put the camera to my eye, aimed it at Liz and snapped a picture, then another one.

"You could have at least let me brush my hair and fix my makeup."

I didn't respond and quickly snapped two more pictures of her. I looked at the back of the camera and figured out how to view the four pictures that I had just taken. Cheryl had made a good choice, the camera was easy to use and the pictures of Liz were quite good, considering I was one of the world's worst photographers.

I then opened the box that contained the voice recorder. Loaded it with two batteries and pushed a blue button a small green LED light illuminated. "Testing, testing – one two three;" I said into the microphone on the unit.

I pushed the blue button again and the unit turned off. The only other button on the unit was a red button on the top. I pushed it and heard testing, testing – one, two, three. "That seems to work just dandy;" I said.

Liz smiled.

I picked up the packing from the voice recorder and deposited it in the waste paper basket. I inspected the suitcase and noticed a side pocket on the outside. I picked up the camera and placed it in the side pocket along with the voice recorder, two memory cards, two packages of fresh batteries and the instruction booklets that came with the devices.

I then proceeded to put all the clothes and toiletries back into the suitcase along with the extra batteries and memory cards. I went into the sitting room and grabbed my laptop case and took it back into the bedroom. I put two pens in with the camera and voice recorder and placed my pad of paper on the very top of the clothes.

I looked around the room; there was a small desk. I picked up my laptop and placed it on the desk. Turned it on, waited for what felt like hours for the operating system to load and then clicked send on the email program. Daniel and Joël are taken care of, I thought to myself.

Liz had left the bedroom and I could hear her rummaging through the desk in the other room. In a couple of minutes she returned with a small pad of paper. It had the hotel name on the top of each page, but it was the perfect size to fit in the pocket on the side of the suitcase.

"Thank you! It's perfect."

"At your service;" Liz had a big smile.

I zipped up the suitcase and took it with my laptop case into the other room. Liz followed.

"Liz, I need to ask you to do a few things for me. This requires a glass of champagne and a cigarette."

Liz went and retrieved her cigarettes, notepad and pen from her purse and my cigarettes from my laptop bag. I smiled to myself when Liz with no hesitation and complete comfort opening my bag without even asking. I went and opened the champagne and poured us each a glass. I had taken the Champagne glasses from the Whitehouse!

I passed Liz a glass of champagne. "To a very special lady;" Liz smiled and we touched glasses.

I took a very big inhale of my cigarette. "Liz, there are a couple of mundane matters and one very serious matter that I need you take care of for me." I inhaled again. "My car is parked at the Flyservice terminal at the Toronto airport. I would like to have it returned to the garage at my home." I handed Liz a piece of paper with my home address, license plate number and description of the car. I went over to my laptop bag and pulled out a set of keys handed them to her and pointed out which key was for what.

"Consider it done;"

"I would like you to take my laptop and its case with you. I've decided that I'm not going to take it with me. The batteries will die in a few hours, and it is just something that I don't see a big value in having with me. I would also like you to hold on to my wallet, the small amount of cash I have and passport. I really don't see a need for any of them. I doubt the aliens will ask for formal identification."

Liz chuckled as I reached into the back pocket of my pants and pulled out my wallet and passport and the side pocket to get the cash. Before I handed them to her, I pulled out a picture of Barbara from the inside of the wallet. I looked at it for a few seconds and before I could put it in my pocket Liz asked if she could see it. I handed it to her with the wallet, cash and passport.

"Pretty girl."

"Yes she is."

I took the picture back from Liz and put it in my shirt pocket. If I starred at it to long I thought I might start to cry.

Liz saw that I was getting choked up and tried to get my mind off the situation, she quickly downed the champagne left in her glass and asked me to refill it. I filled both our glasses.

"Liz I am going to ask you to do something for me that maybe above and beyond the call of duty. If something should happen to me and I don't return and the world is not annihilated I don't want Barbara to hear about my demise over the phone. I am asking and I know it's an enormous request and is really not fair to you, to tell her in person. Explain as best you can, what happened and tell her that I loved her more than she can ever imagine".

I could hardly get the words out of my mouth, tears were flowing down my face; it hit me hard when I realized that I may never see my daughter again.

Liz had tears rolling down her cheeks as well. She got up from her chair and put her arms around me, her head on my shoulder.

Liz pulled away from me a bit.

"I'm sorry; "I said.

"There is nothing for you to be sorry about. You love your daughter very much. The fact that you can share and show your emotions, something that few men can do makes me feel very special. If it comes to that, I will do it, but I'm sure that you will be back safe and sound. I'm counting on it Will. This is not going to be a short friendship; it is going to be a long relationship. I know it in my heart". She kissed me very tenderly on the lips.

"Definitely time for another cigarette and some more champagne;" I said.

I filled up our Champagne glasses which emptied the bottle, retrieved another bottle from the bag and placed it in the ice.

Liz had moved to a loveseat and I sat down beside her. She moved up against me so that the lengths of our bodies were up against each other. Nothing was said as we sipped our Champagne and smoked our cigarettes.

The Champagne was definitely having a relaxing effect on me, I was beginning to feel very mellow, the situation with Barbara had all but left my mind and I began to think about this extremely attractive lady sitting up against me.

It was after ten but I wasn't feeling physically tired, I was mentally exhausted and I felt rather grungy.

"If you will excuse me for a couple of minutes, I'm going to take a quick shower."

I took my suitcase back into the room and pulled out the toiletries bag.

I hadn't been in the washroom off the bedroom yet. I opened the bathroom door and was duly impressed. It must have been recently renovated. There was a large stall shower, at least six feet by four feet and a whirlpool tub plenty big enough for four adults.

I dropped my clothes on the floor went over to one of the sinks, there were two, and turned on the hot water tap. I pulled the shaving gear out and cleaned my face of the stubble. I had stubble five minutes after I shaved! With a clean shave, I opened the door to the stall shower. It was equipped with a multi-head water sprayer contraption that I had only seen in magazines. I turned the water on, adjusted it to a nice temperature and then flipped the lever that I thought would direct the water through the overhead showerhead. Well, I was close, but no cigar, water came out of every nozzle. I pushed and pulled on a few more levers and finally got the water to spray from the showerhead. I stood under the water with my eyes closed and just allowed it to cascade down my body. I did some of my best thinking in the shower and whenever I had a problem I would stand in the shower until the answer was delivered from above.

All of a sudden I lost water pressure and the water went cool. Before I could react, the pressure was back and so was the water temperature. I wondered what had happened but more importantly I wondered if it would happen again.

Now I felt a cool breeze enter the stall shower, what the hell is going on I thought to myself. I opened my eyes and there standing before me was Liz.

"A shower sounded like a great idea;" Liz said. "I don't think that I have mentioned it, but I'm an environmental conservationist and I believe that water is precious, a natural resource that should not be wasted. You don't mind if I shower with you?" Her face was beaming, she looked exquisite.

"I have just recently become an environmental conservationist actually it's as recent as a few seconds ago. I believe that it is our duty to help conserve water. It's of course the only reason that I would allow you to shower with me."

This was the first time I had been able to look at Liz's naked body with plenty of light. It was as close to perfect as you could imagine.

Liz looked at me with a sultry expression, "Soap me up"

I couldn't think of anything I would rather do. I moved out of the path of the water, placed my hands on Liz's waste and positioned her under the showerhead. Once she was completely drenched I moved her to a dryer part of the stall shower and commenced to lather her body with body wash that was provided compliments of the hotel.

I started with each arm and then moved to the top of her shoulders. I slowly massaged the lather over her soft skin. I worked in small circles, allowing the circles to move lower with each pass. I was in no rush! The lather circles reached the top of her breasts, then over them until I was making circles around her nipples. I stopped leaned over and took one of her nipples between my lips and flicked my tongue over it for a few seconds. I raised my head and looked at Liz, her eyes were closed but I could see from the expression on her face that she was enjoying it. I leaned down again and repeated the process on the other nipple. Liz let out a small moan.

I finished lathering her breasts; they were nicely firm and fit comfortably in my hands. I worked the circles down her tummy and even lower. When we were in the Learjet I was aware that Liz was almost clean shaven, but I had felt some hair, but really couldn't make it out in the shadows. Liz had a small landing strip, about an inch and half long and three quarters of an inch wide very neatly trimmed. It really turned me on for some reason, as I lathered it. I made sure I lathered her sides and hips, my hands never left her body, I moved back to the bottom of her tummy and Liz moved to spread her legs apart a bit. I didn't continue where she expected, but instead worked the lather circles down one leg and then back up the other. As my hand reached the top of the inside of her thigh I allowed it to touch her, slowly and gently, she tried to push her body towards my hand but I moved it to just above her tummy.

I put my left arm around her waist and pulled her towards me so that the right side of her body was tight up against mine, her shoulder against my chest. I put my lips tight against hers our mouths opened ever so slightly. At the same time my right hand moved lower, until it wasn't on her tummy anymore. My fingers had reached the most sensitive of areas, I moved slowly at first and then faster, Liz was trying to break my kiss but my left arm had moved from her waist to the back of her head, I held her firmly in position. Her body began to vibrate against me. She managed to pull her lips off mine and screamed. I was sure everyone in the hotel heard it. She went limp and I had to grab onto her to prevent her from collapsing on the floor. She put her arms around my neck, her head against my chest and held herself upright.

Liz was gulping for air; "Wow and double wow" still trying to catch her breath.

In an instant she went from limp to fully alert, without warning she opened the shower door and ran out. I noticed that the shower suddenly had more water pressure. She opened the shower door, grabbed my hand and literally pulled me out. The little devil had been running the water into the whirlpool tub, complete with a bubble bath. The soap bubbles were higher than the top edge of the tub.

"Caught it just in time;" she said with a big smile on her face. "Get in!"

I was a little concerned that if I got in, the water would flow over the top of the tub. I cautiously stepped into the tub. I could hear the water running down the overflow tube. Could have been messy I thought to myself. The water was hot and I had to lower my body into it slowly to allow it to acclimatize itself to the water temperature. As I was trying to sit down, Liz had brought the ice bucket and Champagne into the bathroom. She went over and poured us each a glass. By this time I was sitting in the tub, soap bubbles were lapping at my chin. She passed me both glasses of bubbly, went back and retrieved the loaded ice bucket and placed it on the floor within my reach. With that accomplished she began to climb into the tub.

"Don't make any waves!" Liz looked at me with a big smile.

Liz sat down beside me and put one leg over mine. I passed her a glass of Champagne and we just relaxed, not saying anything. Her body felt extremely nice against mine.

"You know;" she said, "I messed up, I should've had Cheryl buy some candles!

"It's not the ambience, the whirlpool tub or the room that is making this a night I will truly never forget. It's you!"

Liz responded by pushing herself even harder against me.

Now you are probably thinking that this is all far too good to be true and that a beautiful, intelligent woman wouldn't be throwing herself at me and telling me that she was falling in love, after knowing me for less than a few hours. I must admit that thought had entered my mind more than once, part of me was truly curious about the sincerity of all of this, yet another part, the one that controlled my male hormones decided that at this moment it really didn't matter. This may be the last mental and physical relationship that I ever have with a woman and there was no reason not to enjoy it. I wasn't forcing myself on her, if anything, she had been the aggressor and the fact that she was beautiful and intelligent made it all the more enjoyable. Why be a fool and worry about the reasons or sincerity at this time. I decided to just lay back and enjoy life, what little I may have left.

"Will, I assume you know that I have read a dossier about you, it was put together very quickly when your name first appeared on the lists created by the Security Council members. But because the researchers only had a very limited number of hours to compile it, other than the fact that you are a super salesman, have had your name appear in Who's Who, have been the Vice-President of Sales and Marketing for Tricon Inc., for eight years, a widower, with one child in university, you are financially secure, but far from wealthy and that you don't have a criminal record; I know very little about you." She paused for a moment to sip her Champagne. "Who is William Dafoe?" she asked with a grin on her face and snicker in her voice.

It had never crossed my mind that Liz would have read a dossier about me. But it made sense and it didn't bother me I had no hidden past or skeletons in the closet that I was ashamed of.

"I'm not very adept at talking about myself. Would you like to ask me some questions? That might make it easier."

I reached over removed the bottle of Champagne from the ice bucket and topped up our glasses.

"Have you always been in sales and marketing?" Liz asked.

"Do you want the long or short answer?"

"I would prefer the long answer;" and with that she gave me a kiss on the cheek.

"In my teens I thought that I was best suited to be in one of the trades; carpentry, electrical or mechanics. As far back as I can remember; I was very good at working with my hands."

Liz quickly interjected; "You are far beyond *very good* at working with your hands;" she squeezed my thigh.

I am sure I was blushing, but thanks to the temperature of the water in the tub I don't think Liz noticed. I paused for a sip of Champagne and continued. "I attended a trade high school. Its basic mandate was to prepare teens to enter trade apprentice programs. Besides the three Rs, we were exposed to a variety of different trades. My father passed away when I was only seventeen. I finished high school and worked for numerous companies for relatively short periods of time trying to find a trade that I really liked and could make a career out of. My father had worked at a job that he hated in order to support the family. I definitely didn't want to follow in those footsteps.

"From the time I was eleven years old, I used to spend my free time at a local small independent hardware store. For me it was better than being in a candy shop. I would read the labels on products and watched intently as the owner repaired windows and screens and listened as he served the customers. When I was fourteen, I was hanging out at my usual place, the hardware store. It was far busier than normal and the owner was having a real problem serving all of the customers. I just jumped in and started helping customers, telling them which products they needed to accomplish what tasks, I knew where everything was in the store. I helped out all day and really enjoyed it. At the end of the day, the owner offered me a part time job working at the store. I would go there every day after school and on Saturdays. Those were the days when stores opened and closed at rational hours and did not open on a Sunday. I worked there until I finished high school.

"I must be boring the life out of you?"

"If I get bored I'll let you know." She leaned over and kissed me, not on the cheek this time but flush on the lips. She held the kiss for at least twenty seconds. It took my breath away.

I caught my breath and continued; "I realized that working in a trade was not really for me. There was little if any true interaction with people, and although the people I worked with were okay, we had nothing in common. I didn't want to go to the bar after work, down a few beers and talk about sports. I was working for Ontario Hydro as an apprentice lineman and although the pay was very good, the working conditions, and the winter that we had just gone through, were not enticing.

"I considered going back into retail, but the pay was just a little better than minimum wage. I saw a job advertised for an inside salesman for a small electronics parts manufacture. I applied and got the position. That was my introduction to industrial sales, I really liked it and I was good at it. Within three years, at the ripe old age of twenty-two, I had moved into the position of North American Sales Manager, a position which I had basically created.

"Over the years I was very lucky to be in the right spot at the right time and my sales career grew from there. I enjoy selling and I am not embarrassed to say that I am a salesman, which reminds me of a joke. I warn you now; I have a joke repertoire that would fill volumes of books!

"Two guys bump into each other on a sidewalk and realize that they went to the same public school. One guy looks at the other and says; "what do you do for living?" The guy looks back over his shoulder and then across the road. Very softly he says "I'm a salesman. But don't tell my mother, she thinks I play piano in a brothel."

Liz chuckled.

"Other than that I am a true romantic, I prefer live theater over most other types of entertainment. I listen to the classics; my favorite piece of music is Tchaikovsky's 1812 overture, I don't care for opera but I do enjoy a hearing a symphony and I will attend the ballet. I enjoy walking and seeing the sights and I can spend countless hours in art galleries and museums. My favorite city is London, probably because of the abundance of live theater, art galleries, museums and restaurants. I sleep naked; I don't drink beer, seldom drink hard liquor, and love wine. I am an amateur chef, I love to cook and my favorite cuisine is French. My best friend lives in England; needless to say we don't see each other that often."

I paused for a second to take a gulp of needed air.

"Up until this morning at 11:17, the only truly important person in my life was my daughter Barbara. I'm a workaholic. That's the end of my history and life lesson."

I took another sip of Champagne.

"Besides the fact that you are by far the most captivating lady I have ever met, very beautiful and extremely intelligent, I know less about you than you do of me. No one supplied me with your dossier! It's your turn. Who is Elizabeth Montgomery?"

Liz squeezed my thigh again, the water may have been hot, but she was defiantly blushing.

I filled our Champagne glasses again.

Liz looked at me her eyes had a sadness about them. "There really isn't a lot to tell. I'm an only child. My parents have been in politics all their lives. My father was a senator for thirty-four years. He left the senate due to his health but still is very active in the Republican Party. He spends his time consulting with other politicians, industry and public speaking. My mother is in the state senate.

"I guess I would say I had an upper middle class lifestyle. I was sent to a girl's only boarding finishing school when I was fourteen, from there I attended Brown where I received a Masters in Political Science and then I went to Harvard and received a Law Degree. After completing my law degree I took a position with REND as an Associate of Political Science. I worked there until this administration was elected when I was asked to join The President's cabinet; I believe that it was my Dad who arranged it, although he vehemently denies it. Officially, I am on a leave of absence from REND.

"I generally work ten to twelve hours a day, seven days a week. I have very few close friends. Let me amend that last statement, to be honest, I don't have any close friends and no life outside of the Whitehouse. People say that I am a very difficult person to get to know.

I wouldn't say my life was perfect by any means.

"I enjoy the classical composers as well, although I lean towards Brahms, Mozart and Beethoven. I enjoy live theater, although I haven't been in years. I do like walking and have spent hours at the Smithsonian. I am definitely not a good cook; I have problems boiling water. I don't drink beer either; I do enjoy a vodka martini at the right moment, but wine is definitely my beverage of choice. I sleep in my birthday suit, and no matter how cold it is outside I like to have the window open in my bedroom. I have never been to an opera or ballet, so I don't know if I would enjoy them or not."

Liz had always seemed very upbeat, a person who loved life and her job, this was a real insight into her persona, the Liz underneath the government uniform.

I put my arm around her and held her tight against me, she reciprocated. "Liz, can I ask you a question?"

Liz looked anxious as if she wasn't sure if she should say yes. With some uneasiness in her voice; "You can ask me anything you want."

"I have noticed that you refer to yourself as Elizabeth and that the President addressed you as Elizabeth. Yet you asked me to call you Liz. Would you prefer if I called you Elizabeth?"

Liz looked relieved; this apparently wasn't the question she didn't want to answer. "No! My parents call me Elizabeth and I don't have a very good relationship with them. My colleagues and the President call me Elizabeth. I find it very formal and totally lacking any warmth, which believe it or not is what I want. When I meet people I tell them to call me Elizabeth, in my mind it creates a barrier and as I said at the Whitehouse, I am not an easy person to get to know, when I meet people I immediately put up a defensive shield around myself. For some reason, which I am unable to explain, I didn't want to put that shield up when we met, for me that meant having you call me Liz and not Elizabeth. Will, I don't remember the last time I asked anyone to call me Liz when we first met, not even girls."

I was a little surprised to find out that Liz didn't have a good relationship with her parents and I wondered why. She didn't volunteer an explanation and this wasn't the time to ask. I was also curious as to the reason or reasons behind her desire to put up defenses when she met someone.

The water in the tub was beginning to get cold and looking at my fingers I noticed that I was turning into a prune.

"I think it's time to get out of the tub."

"Uhu;" Liz responded. But she didn't release her arms from around me. I wasn't going to push her and just lay there enjoying the feel of her body against mine, her arms around me and her head on my shoulders.

After a couple of minutes, Liz released her arms and sat up.

I looked at her and in a very firm tone; "Stay in the tub."

I swung myself over the edge of the tub and removed two large bath towels from the heated towel rack. I draped them over my arm. I went back to the tub and offered my hand to Liz to help her out.

Liz, reached for one of the towels over my arm, but I moved my arm out of her reach.

"Stand there and don't move"

I took one of the bath towels and began drying her body. Gently I patted the water droplets off her shoulders. I took one of her arms and dried it, then the other. Liz had this big grin on her face. I took the other arm and dried it. I dried her chest, tummy and then went down on my knees and dried each leg and foot. I dried each toe independently, which made Liz squirm a bit. I stood up, told her to turn around and I dried her back and derrière. Once she was dry, I retrieved one of the very plush terrycloth bathrobes, also compliments of the hotel, from a hook on the bathroom door. I held it behind her as she put her arms in the sleeves. I turned her around, closed the bathrobe tight around her and did up the waist tie.

I then took her by the hand and seated her in front of the mirrored vanity. I quickly dried myself and put on the second bathrobe.

"I'll be right back."

I went into the sitting room and brought back Liz's purse.

"A hair brush, if you please madam."

Liz reached into the purse and pulled out a hairbrush and handed to me. I could see the reflection of her face in the mirror. She definitely didn't need the makeup that she wore. She was naturally beautiful. Liz seemed to be beaming from ear to ear.

I removed the hair dryer from its wall bracket and with the hair brush in my other hand I started to dry and brush her hair. While this may sound somewhat unusual, I had a lot of practice at drying a woman's hair. When my wife was ill, I used to wash and dry her hair all the time.

Liz had very thick hair and it took about fifteen minutes to dry and brush it, I enjoyed every minute. When I finished I reached around and handed Liz her hair brush and placed the hair dryer back in its mounting bracket on the wall.

Liz stood up and grabbed the lapels of my bathrobe with her hands and said; "Sir, I would like to give you a tip for the excellent work you have done. But I don't seem to have any cash, is there another arrangement we might make?"

She put her arms around me and kissed me with a passion that I had not experienced in a very long time, if ever.

She took my hand and led me into the bedroom. She pulled back the covers off the bed looked at me and with a very commanding voice said; "Drop that robe and get into bed."

I did as instructed. Liz dropped her robe and climbed into the bed beside me. I turned off the lamp on the night table. Liz put her head on my shoulder, wrapped her legs around mine and placed her arm over my chest.

"I want us to make love all night." She whispered.

And, that's exactly what we did.

Chapter 3 – Day 3

I woke to the delightful feeling of lips against mine.

"I think we should get up;" Liz said.

I glanced at the clock on the nightstand; it was 7:45 a.m. I could see threads of light penetrating the edges of the drapes on the window.

"I would much rather just stay in bed and make love to you."

I placed my arms around her and drew her tight against me. We kissed like a couple of teenagers in heat.

Liz pulled the covers back. Feeling Liz's naked body against me and her tongue in my mouth had aroused me again.

Liz looked at me with bedroom eyes; "I'll take care of that!"

She kneeled next to me with her head facing my feet and took me in her moist warm mouth. My eyes rolled back in their sockets. It didn't take long for me to finish.

Liz gave me a slap on the side of my butt "up! She said. I'm going to order breakfast from room service, you start the shower".

I went into the bathroom. I could hear Liz on the phone ordering breakfast. I ran my hands over my cheeks and realized that I should shave again. Before I finished Liz came into the bathroom, smiled at me and walked into the stall shower. I finished shaving and joined her. Besides some light kissing, touching and playfulness nothing more happened.

We dried ourselves; I took my toiletries bag back into the bedroom, opened my suitcase and took out a fresh pair of clothes and put them on. I removed Barbara's picture from the pocket of my soiled shirt and placed it in the pocket of the shirt I had just put on. I found a plastic laundry bag in the closet and put my soiled clothes in it. Tucked my toiletry bag and the plastic bag into the suitcase and zipped it up.

Liz was still in the bathroom when there was a knock at the door. I answered it, it was Cheryl.

"Good morning Sir;" she said, very bright eyed and cheery. "I have an envelope for you; she handed it to me. She then made an abrupt turn and headed towards the elevators".

As I was closing the door, I noticed a food service cart being pushed down the hall. Our breakfast I thought, I waited to see if it was headed towards our room.

The bellhop stopped at our door and I opened it to allow him to push the cart in. He immediately set it up. I didn't have any US money with me, and I had given the little Canadian money I had to Liz with my wallet.

The bellhop handed me the service check, I signed it and added a 25 percent tip. What the hell I thought. It's the US government picking up the tab. They can afford to be generous!

The bellhop glanced at the service check and gave me a big thank you and exited the room closing the door behind him.

Liz was still in the bathroom so I decided to check the contents of the envelope that Cheryl had delivered. The envelope contained the legal agreement pertaining to Barbara's well being, should anything happen to me. I read the document. It was only three pages in length, but very well written. It appeared to cover everything I had asked for. It had the Whitehouse seal on the bottom over the signature of the President.

Liz came out of the bedroom; she had put on a clean outfit with a brightly colored scarf around her neck. It reminded me of the scarves that the flight attendants on American Airlines once wore. Liz had freshened her makeup and had brushed her hair. She couldn't have looked better.

"What have you got there?"

"It's the agreement with respect to Barbara's security."

"Are you happy with it?"

"It looks good to me, but would you mind perusing it with your lawyer hat on?"

"It would be my pleasure, Mr. Dafoe."

I handed Liz the document, pulled out her chair from the table and moved her in. I took one of the folded napkins off the table unfurled it and placed it on her lap. Liz looked up at me and smiled.

"Eat your breakfast before it gets cold." I removed the metal lid that was keeping it warm.

Liz had ordered us Eggs Benedict one of my favorite breakfasts. She hadn't asked me what I wanted, I wondered if she also read minds.

Liz read the document as she ate her breakfast. I didn't talk to her; I didn't want to interrupt her concentration.

Liz dabbed her lips with napkin. "I think it covers everything you asked for."

"I would like you to hold onto it. There's no reason for Barbara to see it if everything works out the way I want it to. In the event things don't work out, you can give it to her at the appropriate time."

"I'll look after everything."

"You will be coming with me to the departure point won't you?"

"Nothing will keep me from your side."

"Liz, I am going to miss you very much."

Liz jumped out of her chair and ran into the bedroom, I followed her, she was sitting on the bed, holding a pillow and crying. I went over to her, sat beside her and put my arms around her.

"I don't want you to go."

"I have no choice. I'll be back before you know it."

She held me very tight, sobbing a little, but I finally felt her relax and the sobbing subsided.

"I would like to give you something;" she said. She stood up, grabbed her purse and opened it. After rifling around in the purse for a few moments she pulled out a picture wallet. She flipped past a few pictures, stopped at one and said; "this is my Mom and Dad." I had less than a second to look at it before she flipped to another picture. She separated the plastic envelope that held the picture and pulled it out. She went over to the desk and wrote something on the bottom of the picture.

"I would like you to have this with you;" handing me the picture. It was of course a picture of Liz. It had obviously been taken by a professional. She looked absolutely stunning. On the right hand side of the picture Liz had written; *To Will, The man of my dreams. Yours forever, Liz.*

"Thank you, it will be next to my heart as long as we are apart." I placed it in my shirt pocket with Barbara's picture.

Liz was still sitting on the end of the bed. She put the photo wallet back in her purse and pulled out her cell phone. "I want some pictures of you;" Without waiting for a response she stood up, brought the cell phone up to her face and took at least six pictures.

"There's something else I want Liz! I want your scarf, the one that is around your neck."

Liz didn't hesitate. She undid the scarf and handed it to me. I brought it up to my nose; her scent was in the scarf just like I thought.

"Please put it on me." Liz stood up and took the scarf from my hand.

"Are you sure you want to wear it?"

"I'm beyond sure. I want to make a fashion statement to the extraterrestrials."

Liz laughed.

Liz put the scarf around my neck and tied it. She was very close and I took the opportunity to draw her against me and kiss her. She didn't object.

"Tit for tat;" Liz said. "I want the shirt that you wore yesterday. I must be honest though, I won't wear it to work. I'm really not into making fashion statements. I'll wear it when I'm at home and when I sleep."

I retrieved the shirt from the laundry bag and handed it to Liz. She folded it very neatly and placed it in her overnight bag.

The clock on the nightstand caught my eye, it was 10:45.

Liz looked around the bedroom and grabbed the rose that she had placed on the nightstand and wrapped it back up in the linen napkin and went out into the sitting room. She came back with my laptop bag and the envelope with the legal document for Barbara. She pushed on the top of her clothes a little and managed to get them both in her overnight case. She put the napkin wrapped rose in her purse.

She looked at me and answered a question that I handed asked; "less items to carry."

I took my suitcase and Liz's overnight bag and placed them next to the entry door of the room. Liz went back to the bathroom to correct her makeup and then followed. She placed her purse next to the bags.

We sat on the loveseat our bodies touching tightly holding hands, neither one of us said anything.

"Liz, will it embarrass you or create any sort of problem for you if I kiss you with other people present just prior to departure?"

"It will hurt me very much if you don't." With that she squeezed my hand even tighter.

It was 11:10, Liz looked at me. "We should make our way down to the lobby. The limo will be here at 11:15."

I took Liz's coat out of the closet and held it for her as she put it on. I then put my coat on, picked up Liz's overnight bag and my suitcase. We did the standard room once over to check for forgotten items and closed the door behind us.

We didn't speak in the elevator, I held Liz's hand.

When the elevator door opened at the lobby level, I immediately noticed Cheryl sitting in a chair just out of the way of foot traffic. She stood as soon as she saw us.

"The limo's not here yet;" Cheryl said to both of us.

Liz handed Cheryl the keycard to the room. "Do one final check of the suite before you leave the hotel and make sure nothing was left behind. Oh, there is one thing; we left one of the nylon wine bags and two champagne glasses somewhere in the room. If you can find it take it back with you to the Whitehouse and give it to Donny in the kitchen."

Cheryl nodded in response.

I instantly realized that the champagne glasses were in the bathroom on the floor next to the Whirlpool tub. What would Cheryl think? I hoped it wouldn't cause Liz any embarrassment. I didn't really care what Cheryl though of me.

My coat was open and Cheryl looked at Liz's scarf around my neck. "Fashion statement?" she asked, and then thinking that she may have overstepped herself quickly tried to cover her faux pas, "sorry, it's none of my business".

Liz and I broke out laughing. Still laughing I looked at Cheryl. "You hit the nail on the head."

Glancing around the lobby, I am a people watcher. I noticed a number of men and women that were standing in different corners and nooks that appeared to be out of place. Closer examination revealed little white cords extending from one ear of each of the individuals.

"Security;" I said just loud enough for Liz and Cheryl to hear.

Liz looked at me; "What did you say?"

"Security! There must be at least fifty secret service or FBI people covering the lobby."

I whispered in Liz's ear; "A lady as ravishing as you are deserves this type of protection!"

She smiled and poked me in the kidneys.

Liz was holding my hand. Cheryl had noticed, but didn't flinch or change the expression on her face. She did, however ensure that her eyes did not look in that direction again.

A man with a plastic cord dangling from his ear walked over to us. "Your limo is here Mr. Dafoe. Please come with me"

He took my suitcase. Liz and I started to walk towards the revolving entrance doors of the hotel. He abruptly stopped, turned and looked at Liz, in a very stern voice; "We'll take it from here Ms. Montgomery. You can return to Washington."

"Excuse me!" I blurted out in a very loud voice. "We need to talk."

"It's okay!" Liz said.

"It's not okay, wait right here."

With that I walked briskly towards a pillar and the plastic ear cord followed me. I was fuming to say the least.

"Mr. Dafoe;" he said sternly. "I am under instructions directly from the President of the United States. I am in command. It's my responsibility to get you to the park on Roosevelt Island and to make sure there are no problems with respect to your departure. Ms. Montgomery is no longer part of the exercise."

There are two things that I failed to mention to Liz when I was telling her about myself. The first is that I have no respect for anyone who is a pompous ass and secondly I have a vicious temper when provoked and this poor excuse for 007 had definitely just provoked me!

"Do you have a direct telephone line to the President?"

"Why do you want to know?"

"You get him on the phone right now, or the only place I'm going is to the airport to catch a flight back to Toronto. Do you understand?"

He definitely wasn't a happy camper, but he removed his cell phone from his jacket's inner breast pocket and pushed a couple of buttons; he obviously had the President's number on speed dial.

Someone answered the phone very quickly. "This is senior agent Fitzgerald, I need to speak with the President urgently." There was a few second pause; "Mr. President, this is senior agent Fitzgerald, I'm at the Century UN Plaza Hotel with Mr. Dafoe, I'm sorry to bother you but we have a situation" Before he could continue, I grabbed the phone out of his hand.

"Mr. President, William Dafoe. I want the Secret Service, FBI and any other security force involved removed from the assignment immediately. A New York police escort for the limo to handle traffic control is all that is required. Ms. Montgomery will be accompanying me to the departure point. If any of your armed services have installed weapons around the departure area, I want them removed as we discussed and you agreed to at our meeting yesterday. I don't want to see anyone with a weapon of any kind within a mile of the departure point. How the hell am I going to convince the aliens that we are a peaceful group of beings if they are met with a host of armed soldiers and weapons?"

"I apologize, everything will be handled as you think best;" was the President's response. "Please put agent Fitzgerald back on the phone."

I handed the phone back to agent Fitzgerald. I didn't wait to hear the outcome of his conversation with the President. I did hear him say "Yes, Mr. President, I understand," he said that phrase a number of times as I turned and walked back towards Liz.

I took my suitcase in one hand and Liz's hand in the other.

I looked into Liz's eyes, "situation resolved; our limo waits!"

Liz gave me a big smile and squeezed my hand as we walked towards the exit door of the hotel.

Once outside, the area in front of the hotel looked like a black SUV parking lot! I couldn't believe my eyes, there were at least twenty vehicles.

The driver was standing by the open back door of the limo, the trunk was open. He reached for Liz's overnight bag and then for my suitcase.

"I'll take mine into the limo if that's okay?"

A very formal "As you wish sir;" was the response.

Liz climbed in and I followed. We sat up against each other holding hands.

Once the limo started moving, Liz looked at me. "That's a side of you I hadn't seen before." She squeezed my hand.

"I hope it wasn't a turn off?"

"On the contrary, I'm very impressed by the way you handled the situation."

The New York policemen on motorcycles were providing us with an easy drive. We were waved through any red lights as they stopped the cross traffic.

As we went over the bridge to Roosevelt Island I noticed a convoy of military vehicles headed in the opposite direction. My suspicions were confirmed, the military had set up camp in the park. I nudged Liz and pointed at the convoy.

"Assholes" I said under my breath.

In less than 15 minutes we are at the entrance to the park. There was a very large sign by the entrance, *Park Temporarily Closed By Order Of Homeland Security.*

A black SUV was parked, blocking the park entrance road. A man, dressed in a dark grey suit with a plastic white cord in his ear, came up to my side window of the limo. I pushed the widow down button. He looked in the car and said; "Mr. Dafoe?"

"Yes"

"Please exit the limo, the road into the park is narrow and has a lot of bends. It will be much easier for you to get to your departure point on that golf cart rather than this limo." He pointed to a golf cart on the other side of the black SUV. There was a driver waiting in it.

"I was told to inform you that there are only eight people around the circumference of the park at this time and that's including me and the golf cart driver. We are needed to ensure that the public does not enter the park from any direction."

I nodded my concurrence.

I lowered the privacy partition that separated the limo driver from the passengers. Please wait here, the lady will return around 12:15.

The man opened the door of the limo and Liz and I got out. With my suitcase in hand we jumped on the back of the golf cart.

The driver turned his head "Okay to go?"

I looked at Liz and she smiled.

"We're ready!"

The agent at the gate wasn't kidding. It was like riding a roller coaster, up, down, to the right, to the left and then all over again.

Finally we came to a stop. Liz and I jumped off the back of the golf cart. The driver stuck out his arm and pointed towards a green triangular flag on a thin white pole; "That's the exact triangulation of the longitude and latitude points given."

I walked over to the golf cart driver and told him to return at 12:05 to pick Liz up. He acknowledged my request, turned the golf cart around and off he went, disappearing behind some bushes.

Hand-in-hand Liz and I sauntered over to the flag, we were early so there was no rush. The departure point was in the middle of a large open grassed area, very peaceful for New York.

I looked around. Off in the distance I could see one individual with his back to us. It appeared he was standing at a small boat dock. No one else was visible. One small Coast Guard boat was moving slowly past the island. The level of security was acceptable.

During a sales call to the US coast guard I was educated in the primary difference between a boat and a cutter. A boat is 64 feet or less and a cutter is 65 feet or more in length. I'm just a wealth of trivia!

I glanced at my watch, it was 11:51.

I squeezed Liz's hand.

Liz looked at me; I could feel the anxiety emanating from her eyes. "Are you nervous about the voyage?"

"Not really".

For some reason I wasn't apprehensive about the flight to the alien planet, after all I had flown Aeroflot many times prior to the break-up of the Soviet Union and I had flown Mohawk and Allegany airlines in the US. What could the aliens possibly do that would provide a worse flying experience than any of those airlines.

Liz looked at her watch. "Only a couple of minutes, maybe they've changed their minds and there not coming."

She threw her arms around me and kissed me passionately. She held me very tight and whispered in my ear. "I've fallen deeply in love with you William Dafoe. If you don't come back to me, I will never forgive you."

I held her tighter.

There was absolutely no noise or air movement, but there it was on the ground, less than two yards from us.

It wasn't what I had expected, although I'm not sure what I did expect. It's difficult to describe its shape because it didn't match any craft in any of the sci-fi movies I had ever watched. The best description that I can come up with is that it reminded me of a very big igloo, a dome, with a protruding shaft with a rounded top, which was facing me. It was a pastel green; obviously the extraterrestrials had read the study on colors.

There were no windows or doors, it was solid. There were no emblems or writing of any kind on the outside of the structure.

All of a sudden a sense of panic enveloped me. What the hell have I gotten myself into?

I kissed Liz, and before releasing her from my arms I imprinted a picture of her face in my memory. "I'm in love with you too. I will be back!"

I hesitantly released Liz from my arms, and walked the couple of yards to the front of the domed shaft. I didn't see or hear a door open but it was now an open entrance into the spacecraft. I turned around and looked at Liz, she was crying, I waved, she waved back and I stepped into the craft.

Chapter 4 – Day 93

I arrived back on a much larger spacecraft than I had left on. It had to be larger as I had brought back a lot of what I will term at this point as gifts. The aliens were more than generous and although there were some items that were mine, the bulk of the items were for the people of earth. They were an integral part of the compromise that I had negotiated.

It didn't take very long for me to negotiate a reprieve from the aliens. I was right in one of the assumptions that I had made before I left. They were highly civilized and really didn't want to annihilate humanity. All they needed was a reasonable compromise that made them feel secure.

I had developed a deep friendship with many of the aliens and they all treated me as if I was a king.

Although I enjoyed the three years I had spent with the aliens; yes I said three years, as the aliens had developed a form of time travel, so that the 93 days that I was away in earth time was 45 days to get there, three days for meetings and 45 days to get back. The time travel turned the three earth days for meetings into three years with the aliens. The three years without any contact with my daughter was excruciating painful. I missed her deeply and my thoughts about Liz were not far behind those of my daughter. I only knew Liz for a little more than twenty-four hours, yet I truly missed her and I wondered if she was still interested in me. I could only hope so. I had to keep reminding myself that Liz had only waited 93 days for my return not three years.

Over a three year period, your mind can play hellish tricks. I had severe doubts about Liz's sincerity when she said she loved me. I wondered if the sex was part of her assignment - was she playing a role, would she be there when I returned. I would go in and out of the questioning mental states on an irregular schedule.

I had no idea what sort of reception I would receive on my return, it had never been discussed. I hoped that Liz would be there to meet me. As the time drew near to leave the aliens I envisioned being met by Liz and Barbara although I was sure that wouldn't case. It would have been horrible to bring Barbara to the arrival point and then not have me show up.

I will not reveal everything that happened during my three years with the aliens, that's a story unto itself. However, you will be made aware of the details of the elements of the compromise throughout the rest of the story.

I was standing in a designated waiting area inside the spacecraft. It was truly remarkable there was absolutely no sensation of movement or landing. The only way I would know when the spacecraft landed would be the automatic opening of the door. There wasn't even any visual indication that there was a door, no thin lines defining the door from the rest of hull of the spacecraft.

I could see daylight! I was home, well almost. I walked out the door and felt my feet rest on the soft grass. Two men were standing in front of me dressed in hazmat suits. Before I acknowledged there existence, I turned around, the spacecraft was gone and there stacked neatly on the grass were 101 cargo containers custom built by the aliens to match the size of a standard ocean cargo container, 40' x 8' x 8.5'. They were stacked in four rows of five containers, four deep, plus one smaller container, which contained my personal stuff.

I told the aliens that having standard size cargo containers with internationally accepted fittings would make transporting them a breeze here and they had no problems in complying.

I turned back around, and surveyed the area, no Liz! However, the park, at least the area I could see was inundated with well armed men in hazmat suits.

A real bunch of assholes! The most powerful leader in the world couldn't organize a piss-up in a brewery. I thought to myself.

"Mr. Dafoe?" One of them said.

I felt like responding; "No, I'm Zarton. This doesn't look like Mars. Did I get off at the wrong stop?"

I nodded.

"Remove your clothing."

One of the men standing next to me had opened a plastic trash bag and stood there waiting to accept my clothes.

"Not likely!"

Before I knew what was happing, one of them grabbed my arm and started pulling me towards the back of a transport truck trailer.

"What the hell do you think you are doing?"

"You have to be decontaminated;"

I pulled my arm free from his grip. "Not in your life time!

A shot rang out.

"Hold your fire! Hold your fire!" a voice shouted!

Someone had just taken a shot at me. I glanced around, there were at least twenty assault weapons pointing at me. Laser beams were bouncing all over my torso.

The bullet hadn't hit me, but I was sure that it wasn't because the sniper firing it was a bad shot.

A few days before I left the aliens to journey back to earth the Council held a formal reception for me, a goodbye party. The Chairman of the Council had warned me that many of the people on earth would be extremely paranoid about my presence when I returned. I dismissed it. However, he had said that the Council had decided to provide me with protection on my return. A spacecraft would be monitoring my every move and if I was in any jeopardy they would protect me from harm. I knew, from information I had gathered at some of the scientific institutions that I had visited that they had the technology to vaporize a speeding bullet before it hit its mark, for them it was child's play.

A moment later all of the men in the hazmat suits that had been carrying any type of weapon were vaporized into thin air.

The guy in the hazmat suit that had grabbed my arm earlier stood there frozen in his tracks, in total disbelief. He had been looking in the direction of the snipers when they disappeared in front of his eyes.

"Listen very closely;" I was speaking calmly and in a low voice. "Take the hazmat head gear off. I want to speak to the President right now. Call him!"

He took his head gear off and struggled to find his cell phone under his protective garment. Finally he pulled it out, pressed a couple of buttons and waited.

"Secretary Bryant, this is agent Edwards we have a situation with the arrival of Dafoe. He is demanding to speak with the President."

I could hear the response; "Let me speak to him."

The hazmat suit passed me his cell phone. Before this Bryant character could say anything I spoke. My voice was firm and unyielding.

"Put the President on the phone – NOW!"

He didn't say anything to me, but I heard him say; "Mr. President, Dafoe wants to speak with you."

Obviously the President and Bryant were in the same room together.

"William, welcome back. Was your trip a success?"

I was beside myself, totally outraged. "One of your snipers just tried to kill me!"

"What? I don't understand?"

"I don't know how to be more articulate. One of your snipers just tried to kill me. What part of that don't you understand?"

I paused and continued. I calmed my voice, but remained very direct and firm.

"Now this is what you are going to do. I want a suite booked at the Century UN Plaza Hotel. Have the keycard left at the front desk for me to pickup. I do not have any identification with me. Make sure they don't require any in order to give me the keycard to the room. I want a limo sent to the entrance of the park, the entrance that is right in front of the bridge. The driver is not to be armed. He should be instructed to take me directly to the hotel. You can provide a reasonable police escort for the limo, if you wish, that's no more than four police officers."

I glanced at my watch. "It is now 12:17. I will meet with the entire Security Council, permanent and non permanent members at the UN building at 3:00 pm. Arrange to have someone meet me at the front door of the UN building to direct me to where the Security Council room is. As soon as we finish speaking I will start walking towards the park gate. If I encounter any problems or I am intercepted on my way to the gate, you will be condemning the human race to total annihilation. Do you understand?"

"Yes!"

I handed the cell phone back to the guy with the hazmat suit, he hadn't moved, I'm not sure if he was breathing. His mouth opened slightly and I thought he was going to speak, but he didn't say anything, he was at a loss for words.

With a smile on my face, as if nothing had happened, I looked him straight in the eyes. "Have a great day!"

I turned and started to walk towards the front entrance to the park.

I knew that the powers that be would try to open and possibly even move the shipping containers. I wasn't concerned. The container doors were locked and opening required my palm print, DNA, a matching image of my eye retina and a 256 alphanumeric pass code. The containers were made of an alloy that was not available on earth and I knew that we didn't have the technology to cut through it. If they tried to move them they would soon find out that the containers were locked together; this meant that the total grouping was 200 hundred feet long, 40 feet wide, 32 feet high and weighed approximately two thousand tons. The world's largest mobile crane only has a capacity of twelve hundred tons.

It was a beautiful March day in New York. The sun was shining; the temperature was about 75°F with a light breeze. The plants and trees were beginning to come to life after being dormant for winter. I walked slowly along the path leading to the front entrance gate. I knew it would take some time to arrange for the limo and for it to get to the park. I had just spent 45 days in a spacecraft and although it was a pleasant and uneventful journey, I am a bit of a fresh air fiend and there is no fresh air on a spacecraft.

I meandered along the path; my thoughts were centered on Barbara and Liz. I had been upset that Liz didn't meet me, but after what had just occurred, I was reasonably confident that she wasn't allowed to. That of course didn't mean she wanted to.

After I had negotiated the compromise solution with the extraterrestrials and throughout the entire three years that I was with them the song Aquarius, from the Broadway musical Hair kept playing in my head. It seemed to be very appropriate and I would catch myself humming it during the day.

Before I proceed, there is a trivial piece of information that you should be aware of.

The aliens are very technically advanced as compared to us; somewhere between twelve and fifteen thousand years ahead. But, as advanced as they are technically they are extremely backward when it comes to fashion. The clothing that I took with, that I needed for 93 days, turned out to be needed for three plus years. Of course few of the items survived and I had to purchase new items from the clothing that was available on the alien planets.

As an aside, the aliens had provided me with an escort to guide me through the maze of corridors at the building where the Council met, similar in original function to Liz. However, this alien was no Liz, not by a long shot. The escort was female, I think, and had the efficiency of Cheryl, Liz's administrative assistant and the face of Godzilla, with no personality whatsoever!

I don't want you to get the wrong impression. The aliens were not amphibian creatures, this is not a sci-fi movie script; they looked very similar to humans. There were tall ones, short ones, thin ones and heavy ones. There were no fat ones, obesity had been eliminated. There were attractive ones and some that were downright ugly; my escort fit under that heading.

I digress, back to the clothing. I purchased a few sets of basic alien fashion ensembles. The pants come up to the upper middle of my chest. The shirts only have long sleeves, with holes for the elbows and have a very wide double breasted collar. The shirt is an off white with an assortment of brightly colored circles of different sizes ranging from about a quarter of an inch to one inch covering the entire garment. The pants are also an off white, with brightly covered squares instead of circles. There are two back pockets on the pants, no front or side pockets. The shirt didn't have any pockets.

Now, as I mentioned earlier on, the aliens had treated me like a king and my guide was as efficient as Cheryl. My guide Quanch, had realized early on that I carried two pictures in my shirt pocket. She, completely on her own merit, I had said nothing about a shirt pocket, had my shirts modified so that it would have a pocket. In her efficiency, she had the pocket placed on the inside of the shirt so that the pictures of Barbara and Liz could be closer to my heart; that is what she told me.

I hope you have a good imagination so that you can picture me walking down the park path, wearing a pair of weird pants with brightly colored squares, an unusual shirt with brightly colored circles and of course the scarf that I took from Liz before I left.

Yes, I looked like a clown on my way to the big top! The only thing lacking were oversized shoes.

Liz's scarf had never left my neck, I don't think, my memory about some of the details of my visit were confused. I believe that I even slept with it on. I did take it off when I bathed and when I had a couple of medical procedures, but as far as my memory would relate, they were the only exceptions.

That brings me to the toiletries. Although Cheryl had increased the supply of tooth paste and shaving cream, it wasn't enough to last me for three years, nor were there enough razor blades for the length of the trip. I ran out of shaving cream first and although I had used soap in the past, I had very sensitive facial skin and using soap for a lengthy period of time would not have been an enjoyable experience to say the least. When I told my guide, she had a great deal of difficulty comprehending what shaving cream was. I finally had to explain, in detail, how I shaved the whiskers from my face.

In response to my explanation of shaving cream the guide took me to a building that I supposed at the time sold shaving cream. Wrong! I received an advanced form of electrolysis, completely painless, took less than five minutes and I haven't had to shave since. I must admit that the precise details of the electrolysis treatment are muddled in my memory. I was informed that the treatment would last for at least twenty years. Gillette, Schick cry your eyes out!

There were a number of things that the aliens didn't understand or couldn't comprehend. One of the items that truly stick's out in my mind came out at one of the formal meetings I had. The aliens could not understand how we could spend trillions of dollars on weapons each and every year and spend so little on medicine and the well being of all humans. I remember at the time they made the statement, the only answer I could think of was; because we're stupid; although I didn't communicate it to anyone.

But, I digress again.

When I asked for toothpaste a few weeks later the guide informed me that it was not required. Cavities and gum disease were things of the past. They didn't even have dentists. She gave me a bottle of liquid and told me to swish it in my mouth for about twenty seconds, once a day for a month. My mouth and teeth have never felt cleaner, and being someone who had always suffered from plaque build-up and had to go to the dentist every four months for cleaning, I was truly amazed!

I had reached the front entrance gate and there was absolutely no one around. I noticed that the bridge to the island was void of vehicles. They shut the island down, I thought to myself. I stood there humming Aquarius. A few minutes passed and I saw two motorcycles appear at the crest of the bridge, quickly followed by a white limo and two more motorcycles.

The convoy arrived in front of me and the driver got out, gave my outfit a confused stare.

He looked at me, "Mr. Dafoe?"

"Yes."

He opened the limo door and I hopped in.

A few minutes later we arrived at the hotel.

I retrieved my keycard from the front desk without any confrontation; it was the same suite that Liz and I had stayed in, the Piedmont, room 2716. My outfit was receiving the stares that I would have expected. I was surprised that it didn't make me feel extremely uncomfortable, but for some reason, it didn't bother me in the least.

I took the elevator up to the 27th floor, briskly walked along the corridor to the room, released the door lock with the keycard and went in, straight over to the desk with the telephone.

I immediately dialed Barbara's cell phone. It went straight to voice mail. Damn! I listened to her short greeting; even that brought a grin to my face and left her a message.

"Barbara, its Dad. I'm in New York, safe and sound. I have missed you so much. Hope you are okay. I have some things to do, I will call you later this evening, it might be late, but I will call no matter what time it is. Love you deeply, speak to you soon. Bye!"

For some reason just leaving a message on Barbara's cell phone made me feel very good inside. I felt connected to my daughter again; three years is a long time.

I paused for a moment and then dialed Liz's cell phone number. She answered before the first ring was completed.

"Elizabeth Montgomery."

"William Dafoe."

In a highly panicked voice; "Will, where are you? Are you okay? I'm sorry I couldn't meet you, they wouldn't let me. I have missed you so much.

"I'm fine, actually much better than fine now that I can hear your voice. I'm at the Century Hotel, in the Piedmont suite, our room. Where are you?

"Two floors below you, I'll be there in a few seconds, my darling."

I needed to use the facilities and thought I would have just enough time to eliminate the pressures of life before Liz arrived.

As I came out of the bathroom there was a knock on the door, I glanced out the security peephole and there was Liz, looking more beautiful than ever.

"One second!"

I turned the deadbolt knob and pulled the door open expecting to get a hug and kiss from Liz. But that wasn't the case. Barbara was standing there with a big smile on her face.

I grabbed Barbara, and held her tight against me.

"I missed you so very much Barbara."

Tears of joy were exiting my eyes and running down my cheeks. I pushed her back and scanned her up and down. She looked good.

"Everything okay?"

"Everything is good Dad. Dad you are never to go away like that again; understand?"

"I won't, I promise!"

I kissed her on the cheek. It was salty, she had tears as well.

"You need to say a proper hello to someone else Dad."

With that she stepped to the side.

Liz was standing there looking radiant. She quickly stepped into the room, placed one hand behind my head, the other around my back and pushed her lips against mine. I loved Barbara, but I was in love with Liz, there is a big difference.

We stood there kissing for a longtime.

Finally we broke our embrace. She stepped back and holding both my hands looked at me, up and down; "What in god's name are you wearing?"

The three of us broke out laughing.

"It's the latest in alien fashions. Do you like the scarf?"

"Not with that outfit!" Barbara said, still laughing.

I looked over at Barbara; "You have no sense of fashion."

Tears were streaming from Liz's eyes. I kissed her cheeks to absorb them.

"Come in;" I reached around, closed the door and put the latch in place.

"Dad, I have to leave in a couple of hours to go back to Toronto. I have a mid-term paper that is due in a few days."

"That's fine, I will have a lot of work to do here, but we will talk every day, right?"

"You better call me every day!"

Liz interjected. "You two talk, I brought some Champagne to celebrate our reunion. I'll go get some Ice."

With that she grabbed the ice bucket and left the room, in doing so she moved the dead bolt so that the door would remain slightly open and she wouldn't have to interrupt us to get back in.

Barbara and I sat down on the loveseat. I held her hand. It was so good to see her.

"Dad, Liz is a wonderful person. "You can't imagine how good she has been to me. She has been the big sister I never had. She called me every day and she arranged for me to come here. She loves you very much. Don't lose her!" Barbara paused for a second. "I don't have any objections if you want to make her a permanent part of our family." She paused again. "Dad, do you love her?"

"Yes; very much!"

"Then don't be a duffus, ask her to marry you!"

I smiled at Barbara, "I might just do that."

Barbara was looking at my face, "You look great, years younger."

"Technically I am younger, it's a long story, but I underwent a rejuvenation procedure when I was away, the aliens took 13 years off me, so unofficially I am now 38. I don't need any medications anymore. I don't have glaucoma and my 20-20 eyesight is back, without any glasses!"

Liz returned with the ice bucket in hand. She placed it on the desk, retrieved one of the bags she had brought with and pulled out a bottle of Champagne and three glasses.

"None for me Liz;" Barbara said.

Liz didn't question Barbara's refusal. She poured two glasses and brought them over to the loveseat. She stood in front of me and passed me one glass.

"Welcome home Mr. Dafoe."

We touched glasses and each took a sip.

"It needs chilling;" Liz said.

"Dad, are those the only clothes you have?"

"I have more of the same!"

"You can't wear those clothes, Dad, honest."

"I saw a menswear store in the lobby, I'm going to go down and buy you something to wear. You and Liz get reacquainted."

She stood up and walked to the door, grabbing the room keycard from the top of the desk.

"My waist is now 34;" I blurted.

She turned and nodded, then left the room.

I wasn't sure if Barbara really thought I needed new clothes or if she used it as an excuse for leaving Liz and me alone.

Liz sat down beside me, her voice was very somber; "Will, tell me that we will have more than a few days together."

I looked at her face; she looked so beautiful; her eyes were beginning to moisten again. She was definitely thinking the worst.

"Trust me when I tell you that we will be together for a very long time. I guarantee it!"

I could see the relief in her face. "I don't want to hear the details now." She took my Champagne glass from my hand and placed it on an end table beside the loveseat. She turned around and put her arms around me.

"I'd like to have you out of those clothes too;" she said with a smirk on her face.

She kissed me, very passionately, it wasn't a heated let's have sex kiss, it was a tender, I love you kiss. I loved the feel of Liz's lips against mine. It had been over three years since I had the overwhelming pleasure.

She broke the kiss and placed her head on my shoulder with her arm around my chest. I held her tight against me. She smelled so good.

"Liz, please listen to what I have to say. I am not the exact same man who left you here three months ago. Most of what I am about to share with you I am not going to share with anyone else, including Barbara."

Liz tightened her arm around me.

"Physically, I am in much better shape than I was. I am medication free. In fact the aliens took 13 years off my appearance and physical well being. I told this to Barbara when you went to get ice."

"I thought you looked younger!"

"I have changed mentally as well, I have not told any of this to Barbara. You are probably aware that most humans use approximately ten percent of their brain. The aliens use approximately 86 percent of their brain. I am now at 68 percent. The added mental processing power has given me some new attributes, some that you may not find acceptable. I have telepathic abilities. I can communicate with you without using my vocal cords. I can tune into your thoughts. Neither one of these abilities operate from great distances, but within a room.

I can understand any language, not verbally but by using my telepathic powers. As I have the ability to turn my telepathic attributes on and off, I have decided not to use them unless it is absolutely necessary.

The increased brain power has heightened my senses. I can hear things from farther distances, see farther, and my senses of touch, smell and taste are very acute.

My memory has expanded 10,000 fold and I have become extremely observant, without applying any conscious effort. As an example, you took 27 steps to get to the ice machine and only 26 to return. You used the ice cube scoop three times to fill the ice bucket. For breakfast you had eggs, ham, rye toast with butter and blueberry jam, orange juice, a piece of cantaloupe and coffee with cream and no sugar. I could taste it on your lips when you kissed me.

You stand exactly, five foot, five and three-quarter inches tall without your shoes. You have exactly 108,762 hairs on your head.

The security codes that I am using are 256 alphanumeric characters in length and I have no problem remembering them."

I paused for a second; Liz hadn't flinched during my monologue.

"Most important of all, is that I know without a doubt that you are the most beautiful and wonderful woman in the whole world and I don't want to spend a minute more of my life without you!

Do you think that you can be with the new improved version of me?"

Liz didn't respond instantly, but considered what she was going to say.

"You may think faster and have heightened senses, but nothing you have told me would change who you are inside, your ability to love and be loved are the only things that truly matter to me. I love you William Dafoe, with or without your new found attributes."

I slid her arm off my chest and stood in front of her. I reached into the back pocket of my clown pants and pulled out a small plastic baggy. I opened the baggy carefully, took out the contents and placed in the palm of my hand, clenching my fist around it so Liz couldn't see what it was.

I kneeled on one knee in front of her and took one of her hands in mine.

"Elizabeth Montgomery, will you do me the great honor of joining me in wedded matrimony for better, for worse, for richer, for poorer, in sickness and in health, until death do us part?"

Tears started running down her face, she was glowing.

In a choked up voice; "Yes; Yes; Yes!"

I opened my clenched fist and took the ring, the contents of the plastic bag, and placed it on her ring finger.

Liz raised her hand and looked at the ring on her finger.

"Oh Will; it's the most beautiful ring I have ever seen!"

Liz jumped off the loveseat and pushed me off my knee with my back on the floor as she put her lips against mine, her mouth was open and her tongue separated my lips and pushed its way inside my mouth. We lay on the floor, Liz on top of me in a very heated embrace.

Now some of you may think that this is ridiculous, I barely know the woman and I am asking her to marry me. You have to remember a few things. I can read Liz's thoughts; I knew she truly loved me deeply. I'm not sure how, but I knew in my mind the sincerity of her words and actions. I had been away for three years and besides Barbara, Liz was always on my mind. I had opportunities presented to me when I was with the aliens and as I said previously, some of them were attractive, but I didn't even have a moment's transgression, I only wanted Liz.

All of a sudden I heard the door open. Liz broke the kiss, but stayed on top of me.

"Oops, sorry for interrupting;"

Barbara had returned. She had half a dozen bags in her hands.

Liz, who still hadn't moved from on top of me, looked at Barbara, "You better get used to it. Your father and I are getting married."

Barbara dropped the bags and ran over to us, Liz stood up and they hugged. I remained lying on my back on the floor.

"I am so happy for you, for both of you! Second smartest thing you have ever done Dad!"

"What was the first?"

"You had me as your daughter."

We all laughed.

Barbara, with a big grin, turned to Liz, "Can I call you mommy?"

"Only if you want to live without an allowance!"

"Okay! Liz it shall be."

I listened to the banter between them. I was in love with Liz and I loved Barbara seeing them together as friends, close friends, made everything seem perfect in my life.

"Barbara." Liz said, "Take a look at this. With that Liz held out her hand to show Barbara the ring."

Barbara took Liz's hand in hers and looked down at the ring. "Dad, you do have good taste! That is really exquisite."

Barbara was studying the ring; "What is it Dad?"

"The band is made from a mineral called Travolite. It is the rarest mineral in the galaxy. Its value is 1,000 times that of gold. As you can see, it actually emits a low level of light, it's iridescent but it's not radioactive. The stone is a 5.2 carat flawless violet diamond; violet diamonds are the most sought after color in the galaxy because they have only been found on one planet."

Liz had a big grin on her face. She was listening to me and ogling the ring simultaneously. It made me feel very good inside.

I had decided not to tell Liz or Barbara about the welcome I had received. It would only worry them and there was no need to do that.

I glanced at the clock, it was 2:15.

"I'm going to shower and change into my new clothes. I have to meet the UN Security Council at 3:00."

"I'm going to take Barbara to the airport."

I walked over to Barbara and gave her a big hug and kiss on the cheek; "Take care of yourself, have a safe flight home, I'll speak to you tomorrow."

Barbara looked at Liz; "I can find my own way to the airport."

"I'm sure you can, but I'm going to see you off anyways."

Barbara smiled.

"Liz, I have no idea when I'll be out of the meeting."

"I'll be waiting right here in the room when you get back. By the way, I am not in the President's cabinet anymore. I resigned my position at the Whitehouse. I'll tell you the story later."

"I took Liz in my arms and we kissed."

Now I knew the real reason Liz couldn't meet me.

Barbara grabbed the handle of her suitcase and with Liz at her side they walked towards the door.

I heard Liz say; "Elizabeth Dafoe! I like the sound of that, has an air of class."

They both turned and said "Bye" and went out the door.

I paused for a second to organize my thoughts. Shower and change clothes, I said to myself.

I went over and grabbed the clothes bags that Barbara had dropped on the floor and went into the bedroom. I showered and changed into the new clothes, the pant legs were a bit long, but they weren't below my alien shoes. Going from a 36" waist to a 34" meant that I could get shorter off the rack pants. Luckily the shoes that the aliens made for men were similar to the ones I could purchase here; at least they weren't clown feet. I took Liz's scarf and tied it around my neck. I then reached into the inside pocket of my clown shirt and took out the pictures of Liz and Barbara and put them in the breast pocket of my new shirt.

I must admit to feeling much more comfortable in these clothes than the alien clown outfit.

I'm as ready as all ever be; I thought. I left the room, went through the lobby, where I noticed a man and woman with white plastic cords in their ears. They didn't look at me so I assumed that they were probably there protecting some dignitary.

A went outside and could see the UN building across the street. I watched as a few people J walked across the street, horns were honking and words were being said. I knew the aliens were protecting me, but did they have the technology to protect me against a New York cab driver? I was a gutless wonder. I walked over to the intersection and waited for a green light.

Even with a green light and the right of way, crossing the road meant dodging cabs turning left and right. Finally my feet landed on the sidewalk on the other side of the street. That was far more harrowing than the flights across the galaxy, I thought to myself.

I followed signs that indicated the direction of the main lobby. Once inside the doors I saw a young man in a uniform holding a sign that read; "Mr. Dafoe". I introduced myself. He welcomed me to the UN and handed me a visitor's badge, which I clipped to my shirt pocket. He then asked me to walk with him to the Security Council meeting room.

It was a few minute walk, but we finally arrived at an open double set of doors. The young man indicated that this was the place and motioned me inside. He immediately turned around and started walking away.

In the room was a group of tables aligned in a circle. People were seated and talking amongst themselves, very informally. Off in a corner were four young girls sitting on chairs in commissionaire style outfits.

The instant I appeared in the doorway Zhang Wei stood up and briskly walked towards me. He grabbed my hand and placed his other hand on top of it.

"It is very good to see you back safe."

"Thank you Ambassador, it's good to be back."

Ambassador Balabanov was now standing beside Zhang Wei. When Zhang Wei dropped the hand shake, Ambassador Balabanov shook my hand.

"Good trip?" He asked in a pensive tone.

"I think so." I replied.

He put his hand on my back and guided me into the room.

All of the delegates were now standing, I glanced around the room and as I did Ambassador Middleton started to applaud, moments later everyone in the room was applauding.

I looked at Ambassador Middleton as she applauded; she mouthed "welcome back", with a big smile.

I must say that I was somewhat embarrassed by the applause and wasn't sure quite what to say or how to react.

Finally I said; "Thank you."

I glanced around the room and my eyes met the President's. He had a very stern look on his face; I didn't acknowledge him and just stared back.

Ambassador Balabanov directed me to a vacant chair at the table and after waiting for the others to do so, I sat down. Each delegate had a folded card in front of them with their name and title on it facing outward so that I could read them. I wasn't sure if this was strictly for my benefit or something that was always done.

Once the delegation was seated and those that required translation had placed their earphones on and there was no more chair movement a voice spoke. I glanced over and without having to read the card on the table I recognized the Prime Minister of Canada, William Harmon.

"Mr. Dafoe;" he said and then paused for a moment. "I could go into a lengthy welcoming process and introduce you to all of the respected delegates from the member nations of the United Nations Security Council that are seated at this round table. However, I am sure that you will understand when I suggest that we do the introductions at another time and that you lead off by telling us if we are facing total annihilation in a few days."

"We are no longer facing annihilation of the human race!"

I paused and glanced around the room. I could see the relief in most of their faces, some were smiling. Some were wiping tears from their eyes.

Prime Minister Harmon stood up from his chair. He looked directly at me with a glorious smile on his face and shouted; "Well done Mr. Dafoe! Well done!" and with that he started to applaud again.

The other delegates rose from their chairs and all looked directly at me and joined in with the applause.

I was very embarrassed.

After what seemed like an eternity, the applause stopped, the delegates took their seats and earphones were put back on.

No one spoke, so I did.

"Mr. Prime Minister, Ambassadors, I am not familiar with the procedures of this Security Council nor do I know the proper protocols for speaking. If I should make a faux pas, and not address someone properly or break a procedural rule, please accept my apology in advance."

I paused for a moment to see if there were any comments about what I had just said. The room was silent. Prime Minister Harmon motioned me to continue.

"Let me first say that the extraterrestrials are a collection of exceptional peoples. They treated me like a king and the negotiations were definitely not one sided. We will have to give up some things, but in my view, at the end of the day, we will have gained a lot more than we have lost.

"As the extraterrestrials outlined in their original message they're primarily concerned about our weapons of mass destruction. Their concern however is not for the 57 planets that make up the Group of Inhabited Planets none of them would have any problems in defending themselves against us. They're concerned about hundreds of other inhabited planets that have not developed our levels of technology and weapons.

"The basis of the agreement is actually quite simplistic. We, being the people of the planet earth, will destroy all of our weapons of mass destruction, including but not limited to, nuclear, chemical and biological and in return we will not be annihilated."

I paused and looked at the delegates; there was a lot of positive head nodding.

I continued. "It's the methodology of the agreement that is more complex and let me say before I get into some of the details, that I will produce an overview document outlining the agreement and the process of implementation tomorrow and distribute it to everyone in the Security Council. I will then create a more detailed document for the implementation of the agreement. I am estimating that it will take me seven to 10 days to prepare the detailed document."

In fact, I had already completed both the overview and detailed documents on my voyage back, they were formatted perfectly in my brain, all I had to do was make a few minor changes and transcribe my brain to paper, but I wanted some breathing space.

"The biggest hurdle in the implementation is the time frame. We only have 276 days from today to gather up all of the weapons. The weapons will be placed in a location that each country defines with special electronic markers. I have brought back a couple of samples of the markers and detailed manufacturing instructions. In 276 days, spacecraft from the Council of Inhabited Planets will arrive and vaporize all the material that is encircled by the markers. The vaporization is a totally clean process and leaves no residue or toxic waste."

Prime Minister Harmon interjected.

"The Ambassador from People's Republic of China has a question."

"Mr. Dafoe, what happens if one country tries to hide some weapons or is not willing to participate in the process?"

"Any country that hides weapons of mass destruction will be vaporized. If a country does not want to be part of the process, and does not have any weapons of mass destruction, nothing will happen to them.

"The Ambassador has highlighted one of the biggest negotiation problems that I had faced. The extraterrestrials could not understand the absence of a governing body that had jurisdiction over the entire planet. They believed, prior to my arrival, that the United Nations was a true governing body; that countries were actually states under the jurisdiction of the United Nations.

"It took me awhile to understand why this made a difference to the aliens. When I finally realized the subtle difference it allowed me to successfully reach a compromise with them.

"I will try to explain the subtle difference. It is based on who is the perceived enemy? If the United Nations is the most senior governing body then the entire human race becomes the enemy. If any government in any specific country is the most senior governing body, than only that country is the enemy. I will try to explain using the United States and the Russian Federation as an example. The United States has its nuclear arsenal located in fourteen different states, California being one of them. The United States attacks the Russian Federation with a missile fired from a Californian missile silo. Is the Russian Federation at war with California because they fired the missile or with the United States because it is the senior governing body? The answer of course is the United States.

"Let's now use an example that involves the aliens. India fires a missile into outer space armed with a chemical warhead aimed at planet X. If the United Nations is the senior governing body then planet X is at war with earth. If India is the senior governing body than planet X is at war with India.

"I convinced the extraterrestrials that any potential war would be with a specific country on earth not with earth as a whole. Hence, the basis of the compromise, any country that retains weapons of mass destruction will be annihilated.

"To take things one step further. If all of the countries that currently have weapons of mass destruction decide not to participate in the agreement, then all of those countries and their populations will be annihilated. That scenario although extremely disheartening, still saves the human race from total annihilation."

"The President of Azerbaijan has a question."

"Mr. Dafoe, I have two questions."

"Why would a country without weapons of mass destruction participate in the process?"

"While the primary intent is the elimination of weapons of mass destruction, the extraterrestrials have agreed to vaporize anything and everything that is located within the markers. That can include anything from used oil, biological hazardous material such as medical waste or just the vaporization of a landfill site."

"Thank you. My second question pertains to security. Will some countries be in jeopardy during the collection process? As an example; Country A has nuclear weapons and has placed them in an area for vaporization. Country B has nuclear weapons but hasn't dismantled them yet. What if country B attacks country A? Country A won't have the threat of nuclear retaliation as a deterrent."

"Three days from now two spacecraft from the 72nd Reconnaissance Armada of the Group of Inhabited Planets will position themselves above the planet."

I wasn't going to tell them that there was already a spacecraft circling the planet now, protecting me!

"One of the terms of my agreement is that no country will be allowed to fire any rocket, missile or any other projectile, during the 271 day process. If the projectile has a conventional warhead, the missile and a two hundred square yard area around the missile will be vaporized. If the projectile has a mass destruction warhead, the country will be vaporized. The projectile will also be vaporized at lift off."

Prime Minister Harmon looked at each of the delegates. "Please carry on Mr. Dafoe."

I poured myself a glass of water from one of the pitchers that was on the table and took a few sips.

"I want to emphasis that absolutely no projectiles can be fired from earth during the 271 day period that includes satellite launches. I did however negotiate one exception. I did not know the status of the ISS, but I assumed that it was currently manned. We are allowed to send one and only one rocket to the ISS, it can contain a change of crew and supplies that will allow the crew to stay in orbit past the 271 day period or it can be used to return the crew to earth. I have a special beacon, about the size of a cigarette package that must be placed in the space capsule before liftoff. The aliens will allow it free passage to the ISS. If the aliens detect a warhead on or in the rocket or that the rocket has a mission other than going to or coming from the ISS, they will annihilate the human race."

I paused to see if there were any comments or questions about what I had just said. No one spoke out so I continued.

"The last major item in the agreement will lead us into what the extraterrestrials have provided us in return. Although it is the intent of the aliens to monitor the planet on a random basis, they don't want us to have easy access to processed uranium. The world has a vast number of nuclear power plants that are using processed and enriched uranium. Those power plants must be closed down and the enriched or processed uranium is to be delivered to an area that is identified as a vaporization area. This includes all spent fuel rods and nuclear waste."

I looked around the room, I could tell, by the expressions on the delegate's faces, that the loss of the nuclear reactors would not be accepted easily.

"When the aliens requested this as one of their conditions, I advised them that honoring this request would place an enormous hardship on humanity; that the amount of electricity generated by the nuclear power plants would take years if not decades to replace.

"The aliens had and have no intention of creating hardship on any of us. They responded by providing us with solar technology that we currently don't have. I have detailed engineering drawings with me that will allow us to manufacture a proven type of solar collector system. It has been in continuous use on 46 planets for more than 5,000 years. This new solar collection system will convert extremely low levels of radiation from the sun into electricity. It will also store high levels of electricity for extended periods of time, at least six months, and provide it when the sun's radiation levels aren't sufficient to generate additional electricity. Using the alien technology we will be able to manufacture a solar collection system capable of delivering 512 megawatts of electricity for less than 5 million dollars with a maintenance cost of less than 250 thousand dollars per year and a minimum fully operational life of twenty-five years. The physical size of the solar collection system complete with its storage unit is less than sixteen feet long, three feet deep and two feet high. In my estimation, there should be no problem in delivering 750 of these units within the first four to six months of production.

For clarification, all nuclear power plants include those that may be used aboard ships."

I paused and took a drink of water. I wanted to give the delegates plenty of time to absorb what I had just said.

I had decided earlier that I wouldn't tell them at this time that there were also solar collector systems that were much smaller. These systems could easily replace the need for gasoline in automobiles and fuel oil in trucks and ships. The systems could be used to directly power homes and commercial or industrial complexes. Although I considered the technology to be very exciting as it would alleviate the world's dependence on fossil fuels. It would create a global economic crisis.

"The Ambassador of New Zealand has a question."

"Mr. Dafoe, I have three questions. Could you please define what you mean by vaporize?"

"That is the term that the extraterrestrials use. I do not understand the technology or science as it is way beyond anything we have here on earth. However, in laymen's terms, the aliens can breakdown any matter into subatomic particles, electrons, protons and neutrons, which reduces the material to less than an atom in structure. As all material is made up of atoms, the material ceases to exist. The subatomic particles just blend into the atmosphere."

"Thank you Mr. Dafoe. My second question; to what depth do they vaporize?"

"There are two types of markers. A master station marker and a slave station marker. Every area designated to be vaporized will require four markers, one master marker and three slave markers. The master marker has a numeric keypad that is used to define the depth of the vaporization, in millimeters, centimeters, meters or kilometers. The vaporization can be set to zero if no ground material is to be vaporized or as deep as twenty-five kilometers. It is accurate to one millimeter from the top of the head of the marker. The master marker also identifies the marker group."

"My final question Mr. Dafoe
We need nuclear reactors in order to make radioisotopes used in nuclear medicine. How are we going to produce those materials without nuclear reactors?"

"The aliens have supplied me with twenty tons of an element that they call Corbolite. They have told me, and I can only accept their word, that the Corbolite can be used in place of the current radioactive materials that we use in nuclear medicine. I have detailed processing instructions. According to the aliens we have the technology to perform the processing.

I would also like to point out that we do not have to destroy any radioisotopes that we currently have in inventories or in laboratory equipment and that we can continue to utilize our nuclear reactors to make the radioisotopes right up until the 271 day deadline."

Surprisingly there were no questions.

I looked over at Prime Minister Harmon. "Could we take a ten minute break? I will then explain all of the other things that we will receive from the extraterrestrials."

"This is probably a good time for a break." He looked at his watch, it was 6:00 p.m. "I adjourn the meeting at this time. We will reconvene at 6:15 p.m."

Everyone stood-up and some were heading to the door to the room. I followed the group. I figured that they were heading for the washrooms; sounded like a very good idea to me! As I walked towards the door, delegates were walking up to me and shaking my hand, most with big smiles on their face.

Just down the hallway were washroom signs. I followed one of the delegates into the washroom. We ended up washing our hands at the sinks at the same time.

In a very heavy Italian accent, and with a big smile; "Mr. Dafoe, my name Pascal Marino, I Ambassador Italy, excusa - my English not so good."

I smiled at him, quickly dried my hands and extended a hand to him.

"You cigarette?" He took a package of cigarettes out of his jacket pocket and pointed to them.

I hadn't had a cigarette for over three years. The aliens had something that resembled a cigarette, but I think they used tunnis dung as the main ingredient, it smelt and tasted awful. A tunnis is an animal on one of the alien planets that very closely resembles a camel and may even be the forefather of the camel. I had thought I had quit smoking. The alien rejuvenation procedure had given me a clean set of lungs, but then I thought what the hell, just one cigarette won't hook me again.

"Yes; thank you."

We exited the washroom and with the palm of his hand on my back he guided me farther down the corridor to a building exit door. A security guard stood at the door and as he saw us coming he opened it for us. Outside, we quickly walked over to an area where a few other people were standing. Pascal opened his cigarette packet and offered me one.

I removed it, put the filtered end between my lips, Pascal held up a lighter and I was smoking again!

I was enjoying the fresh air, smoking my cigarette, looking around and thinking about what exactly to say next.

Pascal looked at his watch, "Go back now."

We put our cigarettes in the upright cigarette butt canister that was provided, walked back to the room and took our seats.

Prime Minister Harmon called the meeting to order.

"Ambassador Middleton has a question."

"Mr. Dafoe, I have four questions."

"Moving quantities of nuclear materials and waste around the country can be a dangerous, complex and costly exercise. Was any consideration given to these challenges?"

"The aliens didn't seem to give it any consideration, but I have. The materials do not have to be moved. You can designate any area to be a vaporization zone and there is no limit on the quantity of vaporization areas any one country can create. If you place the markers around the complex that is currently housing the nuclear material the aliens will vaporize the structure and its contents.

The same applies to nuclear warheads in storage or sitting on top of missiles. There is no need to transport the nuclear warheads. Designate the areas holding the missiles or warheads as a vaporization area.

I don't believe that I mentioned it before, but the accuracy, with respect to the boundaries of the vaporization area is less than one millimeter."

"Thank you. My second question is; are we only allowed to use the solar collector systems to replace nuclear generating plants?"

"Absolutely not! The technology is ours to use as we want. I would however suggest that priority be allocated to the nuclear power plants."

"Thank you. My third question; is there a method where we can vaporize something in a building without having the building vaporized?"

"I'm sorry to say no." That wasn't actually the case. The aliens had the technology to vaporize objects within any building structure. However, the complexity of identifying the object was extremely complex due to a requirement to enter in exact, to twenty decimal points, the height of the object and the bottom of the object relative to sea level. The aliens and I agreed that it was far too easy to miscalculate the required information and accidentally vaporize something that wasn't to be vaporized. I couldn't see any real value in providing the markers that would be required to perform an in structure vaporization.

"Thank you. My fourth and final question; is there a safety zone around the area? As an example should we evacuate people within a one mile radius of the vaporization zone?"

"In theory as long as a person is standing more than one millimeter from the vaporization zone they are 100 percent safe. I however would not stand that close, not because I am afraid of being vaporized, but because I might inadvertently lift my hand to scratch my nose and in doing so cross the vaporization zone boundary. I would suggest common sense be used. Keep people far enough away that they cannot accidentally or on purpose enter the zone, a few hundred meters."

The Ambassador of Columbia has a question.

"Mr. Dafoe, how long does the vaporization take at a specific site?"

"It depends on the size of the site and the depth of vaporization. But as an indication they can vaporize ten hectares to a depth of one hundred meters in approximately one nanosecond.

Prime Minister Harmon scanned the delegates for more questions. "Mr. Dafoe would you like to continue."

"There is a long list of technology and other benefits that we are receiving from the extraterrestrials. I have not tried to prioritize them. I would prefer not to get into the nitty-gritty details of each one at this time. Doing so would require that we be here until the early hours of the morning."

I paused and looked at the delegates to see if anyone had a problem with that. Everyone was listening to me intently and the salesman in me couldn't find anyone holding back a comment.

"The aliens will repair the ozone layer surrounding the planet and bring it back to the thickness it was a few hundred years ago without any holes.

"They will clean our oceans, seas, lakes, rivers and our atmosphere removing all contaminants.

"They will also eradicate the space junk and debris that is currently orbiting the earth."

I paused to allow the delegates to ponder and absorb what I had just said.

"Besides the solar technology they have provided me with the formulas for medications and other preventative medicines.

"They have provided us with the formula for a vaccine which will immunize us from all known viruses that we may encounter, including the common cold.

"They have provided us with the formula for a medicine that will regenerate our immune systems. It is a cure for AIDS as well as other immune deficiencies.

"I also have formulas for medications that will cure glaucoma, clogged arteries and diabetes. A number of diseases will be eradicated by the use of the immunization vaccine; however that won't help anyone who has contracted the disease prior to immunization. The aliens have provided me with formulas for medicines that will cure

Poliomyelitis, Influenza, Ebola virus, Systemic lupus erythematosus and Creutzfeldt-jakob.

"And I have formulas for medicines that will cure acne and migraine headaches."

I paused, waiting for questions.

"The Ambassador from the Russian Federation has a question."

"Mr. Dafoe, you say you have the formulas with you. We are being provided with the formulas prior to our elimination of the weapons of mass destruction? Why? What do the aliens get in return?"

"Absolutely nothing! The extraterrestrials are providing us with all of this as a gesture of goodwill. The human race will not be annihilated and those remaining, hopefully it will be everyone, will be able to enjoy the long term benefits of these gifts.

Prime Minister Harmon looked at me. "I have a question. When will the aliens clean the oceans and thicken the ozone layer?"

"It is my understanding that a number of spacecraft from the 72nd reconnaissance armada will arrive in 271 days. They will start scanning the planet at preciously 12:00:000 p.m., which is exactly 1 year from the date and time we received the original message. I do not know the exact number of spacecraft that will arrive, but it will be a relatively large contingent. Included in the group will be spacecraft with the onboard technology to accomplish those specific items, I don't know how many spacecraft will be required to complete the entire project. I was told that the entire procedure of scanning the planet for weapons of mass destruction, thickening the ozone layer, cleaning all the bodies of water and the atmosphere will take approximately eighteen hours."

The Prime Minister thanked me and asked the group if there were any other questions. "Please continue Mr. Dafoe."

"The aliens have provided us with technology that will allow us to predict volcanic eruptions and earth quakes to an accuracy of 99.97 percent, at least eight weeks before they occur."

Someone in the room blurted out; "Unbelievable, that alone could save thousands of lives!"

"There is one final benefit which is much longer term. The extraterrestrials would like to investigate the potential of ongoing commercial trade with earth. In order to accomplish this there are a lot of complexities that would have to be resolved, primarily by us. I would suggest that we don't concern ourselves about potential trade with the aliens until we have resolved the elimination of the weapons of mass destruction and nuclear material stock piles."

"The President of the United States has a question."

"Mr. Dafoe, will we be invited or expected to join the Group of Inhabited Planets?

"No! Not in the foreseeable future."

"Can you tell me why not?"

"At this time we are considered to be far too uncivilized." A few hours ago you tried to kill me and you wonder if the aliens would want us to join them. You truly are a horse's backside. I wanted to say it out loud but decided that he probably wouldn't understand anyway.

I looked at my watch it was 7:15. I really wanted to be with Liz.

"Ladies and Gentlemen;" I said. "It is after 7, and I have to prepare the written overview document for you this evening."

Prime Minister Harmon looked around the room. "I believe that this is a good time to adjourn the meeting for today. We all have a lot to think about and I am sure many of us must report back to our respective governments.

"Mr. Dafoe, I want to thank you for your outstanding successful negotiations with the aliens it would appear that we will benefit greatly from your trip. I would also like to thank you for an excellent briefing and being so forthright.

"Is 10:00 a.m. tomorrow a convenient time for everyone to return?"

He glanced around the room and everyone nodded their acceptance.

"I call this meeting adjourned until tomorrow at 10:00 a.m. Mr. Dafoe, would you be available to join some of us for dinner this evening?"

"With all due respect Mr. Prime Minister I have a great deal of writing to accomplish before we resume our meeting tomorrow."

"I understand; we will make it another time."

Everyone stood-up and aimed for the door. A number of the delegates shook my hand and said things like, excellent, brilliant and superb.

I followed some of the delegates out of the building and stood for a moment to get my bearings. We had exited from a different door than I had entered.

That went reasonably well, I thought to myself. I started humming Aquarius again.

I figured out where the hotel was relative to where I was now standing and made a beeline towards it; crossed the street at the lights, dodging a few taxis, and entered the hotel lobby. I didn't have my wallet with credit cards or any cash; I had neglected to ask Liz for them. I went into the store in the lobby and told them I had forgotten my wallet and cash in my room and asked if I could charge a purchase to my room. They had no problem having me sign for a purchase. They had Canadian cigarettes, I asked for four packages. I picked a disposable lighter from a POS display and placed it on the counter. They had an upright cooler in the corner with flowers. I asked the attendant to give me a dozen of the long stem red roses and a glass vase. I signed the receipt and headed for the room.

I sure hoped Liz was there, she had the keycard for the room. No Liz, and I'd be sitting in the hallway.

I arrived at the door to the room and knocked. I didn't need my newly acquired acute hearing to know she was running towards the door. There was a momentary pause when she got to the door, as she looked through the peephole to see who it was. No dummy, I thought to myself. The door opened, she placed her hand inside my pants at the belt buckle and pulled me tight up against her, being loaded down with a bag of cigarettes a glass vase and a bouquet of roses meant I couldn't put my arms around her. She kissed me passionately. She stood back a bit, I swung around her and she closed the door and locked it.

Liz's eyes were red and puffy. There was no doubt in my mind that she had been crying not just a few tears, but torrents.

I had to make a quick decision, pretend I didn't notice and wait for Liz to tell me what's going on, immediately confront her about her puffy eyes, or use my mental telepathy and read her thoughts. I decided to go with the first choice; I'll let Liz tell me when she's ready.

With a big smile on my face I passed the roses to her; "I love you!"

Liz' voice created a sense of sadness in my mind; "What are these for?"

"Do I need a reason to give my fiancée flowers?"

"You're spoiling me Mr. Dafoe!"

I reached into the bag and pulled out the vase.

"Thought you might need this;" as I passed her the vase.

"You're so thoughtful."

She took the vase and the flowers and disappeared into the bedroom, then into the bathroom. She had been in there for quite some time; she came out carrying the vase and roses and placed them on the desk. I looked at her eyes, they were wet, she had been crying in the bathroom.

Liz, adjusted the position of a couple of the rose buds; "They're beautiful!"

"I thought so, but when you stand next to them, I realize that they aren't half as beautiful as I thought they were."

Liz smiled, there was a glow coming off her face and eyes. "I am the luckiest girl in the world. You have made me happier than I ever imagined possible."

So why are you crying? Why do you have a note of sadness in your voice? I didn't say any of that out loud.

She gave me a kiss that made my knees weak. We broke the kiss after a few minutes.

Liz had both her hands in mine, she gave me a puppy dog look; "what would you like to do?"

She was more than ready to make love, and although I was physically excited, I wasn't mentally ready, I needed time to unwind from the meeting.

"Let's go for a walk and get something to eat."

"That seemed to catch Liz off guard, but she smiled at me; "Okay!"

"Liz do you have my wallet and the little cash I left you?"

She immediately turned and picked up her purse from near the loveseat, quickly opened it, rummaged around and pulled out my wallet. She had placed an elastic band around the wallet and had folded the money and placed it underneath.

She handed me the wallet, "I didn't want anything in the wallet to fall out and end up scattered throughout my purse."

I put the wallet in my back pants pocket; the cash in my side pocket and the keycard from the desk and placed it in my other back pocket. I took Liz's jacket out of the closet and helped her on with it.

I had started my journey to meet with the aliens with a coat, but sometime during the visit, I mislaid it. I had purchased a sweater type item from one of their stores, but I inadvertently left that on the spacecraft when we landed.

I took Liz's hand, which she squeezed very tightly and we left the room. When we reached the lobby Liz's hand still in mine, we went over to the menswear store.

Looking at Liz; "I need to buy a jacket, coat or sweater."

It was a very high class store. We walked over to the section with jackets and coats.

"What should I buy?"

"Whatever you want!"

"Sorry my love it doesn't work that way. You are now responsible for my wardrobe! It's one of the responsibilities that comes with being my wife!"

Liz beamed and kissed me on the cheek.

She started to remove one jacket at a time from the rack, looked at it inside and out, felt the material, looked at the fasteners, put it back and then picked up another one and repeated the process all over again.

Liz was obviously taking this new found responsibility very seriously. After her detailed inspection of most of the jackets, she went back and took a dark brown leather jacket that had apparently passed muster from the rack.

"Try this one on."

She handed me the jacket and I put it on. It fit quite well. I have a 44 inch chest and it was unusual to find a jacket that was comfortable across my chest with a sleeve length that wasn't too long. The smell of the fresh leather was almost intoxication. I zipped up the jacket. Liz motioned me to turnaround.

"Does it feel comfortable?"

"Yes!"

"It looks very good on you and its very good quality. I think you should buy it."

I took the jacket over to a salesclerk and paid for it. He cut the sales tags off it while it was still on.

I took Liz's hand in mine and we walked out of the hotel and on to the sidewalk.

I looked at Liz, "I have no idea where we are or what's around here."

Liz squeezed my hand, "Neither do I. Barbara and I, had all our meals delivered by room service."

There were a lot of neon light type signs down the street to the left and without saying anything we started walking towards them.

"Is there anything specific you would like for dinner or any type of cuisine that you have an urge for?" I asked.

"Nothing heavy"

As we walked I started to hum Aquarius. Liz squeezed my hand; "Very appropriate!"

"I think so, if we need a theme song for the meetings that would be it!"

We had walked in the right direction. We crossed a side street and encountered a row of restaurants. We walked past a Jamaican and East Indian restaurant. Next there was a liquor store.

I gave Liz's hand a slight squeeze; "We'll hit this on the way back."

Adjacent to the liquor store was a Bistro. We stopped and read the menu that was posted outside.

"Anything here look interesting?"

Liz hadn't finished reading yet. "They have quite a few salads. This will do fine."

We walked into the Bistro and young lady sat us at a booth in the corner, we sat across from one another. The Bistro was relatively dark and the only light came from a candle flickering on each table.

We opened our menus and began perusing them. Liz had kicked off one of her shoes and was running her foot up and down my leg. She glanced up from her menu and I gave her a big smile.

Liz closed her menu first.

"What have you decided on?" I asked.

"I'm going to have the chicken Caesar salad and an iced tea."

The waitress seemed to appear out of thin air, order pad in hand.

Liz went to speak, but I spoke first.

"The lady will have the chicken Caesar salad and an ice tea, no sugar."

Liz smiled.

"I will have the Bistro Burger with cheddar cheese, mushrooms, mayo and tomato, a large coke, no fruit in the glass please."

The waitress made her notes, thanked me for the order, picked up the menus and walked away.

I put my arms on the table palms up and Liz placed her hands in mine, her foot was still rubbing on my legs. Her engagement ring had a light iridescent glow that shone up though the purple diamond in the dim lighting, it really did look fantastic on her finger.

"Will, you know that I have a million questions for you. I know you will tell me what you can when you can."

"I have no intention of ever keeping anything from you. If I swear to someone to keep a secret that will never include you. In my mind we are no longer two people, we are one person. We will share everything together, no secrets and no hidden agendas."

Liz squeezed my hands.

"Liz, I will tell you anything and everything about what occurred when I was away, all of the details. Please give me a few days to put the UN Security Council crap behind me."

I paused as the waitress brought our drinks to the table.

"Why did you resign from the President's cabinet?"

"After seeing you off, I went back to Washington on a commercial flight. The next morning the President summoned me to his office. The Secretary of Homeland Security, Bryant, was there when I arrived. In front of the President, Bryant tore into me about the incident at the hotel. The President thinks the sun shines out of Bryant's ass, and I swear that it's Bryant who is running the country through his puppet, the President."

So Bryant, the guy in charge of my fantastic arrival is the Secretary of Homeland Security, hmmm, I thought to myself.

"The President said that he expected more from me, a better attitude and working relationship with other government departments.

I went back to my office and wrote a letter of resignation put it in my outbox addressed to the Chief of Staff, collected my personal belongings and left the building."

"Are you back working at REND?"

"No, officially I'm still on a leave of absence."

"What have you been doing for the last three months?"

The waitress arrived with our meals. We broke our grip so that she could place the meals in front of us. She asked if we needed anything else, hearing a no, she disappeared again.

Liz took a couple of mouthfuls of her chicken Caesar salad; "This is very good! I thought about returning to REND and then thought, what if you don't return, what if the world comes to an end in three months, what do I really want to do for the next three months while I wait for you to come back to me?

She stopped and started to eat again. I was taking my second bite of an excellent burger.

"I hadn't had a chance to make any arrangements to retrieve your car from the airport parking lot. I could have contacted Cheryl and asked her to take care of it, but I didn't. I decided that I would fly to

Toronto and retrieve your car myself. When I was driving it back to your home I thought about what was truly important to me. I instantly realized that the only thing that had any importance to me was you and I wanted to remain close to you. I called Barbara, told her I was a friend of yours and if she could spare the time I would like to take her out for dinner. I knew how important Barbara was to you and for some reason, that I can't really explain, I wanted to spend some time with her, to get to know her, she was my link to you."

Liz had been pausing during her dissertation to eat her Caesar salad and had just finished it. I had finished my burger. I hadn't realized how hungry I was.

"Barbara and I had dinner together, we hit it off instantly. I made the decision to tell her how I felt about you and what was really going on. I wasn't sure what her reaction was going to be when I told her that your life was in jeopardy. She took it like a trooper, her eyes had moistened, but she didn't cry. She couldn't stop thanking me for telling her the truth. We were together until well after three in the morning. The only subject we both wanted to talk about was you. We decided that we had to keep in contact, we had a common link, a link that was the most important thing for both of us – you. She invited me to use the house as if it was mine. I stayed there for about ten days, saw Barbara three more times and spoke to her at least once a day on the phone.

I returned to Washington because I had committed to attend the wedding of an acquaintance of mine and I had made arrangements to have dinner with Cheryl.

Barbara and I continued to speak on the phone every day. She really is a great kid, young adult.

I returned to Toronto and stayed in your house. Being there comforted me in some way. Barbara and I would get together at least once a week and speak every day. We developed a very close friendship. I told Barbara that I wanted us both to be in New York for your return. If you didn't return I wanted to be with her, we would be together if and when the world came to an end.

I shook my head in amazement; "You truly are a remarkable woman!"

The waitress appeared with the bill and I paid it with a credit card. I helped Liz on with her jacket and we left the Bistro. A couple of right turns and we were in the liquor store. We bought six bottles of Pinot Gris, Grand Cru and walked slowly back to the hotel.

"Liz, all this flying back and forth, hotel rooms and taking Barbara out must have cost you a fortune. Please allow me to reimburse you."

Liz squeezed my hand very tightly; "I don't have any money and I hope you don't have any money."

I stopped and looked at her.

Liz continued; "We are a partnership in everything I hope. I want it to be our money, not my money or your money. Can you accept that?"

"That suits me just fine. It is something I actually believe in strongly." I never understood my married friends that had separate bank accounts; his money and her money. My wife and I shared all of our bank accounts and never had our own funds. It was always the family's assets.

We continued our slow walk back to the hotel, hand in hand.

"Will, there is something I want to tell you. We are quite wealthy. My grandfather left his entire estate to me. I was his one and only grandchild and the light of his life. I have investments with a net worth well over 375 million dollars. It's no longer my wealth, it's our wealth."

I squeezed Liz's hand and smiled at her. I've never really desired to be rich, just comfortable. I had always had an above average income. I could afford a house and a new car every two or three years. Barbara didn't have to borrow money from the government to go to university and I was able to take the family on yearly vacations. I was debt free and had some savings. Although I believed in common assets, for some reason I felt uncomfortable being handed the access to 375 million dollars. I would have to consider my response.

We arrived at the hotel and headed straight for the room.

I took Liz's jacket off and hung it in the closet. I hung my new jacket next to hers.

I grabbed the ice bucket and scampered down the hall to fill it. I like my Pinot Gris chilled. When I returned Liz was nowhere to be seen. I buried the bottom portion of one of the wine bottles in the ice bucket.

"Liz, I called in a low voice."

"I'm in here;" the voice came from the bedroom.

I walked into the bedroom to find Liz lying in bed. She was on her back; her head elevated slightly by a pillow and the covers pulled up to her neck. A pile of clothes lay on the floor by the bed. Inventorying the items with my eyes, I knew Liz was completely naked under the covers.

"Do you need a formal invitation, want me to send you an email? Take your clothes off and get into bed!" She said with the sternness of an army sergeant giving orders to a new recruit. She had a big grin on her face.

Only the night table lamp was on. It was a 3-way bulb on its lowest setting.

I quickly kicked my shoes off, undid my belt buckle and the button on my pants, slid the fly down and dropped my underwear and pants to the floor in one continuous motion; I unbutton my shirt and dropped it off my shoulders to the floor, bent over and removed my socks.

I pulled the covers back and slid into bed, pulling the covers back over me. Before I was settled Liz had launched herself on top of me, her lips met mine, our mouths opened and we kissed and tongued each other in a heated frenzy. We couldn't get enough of each other.

Liz slid her hand down my chest and across my belly and put her hand around my throbbing erection. She broke the kiss with a start. Her mouth was inches from mine; "My goodness Mr. Dafoe, how you have grown!"

"An engagement present for you from the extraterrestrials!"

Now I must admit that I was, until going away, equipped with an average sized penis both in length and breadth. During the rejuvenating procedure I was asked if I would like to be enhanced. Why not, I figured. A man doesn't get this type of opportunity every day, no detailed discussion took place on what enhancement meant to the extraterrestrials. On inspection, after the rejuvenating procedure I realized that they had not made me much longer, maybe half an inch, but had made me broader, just a little near the head, but towards base it was substantial.

"I hope you like it?"

"To the touch, I think it is perfect, let me try it on and see how it fits!"

With that she raised herself up and straddled me. She positioned the tip inside her and slowly lowered herself down until I was completely inside her.

Liz leaned forward and began to ride me, her mouth opened slightly and small but heated moans of ecstasy escaped. I could feel that she was going to finish. I placed my hands on her cheeks and drew her head towards me. I captured her lips with mine, she was panting into my mouth, I loved the sensation, she tried to pull her lips away, but I held her lips tight against mine. She exploded, with a force I had never felt before. She pulled away from me and fell onto her back beside me.

"Who do I send the thank you card too?" She asked in a choppy voice trying to catch her breath.

"Will, would you be an angel and get me a glass of water?"

I quickly went into the main room where there was a small bar fridge, opened it and took out a bottle of Perrier, unscrewed the cap, poured into a glass, rushed it back into the bedroom and handed to Liz. Liz sat-up and drank at least half of the glass without a break.

"Thirsty?" I said with a chuckle.

Liz nodded and finished the rest of the water.

"More?"

She shook her head no. She placed the glass on the night stand and lay back on the bed, still breathing heavily.

I went back into the sitting room and poured two glasses of Pinot Gris and took them into the bedroom. I placed one on the night stand next to Liz, took a sip and then placed mine on my night stand.

I lay back on the bed and Liz rolled over and put her head on my shoulder and arm around my chest. She placed one leg over mine. She was so very wet I could feel her juices dripping down my leg.

"I'm so sorry!" Liz said.

"Sorry about what?"

"I didn't let you finish."

"Are you saying that you're finished making love with me this evening?"

"Absolutely not!" Liz pinched me.

I squeezed her against me; "The night is very young, my love, I am sure I will not have to go to sleep sexually frustrated."

We lay there without moving or talking for at least twenty minutes. Liz smelled of a sweetness that reminded me of honey.

"Liz, are you sure that you want to share your grandfather's inheritance with me, it's such a large amount of money?"

"Darling, I am very positive and I don't want you to question it again. Please." She raised her head and looked me in the eyes; "I love you so much!" She kissed me so very tenderly and then put her head back on my shoulder.

After a few minutes Liz started to change positions; she sat up and then slid out of bed, taking a sip of the wine. "I need a shower and I need someone to wash me all over, including my hair, it has to be someone who is currently in this room."

I got out of bed and stood there in my birthday suit with my arm raised, waving my hand in a panic.

Liz looked at me and then scanned my body slowly up and down a few times. "You'll do just fine. Come over here!"

I walked around the bed and stood in front of her, she wrapped her arms around me pulling me tight against her, I loved the feel of her supple breasts against my chest. She kissed me passionately; took me by the hand and walked me into the bathroom.

Liz walked over to a group of hotel complimentary lotions and bottles on the vanity and began reading them. I opened the stall shower door and turned the water on. I flipped the correct valve to have the water directed out of the showerhead.

"Can you believe that I left my shampoo and conditioner at your house in Toronto?"

"No, but I could believe that you left your shampoo and conditioner at our house in Toronto."

Liz turned and smiled; "My mistake! It was at our house."

Liz picked two of the bottles and brought them over and handed them to me. "Only use half of the bottle of conditioner."

We stepped into the stall shower and I pivoted Liz under the showerhead, placing the bottles of conditioner and shampoo on a small shelf. She shut her eyes as the water streamed down her face and cascaded down the rest of her body. There was a small waterfall from each of her nipples.

I put a big dab of the body wash on my hands and started to wash her, I loved the feel of her skin under my hands. It was obvious that Liz had not fully recovered from our last love making bout. There were no moans or body movement as I placed the body wash on even the most sensitive parts of her body. I turned around and washed her back, derrière, hips and thighs and then pivoted her under the showerhead again to rinse her off.

I guided her out from under the cascading showerhead. Liz had her eyes closed.

"Keep your eyes closed, I'm going to shampoo your hair."

I removed the top of the shampoo bottle, turned it over and put a few globs on different parts of her hair. Put the bottle back on the shelf and began working the shampoo into a lather and then I worked my finger tips through her hair all the way to her scalp. Liz's hair was very thick, but it was soft and silky to the touch. I flipped the hair on the back of her head up and over to ensure that I lathered it underneath.

Liz moaned a little, "This is so nice, you have wonderful fingers!"

I continued until I was confident that no strand of hair remained unwashed.

I took the handheld shower head from its holder, looked at the various levers on the wall and pulled on one. Right the first time, simply amazing I thought to myself. With the handheld shower nozzle in one hand and my hand in the other I flushed all of the shampoo from Liz's hair.

I took the conditioner bottle and basically repeated the same washing steps as I had done with the shampoo. Another rinse with the handheld showerhead; "You're done!"

Liz shook her head to settle her hair back in place and wiped the water from around her eyes. "Your turn!"

Liz took the handheld showerhead from my hand and drenched me. She put a big glob of body wash on her hands and began running them around my neck and down my chest. Her hands floated over my upper torso, my eyes closed and I just relaxed and enjoyed the sensation.

She moved her hands everywhere, she had an extremely delicate touch and when she ended up in the sensitive area, she stroked me with a lathered hand, a lot more than was necessary just to wash me. She washed my testicles ever so gently. Her hands moved down my thighs and leg and then back up the other one. She turned me around and washed my back, when she finished my butt; she slid her hand between my legs and clutched me again for a minute or so.

She washed the soap off me with the handheld shower head and then without warning saturated my hair. She reached for the bottle of shampoo and lathered my hair. She was no slouch at messaging my scalp with her finger tips. It was very soothing. She aimed the handheld shower head and rinsed me again from head to toe.

"You're done!"

"Stay here for a second and keep warm." I said.

I opened the door to the stall shower and quickly closed it behind me, went to the heated towel rack and removed a bath towel and two regular towels and returned to stand in front of the stall shower door.

"Turn the water off and come on out!"

Liz did as I said and as she exited I wrapped her in the bath towel, with the top just above her breasts, tucking an edge into itself so that it would stay in place.

I took one of the regular towels and placed it over her hair and made a turban out of it.

I took the second towel and wiped her shoulders and arms dry. I then went down on my knees and dried the inside of her thighs, her legs, feet and toes.

I rubbed the bath towel against her to make sure that it had absorbed all of the water droplets. I took a very plush terrycloth bathrobe from the hook on the door, released her bath towel and helped her into the bathrobe and tied the belt in a bow. With that accomplished I took her by the hand and led her to a chair in front of the vanity.

She turned and watched me. I retrieved a fresh bath towel and dried myself including my hair and put the other bathrobe on.

I went over and stood behind Liz and rubbed on the towel turban to help dry her hair.

"Is this a treatment reserved only for your fiancé?"

"No, it's reserved for my fiancé and my wife. You have no idea the pleasure I get from being able to do this for you. Pampering and spoiling you are now my only goals in life."

"What no love making?"

I could see a big grin on Liz's face in the reflection in the mirror.

"No more than half a dozen times a day!"

Liz broke out laughing. "That's what I get for marrying an old man."

"Hey, I wasn't the one that collapsed on the bed awhile ago." Liz laughed even louder. Liz had a fantastic laugh. It had a warmth and sincerity about it.

I dried and brushed Liz's hair and used her brush on my hair, because mine was in my personal container in the Eco Park on Roosevelt Island.

We left the washroom. I retrieved the wine glasses in the bedroom as we went into the sitting room and sat down on the loveseat, side by side.

Liz picked up a remote control that was on a table. "Do you think we can get any music?"

I stood-up and opened the doors of an armoire that was up against the wall, revealing a relatively small flat screen TV.

Liz pushed the on button and a menu instantly appeared on the TV. Liz read over the options, to herself but out load.

"Music!"

She clicked another button and another menu showed up.

"Classical!"

She clicked on that and was presented with another menu. This was beginning to get funny.

Liz chuckled, "Press one for this, two for that and three for something else. Then push one for this and two for that and three for something else, then the next set of options, until you are so frustrated you stop and turn it off. There's no music, I'm sure of it!"

I was looking at Liz and not paying attention to the multiple screen menus, all of a sudden I heard music.

"Well done!"

"Do you recognize it?"

I listened for a few seconds.

"I am pretty sure it's a Vivaldi concerto, Le quattro stagioni, Four Seasons."

Liz looked at me."You win, first prize!" She placed a hand on each one of my cheeks and kissed me, her lips were tender and sweet. "You'll get the rest of the prize later!"

We just sat there. Liz was leaning up against me, her head on my shoulder. I had my arm around her holding her tight against me. I was very content to just listen to the music and sip my wine with Liz in my arms.

My thoughts turned to tomorrow's meeting. "Liz, did you bring my laptop with you?"

"It's in my suitcase. Do you have to do some work now?"

"I will need it in the morning. There is a document I need to produce for the Security Council."

"Will, I called my Mom and Dad, when I returned from seeing Barbara off." Liz's voice was poignant and depressed. "My Dad answered and I asked him to put Mom on an extension because I had something important to tell them. Dad called Mom and when she got on the phone he said that he already knew that I had resigned from the cabinet. Mom asked me why. I could tell by the harsh tone in Mom's voice that she was infuriated with me. I said that none of that matters in the least and that resigning from the cabinet was not what I called about. I said, and these are my precise words, "Mom, Dad I'm engaged to the most wonderful man in the world!" Dad responded by saying that I shouldn't have resigned from the cabinet before I discussed it with him and mother. Mom agreed with Dad."

Liz was choking up. I didn't know what to say, I squeezed her tighter against me. Liz continued; "Then Mom said; you realize that your resignation has had a major impact on both of us! I'm very busy right now so I will have to speak to you at another time, and she hung up. Dad said; you realize that you have probably destroyed any hope of ever running for office. I really don't want to talk with you right now and he hung up.

On the happiest day of my entire life my parents didn't have the time to listen to what I had to say. That's the story of my life. As a family, everything we ever did, every decision that was ever made was done in the name of politics."

Liz was crying. It was obvious that this is what Liz had been crying about earlier, why she sounded poignant; depressed.

I kissed her head, and held her tighter.

I wanted to pick up the phone and call Liz's parents and tell them they would be perfect assholes if they didn't each have a large hemorrhoid sitting on top of their shoulders. How could they talk to their daughter like that? It's exactly these types of people, who have governed the planet earth for centuries, and in doing so created a situation that led us to the brink of total annihilation.

I maneuvered Liz around having her lay in my arms, her legs on the loveseat her torso against mine, her face just a few inches in front of me.

"I love you Will!" She moved her head forward and our lips met, very tenderly at first and then the passion increased until our tongues were entwined together; her lips were burning against mine. Her arms were around my neck and her hand was pushing my head towards hers.

I couldn't believe the unbridled passion that was inside Liz, she was a volcano ready to explode time and time again. We stayed in that locked embrace for what felt like hours, but it was only a few minutes.

She broke our tight embrace and started kissing me very gently on the neck and then my ear lobe. I whispered in her ear; "standup darling."

She stood up and I stood up, I put one arm around her back and the other under knees and picked her up. She immediately placed her arms tight around my neck. I carried her into the bedroom and placed her on her back on the bed, I bent over and undid the belt around her robe and opened it.

I pulled her arms out of the bathrobe sleeves and left her lying on top of the bathrobe. Liz's eyes were fixated on me as I undid my bathrobe belt and let it fall off my shoulders to the floor.

I lay down beside her, on my side. I took each of her arms and placed them above her head one hand on top of the other, with one of my hands gently holding her hands in that position, I whispered in her ear; "don't move your arms and close your eyes."

She lay there staring into my eyes for a moment longer. Her eyes showed a sense of excited anticipation. Then she closed them as I had asked.

Liz and I had been intimate before, but we had always had sex as if we were both in extreme heat. This was my opportunity to make love to Liz; very slowly and with extreme tenderness. I wanted to tease her unhurriedly and bring her to heights that she had never experienced before; heights that she had never even dreamed of.

I waited a second, and then I leaned over and ran my lips slowly and softly across her forehead. A small smile formed on her mouth.

I moved my lips down between her eyebrows and along her cute nose. Then across a cheek to an earlobe which I captured between my lips, sucked on it gently and flicked it with my tongue. I glided my lips back across that cheek over her nose and across the other cheek and then pulled my head away.

Liz's mouth was partially open and I took her upper lip between my lips and drew it gently into my mouth, I ran my tongue across its full length, left to right and then back again. I pulled my head away again. I did the same to her bottom lip. Liz was moving her hips slightly in a rhythmic movement and her breathing was becoming a little heavier. Her mouth was still open and I gave her a quick kiss, she tried to return it, but I pulled my head back before she could. The very tip of her tongue was protruding from between her lips, I bent down and captured it between my lips and with unexpected suction drew its length into my mouth, holding it there, Liz tried to pull it free, but I held it firmly. When I did release it I followed it as it returned to its nesting position in her mouth and kissed her again. Her head lunged forward to return the kiss, but she wasn't fast enough. I backed my head away.

Liz moaned; "You're nasty"

Liz kept her eyes closed and her arms were still over her head, although I had to hold them there she definitely wanted to move them.

I leaned over and put my lips on her chin; I took another quick kiss on her lips and then back to her chin. My lips travelled down her neck and across her shoulders.

I won't bore you with the rest of the details of this evenings love session. Suffice to say, that my lips and tongue didn't miss a square inch of her soft skin and lingered much longer is certain areas, one area in particular was visited numerous times for extended periods of time. It culminated two and half hours later with us climaxing at the same moment at which point Liz screamed so loud I was concerned that the people in the adjoining room may call security.

We lay on or backs completely spent and exhausted. Liz, moved up tight against me, and placed her head on my shoulder and we fell asleep.

Chapter 5 – 270 days to alien arrival

I woke, sometime during the night Liz had rolled over. Her head wasn't on my shoulder anymore.

I used to require at least seven and preferably eight hours of undisturbed sleep. After the rejuvenation procedure I was sufficiently rested after five.

I glanced at the clock on the night stand table it was 6:15 a.m. I carefully, so as not to wake Liz, got out of bed and put my bathrobe on. Went around to Liz's side of the bed and pulled the covers up and over her shoulders. I stood watching her sleep for a few seconds. She looked so very beautiful.

I retrieved my laptop case from Liz's suitcase and took it into the sitting room; plugged the power supply cord into the laptop and found a vacant electrical outlet on the wall near the desk. I set the laptop on the desk, opened it and booted it up.

It had been awhile, over three years, since I had typed anything. I was wondering how long it would take for my fingers to get back into sync with my brain. I had never been a fast typist, about fifty words a minute at top speed.

My brain now operated a bit like a computer. I concentrated for less than a second and brought the previously compiled overview document up in my brain. I could actually visualize it as a completed document.

I placed my finger tips on the appropriate keyboard keys and started to transcribe the document that I could see in my brain to the keyboard of the laptop. To my own amazement my fingers took off with a life of their own. It was rather weird and a bit unsettling. I will try to explain what was happening. If I concentrated on a specific word or sentence within the document, my fingers slowed and typed what I was concentrating on. If I visualized and then concentrated on the entire document, from start to finish, my fingers sped up phenomenally.

I stopped for a second, straightened my back in the chair. I put my finger tips back in position on the keyboard, visualized the entire document, and my fingers took off.

In less than fifteen minutes, I had typed a six and a half page document with no errors. I was impressed!

I rummaged around in my laptop bag and found a flash drive and proceeded to copy the overview document on to it. Harmon will have to make hard copies of the document because I didn't have a printer.

I began to think about the situation and my upcoming meeting. I went over to the bar fridge and took out a bottle of orange juice, popped the lid and drank about half of it. Cigarette, I thought. I found the cigarettes and lighter, sat down on the loveseat and just relaxed for a few minutes.

I put my brain into memo mode and considered what I needed to discuss at the Security Council Meeting.

The UN Security Council would have to tell me what involvement, if any, I was to have from this point on. I had already committed to provide them with a document detailing the agreement and its implementation. I also needed to pass over the medical formulas and explain the use of the items in the cargo containers. In theory once I had accomplished those tasks, they could do everything else without my involvement.

That was the theory. However it was highly unlikely that they would proceed without my involvement. On the premise that I would be involved, there were a lot of arrangements and decisions that they would have to make.

The first item that came to mind was logistics. Did they want me to stay in New York, go back home to Toronto or somewhere else? I needed a location to store the cargo containers. I needed a place to live. It would be great if there was a warehouse with a loft I thought to myself.

The second item was remuneration. I hadn't checked my bank account balance since my return and I hadn't asked Barbara, but I assumed that I hadn't been paid in three months. After all, I hadn't performed any work for the company, why should I get paid? While I wasn't hurting for money, I didn't think that I should have to donate my time, it was a bit of a principle; after all, all of the representatives to the UN Security Council were getting paid.

The third item that I placed on my mental memo pad was; staff. I would probably need some staff, but how many and their skill set depended a lot on exactly what my involvement was going to be.

I paused and finished my orange juice. The clock on the desk said it was 7:35. I wanted to shower and have some breakfast. It was time to wake Liz.

I went into the bedroom; Liz was now on her back. I leaned over and gave her a kiss on the forehead. Her eyes slowly opened and when she saw me leaning over her she had a big smile on her face.

"Good morning, Mr Dafoe!"

"Good morning, Ms. Montgomery! How did you sleep?"

"Like a baby, I haven't slept that well, in years, maybe ever. Will, I honestly didn't know that there was a difference between having sex and having someone make love to you. I can't believe what you did to me, every time I climaxed I was sure I had nothing left inside me and then you brought me back again for another and another and another each time more intense than the last and at the end when I was sure that I was completely void you gave me the largest finish imaginable." Her eyes twinkled. "Can we do that every night?"

"Won't you get bored of the same thing every night?"

"It doesn't have to be identical, just similar." Liz laughed. "Is it time to get up?"

"It's after 7:30 and I need to shower and have some breakfast, I thought you might like to join me, but if you would prefer to laze in bed, I really don't mind."

"There is no way you'll shower and eat breakfast alone - ever, if I can help it."

She pulled the covers back, and stood up. Standing there naked in front of me, I could have easily ravished her again, but I managed to maintain my decorum. Liz put her arms around my neck and kissed me.

We went into the bathroom and showered. We kissed a lot, but managed to keep it from going past that. We discussed breakfast, Liz asked me to order for us, her only request was a pot of tea. While Liz was putting on her makeup, I ordered breakfast from room service.

I put on clean clothes and transferred Liz and Barbara's pictures to my new shirt.

I went back into the bathroom and watched as Liz did the final touches to her face. She saw me watching and grinned from ear to ear.

There was a knock at the door, a quick look through the peephole to ensure it was room service and I opened the door. The table was setup and I signed the bill.

Liz went over to the table, I pulled out her chair, she sat and I pushed the chair in, took her napkin and placed it in her lap. I removed the warming covers from the plates, sat down, and looked at Liz; "I love you very much!"

"Not half as much as I love you!"

I had ordered eggs Benedict for both of us. The aliens did not make anything that resembled eggs Benedict prior to my arrival, although they had all the basic ingredients. Eggs Benedict was one of my culinary gifts to the extraterrestrials. I showed a chef at a restaurant how to prepare it and how to make hollandaise sauce. Within twelve months it was being served in restaurants on four planets. They called it Eggs Dafoe.

Liz and I commenced eating our breakfast while we chatted.

"Do you know how long you will be at the meeting today?"

"Not a clue."

"Do you think you will be back for dinner?"

"I think so. I want to have dinner with you. I will call you, if I can't. Do you have any plans for today?"

"I was going to go shopping to get Barbara a birthday present. You haven't forgotten that her birthday is in a couple of weeks."

"I hadn't forgotten, well not exactly, I knew it was April 20th, I just didn't have a grip on what day it was today."

I would have remembered Barbara's birthday a few days before the date and then scrambled to get her a gift. Barbara is a very difficult person to buy for at anytime.

The room phone rang, I glanced at the clock; it was 8:15.

Liz, looked at me, "It can't be for me, the only person who knows I'm in this room is Barbara."

I went over to the desk and picked up the phone.

"Hello!"

"William?"

"Speaking."

"This is Prime Minister Harmon, I'm sorry if I am disturbing you."

In a very light tone; "You're not disturbing me."

"I wanted to make sure you are being looked after."

"The hotel room was booked by President Wycliffe's staff. I am assuming that they are picking up the tab as no one has asked me for a credit card or pre-payment of any type. I was going to discuss some personal items with you and the other members of the Security Council this morning. To give you a heads up, so to speak.

"I would like to know what my future involvement in this exercise will be. Should I go back to Toronto in the next few days and go back to my job. I am currently on a leave of absence and haven't notified the company of my return date."

With a small chuckle in my voice, "I'm not even sure I still have a job." I continued.

"There are some logistical; matters with regard to the cargo containers that I brought back that are currently sitting on Roosevelt Island. It will be necessary to create a methodology to transfer the medical formulas to an entity so that they can be produced."

"Just so I understand, have you received any remuneration or are you expecting to receive any remuneration for the time you have been away."

"No! It was never part of my agreement."

"I will place you as the first item on the agenda. I would like to ask you to delay your arrival by a half an hour, 10:30 instead of ten. I would like to speak to the delegates about you prior to your arrival. Is that acceptable?"

"Yes! Mr. Prime Minister I have finished the overview document, but I don't have access to a printer or photocopier other than those in the hotel and I didn't think using them would be a great idea. I have copied the document to a flash drive."

"I'll arrange to have it printed from the flash drive at the UN when you arrive. Is there anything else?"

"Not at the moment. Thank you for calling Prime Minister."

"Thank you, William. I will see you in a little while. Bye."

"Bye." I hung up the phone.

Liz looked up from her cup of tea; "Something wrong?"

I looked at Liz; "That was Prime Minister Harmon; a really weird phone call. Something is definitely happening that involves me. My meeting has been rescheduled to 10:30. I'm not going to worry about it now, I will find out in a couple of hours. Why don't you get dressed and we'll go out and try to buy me a disposable cell phone."

"Not before I get another kiss. It's been at least a half hour!"

She stood up; I went over to her held her in my arms and kissed her.

She gave me the biggest smile, turned and headed for the bedroom to get dressed.

I sat at the table and finished my coffee.

Liz came out of the bedroom looking fantastic. Her fashion sense was excellent. I had no fashion sense and I am sorry to say that Barbara inherited that trait from me.

I looked Liz up and down and she did a quick pirouette. "Very, very nice!"

I grabbed my wallet, cash and the UN visitor's badge which I hadn't returned and put the flash drive and room keycard in the appropriate pockets.

I helped Liz on with her jacket and we left the room, hand-in-hand and headed for the streets of Manhattan!

Once outside the hotel we started walking in an arbitrary direction, glancing at store windows. Liz squeezed my hand. "I'm so happy, I feel as if I am walking on air!"

"I want you to always feel like this Liz!"

We found a cell phone store and after being educated on all the latest cell phones, I looked at the clerk and said; "I'm old, I need simplicity. A disposable phone will be perfect." We could see that he wasn't thrilled about my low cost choice, but he pulled a box from under the counter and told me it would probably fit my needs perfectly. I removed it from the box, it looked like a phone to me; there was a telephone number tag in the box, which I passed to Liz. I asked the sales clerk to dispose of the packaging, stuck the phone in my jacket pocket and Liz and I exited the store.

I looked at my watch, it was about 10 o'clock.

"We should start heading back to the hotel".

Liz didn't respond verbally, she gave me a smile and placed her hand in mine and we walked towards the hotel. When we arrived in front of the hotel we stopped and I looked at my watch, it was twelve minutes after ten. "I won't go back up to the room with you, have a good day and miss me lots."

"I will definitely miss you lots. You have a good day my darling." We hugged and kissed. I waited until Liz was inside the hotel lobby before I started my short walk to the UN. I easily remembered how to reach the door that I had excited from the night before. In a few minutes I was walking down the corridor of the Security Council room.

A commissionaire was sitting to the side of the doors and as soon as he saw me walking down the hall. He glanced at his watch. When I reached him, he verified who I was, knocked on the door and without waiting for an answer opened it.

As soon as I walked in, all of the delegates stood up from their chairs, all but one that is, a new face, I quickly realized that President Wycliffe was not in the room, this was most likely his replacement. He sat in the designated United States position at the round table, eyes looking down, banging the tip of his pen gently against the top of the table. I made my way over to the Prime Minister and handed him the flash drive. He motioned to one of the young lady commissionaires sitting in the corner, she quickly came over. The Prime Minister handed her the flash drive and gave her some instructions. She bolted out the door.

As I walked around the table to my vacant seat, a few of the delegates shook my hand while others, farther away, nodded their heads.

Everyone sat back down and I followed suit. Prime Minister Harmon looked around the room to ensure everyone was settled; "Mr. Dafoe thank you for meeting with us this morning. For the benefit of the other delegates Mr. Dafoe has brought us an overview document as he said he would. I have requested copies be made and they should be here in a few minutes. Translations of the document will probably not be available until late this afternoon.

Mr. Dafoe, before we continue our discussions with respect to the agreement and benefits, there is another matter that we wish to discuss. It has been brought to our attention, by the representative for the United States, Mr. Edward Bryant, that there was a serious incident that took place on your arrival. Would you like to comment?"

After what Liz had told me last night I found his arrival very interesting, so this is Bryant! He still had his face pointed down and was still tapping the tip of his pen on the desk.

My voice was perfectly calm; "Are you referring to someone taking a shot at me?"

With anger the Prime Minster shouted; "Someone shot at you?"

"An overzealous agent of the US Homeland Security I suspect.

Luckily he was a bad shot and missed."

"I've heard enough!" Bryant interjected in a loud voice. He had finally raised his head to look at me. "You're responsible for the deaths of 23 United States federal agents."

I reached over and poured myself a glass of water. I hadn't changed the expression on my face and continued to maintain eye contact with Bryant.

"You refused a United States federal agents request to undergo decontamination and you physically pushed a United States federal agent. I have formally requested that the United States Department of Justice immediately start a criminal investigation with the intent of having criminal charges laid against you; 23 counts of murder or conspiracy to commit murder along with other charges that pertain to not following the express orders of and assaulting a United States Federal Agent."

I stood up and looked around the room and then directly at Prime Minister Harmon. In a very calm but firm voice; "Prime Minister, considering that I am under criminal investigation by the United States Department of Justice, I do not believe that it is in my best interests to respond."

I paused.

"Anything that we may discuss here today and in the future could have a bearing on the criminal investigation. I don't believe that it is in my best interests to have any additional conversations with respect to my meetings with the aliens.

I paused again.

"I am therefore, taking my leave." I turned and started walking briskly towards the door.

Before I had taken three steps I heard Zhang Wei; "Mr. Dafoe, before you leave a few of us would kindly request a private meeting with you."

I turned around to find Ambassador Zhang Wei, Ambassador Middleton, Prime Minister Harmon and Ambassador Balabanov walking towards me.

They directed me to a far corner of the room.

Prime Minister Harman spoke, "Mr. Dafoe, on behalf of all but one of the delegates here I deeply apologize to you for what occurred yesterday when you landed and this morning. Mr. Bryant does not speak for all of us; in fact he only speaks for himself. We were only made aware of what occurred on your arrival and his accusations yesterday evening when he joined us for dinner. You had said nothing at our meeting yesterday."

"I didn't say anything because I considered the incident, with respect to the overall situation with the extraterrestrials to be trivial."

"We're all basically in agreement with you and I want you to know that Mr. Bryant did not inform us that one of his agents shot at you. I for one do not consider that trivial!"

"Each one of the people standing with you here took the exact same action, unbeknownst to the others. We're all providing you with full diplomatic immunity. Prime Minister Harmon reached into his coat pocket and handed me a Canadian red diplomatic passport, if you want or need to have any of your relatives declared under Canadian diplomatic immunity, provide me with their names and I will have it taken care of immediately."

Ambassador Balabanov reached into his inner suit jacket pocket and pulled out a red passport and handed it to me; "Diplomatic immunity from the Russian Federation."

"Diplomatic immunity from People's Republic of China;" Zhang Wei handed me a red passport.

"Mr. Dafoe, it is my honor to provide you with diplomatic immunity from the United Kingdom." Ambassador Middleton handed me a red passport. "I am sure that I speak for the other Ambassadors when I say that all of us would be pleased to provide additional immunity to your family if you desire and that you and your family members will be welcome in any of our countries on a permanent or temporary basis at any time."

I glanced and smiled at all the Ambassadors and the Prime Minister; "I want to thank you all, very much."

I shook each of their hands.

There was a definite note of relief in the Prime Minister's voice; "Shall we all go back to the table and resume our discussions?" It was a rhetorical question.

As we walked back towards our seats I reflected on what one of the alien leaders had said to me; "You may have severe problems when you return to earth. Always remember that you and your family have a home and friends here." It would take little more than a thought to be travelling back to the extraterrestrials. I felt more comfort in that knowledge than I did in the diplomatic immunity from four countries.

We all sat down at the table again. Bryant glanced up at me and smirked as if he was the mouse that had just stolen the cheese. My facial expression was of a very happy and content individual. It must have been driving him crazy that he hadn't flustered me. Many of the Ambassadors were talking amongst themselves; no one was talking to Bryant.

"The Prime Minister tapped his pen on the table to get everyone's attention; "Mr. Bryant, you may wish to inform your Department of Justice that Mr. Dafoe has been granted full diplomatic immunity by four countries; Canada, United Kingdom, People's Republic of China and the Russian Federation. Your State Department was informed in the change of diplomatic status for Mr. Dafoe early this morning.

You should also be aware Mr. Bryant that we have been in contact with President Wycliffe and in no uncertain terms have told him that we want you replaced as the representative of the United States."

Bryant surveyed the group around the table, they were smiling and some could be seen chuckling under their breath.

Bryant stood up his face was red; he was furious, he was going to say something but thought the better of it. He began walking, almost running to the door. As he did the rest of the delegates stood and applauded his exit, he slammed the door behind him as he left the room.

I couldn't wait to tell Liz what had just happened to her buddy Bryant.

"The Prime Minister relaxed himself in his chair; "Let's move on to our agenda. The first item pertains to Mr. Dafoe. Mr. Dafoe, earlier the committee discussed the points you had raised with me on the telephone. If I may take a moment I will tell you some of the decisions that we have made."

He paused and poured himself a glass of water.

"Due to the situation with the United States, we were concerned about your current hotel bill. Ambassador Middleton has already made arrangements to cover all of your hotel expenses for as long as necessary on our behalf."

I looked at the Ambassador and mouthed; "Thank you!" She smiled.

"We want your full involvement in this situation for at least the next 270 days, the time frame selected by the aliens. We would like to offer you some sort of one year employment contract to manage the situation and interface with the aliens if necessary. We feel that a fair payment would be 25 thousand US dollars per month. The Canadian Government will provide that payment each and every month and I have agreed that it will be tax free.

The delegates have also agreed that you should be compensated for the period of time you were away and not earning an income. We agreed that a lump sum payment of 100 thousand US dollars was reasonable. The Ambassador for the Russian Federation has been kind enough to commit to making that payment and I have agreed that it will be tax free.

Do you have any questions or comments, Mr. Dafoe?"

"No questions. I believe you are being more than fair!"

"This morning before your arrival, we couldn't reach a final decision on location. We had narrowed it down to either Toronto or New York. We felt both had equal advantages and disadvantages. However, after this morning's episode, we believe that Toronto would be the better location. However, we have decided to leave the final decision up to you. We will of course cover all operational expenses and in that regard we are making arrangements to provide you with an initial sum of 25 million dollars. Staffing would be at your discretion. Comments or questions?"

"I am in agreement. I would like to have 24 hours to consider the location before I commit." Although I liked the thought of Toronto, being close to Barbara, I wanted to discuss it with Liz before I committed.

"I don't see a problem with that. We have not come to any conclusions with respect to how we commence manufacture of the solar systems or circulate the formulas for the medicines."

A knock at the door interrupted us. The female commissionaire who had taken my flash drive had returned with copies of the overview document for all the delegates and a message for the Prime Minister.

The Prime Minister took one of the documents and passed the remaining documents to the individual on his left; each representative took one and passed the remainder of the stack to the next delegate. I didn't take a document; I knew what it said verbatim.

The Prime Minister read the note aloud; "President Wycliffe has called; Vice-President Almont will be joining us this afternoon, he has already left Washington."

I think this would be a good time for a break. Lunch, for anyone who would like to partake has been set-up next door. Mr. Dafoe you are more than welcome to join us."

Some of the delegates rose while others remained seated reading the document that was just delivered.

Cigarette break I thought to myself. I went to the outside smoking patio. Ambassador Marino had beaten me there. We shook hands. Ambassador Marino shook his head; "Bryant, not good man!"

I nodded, "Bryant like many men. Want power, control".

Have you ever noticed that when you talk to someone who speaks in broken English, that you start talking in broken English and you speak much louder?

The Ambassador nodded, "I get you Italia immunity; Italia bureaucracy very large, very slow. You have tomorrow!

I gave him a big grin; "Thank you Ambassador"

Maybe I should call the Guinness Book of Records. Having diplomatic immunity from five countries, at the same time, must be a world record.

When I was with Ambassador Marino yesterday, he looked very familiar, but I couldn't place him. I know what you're thinking; remember I have telepathic abilities. I can't believe he knows another one of the Ambassadors! Today, I realized that he looked like my barber Tony in Toronto, they could easily be brothers.

The Ambassador and I finished our cigarettes and walked to the dining room. They had set the room up as one large table with chairs on both sides. The table setting was very formal. There was a lunch buffet along one wall. I wasn't hungry in the least, I had a big breakfast. I placed a small scoop of a couple of different salads on my plate, found a vacant chair at the table and sat down.

On my left was Ambassador Middleton and on my right was Zhang Wei. There was a lot of idle chit chat at the table. I overheard Bryant's name mentioned a couple of times. Ambassador Middleton was making idle conversation with me about the South of England.

I excused myself, hit the bathroom and went out for another cigarette. I considered what approach I would take and subjects that I would cover this afternoon.

On my return I went to walk into the dining room, to find that only two of the delegates remained. They were in a heated discussion over a football match that had recently taken place.

I turned and went into the meeting room. The delegates had taken their seats and those that could comprehend English were reading the document. I sat down and a moment later the last two delegates walked in and took their seats.

Prime Minister Harmon called the meeting to order.

I was glancing around the room at the delegates and caught the eye of Ambassador Balabanov; he motioned that I should put on my earphones for translation. Although I could now understand any language spoken, at this time I didn't want anyone else to know about my telepathic abilities. I did as he requested and placed the earphones on. I played with the volume level so that the earphones were muted and mentally honed into his brain waves. I wanted to hear what he was going to say directly, not through a translator.

"May I have the floor Mr. Prime Minister? I would appreciate the opportunity to address Mr. Dafoe." Ambassador Balabanov asked in English.

"Please proceed Ambassador."

Ambassador Balabanov switched to his native language Russian; "Я изучал, (I realize that most of you do not understand Russian so I will provide you with the translation of what he said.) I have studied the overview document kindly provided by Mr. Dafoe. I personally want to commend him, at the highest level, not only on his remarkable negotiating skills, but on his principles, beliefs and character. He put his life in jeopardy, knowing that there was no one who would or could come to his rescue, to meet with an adversary who had already planned the total annihilation of the human race.

"He negotiated what he has called a compromise. I do not see it as a compromise. A compromise implies give and take it would appear after reading the overview document that it is all take with no give.

"We are asked to give up weapons of mass destruction; this is something that we should have negotiated amongst ourselves decades ago. We are asked to give up our nuclear power plants. We know from experience; Chernobyl, Kyshtym, Windscale, Three Mile Island, and Tokaimura, that there can be major nuclear power accidents; accidents that can kill tens of thousands of people.

"We are in fact giving up nothing of value!

"In return for giving up nothing of value, we are receiving medical advances that will save countless lives, enrich and benefit the health of us all. We are receiving technology that will save countless lives and give all of humanity the chance to live a better and longer life.

"Mr. Dafoe, every man, woman and child on this planet owes you their reverence."

Everyone in the room stood and applauded!

I was truly choked up, I stood and faced the Ambassador; "Thank you Ambassador! I am honored;" was all I could think of to say. Not overly impressive for a salesman!

The applause finally subsided and everyone sat back down.

The Prime Minister started to speak when there was a knock at the meeting room door and it opened. I recognized, from pictures, Vice-President Almont.

He entered the room, shook some hands and was directed to his seat at the table.

The Prime Minster looked over at me; "Mr. Dafoe, this is Vice-President Almont of the United States." I stood and nodded.

The Prime Minister passed a copy of the overview document across the table to the Vice-President and asked; Have you been briefed Mr. Vice-President?"

"The President briefed me before I left this morning."

"Then let's continue our discussions."

I had decided to start this session of the meeting by discussing the methodology to deliver the technology and medical science to the population; "If I may Mr. Prime Minister?"

"Please continue Mr. Dafoe."

"The agreement and the technologies that we have negotiated and received with and from the extraterrestrials are quite simplistic. In my opinion, the implementation will be extremely complex.

"It's the dissemination of the technologies that I see as a very complex issue. Which country or which business gets what technology. The economic consequences could have an enormous impact on the global economy and therefore must be taken into account. Who will own the technologies? Who will manufacture them? Who will trade with the extraterrestrials?"

I paused and looked around the room at the delegates, many were making notes on pads of paper; others were nodding in agreement.

"I believe I may have a concept that would resolve a lot of these issues.

"I suggest the formation of an international zone, similar to the way the United Nations exists in New York." In the international zone an entity unto itself would exist; similar to the Vatican which is an independent entity within the boundaries of Italy.

"The structure of the entity would be as a non-profit but it would be self sustaining requiring no funding. It may require a loan or capitalization to cover initial cash flow requirements."

I paused, to take any questions; there weren't any so I continued.

"The extraterrestrials have a market economy. I didn't outline the component requirement details of the solar systems previously, but one of the components is not available on earth. It is an element they call Xanfor. I brought back sufficient quantity of the Xanfor to allow us to manufacture one thousand - 512 megawatt units. The element, which has been prepackaged between a specialty glass plate and a sheet of non-conductive material, has been supplied to us by a commercial solar system manufacturing company, paid for by the Council of Inhabited Planets. It is not supplied to us free, but at commercial prices. The aliens provided it to me under a very loosely defined verbal credit agreement. We must pay for it eventually. When I said that each unit would cost approximately 5 million US dollars I included the cost of the Xanfor module which is approximately 1 million US dollars.

"The new entity would become the exclusive trading partner with the aliens. The aliens don't trade with multiple entities on any one specific planet but through a trading agency. This was one of the complexities that I mentioned in my overview.

"A similar scenario applies to the equipment necessary for the detection of earth quakes and volcanic eruption.

"I would suggest that the new entity would go out for a world-wide bid to have the items manufactured for them. In order to control the selling prices of the devices, the new entity would be the buyer. It would then mark up the cost of the items to sell them to power generation utilities, just enough to cover its expenses. That way, no business, with a goal of profit would control the market for any of the new technologies. As well, the new entity could ensure that there is a fair balance of where the manufacturing takes place, so that, within reason, as many countries as possible could benefit.

The medicines would be treated in a similar manner. The entity would go out to bid, purchase the medicines and then sell them with a small mark up, just to cover expenses.

The entity would operate with a Managing Director who would be an employee of the entity and a board of directors who would be chosen from members of the United Nations. How they are chosen is beyond me at the moment!" I heard a few chuckles from the delegates.

Ambassador Zhang Wei raised his hand.

The Prime Minister acknowledged his hand; "Please proceed Mr. Ambassador."

"Thank you Mr. Prime Minister. Mr. Dafoe, your concept and organizational structure has a lot of merit. I can see how it would solve a lot of problems. Would you be prepared to undertake the position of Managing Director of the organization? I cannot think of anyone more qualified or with a better understanding than you."

"I would Mr. Ambassador."

I surveyed the room, nothing was being said, but the delegates were looking at each other.

The Prime Minister broke into the silence. "Mr. Dafoe, is there anything else you would like to say with respect to your structural concept?"

"If you desire to proceed in this manner, I would like to immediately offer Ms. Elizabeth Montgomery the position of Deputy Managing Director of the new organization. Ms. Montgomery is a former member of President Wycliffe's cabinet. She was instrumental in my decision to undertake the original assignment. I would expect that overall staffing would be my responsibility. However, as Ms. Montgomery is also my fiancée I am hereby requesting specific approval to avoid the appearance of nepotism or corruption."

The Prime Minister nodded; "Mr. Dafoe, please do not take any offence, but I think some of the delegates would be more comfortable speaking about these matters without your presence. Could I ask you to excuse yourself from the room? You can wait in the dining room."

"Mr. Prime Minister, delegates, I do not take any offence. However, if it is all right with everyone here, I would prefer to go for a walk and get some fresh air."

I wrote down my new cell phone number on the bottom of the pad of paper in front of me, tore it off, walked around the table and handed it to the Prime Minister.

"That's my cell phone number, call me when you want me to rejoin the meeting, I shouldn't be more than ten to fifteen minutes away."

I left the room and the building. It was a nice day in New York, 73°F with no wind. I lit a cigarette, picked a direction and started off on my walk. I had always suffered a little from what I have always described as a minor case of claustrophobia. It wasn't unbearable in the same manner that others experience. I didn't have problems with elevators or going into small rooms. But being in any closed area for a lengthy period of time made me fidget and somewhat uncomfortable. I always felt much more comfortable outside in the fresh air.

I glanced at my watch to set the time in my head. I didn't want to walk in any one direction for more than fifteen minutes. My increased brain processing power allowed me to monitor the time without a watch or clock, but old habits die hard and I still looked at my watch or a clock to tell what time it was. My watch was very inexpensive, it was my backup. I had a nice watch, nothing fancy and also not overly expensive but the battery had died and I had worn the cheap watch to work the day I ended up meeting with the President. It was on my list to buy a new watch battery, but I hadn't gotten around to it.

I looked at my watch again and decided that it was time to get rid of it. I undid the buckle and chucked it into a street side waste container.

You can easily get a permanent kink in your neck looking at the skyscrapers in New York, it's also an easy way to get run over by a taxi or stampeded by a group of pedestrians. I walked looking in store windows, watching people as they scurried about and wondered what Liz was up to at this very moment. I made a mental note to call Barbara this evening.

I knew it was time to turn and head in a direction that would put me closer to the UN complex. I looked at my bare wrist to verify the time. Damn I thought to myself, you have to stop doing that.

I came up to a small courtyard with benches in front of a skyscraper and decided to park my butt for a few minutes. I lit another cigarette and started to consider the perfect location for this new entity. I pondered the advantages and disadvantages of warehouses, industrial complexes and other possibilities. It didn't take long for me to reason that the best location would be an abandoned or underutilized air force base or commercial airport, just outside a major metropolitan area; large buildings for the cargo containers, an office area and a runway to receive aircraft, plus a level of security and privacy. The negatives would relate to its current condition and how much if any work was needed to bring it up to a commercial complex. I knew that abandoned and underutilized airports were everywhere. It would only be a matter of choosing which country to start in. In the back of my mind I was leaning towards Canada, Southern Ontario to be specific. It would put me reasonably close to Barbara. But, I didn't know how Liz would react to relocating to Southern Ontario and I wasn't going to do anything that would affect her without first having discussed it with her.

As I was relaxing I heard a muffled rendition of the William Tell Overture. I quickly realized that it was coming from my pocket. I grabbed my cell phone and answered "Hello!"

"Mr. Dafoe, Prime Minister Harmon, would you please return to the meeting"

"I'll be there in less than fifteen minutes."

"Thank you." He hung up.

Now I happen to like the William Tell Overture, in my youth I watched the Lone Ranger every Saturday morning on television. But, it's not what I consider to be an acceptable ring tone, probably my old age. I made a mental note to change it to; ring, ring, ring; when I got back to the hotel.

I had only been out of the room for 43 minutes. I didn't look at my wrist! They called me back much quicker that I had expected. I put the cell phone back in my pocket and briskly walked back to the UN complex and directly to the meeting room. I knocked, opened the door and went directly to my seat.

The Prime Minister brought the group to order; "Mr. Dafoe, we have, maybe surprisingly, made some decisions and we are in unanimous agreement."

He started to read from his note pad.

"We want to form an organization as you have described working in a manner as you described. We would like you to be its Managing Director. For the time being the members of the Security Council will take the role of Directors of the organization, this may change at a later date and the individuals representing any specific country may change. The physical location will be completely up to you, but we would suggest that for expedience you choose a location that is in one of the Security Council member countries. That way you would be assured of complete support.

With respect to the employment of Ms. Montgomery; Vice-President Almont gave her an unprecedented reference. We believe that Ms. Montgomery would indeed be an excellent candidate for the position of Deputy Managing Director within the organization. You are free to present her with an offer of employment. I would also like to say that all of the delegates were highly impressed by your concern for complete transparency within the organization."

Wait until I tell Liz about the reference, I thought to myself.

"We would also like to take this time to congratulate you on your upcoming marriage and hope that you and Ms. Montgomery are very happy and have a good life together."

"Mr. Prime Minister I would like to thank all of the delegates for their good wishes and for their faith in my concepts. I will do my very best to ensure that everything is implemented in the best interests of all humanity."

The delegates then gave me a short round of applause. I nodded and mouthed thank you to all of them.

Once everyone had settled down, the Prime Minister spoke again; "Mr. Dafoe there are some questions."

Just then there was a knock at the door, a young lady entered with a handful of documents. "These are the translations that were requested." And with that she distributed specific copies to specific delegates.

The Prime Minister looked at the delegates; "we will take a fifteen minute break to allow the delegates who have just received their copies of the translated overview document to read it."

Out of the corner of my eye I saw Vice-President Almont standup and start circling the table. He stood beside me and I stood up. "Mr. Dafoe, I am Vice-President Almont." He put out his hand and I shook it. "I was wondering if we could have a moment together." I nodded in the affirmative. We walked to a corner of the room. "Mr. Dafoe, on behalf of the President of the United States and myself I wish to apologize for what occurred yesterday on your arrival and this morning. Bryant was way out of bounds in the way he organized your arrival and in the manner in which he spoke to you this morning. The President will be accepting Bryant's resignation as Secretary of Homeland Security this afternoon. I would like to assure you that there is no Justice Department investigation underway and there never will be. This administration had mistakenly accepted Bryant's supposed wisdom without question. We now realize that it was a major error on our part."

He stuck out his hand again and I shook it; "Mr. Dafoe, the President has also asked me to ask you to apologize to Ms.

Montgomery and for you to tell her that if she doesn't want to work for you, she would be welcomed back to his cabinet with open arms."

Wait until Liz hears this, wow!

"Thank you Vice-President and please relay my thanks to the President. Apologies although not necessary are accepted. In a roundabout way, what occurred this morning may have had a positive outcome. It seemed to bond and unite many of these delegates together against a common foe."

I almost looked down at my wrist, but caught myself in mid glance. It was 4.07. I wanted this to end so that I could be with Liz.

I had seated myself at the table, everyone who was reading had seemed to have finished. The Prime Minister must have seen it as well. "Mr. Dafoe, as I said earlier some of the delegates have questions. Are you willing to take them now?

"Yes!"

"Ambassador Marino."

"Thank you Mr. Prime Minister. Mr. Dafoe, better I speak Italiano, okay?"

I nodded and put on my muted earphones. I will translate for those of you who do not understand Italian.

"Mr. Dafoe, are the cargo containers that you brought back from the extraterrestrials secure?"

"I believe so. They are made of an alloy which is not available on earth. According to the aliens, we do not have the technology to cut through it. There are 101 cargo containers and they are locked together making them a single unit of a weight and size that although not impossible it is highly improbable that they could be moved. The doors on the containers have an extremely high level of security, my DNA; my hand print; an image of my retina and a 256 character alphanumeric code, different for each container is required to unlock the doors. I did not make any specific arrangements for them to be guarded, but I am assuming that at least one of the many US security agencies is guarding them."

"Thank you Mr. Dafoe, I have one additional question. You mentioned that we have received the materials on credit. Are there any terms and conditions to this credit, such as interest and a payment date?"

"This was an unusual situation for the extraterrestrials. The materials were provided by the Council of Inhabited Planets who do not process or handle any type of trade transactions. Their exact words were; you can pay us later. I must admit, that I am not one hundred percent positive I understand the words "you" or "pay" in that sentence. I know they don't think that I will provide payment from my personal resources. I do believe that payment will, at sometime in the future, be transacted in an element such as copper, silver or gold, but I could be wrong. I do know the aliens perceived value of the material in US dollars, which is how I came up with the 940 thousand US dollars per 512 megawatt solar collector system. I am sure that there is no interest on the debt."

"Thank you Mr. Dafoe, I yield the floor to the Ambassador for India."

"Mr. Dafoe, are there any special ingredients needed for the medicines? By special I mean not available on this planet."

"The aliens told me that we have all of the available ingredients to make all of the formulas supplied readily available on this planet. I'm neither a chemist nor biochemist; I have taken their word for that. I would like to point out that they have additional medications. The formulas for these medications have not been provided to us because we do not have all the ingredients available on earth. It would require that we set up trade with the extraterrestrials."

"Thank you, a second question if I may."

"What are the skill sets needed to manufacture the solar collector systems? Is special machinery required?"

"Mr. Ambassador; in no specific order the skill sets necessary for the manufacture of a complete solar collector system would include; welding, machining, polishing, metal component assembly, electronic component assembly, and glass blowing. A machine shop that can produce items to reasonable tolerances would be more than capable of manufacturing the platform. Any electronic circuit board and component assembly house could easily undertake the electronic assemblies. The glass dome would require a company that has the knowledge and facilities to blow glass."

"Thank you Mr. Dafoe, I yield the floor to the Ambassador for the United Kingdom."

"Mr. Dafoe, how complex will it be to install a solar collection system at a current nuclear power generating station."

"The installation of the solar collection systems at each generating station may create their own unique challenges which will primary be logistics. In very simplistic terms, the cables that currently connect to the generators at the nuclear power station will be transferred over to the solar system. This will be more complex at some stations than others. A few towers holding the electrical cables may have to be removed in some cases, in other cases cables may have to be extended to reach the physical positioning of the solar system at the generating plant site. In my opinion none of the challenges will be insurmountable. The current generating station engineers should have no problems in overcoming any of the challenges presented to them. They face similar challenges on a day-to-day basis."

"Thank you Mr. Dafoe, I yield the floor to the Vice-President of the United States."

"Mr. Dafoe, you have outlined that you have formulas for medications, do you also have dosage and side effect information? Should we send samples to our regulatory agencies for testing?"

"I have dosage information for all the medications. In almost all cases it is based on the weight of the individual. In one case it is based on gender and weight. Possible side effects of the medication are interesting. I had brought that up with the extraterrestrials when they provided me with the formulas and dosages. It took me almost fifteen minutes to explain to them what I meant when I said side effects. When they finally understood, they said there are no side effects. Later on in conversation they couldn't comprehend why we would produce a medicine that had side effects."

I do not believe that testing is required. I have taken many of the medications. I no longer have type-2 diabetes, glaucoma or high cholesterol. However, I would think that it would be up to the health departments in each country to decide whether or not to release the medication to their populations."

"Thank you Mr. Dafoe, I yield the floor to the Ambassador for New Zealand."

"Mr. Dafoe; "Do you have pictures of the aliens and their planet."

"I took more than 6,500 pictures. The memory cards are in one of the cargo containers. I will distribute the pictures as soon as I can catalogue them and add captions. The pictures without captions will have little meaning."

"Thank you Mr. Dafoe. I yield the floor to the Prime Minister of Canada.

The Prime Minister looked around the room, "are there any other questions or comments for Mr. Dafoe?"

No one asked to speak.

The Prime Minister looked at me; Mr. Dafoe do you have any questions or comments?"

"Yes, Mr. Prime Minister, I do.

"There are many things that I have not related about my visit to the extraterrestrials because they do not have any bearing on the decisions that have to be made. However, one of those things that you may find interesting is that I did not spend three days with the aliens, I actually spent three years, the reason I could take 6,500 pictures. The aliens have a technology or science that allows for what I can only describe as limited time travel. They cannot go back in time, but they can slow time down during space travel, if that makes any sense. It took forty-five days to reach the alien planet. I then spent three years with the aliens and another forty-five days to return. The elapse time on earth was only 93 days, for me it was 1185 days. As well, I did not stay on one planet during my visit. I visited four planets in all. I am sure that you have a lot of questions about the aliens and their life styles. But it is crucial that we don't get side tracked. There is a lot to do in a very limited period of time. We are now at 270 days before the aliens visit us."

The Prime Minister responded quickly; "Your point is well taken Mr. Dafoe, first we must ensure that the crisis situation is under control, it would be easy to get side tracked and waste valuable time. Is there anything else Mr. Dafoe?"

Two items; the first pertains to the new entity, it needs a name. I would like everyone to ponder it over night and hopefully we can come to a decision tomorrow.

The second item relates to Ms. Montgomery, if she chooses to accept a position with the new entity I would like to bring her to the meetings, starting with tomorrow's meeting. There are numerous reasons. She is very intelligent and creative and I believe that her council would be invaluable to us. I think it would be good for her to meet you and be able to put a face to the names. It would save me valuable time, if I do not have to relate everything said at meetings to her. Another important consideration, should something happen to me, you will need someone with as much knowledge as possible of the situation to be able to immediately step in and take over."

Then I smiled; "Lastly, she will be much easier on your eyes than I am.”

Some of the members chuckled out loud.

“I have no other comments or questions at this time Mr. Prime Minister.”

“Thank you Mr. Dafoe; the more you speak the more positive I am that we have chosen the right man to lead us. I am very impressed with your thought processes.”

A number of delegates slapped the table as a sign that they were in agreement with the Prime Minister.

“Do any of the delegates object to the presence of Ms. Montgomery at our meetings?”

No one responded and most of the delegates were shaking their heads no.

“Does anyone object to an earlier starting time tomorrow, 9:30?”

No one objected.

“I call this meeting adjourned until tomorrow at 9:30 am.”

It was ten after six and I was anxious to get back to see Liz. I rose from my chair and started to head for the door, but was intercepted by Ambassador Middleton; “Mr. Dafoe, may I have a moment of your time.”

“Of course.”

We walked away from the exiting traffic.

“Mr. Dafoe; I do not know if you and your fiancée have made any plans for a honeymoon. We would be honored to have you and your wife honeymoon in the UK as guests of the British Government. She then spent a few minutes reminding me about the benefits that would be available should I consider locating the new entity in the UK.”

With that she passed me her business card, she pointed out that she had written her personal cell phone number on the face of the card and on the back was the name of the British Prime Minister’s personal assistant. Should we wish to accept the offer all we had to do was call the individual listed on the back of the card or her and of course she said that I could call her at anytime about any matter.

I thanked the Ambassador for her gracious offer and said that I would keep it in mind when the issue of where to honeymoon became a consideration. We said our goodbyes. I walked quickly out the building towards the hotel.

What a day I thought to myself, I’ll be up all night telling Liz everything that happened.

I knocked on the room door and Liz opened it in a flash. She grabbed my hand, pulled me into the room and kissed me passionately.

There was an energy in Liz that I hadn't seen before. Liz took my hand and walked me over to the loveseat; "I'm so glad you're here, I have so much to tell you. How was your day?"

"I had a good day and I have a lot to talk to you about."

She smiled, "Can I go first? Would you like a glass of wine?"

"Yes to both questions."

Liz poured me a glass of wine and topped up her glass, she had been indulging before I arrived and sat down next to me.

"I was watching RNN this afternoon; around 4:30 they announced that the President had accepted the immediate resignation of Edward Bryant, Secretary of Homeland Security. A spokes person for Bryant said it was for personal reasons, unnamed sources inside the Whitehouse reported that the President and Secretary Bryant had a major falling out."

I smiled at Liz, "I already knew that!"

Liz pocked me in the ribs; "Because of your new mental powers?"

"No because I met Vice-President Almont today and he told me. But that's just part of what I want to tell you when it's my turn."

Liz placed her hand on my thigh and squeezed it; "I love you so much!"

She paused and took a sip of wine; "Mom and Dad called me a little while ago. Dad said that President Wycliffe had called him and Mom. The President apparently apologized to them about the incident that took place at the Whitehouse that lead to my resignation. He told them that although it was Bryant that created the situation, he didn't intercede to stop it. Dad went on to say that the President would like me to return to his cabinet. Of course I could tell by the tone of Dad's voice that he expects me to jump at the opportunity and run back to the Whitehouse. Mom then said they were really surprised when the President congratulated them on my engagement to a William Dafoe; she wanted to know why I hadn't told them. I said I had told them yesterday, but they were so busy yelling at me, that they didn't hear anything that I had said. Mom and Dad apologized the way politicians do, no sincerity whatsoever. Mom wanted to know who you are, what you do for a living and if you were from old money. Dad wanted to know if you are a Republican. I told them that you aren't a Republican, you're a Canadian. I was going to tell them that you were the Vice-

President of an electronic s company, but I had thought about our conversation and I said he's a salesman. Mom asked if I was sure that you were the right man for me. A marriage to you would not enhance my political aspirations. I have never had any political aspirations; they have had political aspirations for me! Mom then said that we needed to start the wedding plans. She would hire somebody whose name I don't remember as the wedding planner."

She paused and took a big sip of wine.

"Will, my mother will try to make our wedding into the political event of the decade. I don't want that."

"Then it won't happen, my love. Our wedding will be what we want it to be. I do have a couple of ideas on the matter."

Liz squeezed my thigh; "If you say it won't happen, I know it won't happen! Mom wanted to know if I had an engagement ring. I told her I did, she wanted me to describe it, but instead I took a picture of my finger and sent it to her cell phone. I'm sure it will blow her mind when she sees how beautiful and big it is! And last, they want us to get together so they can meet you, but they are very busy, so they will look at their calendars and see what dates are good for them."

That's my big news, on the lighter side; I spoke to Barbara, everything is fine, she's expecting a call from you tonight. If we're still here during her spring break she wants to come and visit. That would be her birthday week, so I thought for her birthday I would take her to an upscale spa and give her the total package. What do you think?"

"I think that's a great idea."

"I want to hear about your day, but first I need some loving!"

She put her wine glass down and laid across my lap, I held her in my arms and we kissed. I felt like a teenager in heat. After a few minutes of hot and heavy kissing, we broke our embrace.

Liz smiled; "Okay, that should hold me for a few minutes, tell me all the news".

Liz had tucked her legs underneath her and was staring at me giving me her full attention.

I told her about Bryant and the Justice Department threats and that I now had diplomatic immunity from four countries and that it may be five, if Italy actually gives me a diplomatic passport. I told her that they had offered her and Barbara diplomatic immunity as well. I related the conversation that I had with the Vice-President.

Then I told her about the decision to form an entity to distribute the new technologies that were given to us by the aliens and that I had accepted the position of Managing Director and I told her about the financial compensation I was to receive. At that point I paused and took a large gulp of wine, stood up retrieved the wine bottle and refilled our glasses.

"Liz, you are going to have to make a couple of decisions."

She gave me a big smile, her face was glowing.

"I can locate the operations of this new entity almost anywhere I want; in any country. I am leaning towards southern Ontario. What are your feelings about moving to southern Ontario. Before you answer, my love, you must also decide whether you want to go back to Washington and rejoin the President's cabinet or REND, because if you choose either one of those, it will automatically decide where I choose to put the new entity. I don't have any desire for us to be separated."

I decided that I would not mention that I had a position for Liz with the new entity. I wanted to know if she desired to work in Washington and in politics.

"Take some time and think about it, Darling."

"I don't need any time to think about it. I don't want to work in politics; that was part of my parents' great design for my life. From the minute I was born, they groomed me to be the first woman President. I will be at your side no matter where you want to set up this new business."

Liz paused and laughed; "as long as it's within driving distance of a nail salon. Southern Ontario is probably an excellent location as it would place us close to Barbara, which I think is important. There are nail salons in southern Ontario aren't there?"

"I laughed as well; "Yes! There are nail salons on every street in southern Ontario. I asked and received permission to offer you a position with the new entity; Deputy Managing Director. Would you like to do that? Would you like to take some time to think about?"

Liz's voice was filled with a combination of joy and excitement; I don't need any time to think about it. Oh yes; very much!"

"I want you to know that Vice-President Almont gave you a glowing recommendation. From this point on, you will be attending all of the meetings with the UN Security Council."

Liz's cell phone rang. With a questioning look she picked it up from the desk and looked at the screen; "It's Barbara!"

They talked about nothing for a minute or two and then Liz passed me the phone.

Barbara told me that she wanted to say hello before she went to the Library, something about a term paper. We expressed our love for one another and then she asked me to pass the phone back to Liz.

Liz listened for a second and then turned her back to me; obviously she wasn't considering my enhanced hearing. I heard her say; "No not yet, the opportunity hasn't presented itself yet, I will, I'll call you tomorrow and tell you all about it. Bye." She turned and looked at me with a silly grin on her face and I think she was blushing. Something was up; my two girls were hatching a plot. I figured I'd find out when they were ready.

Liz came over and gave me a kiss, as if to get my mind off the conversation I may have overheard; "If you are going to be a Managing Director we need to get you some clothes, a few suits, dress shirts and ties. Let's go down stairs and see if we can get you something at the menswear store.

We entered the menswear store and Liz headed straight for the suit racks and started to peruse the collection. A salesclerk came over, but Liz said she would call him when we needed him, he didn't disappear, he stepped back a few yards and waiting to be summoned. I stood back and let her do her thing. It didn't take her long to pick out two dark blue suits and a deep chocolate brown. "Try these on!"

I did as I was instructed.

I tried the chocolate brown suit on first, the jacket fit fine across the chest. The sleeves would have to be shortened. I came out of the dressing room, Liz gave me a once over asked to see the back and then sent me to the dressing room to try on another one.

I put one of the blue suits on, it felt more comfortable than the brown; of course the sleeves were too long on this jacket as well.

Liz gave me a once over and handed me a dark grey suit; "I don't like the brown suit."

I tried the second blue suit on and received my inspection and repeated it with the grey suit. When I came out of the dressing room, Liz looked over at the salesclerk; "we'll take the two blue suits and the grey." The salesclerk told me to go put one of the suits on and he would mark it for the necessary alterations.

I did as I was told. Liz watched closely and instructed the salesclerk on the length of the pants, sleeves and a couple of tucks she wanted in the pants and one on the jacket. I did the same with the other two suits.

Liz took the jackets and went over to the shirts, asked me my neck size and proceeded to pick out three French sleeve shirts for each suit. She did the same with the ties. On her way to the ties she had selected three packages of socks.

The last item was shoes and Liz was sure of the style she wanted. Luckily the store had my size.

At the checkout counter Liz told the salesclerk that we needed one of the suits tomorrow. He moaned but she was firm; no was not an acceptable response. Liz paid for the items with her platinum American Express Card, a little over $7,300. I let out a gasp when I heard the amount.

We exited the menswear store with the nine shirts and ties; a dozen pairs of socks and a pair of shoes. Liz wrapped her hand around mine; "we really need to go to a tailor to have your suits made for you! Do you have cufflinks for the shirts?"

"Not here."

Liz, holding my hand aimed for a jewelry store. Once inside Liz quickly determined which showcase had the cufflinks. A salesclerk lifted out some trays and placed them on top of the glass countertop. Liz picked up a few of the individual sets and studied them closer. Liz pointed at three sets of cufflinks; "We'll take those."

While the salesclerk fumbled around finding the boxes, Liz squeezed my hand; "two of them are for work and one for when we go out."

Liz had excellent taste in men's jewelry. I went to pay for them, but Liz had already given the salesclerk her American Express card. The three sets of cufflinks came to a little more than twelve hundred dollars.

"You're spending too much money on me!"

"It's our money and you need to look the part of a Managing Director! Plus, I bought the clothes with you not for you."

We went back up to the room, once inside, I remembered the William Tell Overture on my cell phone. I played around with the menu keys, found ring tones and set the phone to a basic ring pattern.

Liz had opened the armoire and was hitting keys on the remote to find the music. I went over to her; "thank you for choosing my wardrobe," and gave her a kiss.

"Your welcome, it was fun! I've never shopped for men's clothes before, other than your jacket. Can we have room service for dinner?"

I went over to the desk and opened the room service menu; "Is there anything specific you'd like?

"I looked at the menu earlier, I would like the tiger shrimp cocktail, the medallions of veal and an ice tea."

I really liked that about Liz, she made quick choices and didn't hem and hah about things.

I called room service and ordered two tiger shrimp cocktails, two medallions of veal, an ice tea and two cokes.

I was just about to sit down beside Liz for some much needed cuddling when her cell phone rang. She looked at the screen; My mother! Liz's voice became anxious; "Hi Mom, twice in one day, that may be a record."

I tuned my hearing so that I could hear Liz's mother on the other end of the line. I don't believe Liz was aware that I was listening. Liz was beginning to pace the room.

Liz's mother had a frustrated tone to her voice; "I called your apartment and got your voice mail, telling me to call you on your cell phone. Where in god's name are you?

"I'm in New York at the Century UN Plaza Hotel with Will."

"Are you together?" There was disapproval in her voice.

Liz continued to pace; "Yes Mom, we are staying in the same room together."

Her Mom's voice had changed, she sounded like a public school teacher talking to a student; "You don't want to have any accidents, are you taking precautions?

"Mom, I'm a big girl, I know about birth control."

Now Mommy Senator spoke; "Liz your Father and I have checked our calendars and although we will have to cancel some commitments we want you to come on April 15th and 16th.

Liz's voice was getting more and more anxious with every word spoken. "Will and I are in the middle of a very complex assignment and I really don't know if we will be able to make it on those dates."

Mommy Senator continued, she completely ignored Liz's comments about the dates; "There are a lot of arrangements to make for your wedding and you must book the church. We'll want the wedding at Atlanta Presbyterian and they are booked well in advance. Luckily your father has some close friends there; he should be able to move your date forward.

Liz was beginning to choke up; "Mom, I don't want a big church wedding."

I motioned to Liz to pass me the telephone.

"Mom; Will is standing beside me and would like to say hello." She passed me the cell phone without waiting for a response.

"Senator Montgomery, it's a pleasure to speak with you, Liz has told me all about you and her Father."

"We can't wait to meet you." She sounded just like a Politian who wanted my vote.

With a voice of utter disgust; "Liz said you are a salesman, what do you sell?"

Now's the time for some fun I thought. Liz had just downed a glass of wine, but was still pacing.

"Cemetery plots! I said in my salesman's voice. Have you and Mr. Montgomery considered where you want to rest for eternity. I have access to some of the most beautiful cemeteries in the US. Plots that are under stately oak trees or maybe you would prefer to rest with a view of a river or lake, I would"

I looked at Liz. She was looking at me as if I had lost my mind. She mouthed; "What are you telling her?" I gave her a big smile. Liz started to chuckle.

Liz's Mom interrupted my sales pitch. She was definitely flustered; "I am sure they are all wonderful locations. I understand you are acquainted with the President"

I could tell that I hadn't made a sale!

"Yes, I sold the President a cemetery plot for his dog a number of years ago."

With panic in her voice; "I was telling Liz that it was crucial that we start planning the wedding now. We have to book the church."

"Senator, I understand your desire to book the church and under any other circumstance I would be pushing Liz to do so. I don't know if Liz has told you, but I'm a widower and a big church wedding just wouldn't be appropriate."

I have absolutely no idea why being a widower would make a church wedding inappropriate. However, I do know that bullshit baffles brains. That's not only a salesman's credo but a politician's credo as well.

Liz's Mom paused. I think she was trying to figure out the relationship between widowers and church weddings in her own mind.

I knew, that as a politician, she would never admit that there was something she didn't understand.

When she did speak, I knew that I had totally befuddled her; "I wasn't aware that you were a widower, now I understand why Liz doesn't want a big church wedding."

Explain it to me please, I thought to myself. I almost laughed out loud. If the big church wedding raises its ugly head again I will resort to the; I'm a devote Druid and my faith will not allow me to enter a church.

"It was so nice to speak with you Will, please put Liz back on the phone."

I passed the phone to Liz.

"Liz, you should have told me Will was a widower earlier; it would have saved me a lot of embarrassment! Your father will be disappointed he really wanted to walk you down the aisle. I'll see you and Will on April 15th, I've got to go, Bye!" she hung up without waiting for Liz to say anything.

Liz had stopped pacing, but she was still anxious. I held her in my arms; "I'll deal with your parents."

She held me very tight and in a very soft voice. "I love you so much!"

We stood locked in a hug for a couple of minutes, Liz's head resting on my shoulder. I could feel her begin to fully relax.

A knock at the door interrupted the sharing of true love that we were experiencing.

A waiter pushed a food service cart through the door and quickly set it up. He informed us that the entrees were in a warming box under the table, had me sign the bill, wished us a Bon Appétit and left. I pulled out the chair for Liz and seated her, napkin and all.

I removed the plastic wrap covering the tiger shrimp cocktails. There were three tiger shrimp hanging off the glass, with some cocktail sauce in the center. The tiger shrimp were enormous, Liz and I dug in!

Liz had a puppy dog expression on her face; "These are excellent."

She paused to have another bite of shrimp. "Did you actually tell my mother that you sold cemetery plots?

"I did!"

Liz started to grin; "What did she say?"

"She changed the subject after I told her that I had sold a cemetery plot to the President for his dog. I am sure that your mother thinks that I am the lowest of the low, white trash, just slightly above road kill."

"Liz broke out laughing, hardly able to speak; "I wish I could hear the conversation she will be having with father. I can just see them going out and buying a dog, just so they can purchase a cemetery plot for it, next to the President's dog plot of course!"

I had finished my last shrimp; they were so big; I was almost full. I rested while Liz finished hers.

"Liz, I know you don't want a big church wedding, which is fine by me. Do you have a dream wedding that I can fulfill?"

"I don't have a lot of specifics, but I picture it taking place on a tropical island, looking out over the ocean. What would you like to do?"

"We think very much alike, my love. Are you familiar with the Fern Grotto weddings on Kauai, one of the Hawaiian Islands?

"A little bit, many years ago a girl friend in college got married there. I had forgotten about it. I couldn't go for one reason or another, but I remember the pictures she brought back, it was very beautiful. That would be perfect Will!"

Liz stood up before I had time to pull her chair out. She walked around the table and gave me a long tender kiss. "I need a break before we start the entries, I'm stuffed! I'll be back in a minute. Wait for me on the loveseat."

She turned around and walked into the bedroom. I went over and plunked myself down on the loveseat, I was stuffed as well. I took a sip of the wine that had been sitting there for quite some time; it was warm. A moment or two later Liz reappeared from the bedroom; she had a hand behind her back. She stood in front of me; "close your eyes and stick out your left arm." I did as I was instructed. I felt something slide over my hand and tighten around my wrist. My first notion was handcuffs, naughty girl I thought to myself.

"You can open your eyes now."

I opened my eyes and looked at my wrist, it wasn't handcuffs and believe me when I tell you that I wasn't in the least disappointed. It was the most elegant wristwatch I had ever seen. It wasn't in the least ostentatious like many wristwatches are; it immediately exuded an extremely high level of class, and sophistication. It said "The wearer is successful". It was silver, with a silver gold expansion band. It had a small black face with diamonds at the three, six, nine and twelve marks. I needed a watch with a small face because I had small wrists and hands. A large face watch looked out of place. I studied it carefully, it was a Patek Philipe. I had never even owned a Rolex, never could consider spending the money on a Rolex and now I was the proud owner of a Patek Philipe. My head was spinning.

"It's your engagement present! Do you like it?"

I shook my head, I was grinning ear to ear and I was basically speechless; "Liz it's awesome, you shouldn't have, I can't take my eyes off it, thank you so much."

"There's an inscription on the back."

I removed the watch very carefully as if it was made of crystal and might break into a million pieces and flipped it over; "*Will, There will never be enough time to tell you how much I love you! Your Liz.*"

Tears came to my eyes. I put the watch back on my wrist, stood up and took Liz in my arms. I kissed her passionately and then held her close against me; "There is no doubt that I am the luckiest man in the world. No other woman can even stand in your shadow Liz."

We kissed again.

We sat down on the loveseat and I held Liz in my arms. In a very soft voice and somewhat choked up voice she whispered, "Never stop showing me how much you love me Will, please! I need to feel your arms around me, your lips against mine, to feel you touch me, to know you desire me."

Liz was crying out for the love and security she had never received from her parents or anyone else it would seem. I couldn't understand why such an attractive, intelligent and wonderful person had never found love. It spooked me a little, was I missing something, was she going to turn into another person. Was Liz trying to buy my love with all the gifts? I realized that I was being a jerk. It was stupid of me to even think about something I had no control over. I loved Liz, with all my heart what would be would be.

I pulled her even tighter against me; "Liz, my darling Liz, you are not a short term infatuation, I am obsessed with you and totally and utterly captivated by you. You are constantly in my mind. I was away from you for over three years, and not once did my love for you ever waver. It was the thought of spending the rest of my life with you that kept me sane. I was alone in a world of aliens. I impregnated your face on the back of my mind, so that you would be with me no matter what I faced. You have no idea how depressed I felt when I didn't see you when I stepped out of the spacecraft on my return. I was sure that I had lost you. Did I not bring you an engagement ring on my return?

"You could have given that ring to anyone?"

I laughed out loud. "Only if there name was Liz."

"Liz was getting upset; "Why are you laughing at me?"

"Obviously you didn't read the inscription on the inside of the ring!"

She pulled away from me, her voice was angry. "What inscription, you never said anything about an inscription!"

She pulled the ring from her finger; she stared at the inside of the band. There was a level of panic in her voice. "I can see an inscription, but I can't focus on it to read it!" Her eyes had tears in them. "Damn it Will, what does it say?"

"*Liz, forever yours, Will.*"

She started to cry. I reached over to pull her against me but she moved away.

"I'm such a fool Will. I don't know what's wrong with me. There are times that I know that I don't deserve you and times I feel that I am not good enough for you. If you haven't realized it yet, I'm very insecure with one-on-one relationships.

I got up and retrieved the tissue box from the bedroom and passed it to Liz.

"Thank you." She wiped her eyes. "There is something that I haven't told you about myself, I've been afraid that if I tell you I will lose you, but you have to know, it's not fair to you to keep it a secret."

"Do you want to tell me now?

"I don't want to tell you ever, but I have to tell you now."

"Well, Ms. Montgomery, I have a rule about situations such as this."

Liz sounded uneasy; "Rules?"

"Bad or upsetting news is only conveyed between us is while we are lying in bed, in each other's arms."

I clasped her hand tightly in mine and gently pulled her into the bedroom.

"Lie down on the bed."

Begrudgingly she lay down. I lay down beside her. I maneuvered her so that her head was on my shoulder and my arm was around her. She was fighting me mentally and physically; "Put your arm around me!" She finally did. "You are not to move from this position until I say you can; understand?"

She responded with a whimper; "Yes."

"Talk to me, don't rush. I know it's not easy but try to relax a bit."

I held her very tight against me for two reasons; I was attempting to provide her with a feeling of security and secondly I was afraid she would run away.

I just lay there waiting for her to muster the courage to tell me this horrible thing that she has kept buried for the past two days.

Liz's body was shivering as if she was cold. Her voice was timid; I could tell she was really frightened.

Finally, "Will, since my early teens I have faced severe periods of depression. When I was seventeen and then again when I was twenty-four I tried to commit suicide."

She moved her arm which was just lying on my chest so that she could actually hug me. That was a good sign. I held her firmly and squeezed her against me a little bit harder.

"I have been in and out of psychiatric institutions ever since I was fifteen. I take the antidepressant Prozac twice a day, which I have been hiding from you. When I'm at home, I visit my psychiatrist twice a week. According to the psychiatrist my depression is the result of very low self-esteem. There is no cure; I have to learn to live with it."

Liz paused for a few seconds. I just kept holding her tight.

"In the past when I have met someone I like, male or female, as soon as they find out that I have a mental disorder, they disappear. They stop calling me, stop returning my messages; usually they use the excuse that they have gotten very busy.

"There has recently been one exception to the rule. Your Barbara accidentally found my prescription bottle of Prozac and asked me about it. I told her about my illness. She jokingly said that I looked and acted saner than most of her friends and all of her professors. She didn't change her attitude towards me or comment about it again. Barbara is the only true friend I have ever had and that is a sorry state of affairs.

"The only person that I have ever loved or felt that they loved me, before I met you is my grandfather. I really went to shambles when he passed away. I was in an institution for almost six months.

"My parents are the biggest trigger to my episodes. They seem to know exactly what buttons to push, to send me reeling into a deep state of depression and I let them get to me every time.

Liz stopped talking, but she held me a little tighter, she was still shivering, but not quite as badly as before; "Aren't you going to say something?"

"I'm waiting for you to tell me something that is overwhelming dreadful about yourself."

"Please don't make fun of me Will."

"I'm not making fun of you, not in the least. I knew all about the depression, the Prozac the psychiatrists, mental institutions and suicide attempts. I knew all of this before I asked you to marry me."

"Did Barbara tell you?"

"She, very unintentionally made me aware. When I met Barbara on my return, she talked to me about you, she told me how wonderful you were, that she would gladly welcome you into our family and that I would be a jerk not to marry you. Actually she used the word duffus. But I sensed something in the way she spoke that made me uneasy. This wasn't a sense that came from being with the aliens. This was a sense that occurs when a daughter speaks to her father. I thought that she might be in some sort of trouble or have a major problem that she didn't want to talk about. I decided to use my new found telepathic abilities. The biggest thing on her mind was that she had broken the side mirror on the car when she had backed it out of the garage and was hoping that I wouldn't come back to Toronto until she had it replaced. I then picked up a thought that she was concerned about you because you were ill.

"That really scared me, because of my love for you. I didn't want you to be sick.

"When you returned to the room, I'm sorry to tell you, that I delved into your thoughts. Your illness was right in the forefront, well not actually the illness, but your fear of telling me about the illness.

"I also know that your parents are a major trigger and I didn't need mental telepathy to figure that out. You became depressed and very anxious every time you spoke to or about your parents.

"I wasn't going to tell you that I knew about your illness. I thought it was very important that you told me when you were ready and I knew you would eventually.

"You say there is no cure, well there may be no cure on this planet, but I have a little surprise for you; my alien buddies can cure depression with one pill, which I will get access to tomorrow or the day after at the latest. It is in my personal container on Roosevelt Island. But, even if there was no cure, I love you deeply Liz and I want you to be with me. If you remember, when I asked you to marry me I specifically said in sickness and health and I meant it. Together we would have avoided the triggers. I would have deflected your parents' attacks and anything else that could harm you in any manner.

I don't want to lose you, now or ever!"

I paused for a couple of seconds. Liz was crying, but I could tell that it was a joyful cry.

"Liz, I really need a kiss!"

Liz raised her head and put her body on top of mine, she looked me in the eyes; tears were rolling down her cheeks, but she had a warm smile on her face. "You are the most wonderful, caring man in the whole world, I am so very lucky to have found you." She placed her lips against mine, they were warm and moist; it was by far the best kiss that I have ever had the pleasure of receiving.

We lay there together for quite awhile, Liz lay on top of me, her head on my shoulder; every now and then she would kiss my neck.

Feeling her body against mine, her warm breath on my neck was making me excited, but I knew this was not the time; "Darling, shall we go into the sitting room and finish our dinner?" She lay there awhile longer, and then straitening up and gave me a big kiss; she looked me in the eyes, her face just inches from my mine; "I like this rule are there others?"

"There are a few others, not to many."

She gently climbed off me; "I need to use the washroom."

When she entered the sitting room, she looked absolutely radiant. She had refreshed her make-up and restyled her hair, she had a bun on the top of her head. She looked regal. I couldn't help but gawk.

Liz caught me ogling her; "do I look okay?"

"Far beyond okay!"

She smiled. "What you see is what you get, and you Mr. Dafoe can get it any time you want!" She had emphasized the words "get it".

I pulled out her chair and made sure she was comfortably seated; "Would you like me to order you a fresh ice tea?" All the ice had melted in her glass.

"No, I'd like some wine, please."

I poured us each a glass of wine. I opened the warming box under the table and removed Liz's entree and placed it in front of her, then did the same with mine.

I couldn't stop gazing at her; Liz knew it and absorbed every ounce of my stare energy! She had this very sultry look on her face. I could have easily lost control and ravished her right then and there.

I'm sure that the medallions of veal would have been very good if they hadn't sat in the warming oven for over ninety minutes. Liz ate about a third of the meal, I ate about half. Liz went to push her chair back, but this time I was quick enough to get behind her and move the chair out from the table.

Liz walked over to the loveseat and sat down. Liz started playing with the remote control again, she hadn't found the music channel before her mother had called and interrupted us. I collected all the dishes and glasses, put them in the center of the food service cart and wheeled it out to the hallway.

I picked up my wine glass and sat down beside her so that our bodies were touching.

Liz seemed to have fully relaxed. For the time being at least she had put her depression behind her. She had a sheepish grin; "tell me what other rules I will have to follow?"

"Hmmm, in the unlikely event that we have a heated argument, we must immediately go into the bedroom, turn all the lights on and strip naked. We stand facing each other about three feet apart. I defy anyone to have an argument while standing in a lit room completely naked!"

Liz broke out laughing; she had been holding her wine glass and had to quickly put it down before it spilled over the top. Liz had tears rolling down her face she was laughing hysterically. I really didn't think it was that funny. Liz was barely able to catch her breath; "For some reason, I immediately pictured Mom and Dad naked standing in the bedroom arguing!" She continued to laugh, it was subsiding a little.

Liz had gained her composure, her cheeks were red. It was good to see her laugh so hard.

"I don't remember ever laughing so hard. I like that rule too."

She paused for a second, I thought she was going to break out laughing again, I could see that she was fighting to maintain a level of self-control.

"What's going to happen tomorrow?"

"We have a 9:30 a.m. meeting with the Security Council. I will inform them that we have decided to look at the potential of locating the new organization in southern Ontario. I also need to access my personal cargo container, which I am sure is being guarded. Arrangements will have to be made, so that I can access it when I want."

"Do you expect problems with your choice of southern Ontario?"

"It's our choice!" Liz gave me a big smile and squeezed my thigh.

"I am not expecting any objections, there are a few good reasons to put it in Canada, you outlined some of them yourself when you explained to me that choosing a Canadian as the emissary to meet with the extraterrestrials had advantages, but I am sure there will be some disappointment. Every country would like to host the new organization. Besides the prestige of having the headquarters for the new entity located in your country, there is bound to be some economic fallout. Basic services such as construction, transportation and communications will automatically go to local companies for convenience and ease of logistics.

I will remind them that the entity will not be the manufacturer of any product. I don't expect the entity to have more than fifty full time employees. I will also commit that Canadian companies bidding on the manufacturing programs will not have any unfair leverage or advantage over companies in any other country."

I paused to see if Liz was going to comment or if she had questions. I looked at her face; she was listening intently and absorbing everything I was saying.

"This meeting will cover some of the smaller details of the initial set-up of the organization. By the way, I don't want to refer to the new entity as a business."

"Why?"

"The word business has a connotation of profit. For the average person it sounds like Wall Street is involved. This entity is to be structured to enhance all of humanity, not make anyone rich."

"I understand; I will try not to use the word business."

"We have to choose a name for the organization. I asked the Security Council delegates to come up with some suggestions in the hope that we could commit to one at the meeting. Do you have any ideas for a name?"

I was going to say something witty such as; I was going to suggest; Liz & Will's House of Horrors, but decided to keep the conversation on a serious note.

"Liz stood up and went over to the desk, grabbed some paper and a pen and sat back down on the loveseat; "let me think about it for a few minutes."

I went to get us some more wine, only to find an empty wine

bottle. "I'm going to get some fresh ice, you keep thinking."

I returned, opened another bottle of wine and filled our glasses. I buried the open wine bottle in the ice. We have to get some more wine I thought to myself.

Liz was busy writing, crossing out and writing more. She had lit a cigarette that she had burning in an ashtray on the table beside her. By the expression on her face I could tell that she was focused intently on the challenge.

I sat down beside her, closed my eyes and listened to the music. I recognized it immediately. Brahms; Violin Concerto in D major, Op. 77 in three movements composed in 1878 and dedicated to violinist Joseph Joachim. It was Brahms's only violin concerto. I impressed myself with my newly developed mental processing abilities.

I was off in the world of classical music when I felt a kiss on my cheek. "Are you sleeping, my darling?"

I opened my eyes, Liz's face was inches from mine; I leaned forward and kissed her. "I wasn't asleep."

"I think I may have a name. It is very simple and it has a good acronym."

I could hear pride in her voice. "For Humanity, the acronym would be FORHUM. What do you think?"

I thought about it for a second. "For Humanity"; perfectly described the mandate of the organization. The acronym FORUM was easy to remember and easy to pronounce, at least in English. "I think it's brilliant!"

The low self-esteem reared its ugly head. "You're not just saying that because you love me and don't want to hurt my feelings, are you?"

I gave Liz a stern frustrated look; "You are right, I never want to hurt you in any manner. But, if the name didn't thrill me I would have said something to the effect of; "It's a consideration or not bad." I would have never said "Brilliant."

Her head was down; "I'm sorry."

"Enough!" I said loudly. I grabbed her and threw her over my lap, her papers and pen went flying. I gave her backside a couple of gently slaps.

Her voice was bubbly; "Why Mr. Dafoe; I like that!" and she just lay there.

I gave her one more slap and then sat her back up.

"We will present your name suggestion at the meeting tomorrow.

Liz, I don't want you to be hurt or offended if they choose a different name. Always remember that all of their decisions are centered around a level of diplomacy and keeping everyone on side. I learned a long time ago that the phrase, *pick your battles wisely*, is key in any set of negotiations and nowhere it is more appropriate then when dealing with a group of politicians who all have their own agendas. A well thought out organization name would be great, but if it meant loosing the support of even one delegate, it's not worth it."

"Being part of the Whitehouse cabinet I am well aware of dealing with politicians or wannabe politicians. I take it from where it comes!"

I gave Liz a big smile. "That's my girl! If they choose that name, we will ask the delegates to have the acronym checked to ensure it doesn't mean something untoward in another language."

It was 10:45; "I think we should probably get some sleep, we have a busy day ahead of us."

Liz picked up the remote control and turned off the music. I took her hand and we walked into the bedroom, turning off lights as we passed them.

In the bedroom, we got undressed, my clothes hit the floor and I placed my new Patek Philipe on the night table. Liz folded her clothes neatly and placed them on a chair. She undid the bun she had configured on her head and her hair dropped, she shook her head just like a puppy so that it would fall into the proper position. We climbed into bed. Liz laid flat on her back, with her head on her pillow and let out a big sigh. "I didn't realize how tired I am."

"Do you know how to spoon?"

Liz didn't speak for a second; "No!"

I chuckled; "You're going to learn. Lie on your side facing away from me, bend your knees."

Liz did as I asked.

I maneuvered myself into the same position, so that if we were sitting up, Liz would have been sitting in my lap facing forward. I reached over and placed my hand around her waist and pulled her tight against me; her back was against my chest, derrière in my lap, thighs and legs all touching.

Her hair tickled my nose for a second. I quickly moved my arm from around her waist to reposition her hair. I pushed against her; there was a delightful sweet fragrance emanating from her.

Liz wiggled her body a bit so that it fit even a better against mine.

Her voice was very mellow; "I really like this Will! Hold me tight."
It only took a few minutes before we were both sound asleep.

Chapter 6 – 269 days to alien arrival

It was 6:33 when I woke, Liz and I hadn't moved all night. We were still in the spoon position and my arm was still around her. I was somewhat surprised. I had never fallen asleep and woke in the same exact same position. I wasn't complaining; I cherished the feel of Liz's body against mine.

I'd give Liz a few more minutes of sleep, I thought to myself. I laid there snuggled up to her with my arm around her waist and pondered the day in front of us.

At 6:45, I gave Liz a kiss on her neck, then another, I heard a small moan "mmmm". "Good morning darling, did you sleep well? It's time to get up." I removed my arm from Liz's waist and she rolled over on to her back, raised her arms in front of her and stretched.

Liz looked at me just half awake. "Don't I get a good morning wake-up kiss?" I leaned over to give her a light kiss. When I did, she placed her arms around my neck and changed the light kiss into a passionate embrace.

I am definitely not a psychoanalyst. But I am sure that Liz would have filled a few note books even for Freud. She was the ultimate contradiction in terms. One minute her character was extremely strong willed; I know what I want and I'm going to get it, and the next minute she was cowering in a corner.

We showered and got dressed. I put my Patek Philipe on and admired it for a few seconds. It was an absolutely beautiful time piece.

Liz had put on a very stylish but refined business suit. It gave her an air of success coupled with sophistication.

I suggested to Liz that we breakfast in the downstairs coffee shop. We were very comfortable together, we held hands while walking and talked about trivial things during breakfast.

At 9:13, according to my Patek Philipe watch, we headed over to the UN building. I had considered going back through the main door rather than the back entrance because Liz didn't have a visitor's badge. I decided it wasn't necessary, if the security guard at the back door wanted her to have one he could issue it.

We arrived at the back entrance early. We stood out on the smoking patio and each had a cigarette. At preciously 9:28 we entered the building, no security guard, just boggled my mind. We walked to the open doors of the meeting room. I released Liz's hand before we entered. Some of the delegates were seated, others were milling around talking amongst themselves.

Zhang Wei saw us immediately, walked over and shook my hand. He looked at Liz. Ambassador Zhang Wei; allow me to introduce Elizabeth Montgomery, Elizabeth this is Ambassador Zhang Wei representing the People's Republic of China. They shook hands. Zhang Wei studied Liz's face for a second. You were at the original meetings we had at the Whitehouse.

"Yes Ambassador; at that time I was a member of President Wycliffe's cabinet."

"Welcome! It is good to see you again Ms. Montgomery. Please except my best wishes in your upcoming marriage to Mr. Dafoe."

I looked at Liz; she was blushing just a bit. "Thank you Mr. Ambassador."

The Ambassador looked around the room. "We must get Ms. Montgomery a chair at the table." He quickly turned and went over to the wall, I followed him. Together we picked up a chair; brought it over to the table where I had been sitting, we pushed some other chairs closer together and slotted the chair for Liz next to mine."

He shook my hand again and walked towards his chair. Liz and I were standing behind our chairs, when Vice-President Almont came up from behind us.

He had a grin on his face; "It is so good to see you again Elizabeth, I hope that Mr. Dafoe gave you the President's apology for what happened."

"It is nice to see you Vice-President. Yes. Mr. Dafoe relayed the apology from the President. Please inform the President that I hold no ill will towards him."

"I will do that. I am assuming that as you are here today you will not be rejoining the President's cabinet, we have missed you, but the choice was yours and you will be an invaluable asset to the new organization. I wish you success. I would also like to extend my congratulations to you on your forth coming marriage."

"Thank you Mr. Vice-President. Would you please inform the President of my decision?"

"I will, I know he will be disappointed."

The Vice-President looked at me with a devilish grin. "Mr. Dafoe, The President and I consider Elizabeth to be a daughter. You take care of her or you will face the full brunt of our powers!

"You can count on it Mr. Vice-President." We shook hands and the Vice-President walked to his chair, shaking a few hands like the good politician he was.

Other delegates came over and I introduced Liz to them. My new memory capabilities came in handy. I had absolutely no problem remembered everyone's name and title for the introductions.

Just then, the Prime Minister walked into the room and went around to his chair. "I apologize to everyone for being a late; as usual the traffic in New York is atrocious." The Prime Minister glanced over at me and nodded with a smile on his face."

With a rather frazzled voice the Prime Minister tried to bring the session to order; "Will everyone please take their seats."

The Prime Minister paused until everyone was seated.

"Mr. Dafoe, would you like to introduce the lady next to you?"

I stood and so did Liz; "Mr. Prime Minister and delegates, I am pleased to introduce Ms. Elizabeth Montgomery. Ms. Montgomery has accepted the position of Deputy Managing Director of the new organization."

The delegates gently applauded.

Liz and I sat down.

The Prime Minister welcomed Liz on behalf of the group. With a sense of haste in his voice; "The first item on the agenda is a name for the new organization. I think we should just start at one end of the table and go around the room. We will write each name on the whiteboard for consideration."

The Prime Minister motioned one of the commissionaires to go up to the whiteboard.

The Prime Minister looked at Ambassador Zhang Wei who was seated to his right. "Mr. Ambassador would you like to start."

"I spent some time with my staff yesterday evening and the name we suggest is; The United Nations Organization for Health and Prosperity."

The commissionaire printed it on the whiteboard.

The delegate seated to the right of Zhang Wei, Ambassador Chopra from India spoke; "We suggest The United Nations Extraterrestrial Trade Organization."

The commissionaire printed that suggestion below the first one.

We went around the room, and fielded a number of names. When it was my turn, I passed. Then Liz passed. The delegate next to Liz continued. A few delegates said they didn't have any suggestions and one said that his suggested name was already on the whiteboard.

When the last delegate spoke, the Prime Minister looked at the whiteboard. "We'll take a moment to contemplate the names that have been presented." All of the names presented had United Nations or UN as part of the name.

The Prime Minister, still looking at the whiteboard; I'll read off each proposed name and would ask the delegates to raise their hands if they like the name."

With each name read three or four hands were raised. After reading the last name it was obvious that there was definitely not a consensus on any of them. I also knew that there were some politics involved in the selection process.

I scratched *"your going to be up soon"* on my pad and made sure Liz saw it.

"Mr. Prime Minister if I may interject."

"Please proceed, Mr. Dafoe."

"Ms. Montgomery has a suggestion."

Liz immediately rose from her chair and walked to the whiteboard, the commissionaire walked to the side. She had an air of total confidence about her. She turned and looked at the delegates;

Her voice was respectful but firm; "I had considered using the words United Nations or UN in the name, but I remembered that not all of humanity is represented by the United Nations. I also believe the name should be short and very meaningful. For those reasons my suggestion is;" Liz turned as she continued to speak as a teacher would in a classroom full of students and wrote the name on the whiteboard at the same time she was speaking it. "*For Humanity*" she glanced over her shoulder as if to make sure all her students was paying attention. "The acronym would be;" she faced the whiteboard again and wrote "FORHUM" as she said it.

She turned and faced the delegates, catching the eyes of each one of them one at a time. A couple of delegates looked at me. I'm sure they could sense the pride that I was feeling. Liz was handling herself better than I could have even hoped for. That's my girl! I thought to myself.

Liz stood in front of the whiteboard, no one said anything, but she didn't waiver.

The Prime Minister interjected into the silence. "Ms. Montgomery, I for one like it and I'm impressed by your thought process. You are, of course, one hundred percent correct when you pointed out that all of humanity is not represented by the United Nations. It's something that I believe we are all guilty of forgetting from time to time.

If any of the other delegates are in favor of the name *For Humanity* and the acronym *FORHUM* would they please raise their hands?"

All of the hands popped up almost instantaneously.

The Prime Minister looked at Liz, he had a relieved expression on his face; "Ms. Montgomery, I believe that you have just received your first overwhelming vote of confidence. I hereby declare the name of the new entity to be "*For Humanity*" with the acronym of *FORHUM*."

There was applause as Liz returned to her chair.

After the applause subsided the Prime Minister looked over at me. "Mr. Dafoe, do you have any items to present to the delegates?"

"I do Mr. Prime Minister. We think that we should have the UN translation department confirm that the acronym "*FORHUM*" does not have an undesirable meaning in a foreign language, before we commit to it."

"Your point is well taken" The Prime Minister took a fresh sheet of paper and wrote a message on it. Called one of the commissionaires over and handed them the piece of paper. The commissionaire scurried out the door.

"Mr. Prime Minister, Ms. Montgomery and I have decided that the first locations we wish to consider for FORHUM will be in southern Ontario. We would like to find an abandoned or underutilized airport. In that regard it would be advantageous is we had appropriate contacts in the Canadian Armed Forces and the Department of Transport who would know what facilities may be available and be prepared to show them to us. I am hoping that you will identify the personnel for us."

"I will make those arrangements when we break for coffee. Please proceed."

"We will need a bank account in order to accept the deposit of the twenty-five million dollars that is being provided to capitalize FORHUM. FORHUM does not have Letters of Incorporation or a government charter of any type, it is my understanding that Canadian Banks are not allowed to open an account without them. I am hoping that a phone call to one of the major banks from the Minister of Finance could have that ruling waved temporarily for one account."

"I will call the Minister of Finance and have him make the arrangements."

"May I ask Mr. Prime Minister, what is the status of the funds?"

"Mr. Dafoe, the delegates and I have committed to have all of your funds available no later than Monday, April 10th. We will be providing you with certified international cashier checks."

The Prime Minister paused to look around the room. Please proceed; Mr. Dafoe.

"I need access to one of the cargo containers on Roosevelt Island. I have not been there since my arrival but I am assuming that the area is secured. I really don't want to be shot at again." I smiled.

Vice-President Almont interjected. "Mr. Prime Minister I will make immediate access arrangements for Mr. Dafoe as soon as we take a break."

I gave him a nod; "Thank you Mr. Vice-President."

There was a knock at the door and then it opened. Three food service carts were wheeled in with coffee urns, cups, saucers and some pitchers of orange and other juices.

The Prime Minister stood up; "Let's take a fifteen minute break."

I looked at Liz, "Cigarette break?"

"I could use a ladies room!"

"It's on the way."

We walked out the door and down the hall; we stopped at the ladies room and I waited in the hallway, we then went through the doors and outside to the patio area. Ambassador Marino already had a cigarette going. Although I wanted to talk to Liz, it was politically correct to go over to the Ambassador. I introduced them to each other. Liz and I lit our cigarettes.

Ambassador Marino looked at Liz with a grin; "For Humanity name; I like much, you smart lady!"

Liz blushed and thanked the Ambassador without using broken English.

The Ambassador finished his cigarette and pulled out his cell phone and pointed at it. "Make call – excusa." He turned and went back into the building.

"I looked at Liz; "You did an outstanding job in there. I could tell by the expressions on the faces of the delegates, that they were extremely impressed."

Liz smiled, looked around to make sure no one was looking put her hand on my butt and gave it a squeeze; "Thanks boss! What's happening next?"

"I have a couple of more things to cover, but they should be short and sweet. It would be nice if we can get out of here at noon or a little there after."

We finished our cigarettes and went back into the meeting room. Prime Minister Harmon made his way over to us. "William, Elizabeth; I spoke to the Minister of Finance and he said he would discuss banking arrangements with one of the CEOs of a major Canadian bank, he knows many of them very well and doesn't believe there will be any problem. He will call me as soon as he has sorted things out."

"Thank you Prime Minister."

"I didn't want to say anything in front of the other delegates, but an abandoned or underutilized airport makes a lot of sense to me, I think it is an excellent idea. I spoke with the Minister of Defense and the Minister of Transport. They will both identify an individual to be your liaison and send me a text message as soon as they have contact information. The story line, because I didn't want the situation to be revealed at this time, is that you are looking for a location on behalf of a commercial small aircraft manufacturer. The aircraft manufacturer is treating this as top secret, it is imperative that their competition does not find out. I told them the CEO is a personal friend of mine and he gave me a heads up. I think the story line will hold up until the whole thing becomes public. I gave them both your names; you are senior executives of the aircraft manufacturer."

"Thank you again Mr. Prime Minister. Although not urgent, could you please find out what is involved in designating an area an international zone in Canada?"

"Interesting point, I have no idea and I am not sure what ministry it would fall under. I will have it investigated and get back to you. This may take a few days."

"Thank you Prime Minister, there is no rush."

"If you'll excuse me, I must have a word with Ambassador Middleton." He turned and walked away.

Liz let her hand hit my thigh, I looked at her, she whispered; "Efficient."

A moment later Vice-President Almont walked up to us; "Elizabeth, William; "as you suspected there is security at the park. The security unit is expecting your arrival, the guard at the front gate will ask for some identification, driver's license, passport or anything else with your picture on it. If Elizabeth is with you he may ask for her identification. If you need any assistance in transporting anything, they will make the arrangements. They have been told to follow your instructions without question."

"Thank you Mr. Vice-President, I truly appreciate your quick actions."

Everyone began to sit down and Liz and I followed the lead of the others. The Prime Minister brought the meeting back to order.

"Mr. Dafoe, is there anything else you would like to discuss at this time?"

"Yes! Mr. Prime Minister; "I am assuming that you will call the United Nations General Assembly together to disseminate the information and tell them what they must do. When are you planning on having this meeting? I would like to prepare some documentation for each delegate or country that can be distributed during the meeting."

"How long do you need to prepare the documentation Mr. Dafoe?"

"I can have the documentation in 48 hours. But it will have to be translated, copied and bound."

The Prime Minister paused for a moment and surveyed the delegates. Everyone seemed to be at a loss. If you will please remain in your seats, I need to call someone to see how long it would take to perform those tasks.

The Prime Minister stood up and walked to a corner of the room; reached into his jacket pocket and pulled out what appeared to be a small telephone number directory. He found the number he wanted and dialed it. He was pacing and talking simultaneously. I didn't bother to tune into the conversation, the details had little if any value.

He took the phone away from his mouth and from across the room he bellowed. "Mr. Dafoe, How many pages do you think will be in this document?"

I brought the semi-prepared document into the forefront of my memory and quickly counted the pages.

I yelled back, "Twenty-eight, Mr. Prime Minister".

He put the phone back to his mouth and kept talking. He disconnected, found another number and dialed it, had a reasonably short conversation and in a few minutes he returned to his chair. The Prime Minister's voice was harried; "The translation department estimates eighteen hours for full translation to all the languages required. The transcription department which would handle the copying and binding would require twelve hours. That's a total of thirty hours, maybe a little less because the transcription department can start on the English version without having to wait for translation. With Mr. Dafoe's requirement of 48 hours the minimum time frame would be 78 hours."

Ambassador Balabanov leaned forward; "Mr. Prime Minister, how long does it take to notify the 193 members of the General Assembly about a meeting? Are there protocols that we must follow?"

"Good questions Mr. Ambassador, and I don't have the answers off hand."

The Prime Minister didn't get out of his chair this time. He opened the telephone directory and skimmed the pages, paused and then skimmed some more. Finally he dialed a number. He identified who he was and asked what the protocols are for calling a meeting of the General Assembly. He listened and made some notes on his pad. He then asked how long it would take to notify all of the members of the General Assembly that a meeting was going to take place. He made another note on his pad. He thanked whomever he was speaking with and disconnected.

The Prime Minister shook his head in bewilderment; "Apparently there are 137 protocols that are to be followed in order to just call a meeting of the General Assembly, it takes a minimum of three weeks to follow them!"

Ambassador Middleton interjected; "Mr. Prime Minister, this is an unprecedented situation. I suggest we just ignore the protocols."

The Prime Minister looked around the room; "Does anyone have an objection to ignoring the protocols?"

No one spoke.

"I would like to have a show of hands. All those in favor of ignoring the protocols necessary to call a meeting of the General Assembly please raise your hands."

I looked around the table, all of the hands were raised some were raised faster than others.

The Prime Minister had some relief in his voice; "As President of the Security Council I can call the meeting. It will take six hours to have the meeting notices prepared in the required languages. The official meeting notices are sent out, by couriers in one batch. A copy of the notice is either faxed or emailed."

The Prime Minister paused and took a drink of his stale coffee. He pulled out his smart phone and hit a few buttons. "I suggest that we call the meeting for April 12th at 1:00 p.m. That should provide every country with a minimum 96 hours notice. All in favor please signify by raising their hands."

All the hands were raised.

I was relieved to see a consensus as was the Mr. Prime Minister. "Mr. Prime Minister, there is another point which I believe you must consider now."

The Prime Minister looked at me with a horrified expression on his face; "please continue Mr. Dafoe."

"As soon as the meeting of the General Assembly is called, the press is going to want to know what, it's all about. More importantly however, is that as soon as the situation is announced to the members of the General Assembly it will be of the utmost urgency to inform the population. Has any consideration been given on how best to inform the population and how to deal with the press? If we are not careful, we could inadvertently create widespread panic."

The Prime Minister had a pained expression on his face and he looked tired; "Mr. Dafoe, your points are well taken again. We should have a plan to address dealing with the press and informing everyone. Does anyone have any comments or suggestions?"

I interjected; "Mr. Prime Minister, Ms. Montgomery and I have a lot of work to do in order to have the document for the members of the General Assembly prepared within the next 48 hours. I would like to get started right away, may we take our leave?"

The Prime Minister looked disappointed; "While we would truly welcome Ms. Montgomery's and your council in these matters, I appreciate the time constraints that you are under with respect to the document for the members. Does anyone have any objections?

No one objected, their minds were definitely on how to inform the population while avoiding a global panic.

"Mr. Dafoe, may I suggest that we have our next meeting on April 9th at 1:30?"

"That would be fine Prime Minister. Would it be possible to have a contact number for you in case we have any questions?"

The Prime Minister wrote a telephone number on his pad; tore it off and handed it to Liz.

Liz and I stood; "Thank you Prime Minister, delegates!" We quickly left the room, before they changed their minds.

Liz and I walked briskly off of the UN complex. With Liz's hand in mine, I mapped out a route to the courtyard I had stopped at the day before. Once there we sat on the bench, and each lit a cigarette. It was 11:45. Liz placed her hand on my thigh; "You have a lot of work to do."

"Not really, the document is written, I need to make some adjustments and additions to what's in it and then type it up. It will only take an hour or so."

Liz gave me a look of bewilderment; "an hour or so?"

I looked at her; she looked lovely; "yes my love, only an hour or so! The first thing we need to do though is to get some items from my cargo container."

There was an ATM at the front of the building where we had been sitting and smoking; I went and relieved it of some cash so that I could pay for a taxi.

With Liz in hand, I went to the curb and hailed a taxi, we got in and I told him that we wanted to go to the Eco Park on Roosevelt Island. He quickly informed us that the park was temporarily closed and that he could take us to park that was just as nice if we wanted. I told him that we had made arrangements to meet someone at the front entrance of the park.

As we came over the peak of the bridge, the stack of cargo containers stood out like a sore thumb!

The taxi driver informed us that he had no idea what was in the cargo containers, but he suspected it was gold or diamonds, because of all the security at the park and that there were two coast guard cutters constantly patrolling the waters around the island. I didn't comment. I paid the taxi driver, and Liz and I walked over to a guy with a plastic cord in his ear, standing beside a black SUV. He looked at us and said that we would have to move on, that the park was closed. I pulled out my Canadian diplomatic passport; "My name is Dafoe, I believe you're expecting me!" I passed him the passport. He looked at the picture in the passport and then my face and then back to the picture in the passport. "Sorry, Mr. Dafoe, I was informed that you would be coming. Is this Ms. Montgomery?"

"Yes."

Liz went to hand him her passport. "That won't be necessary Ms. Montgomery. Do you want a ride to the cargo containers?"

I looked at Liz, it was a very pleasant day, "That's not necessary, we'll walk."

"If you need anything I would be pleased to oblige."

Liz and I headed down the path towards the containers. In the background I heard; "They're on their way."

Liz and I sauntered down the path hand-in-hand.

We turned a corner to find a higher level of security. Six soldiers with automatic weapons were patrolling in front of the containers. As soon as they saw Liz and I they moved away. I pointed; "That's my container over there." we walked to it.

Liz chuckled; "How come you have the smallest container?"

"The best things come in small packages, you are the proof!"

She gave me a kiss on the cheek.

There was a small alphanumeric key pad almost in the middle of the container end wall. I punched in the 256 alphanumeric codes that would start the container unlocking process. A blank flat screen pad appeared. I placed the palm of my left hand flat on the screen, in less than a second a panel opened. I stood in front of that panel positioning the retina of my right eye directly in front of the opening. With that security entry procedure finished, the complete side of the container disappeared, to clarify, it didn't open or slide and it didn't rise up; it disappeared; providing me with easy access to all my goodies.

"That's really nifty!" There was a sense of wonderment in Liz's voice.

I pulled out my suitcase, the one Cheryl had purchased for me. It had travelled millions of miles, went to a multitude of planets and was still in very good shape. I had put my camera and all of the memory cards in it. I scanned the translucent containers that were inside my container, each about the size of a file folder box, they had been color coded with multiple strips of different colored tape so that I could tell from the outside, exactly what was on the inside of each one.

I spotted the one I needed and quickly shuffled others around so that I could get to it. I pulled it out and opened it. I could sense that Liz was watching my every move. She was now looking inside the container. This container held about a 100 small baggies. Each contained a quantity of a different medication. I found the one I wanted, placed it in my pocket and returned the small container to its position. I scanned the inside of the container for a moment to make sure that there was nothing else in it that I would need over the next couple of days, assuring myself that there was nothing more, I went to the side of the container, placed my palm on the screen and the side of the container reappeared and the sliding security panels faded into the sidewall. All that remained visible was the keypad.

I took the suitcase in one hand and Liz's hand in the other and we started to walk back to the front entrance.

"Liz squeezed my hand, her voice was somewhat anxious. "Is the medication you took for me?"

"Yes Darling!"

We walked briskly to the front gate. The man with the plastic cord in his ear asked if he could be of any assistance. I looked around, there was no traffic; "Could you call a taxi for us?"

"I'll do better than that;" he brought his hand up to his face and said something which I didn't overhear; I was too busy looking at Liz. A moment later a black SUV pulled up. The plastic cord opened the back door; "Agent Treadway will take you anywhere you want to go." I motioned to Liz to get in; I put the suitcase in and then followed. I told agent Treadway to take us to the Century Hotel.

We were back at the hotel in twelve minutes, I thanked the agent and Liz and I got out of the car. We went straight up to the room.

Liz looked at me with a frightened expression on her face, her voice was anxious; "What are we going to do now?"

I'm going to give you the medication."

Liz put her arms around me and gave me a passionate kiss, her body was shaking, she broke the embrace; "I'm scared!"

"There is nothing to be afraid of darling. You know I wouldn't hurt you. I want you to go into the bedroom, get undressed and put one of the bathrobes on.

I pulled up the medication instructions from my memory.

I have to go and get some ice."

I grabbed the ice bucket and filled it. When I returned Liz was sitting on the bed wearing the bathrobe.

I placed a towel over her pillow and obtained a bottle of water from the bar fridge in the sitting room. I made two packages of ice wrapped in hand towels. I placed one of them on the towel on her pillow. Liz was still sitting on the bed, she was definitely shaking.

"Try to relax Liz and I'll tell you the procedure and what you might experience. I am going to ask you to lie down and put the back of your head on the ice. I want you to close your eyes and try to relax, think about our wedding at the Fern Grotto. I am going to place the second towel with ice on your forehead. I will be turning off all the lights and closing the drapes. The ice may be uncomfortable, but you must stay lying flat on your back moving as little as absolutely possible.

After twelve minutes, I am going to ask you to swallow two pills with water.

You will then lie back down and I will put the ice towel back on your forehead, you must lie in that position for ten more minutes. You may experience a sense of euphoria; light headiness; dizziness or a feeling that your mind is emptying. You may also experience a quick sensation of a lot of emotions one after another including fear and panic. These are all expected sensations and will not last very long. Do not sit up no matter what you feel, until I tell you; Promise me!"

"I promise; will you stay with me?"

"I will be sitting or lying beside you, holding your hand throughout the entire procedure. Are you ready to start?"

Liz took a big gulp of air, "As ready as all ever be."

I quickly closed the drapes and turned off the table lamps in the room. It was dark, but not so dark that I couldn't see.

I gave Liz a kiss and then helped her lie down so that the back of her head rested squarely on the iced towel. She wiggled her head a little so that there were no sharp ice cubes sticking into her. I placed the towel with the ice on her forehead. I lay down beside her and held her hand.

I glanced over at Liz. Her eyes were closed as I had asked.

It must have been very uncomfortable to have her head surrounded by ice cubes. But Liz was a trooper, she laid there without moving.

At the twelve minute mark I took the ice towel off her forehead, sat her up and gave her the two pills and a glass of water. She swallowed them without hesitation and I quickly laid her back down and placed the ice filled towel back on her head. I held both her hands in mine. I really didn't know what to expect. She lay there for a couple of minutes with an expression of bliss on her face. Then without warning the expression turned to pain and agony, she clenched my hands and in doing so dug her nails into my skin. I felt so bad for her, I was really hurting inside. I didn't know what to do. Her head was rocking violently side to side I thought she might start convulsing. It seemed to last forever. Then, as quickly as it had started, it stopped. She had been in that tremulous state for exactly ninety seconds. She lay there; calm, at rest, a slight smile on her face; a smile of enjoyment, pleasure and happiness all rolled into one. I glanced at my hands there was blood dripping from them.

When the ten minutes had elapsed I removed the towel from her head and sat her up. I looked at her waiting for her to tell me about her pain and agony. She gave me a big smile and kissed me very tenderly for a long time.

When she stopped, she looked into my eyes, I had never seen her look so calm and at ease. "Will, it has worked. It's hard to explain how I know, but I am sure, one hundred percent sure. Only someone who has ever experienced deep depression can really understand how one's brain feels. It's as if it is tied up in knots, it always feels like that, it never goes away, sometimes it gets even worse, as if the knots are tightening, as if someone is pulling on the ends with tremendous force and you can't stop it. I honestly do not remember never having knots in my brain. I thought that the sensation was normal, that everyone must feel knots in their brains. That the difference between those that suffered from depression and those that didn't was how they dealt with the sensation, some people dealt with it better than others.

Will, there are no knots in my head anymore, not even one small one, none! I feel like I've been reborn."

She gave me another kiss.

"How long does the medication last? How often will I have to take it?"

"It lasts forever my darling; you never have to take it again!"

Liz gave me a devious look; "I need to exercise my new brain!"

She pushed me back on the bed, put her mouth against mine, pushed my lips open with her tongue and teased the inside of my mouth. We had sex, fantastic, unbelievable sex, and not just once, not twice, but I finished three times, each time in unison. Liz had so many orgasms, big and small, that I lost count!

We lay beside each other, on our backs, trying to catch our breath, totally exhausted. "Will, do we have time to have a nap?

It was after three, but there was nothing we had to do immediately; "Yes darling!"

She rolled over with her back facing me, "Spoon me!"

I rolled over and cuddled the front of my body into the back of hers. Our bodies were damp with sweat. I pulled the covers up and over us, and placed my arm around her waist, pulling her tightly against me. We were a good fit.

Liz's voice had a melody to it, "Will, I want you to know that in my knotted brain, I loved you. In my new brain, it is far beyond simple love. I worship being with you, I adore you, I find you irresistible, I want to feel you against me always, to touch you, feel your lips against mine, to make love with you."

Her voice began to fade a bit. She pushed herself against me and fell asleep.

I must admit that I had been concerned from the outset that if Liz's depression was cured, that she might realize that she wasn't in love with me. Taking care of Liz was more important than her love for me. If making her well meant losing her, there really was no choice.

A few seconds later I was asleep.

It was 6:17 p.m. when I opened my eyes. Liz and I were still in spoon position. I adjusted the position of my arm around Liz's waist.

In a very soft voice, "Are you awake Will?"

"Yes. We probably should get up, I need a shower." We didn't move out of position very quickly; we just lay against each other enjoying the moment.

I finally, took my arm from around Liz's waist and got out of bed. Liz got out of bed and turned on the table lamp and saw the blood from my hands on the bed, startled; "Is that my blood?"

"No darling, it's my blood.

"What did you do to yourself?"

I chuckled; "I didn't do anything, during the medication procedure you scratched me a bit. I'm fine."

"Let me see!"

I showed her the back of my hands and the blood laden scars from her finger nails.

"That's not a bit! I'm so sorry Will. I don't remember anything that happened after I took the pills until I felt that my brain was unknotted. Please forgive me for hurting you."

"There is nothing to forgive and it doesn't hurt, honest. Please forget about it."

Liz gave me a look of consternation.

We showered together; Liz danced and sang; "I've got a new brain, I've got a new brain! Now I know how the Scarecrow felt in the Wizard of Oz." Liz looked so happy.

She had me laughing. She told me that she couldn't wait to speak to her Mom and Dad to see how her new brain would react. I wondered that myself.

I dried and brushed Liz's hair; "Are you hungry?"

"Not overly, are you?"

Liz pondered for a second, "Why don't we go back to that Bistro, the food was good and we can get something relatively light. We must remember to pick-up your suit on the way back. We can also pick up some more wine."

I smiled at her in the mirror, "Sounds like a good plan to me!"

We dressed and went to the Bistro where we ordered exactly what we did a couple of nights ago. It was deja vu, eat at the Bistro and buy some wine. On the way back we stopped and picked up my new suit. Liz informed the salesclerk that I would try in on in the room and if there was anything she wasn't happy with we would bring it back.

On returning to the room, the message light on the phone was blinking and the number 4 was lit beside it. I pushed play. Liz stood next to me listening intently.

The first message was from Prime Minister Harmon. He thanked us for our input into this morning's meeting and gave us the name and number of a contact at the Ministry of Transport and another for the Department of Defense, both individuals were expecting Liz or me to contact them. He also said that the Minister of Finance had arranged for a bank account to be opened at one of the major Canadian banks and gave me the name and number of someone to contact when I was ready. He thanked us again.

I pushed play again.

The next message was from the menswear store in the lobby telling us that the suit was in.

I pushed erase and then play.

I heard a click.

I pushed erase and then play.

I heard another click.

I pushed erase.

Somebody was trying to reach us and wouldn't leave a message. I was curious.

Liz had left her smart phone on the desk plugged into her charger when we went out for dinner. She picked it up; "I have a message from Mom." There was absolutely no anxiety in her voice.

"Elizabeth, it's your mother, give us a call as soon as you can."

Liz was staring at her smart phone, and she started to laugh. "I just realized that this phone belongs to the US Government, it was issued to me when I joined the President's cabinet. Gee, they may arrest me for theft of government property!

I could tell by the sound of her voice that she wasn't concerned in the least that she was still using the phone. She put it back on the desk. "Try your suit on."

I put the suit on. Liz examined the fit as if she was checking a piece of equipment for a space shuttle flight.

"It looks very good on you!" She came over and gave me a kiss.

"Take it off and hang it up. I'm going to call my Mom and Dad."

I went back into the bedroom to hang up my suit. I mentally raised the level of my hearing.

"Hi Dad, how are you?"

"Let me put your mother on the extension."

"Elizabeth, we are going to a fund raiser tomorrow night and President Wycliffe will be there, we need to know when you will be rejoining his cabinet?"

"I'm fine, Will is fine too, thanks for asking."

She had a power and strength in her voice that made my head spin. She was definitely a new woman. I thought I'm going to have some fun. I took off my underwear and socks and walked back into the living room in my birthday suit.

Liz glanced around and started to laugh. She motioned me over to her.

"Elizabeth, I asked you a question, I expect an answer."

"I won't be rejoining the President's cabinet! I have decided to work with Will as his assistant in the cemetery plot business."

I was standing beside Liz. She reached down wrapped her hand and fingers around me. Her voice didn't change; she had a big smile on her face.

"Elizabeth, this is your mother, you are being really foolish. Being part of a President's cabinet is the starting point for anything else you may want to do. You are passing up an opportunity that most people only dream about."

"Mom, Dad hang-on one second please."

Liz moved the phone away from her face; went down on her knees and took me in her mouth for a couple of seconds. It was delightful!

"Sorry Mom and Dad. Will had brought in a delight and I wanted to have a nibble of it." She was trying to keep herself from bursting out laughing."

I walked back into the bedroom to get dressed still tuned in on the conversation.

I was so proud of Liz. She wasn't taking anything from her parents but was delivering all the blows.

Liz had composed herself; "Will and I met with Vice-President Almont today. He flew up to New York yesterday expressly to meet Will. He has a Saint Bernard that he wants to buy a cemetery plot for. That's good business for Will because a Saint Bernard is so big that it requires two plots side by side."

I came back into the sitting room.

"The Vice-President has a dog?

"You didn't know? I'm very surprised father. I thought you knew everything there was to know about every politician. The dog's name is Wilbur. When you're at the fund raiser you should ask the Vice-President how Wilbur is, apparently he hasn't been well lately.

Mom, Dad; I have to go now, Will wants to have sex again, he has an extremely high libido and is insatiable!"

Liz hung up the phone without waiting for any response.

She looked at me and started to laugh.

"I really like the new Liz!"

"No anxiety Will! I feel terrific inside; it was wonderful to be able to talk to them without cowering. Thank you for my new brain, my love." We kissed.

"I wish I could be at the fund raiser when Mom and Dad ask the

Vice-President how Wilbur is!"

"Your parents will never talk to me."

"Au contraire! When they find out that you are politically connected and the world's hero, they won't stop talking to you. You will be their son-in-law and they will make sure that everyone knows it. Wait until they ask you for a campaign endorsement."

We went and sat down on the loveseat.

"What's our plan of attack?"

Liz picked up a pad of paper.

"Tomorrow I want to finish the document for the General Assembly. It's probably 95 percent finished in my mind, but requires some small additions and changes and then I need to type it up.

I would like you to call the contacts that the Prime Minister gave us at both the Ministry of Transport and Department of Defense. Ask each of them to prepare a list of airports and military bases in southern Ontario that are abandoned or very underutilized. We would like detailed descriptions of all the properties, pictures if available. Be your forceful self and tell them that the requirement is urgent. They can send them to us piecemeal; they don't have to wait until they have a complete package. Don't forget to mention that we are calling on behalf of the Prime Minister. That might make them move a little bit faster than most bureaucrats.

Also, please call the banking contact. Tell her that we will make contact in the next week or so. We are currently out of the country. You could also find out where she is located.

I looked at Liz; she had been making notes of her assignments. Then I panicked; "Liz, I didn't call Barbara!"

Liz jumped up and grabbed her phone, I'll call her.

I wondered if Barbara was the two hang-ups I heard from the message center.

Liz had Barbara on the line and they were jabbering away. I heard Liz tell her that she had given me the watch, obviously Barbara knew about it. Then with delight in her voice I heard her explain to Barbara all about her new brain and her phone conversation with her Mom and Dad. They talked for more than 45 minutes. Then I heard Liz say; "He's fine, actually I think he's perfect! Do you want to talk to him?" They talked for a few more minutes and then Liz disconnected the phone line.

"Barbara's fine. She was the one who called us twice and didn't leave a message."

Well! That's a nice state of affairs, I thought to myself. My daughter has become closer to Liz then me. Actually it made me feel very warm inside. Barbara needed a woman in her life for guidance someone she could talk to. I couldn't think of a better role model than the new improved Liz.

While Liz was talking to Barbara I made all of the necessary changes and enhancements to the overview document for the members of the General Assembly. I decided that I wasn't in the mood to type it now; I had plenty of time available in tomorrow.

I turned my mind to Liz and her assignments for tomorrow. There wasn't a lot for her to do until we received the information about the airports and military bases. One thought did come to mind. A logo! We must have a logo.

"Liz, how are your graphic design skills?"

"I'd never get a job with Disney."

"We need a logo, would you like to see if you can create something?"

"I don't have a computer with me."

"If you would like to try, there's a computer store not far from here. I passed by it when I was out walking yesterday. We can go over there first thing in the morning and get you a laptop with appropriate graphic design software.

"Then that's what we'll do after breakfast."

It was 11:17 I wasn't in the least bit tired after the three hour nap I had this afternoon. I had slept very soundly. Liz certainly didn't appear sleepy. I passed Liz the remote control and asked her to put on some music. I went and opened one of the bottles of wine we had just purchased.

We sat next to each other. Liz was trying to sketch a logo on a piece of paper, it didn't appear that anything she started was appealing enough to complete. She finally placed the paper and pen down in frustration and cuddled into me.

We didn't talk about anything overly important, Liz told me about her family, that she had an aunt and some cousins on her father's side that she hadn't seen or talked to in years. She told me about her grandfather. We talked about my favorite city, London and my best friend Daniel and his family.

Chapter 7 – 268 days to alien arrival

I was 2:04 in the morning when I suggested we go lie in bed and see if we could dose off. Liz agreed, she lay with her head on my chest and we continued to chat, I felt her drift off to sleep at 2:33. I didn't fall asleep 3:42.

It was 7:05 a.m. when I opened my eyes. Liz had rolled over and was sleeping on her side facing me. I went to adjust her covers and her eyes opened. "Good morning Boss!" She rubbed the sleep from her eyes; "Is it time to rise and shine?"

"It's after seven."

"My morning kiss please."

I leaned over and kissed her. We got out of bed and showered together. I derived a lot of pleasure from being able to run my hands over her body in a nonsexual way.

We dressed and went down to the hotel coffee shop for breakfast. This was the first day back that it wasn't nice out. It was overcast, cool and drizzling. After breakfast we purchased a large umbrella at one of the shops in the lobby of the hotel. We left the hotel and headed for the computer store.

Now you might ask why didn't they take a taxi if it was raining out? Obviously you have never been to New York when it's raining, taxis just aren't available; you can stand on the curb all day and never see a vacant taxi.

Once inside the store, Liz started to investigate the available laptops. A salesclerk, a real techie came over and Liz drilled him on the advantages and disadvantages of each of the models on display. I was impressed by her technical knowledge. Watching the techie's face, I think he was impressed as well.

I wandered away to look at the personal tablets. I didn't want a tablet, but I was curious, I had been away for three months, there were models I wasn't aware of. Over in a corner was a display stand with flash drives and I picked up four.

I glanced up to find Liz and the techies had left the laptops and were now looking at software packages.

I saw the techie walk away and went over to talk to Liz. "Did you find what you want?"

"Exactly what I want!" She brushed her hand against the front of my pants and gave me her devious smile.

"He's gone to get everything."

The techie appeared in a few minutes from behind a curtain. He was struggling to carry a laptop box and three software packages.

He took them over to a cashier, thanked Liz for her business and went to hustle another customer. I placed my four flash drives on the counter next to the software. The cashier rang up the sale. This time I managed to get my credit card in the cashiers hand before Liz could. She gave me one of her looks.

I looked her back in the eyes; "This is a FORHUM business expense."

The cashier bagged the software packages. I passed the umbrella to Liz. I took the laptop box by its integral handle and the bag of software. We headed back to the hotel. Luckily the rain had stopped, but it was difficult to walk without stepping in puddles and getting sprayed by passing vehicles.

Once we were in the hotel room, Liz was like a kid with a new toy at Christmas. She opened the laptop box and flung the packing on the floor. Plugged the power supply into the back and plugged the other end into a wall receptacle near the loveseat. She looked at me and answered a question I didn't ask; "They're never fully charged when you get them."

She then cleaned up the mess she had made.

She stood there looking as beautiful as ever, big grin and completely relaxed. "Ready for work?"

I looked at her sheepishly; "No, I need a kiss first!"

Liz flung herself into my arms; we kissed for a few minutes. "Now are you ready for work?"

"Yep!"

She went over to the phone and replayed the saved message from the Prime Minister, writing down the names and telephone numbers.

"You start your typing I'll go into the bedroom to make the calls, so I don't disturb you."

I sat down at the desk in front of the computer. Brought the document to the forefront of my mind and let my fingers loose on the keyboard. My fingers stopped when I reached a note that I had placed in the document for a picture of the marker. I had taken a number of pictures of the marker when the aliens showed it to me. I went over to the suitcase and opened it. I had numbered each of the camera's memory cards. I closed my eyes, and began to run through the pictures in my mind, the process was quite quick, I was reviewing about fifteen pictures a second. In a couple of minutes I had found the pictures of the marker. Memory card 43. I found the memory card, put it in the camera, then took the camera cord and connected it to my laptop. I selected an appropriate picture, placed it in the document and let my fingers loose again.

I stopped again and repeated the exercise when I needed a picture of the solar collector system.

Liz came out of the bedroom while I was typing and went over to her laptop with the bag of software packages. I could sense her working on her laptop while I completed typing the document.

I finished the document and glanced at the right hand corner of my computer screen, it was 1:17 p.m. Damn, I've got to stop doing that, I said to myself! It had taken me less than three hours to put the document together, with pictures it was twenty-nine pages. I hadn't included the pictures when I had told the Prime Minister that the document would be twenty-eight pages in length.

I copied the document and picture files to a flash drive.

I glanced over at Liz. She was busy on her laptop. "Liz, do you want some lunch?"

She raised her hand and motioned me not to interrupt her at the moment.

I sat in the chair and watched her work. The concentration level was awe-inspiring.

She stopped and looked over at me in a very businesslike manner; "Do you want an update on the telephone calls I made?"

She didn't wait for a response. She picked up her notes. "The guy I spoke to at the Ministry of Transport initially responded like a true bureaucrat. He would look into it, but he was very busy and didn't know when he would be able to undertake collating the information. I nonchalantly told him that I would put that information in my report back to Prime Minister Harmon. That put a firecracker up his backside. He said he had checked his calendar and surprisingly he had some free time this afternoon and tomorrow. He said he'd be sending a partial package by the end of the day tomorrow, and the balance in three to four days."

Liz looked up from her notes; "it was all I could do not to break out laughing.

The other fellow turned out to be a Major in the army air force, I think. Anyways, he asked a lot of questions and I answered them as best I could. He was very military like, saying yes ma'am and no ma'am at the beginning or end of every sentence. He said he would assign it to a couple of staff as soon as he was off the phone. He said most of the information was readily available and it was only a matter of collating it. He said we should have a complete package by the end of the day tomorrow.

She paused and took a breath of air.

The bank lady, turned out to be the Vice-President of Commercial Accounts. She sounded pleasant enough and said she would be there anytime we wanted to speak with her and make arrangements. Do you want me to send you written memos about this stuff?"

"Absolutely not, I am trying to save the forests."

"What about electronic memos?"

"Liz, you are not my secretary!"

"Yes Boss! Did you say something about lunch? I have an urge for a cheese burger and onion rings. Let's order from room service, I'm on a role with the logo."

"Ice tea? What do you want on your burger?"

"Two ice teas, no ice. On the burger, the works, no onions. I have a hot date tonight!"

Liz immediately went back to work on her laptop.

I called room service and ordered two cheese burgers; one with the works no onions and one with tomato and mayo; onion rings, fries, two ice teas and two cokes all with no ice.

I sat there, watched Liz hard at work and pondered what I should do next. I also considered whether or not to call Steve and tell him I wouldn't be back. Then there was Daniel in England and Joël in Switzerland. I decided not to contact anyone yet.

Lunch arrived, I filled the ice bucket added a few cubes to one of each of our drinks and Liz and I sat down and ate lunch.

"I am very curious Will; can you tell me what the extraterrestrials look like, or is this something I don't want to hear over lunch?"

I almost choked on my burger; "There is nothing untoward in their appearance. Remember I visited a number of planets and there were some noticeable variations in appearance. Let me start with the first planet I went to, which is the location where the Council has its facility.

"The people are smaller than we are, in general between four and 5 feet, a very tall person would be five feet, three inches. Facially, they have smaller ears than we have, faces vary, from what I consider attractive, to what I consider very unattractive, the guide that looked after me at the Council building looked a little like Godzilla!"

With that Liz almost choked on her burger.

"I don't recall seeing any female that I thought was beautiful or any male that I would have considered hansom.

"Other than on their heads, they have no body hair, men don't have any facial hair due to an electrolysis process that I was given as well, males and females wear their hair long. On that planet the hair color was black, there are no variations and I didn't see any hair coloring products. Proportionately, I think their arms were slightly longer than ours. Females seemed to have smaller breasts, but bigger butts. However, they are like humans, there is a wide variety of builds. They have eliminated anorexia and obesity. All the people, other than visitors from other planets are Caucasian. The males are heavily tattooed from the top of their shoulders to the bottom of their ankles; the females do not have tattoos. In general females grow their fingernails longer than most human females, I saw few with nails extending less than one inch and I would say most extended at least an inch and a half. Single females decorate their fingernails with jewels, decals and nail polish if they are actively looking for a mate. Males have short fingernails and do not decorate them."

I looked at Liz she was listening intently. I took a couple of bites of my lunch and continued with my description.

"They procreate in the same manner as humans.

"Females will have their first sexual experience between the ages of fourteen and sixteen and males between the ages of sixteen and eighteen depending on their mental maturity. There is a lot of pomp and ceremony for an individual's first sexual escapade. They actually have special facilities that I can only describe as brothels for males and females that have not yet found a mate. There is no taboo in having sex and it's a frequent topic of discussion when friends gather.

"They have birth control that is 100 percent effective and no one would consider having a child outside a permanent union.

"They have a high regard for family values. Once in a permanent union; their relationships are totally monogamous. The aliens had a problem understanding the concept that a male and female once united would not want to be together for the rest of their lives. They don't have a mechanism for divorce.

"They believe that something outside of the universe initially started its creation, the best description of their beliefs that I can offer is a dormant god. He started the creation but is no longer involved in any manner. They do not have any religions, nor do they worship anything or anyone. For the most part they seem very happy with their lives. They live from one hundred and fifty to two hundred years. At one hundred and fifty they stop receiving medical treatment that will prolong their lives. If they live to two hundred they are euthanized."

Liz let out a small gasp.

"A normal work week is fourteen hours. They are only allowed to have one child. In the unlikely event that the child passes away before the age of fifteen, they are allowed to have another. Most aliens go to school until they are 35 years old. They don't have any poverty, the lowest class is middle class and they don't have any super rich. For the most part they are very friendly and charming."

I stopped to finish my lunch.

Liz had finished eating; "Do they have homosexuals?"

I gulped down the last of the burger that I was chewing on; "I asked the aliens the same question. They told me that a very long time ago they found out that homosexuality was caused by a defective chemical receptor in the brain. They developed a method of correcting the disorder and anyone who had homosexual tendencies was mandated to have the procedure to correct the defective receptor. About 500 years ago, they decided that they would not make the procedure mandatory. Although 99.9 percent of the aliens on this planet continue to get the procedure, on other planets that is not the case."

"Do they have crime?"

"That was one of the few conversations that I had where I had to fight to maintain my composure and not break out laughing. I forget exactly how the conversation started but somewhere along the line, I asked about crime on the planet. They became very subdued and said that they wanted to apologize to me, because last year the crime on the planet had risen. It almost doubled from the year before. With a very embarrassed expression on his face the extraterrestrial told me that he was ashamed to have to admit that last year they had eight murders, fifteen assaults, and twenty-three robberies. Liz, that is for the whole planet, a population of over sixteen billion beings. That would be a very quiet weekend in Detroit! I remember reading somewhere that there are forty-five murders each and every day in the United States alone."

Liz shook her head in disbelief. "We are uncivilized aren't we?

"Can I change the subject for a minute?

"With your new brain power why aren't you designing the logo?"

"You may be under the wrong impression about my new brain power! I will try to relate it to a computer. I have a much higher speed processor and faster memory, but I don't have any new software programs. Before I went to visit the extraterrestrials I couldn't draw a horse. Now, I can't draw a horse a lot faster."

Liz began to laugh.

"The things I can do with my brain now are only because of the processing speed. I have all the pictures that I have ever taken in mind's memory. But, so do you. The difference is that I can access them at a phenomenal speed."

Liz gave me a look of complete and utter confusion. "I don't remember all of the pictures I have ever taken."

"Actually you do."

Liz had an expression of disagreement on her face. She wasn't going to argue with me, she was going to humor me.

"Let me give you an example Liz. Have you ever picked up a photo that you took at a party when you were in high school or even public school? When you looked at the photo, didn't it look familiar? Didn't you, in your mind, start putting names to each of the faces in the picture? Your mind would have also brought back some memories of your interactions with those individuals. Given enough time, you would probably be able to name everyone in the photo and the location. You were doing exactly what I do. The difference is that I can do it at a much higher speed than you can.

"Does that make any sense to you?"

"But, you have other new mental abilities."

"Such as?"

"You can speak all languages."

"That's not true. I can only speak English. This is complicated to explain. When you think of the word *house* a set of electrical impulses race around your brain. If a person who speaks Spanish thinks about the word *casa* which has the same meaning as house, the exact same electrical impulses race around their brain as the ones that raced around yours when you thought of the word house. The electrical impulses not only scurry around your brain, but they emanate from your brain. I pick up the emanated pulses and I hear the word house. I hear the word house even from the person speaking Spanish who was thinking the word casa, because they both emanate an identical electrical field.

Have I totally confused you?"

Liz pondered what I had said for a moment and smiled at me. "I think I'm beginning to understand."

"Every human has the inherent ability to read other people's thoughts. The primary reason they can't is because they are unable to process the emanated electrical pulses fast enough. Again, it is the speed at which I can process information that makes me able to do it. The more people in a confined area the harder it is for me to tune in on any specific set of electrical brain pulses, because everyone in the room is generating their own unique electrical pulses.

"The aliens told me that I must practice my telepathic skills in order to be able to hone in on any specific set of electrical pulses.

"I can learn faster, so if I wanted to learn to understand another language it would only be a matter of reading a translation dictionary and storing the information in my memory. I would be able to access the translations at ultra high speed. But, I couldn't speak the language, because there is a big difference between being able to translate a foreign word and pronouncing it and using it grammatically in a sentence.

"I might be able to learn to write in the foreign language by reading and memorizing a book that detailed proper grammar for that language. But that would still not help me pronounce the words so that I could speak the language.

"I have no more intelligence, intellect or creativity than I had before I visited the extraterrestrials. I can just access what I have faster!"

Liz looked at me as if a light had just gone on in her brain. "By relating it to processing power and memory it all makes sense to me."

Our conversation was interrupted by Liz's phone. She quickly got up and answered it. Her back was to me as she talked and I didn't bother to adjust my hearing so that I could overhear the conversation.

Liz walked back to the table; "That was Major Phelps, you know; our contact with the Department of Defense. He has identified a few additional potential locations in central Ontario and wanted to know if we were interested in reviewing them. I told him to send the information. He said we should expect an email in about an hour."

"I like his efficiency."

Liz smiled, she seemed to be floating when she walked; "I'm going to work on the logo." She turned, headed back to the loveseat, where she quickly went back to work.

It was 3:23. I decided that enough time had elapsed for me to have completed the document for the members of the General Assembly, without any additional mental capabilities. I went to the desk phone and called Prime Minister Harmon's cell phone. After the cordial hellos I told him that the document was ready and asked who I should deliver it to. He said that he would make arrangements to have someone pick it up from my room. He thanked me a few times for my speedy work and my commitment to the overall process. He also informed me that the delegates had successfully drafted an invitation for the proposed meeting.

I disconnected the line and was about to place the handset back in its holder when it rang. A young female voice asked if I was Mr. Dafoe, I acknowledged and she asked me to hang-on for Ambassador Middleton.

"Good afternoon William! I hope you and Elizabeth had a good evening."

"Good Afternoon Ambassador; Yes we did, thank you for asking."

"William, the British Ambassador to the United States, Sir Edward Evans, arrived in New York from Washington this morning. He is having a small dinner party this evening and would be honored if you and Elizabeth would attend."

She paused and waited for answer.

"Is it a formal dinner, I don't have a tuxedo with me?

"Ambassador Evans will be not be wearing a tuxedo."

"May I ask you to hold one second Ambassador; I need to ask Elizabeth. I know she has a lot of things she wants to accomplish."

"I would think that you both need and deserve a break. Please check with her."

I pushed the mute button on the telephone set.

"Liz!"

She raised her head from her concentration on the laptop screen.

"We have been invited to attend a dinner party with the British Ambassador to the United States, Sir Edward Evans, this evening. Would you like to go?"

Liz's face lit up, her head was nodding up and down. "Very much!"

I pushed the mute button to release it.

"Ambassador, we would be pleased to attend. Where is the dinner and what time would you like us to arrive?"

The Ambassador's voice sounded relieved. "I will send a car to pick you up at 7:45, is that acceptable?"

"Perfect Ambassador, I look forward to seeing you this evening."

"Goodbye."

"Goodbye"

Liz was still looking at me; I could tell she was very excited about the dinner party invitation. "What time and where?"

"A car will pick us up at 7:45."

Liz glanced at her watch. "I need to get my hair and nails done."

She stood up and grabbed the room phone and hit a few buttons; after a very brief conversation she hung-up.

"They can take me right now."

Liz gave me a big but very quick kiss, grabbed her purse and literally ran out of the room.

I put all the food service items on the table, dropped the side leaves and wheeled it into the hall.

I decided to start working on the RFQ's for the solar systems and the markers, in my mind. I had just started the documents when there was a knock on the door. I opened it to find an attractive young lady in a UN commissionaires outfit. "Mr. Dafoe, Prime Minister Harmon asked me to collect a document."

I went to the desk and unplugged the flash drive from my laptop, returned to the door and handed it to her. She thanked me and headed back to the elevators.

I had just sat down and the room phone rang. It was the menswear store telling me that my other two suits were ready. I told them I'd be right down. I thought that Liz would want the opportunity to choose which suit was best for the occasion.

I returned from the lobby, hung the suits in the closet, poured myself a glass of wine and proceeded to continue to draft the RFQ's.

It was 6:17 p.m. when a click on the door lock broke my concentration and I stood up. The door opened, it was Liz. I am hard pressed to describe how she looked. I can tell you that my mouth fell open. Her hair was up, her eye make-up made her large brown eyes even bigger, her complexion was flawless, her lips were a tantalizing deep pink and above all she was radiant. She was carrying a garment bag and three store bags. I could see that her finger nails had been extended and painted to match her lipstick.

I grabbed the bags from her.

"What did you buy?"

"I had to get an appropriate dress and shoes, I hope you like them."

I looked her up and down, "You look positively exquisite; regal in fact!"

She gave me a big smile and in a very sincere voice; "I want you to be proud of me."

"Liz, I'm always proud of you."

"What time is it?"

"6:14; I picked up my other suits."

"Excellent, I was going to suggest that you call down and see if they were ready. Can I have a glass of wine please?"

Liz went over to the loveseat and dropped herself into it, she looked exhausted. "I can rest for awhile. Try on your suits so that I can pick which one I want you to wear this evening and bring out the shirts, ties and cufflinks please."

I brought the items from the bedroom that Liz had requested and then tried on each suit in turn. She picked one of the blue ones and asked me to bring her the jacket. She laid the jacket on the loveseat and did a mix and match puzzle with the ties and shirts, laying each set on the jacket.

I consider myself very observant; it is one of the traits of a good salesman, but for some reason I had never taken real notice of Liz's earrings. They were small diamond studs, maybe a quarter of a carat each; nothing special.

"I have to go down to the lobby, you continue your sorting."

Liz didn't lift her head she was in deep concentration on a specific shirt and tie combination.

I left the room and took the elevator to the lobby and went straight for the jewelry store that we had purchased my cufflinks in.

I believe that I have good taste in ladies jewelry and I am an impulsive shopper. I hastily found the glass display cabinet housing the earrings. A female salesclerk pulled out a number of trays and I started to peruse them with my eyes. I quickly scanned the first tray and moved on to the second and then to the third. Half way down the third tray a pair of earrings told me to stop looking any farther. I pointed to them and asked the sales clerk to try them on for me. She did without hesitation. I thought they were perfect. They dangled down one point nine inches below the ear lobe. They were white and yellow gold, with a star at the bottom dangling from a white and gold braided rope; in the center of the star was a solitaire ¾ carat diamond mounted in yellow gold. The outside of the star was made up of white gold with small brilliant red rubies, not chips but stones.

I told the sales clerk that I would take them. She complimented me on my choice. I paid for them and scurried back to the room.

I decided that I would wait for Liz to get dressed before I gave them to her.

Back in the room, Liz showed me what she had chosen for me. A light blue shirt, a deep blue tie with a cross weave pattern on it and the tiger face cufflinks with the small ruby stones in the eyes.

Liz leaned back on the loveseat and closed her eyes.

A little while later she opened her eyes, looked at her watch; "It's time to get dressed."

Liz took off her clothes, including her bra, panties and silk stockings. She went to one of the bags and pulled out a new pair of thong panties, silk stockings and put them on. She then went to the closet where I had hung her garment bag; she laid the garment bag on the bed, unzipped it and removed her new dress. She stepped into it and pulled the front up to the top of her shoulders and slid her arms inside the straps that went over the shoulders, there were no sleeves. "Zip me up, please!"

I went behind her and reached for the zipper and pulled it up. The top of the zipper only went to a spot about four inches above the top of her cute tush. There were two straps, skin colored that crisscrossed to hold the dress on her shoulders. You had to look hard to see the straps which made her back look completely bare. The dress was a soft gold in color, the material felt like silk. She turned around and I could see that it fit her like a glove, I could see the outline of her firm breasts, but there was no sign of her nipples. It was full length. Liz pulled a little on the dress in places to make sure it fit the way she wanted. There was a full length mirror behind the bedroom door, Liz stood in front of it and studied how she looked in the dress.

She slipped on a new pair of shoes that she had retrieved from another bag.

She reached into another bag, opened a box and took out a white finely knitted shawl, which she placed over her shoulders and draped in front of the dress.

There are no words that can describe how she looked, elegant just doesn't do it justice.

I had finished dressing and was tying the last bow on a shoe lace.

Liz looked at me; "Do I look good enough to take out?"

I went over to her, walked around her; looked her up and down. "There's something missing."

Liz's jaw dropped, she looked so sad and defeated.

"I think I know what it is!" With that I reached into the pants that I had dropped on the floor and pulled out the small box containing the earrings.

I stood in front of her and opened it. I thought Liz's eyes were going to pop out of her head. The defeated look changed to delight. "They're beautiful Will absolutely precious." She removed her diamond studs and carefully fastened the new earrings to her ear lobes. She stood in front of the mirror and moved her head from side to side. "They are the most exquisite earrings I have ever seen. I will thank you properly when we get back!" She was beaming from ear to ear. I must say in all modesty that the earrings did look exquisite, especially dangling from Liz's ears. Liz took a lipstick from one of the bags and touched up her lips. Reached into another bag and pulled out a small but classy clutch handbag, put the lipstick in along with some additional make-up and her cigarettes.

She looked at me and smiled; "You really look good in a suit!"

We left the room and headed down to the lobby in the elevator. It stopped at the 16th floor and a man in his mid twenties went to step inside, he stopped in his tracks when he saw Liz and his mouth fell open. He composed himself and stepped into the elevator his back to me. I glanced at Liz; she had a smile on her face like a Cheshire cat.

When the doors opened at the lobby and we started to walk to the front door, I could feel the eyes ogling Liz. I smiled to myself, thinking she's all mine; dream all you want, you can't have her!

It was 7:43 when the doorman opened the door for us to exit the hotel. Parked in front of the hotel was a white stretch limo. A chauffer was standing beside the open back door. I bent a little and saw Ambassador Middleton in the back with a man that I didn't recognize. I took Liz by the hand and we walked over to the door. The Ambassador and the man were in rear facing seats, the Ambassador motioned us to enter. I helped Liz in and then climbed in myself, we sat facing the Ambassador. The chauffer shut the door and walked around to the driver's door, got in and off we went.

The Ambassador was dressed expensively, but not elegantly. The man beside her was staring at Liz. Elizabeth, William allow me to introduce my husband. Liz and I smiled and shook his hand. While the limo maneuvered through the streets there was some idle chit chat about driving in New York. The Ambassador complimented Liz on her hair, and they chatted about hair emporiums for a few minutes. Liz was very at ease and she made everyone else comfortable.

The limo pulled over to the curb and stopped. A doorman opened the door. Liz got out first, then the Ambassador, I motioned to the Ambassador's husband to exit and I followed. We stood for a moment in front of the building, it was very nondescript. We entered and I soon realized this was the Ventura Club, I had heard about it. It was New York's most exclusive business club and it cost a hell of a lot to be a member, if you were invited to join.

Inside we were led to a room where a number of people were standing together in small groups talking, the men definitely out numbered the women. There was a long table in the middle of the room, very formally set to seat 24 people. As we entered the room all eyes were on my Liz!

A man at the door, wearing a tux and white gloves, asked if he could take Liz's shawl. She slid it off her shoulders and handed it to him; he laid it across his arm and disappeared into a side room. Moments later a waiter, came over with glasses of champagne, I allowed the Ambassador and her husband to each take a glass. I took two and passed one to Liz.

A stocky older gentleman with balding grey hair wearing a finely tailored English wool suit that had been standing talking with a group, glanced over and caught the eye of Ambassador Middleton, I noticed that she gave him a nod. He quickly said a parting word to his group and walked towards us. He had a serious limp and walked with a cane. You could see that walking was not pleasurable for him. On his side was an older woman, expensively dressed, but it was an older outfit that I believe had been worn many times before. She was wearing far too much jewelry.

Once he had made it over to us, Ambassador Middleton introduced us. It was, as I suspected Ambassador Evans and his wife. There was a lot of hand shaking. Ambassador Evans looked at me. "I am so pleased that you and Elizabeth could join us. The others in the room are senior executives, a few of their wives and some senior British government people representing British Industry. They are here in the United States on a trade mission. The only thing they know about you and Elizabeth is that you are senior executives; from a North American Corporation that will be releasing large value RFQ's in the near future and that you will not be able to discuss anything with them until you have completed some necessary US SEC filings. I felt that it would benefit everyone to at least meet so that you could if possible put a face to a name in the future.

I didn't comment, but being set-up went through my mind and I wasn't pleased.

It was also a good excuse for my wife and me to personally meet and shake the hand of the man who saved all humanity.

He held out his hand again and shook it with a very tight grip.

It was obvious that Ambassador Evan's wife was used to gatherings with her husband. She stood beside him, but about half a step back. She looked at Liz. "My dear, I understand congratulations are in order, that you have just gotten engaged to William." She said it as if I wasn't standing beside Liz.

Liz grinned; "Thank you." Liz raised her ring hand to show the proof of the engagement.

The Ambassador's wife took her hand in hers and looked at the ring. Her eyes had the look of utter amazement as she glared at the ring. "That truly is magnificent, my dear!" Her reaction to the ring was very sincere.

The Ambassador gently grabbed my arm; "Allow me to introduce you and Elizabeth to some of the other guests." Here it comes, I thought to myself. The four of us slowly walked with the Ambassador to the small group of people he had been talking to when we arrived. The Ambassador introduced us all, including Ambassador Middleton and her husband to the group. We left that group and moved on to another, until we had been introduced to everyone in the room. The moment we stepped up to any group all of the men, including the ones with their wives present would ogle Liz. To my surprise and pleasure, no one talked any business. I thought maybe I had read the situation incorrectly. The salesman in me was disappointed; I don't like to read situations incorrectly.

I noticed a waiter come out from behind a set of doors, motion to one of the ladies in one of the groups. She spoke to him for a moment and then walked to the Ambassador and in a very low voice; "They're ready to serve."

The Ambassador backed away from our group; "Ladies and gentlemen would you please be seated."

There were name cards at each of the place settings. It was quite obvious that the others had found their seats previously because they headed straight for them. The Ambassador touched me on the shoulder, "you're next to me and Elizabeth is next to you." He looked at Ambassador Middleton, you're next to Elizabeth and your husband is next to you."

We followed Ambassador Evans. He stood behind a chair at the head of the table. His wife was standing behind a chair at the far end. I was on the Ambassadors right. As soon as we were all standing behind our chairs, the Ambassador pulled out his chair and began to sit; it wasn't easy for him to place his leg under the table. I helped Liz into her chair and then sat down.

Liz reached under the table and squeezed my thigh without changing her facial expression.

Waiters came out from the kitchen and placed a shrimp cocktail in front of each of us and poured us a glass of wine. As we ate Ambassador Evans was chatting with me about London. He managed to slip in the fact that the UK, due to austerity measures, had recently closed a number of military air bases across the UK and in the unlikely event that we cannot find a suitable facility in Canada he would be pleased to make arrangements for us to visit the closed bases in the UK.

I was sure that there are a lot of closed military bases around the world due to austerity measures. Ambassador Middleton was talking to Liz, I didn't know about what.

After the shrimp cocktails were cleared we were served lobster bisque and a different wine.

The main course was fillet mignon, perfectly cooked, with a portabella mushroom sauce, and tiny veggies the wine was a French Burgundy. The meal was surprisingly very good; usually I find that meals served to a large number of people are mediocre at best.

The table was cleared of the entree and platters of cheese and fruit were placed on the table, well within everyone's reach. Then to my delight, they brought out decanters of port. I leaned over to be able to talk quietly to Ambassador Evans. In a very whimsical tone; "If you're trying to bribe me, it's working."

"Do you like port?"

"If it's good port!"

"This is Graham's 1962. Please enjoy."

A waiter asked me if I would like him to fill my glass.

"Yes please!"

I leaned over to Liz, "Do you like port?"

"I don't think I've ever had port."

"Try this."

The waiter filled her glass.

Liz took a sip; "Very nice."

I smiled; "Just watch yourself; port can sneak up on you."

I leaned back in my chair and sipped the port, it was excellent, a very good vintage.

"Mr. Dafoe."

The gentleman sitting across from me caught my attention. His name was Vincent Marlboro, a tall slim man with strong features. He was a VP at Transglobal Enterprises. They were into a lot of high tech manufacturing and had plants throughout the EU. I could see that Liz had turned her attention to him as well.

"I understand that you will be releasing some RFQs for the manufacture of some high tech equipment in the near future."

"That's correct."

"I have been advised that you can't say what the product or products are, but could you give me your estimated value of the orders?"

"Somewhere between 250 and 500 million US dollars."

Most of the other's at the table were listening to our conversation.

I could tell that an order of that size impressed Marlboro.

He looked at me and leaned in towards the table; "Over what period of time, if I may ask?"

"We will need the products as soon as possible, four to six months max!"

"Can a manufacturer rationally gear up to deliver that much product in that period of time?"

"I have little doubt that there are manufacturers who could probably do it in three months if they put their minds to it. However, that being said, if necessary we will split the orders to multiple manufacturers."

"How confident are you that you will actually place the orders?"

"One hundred percent"

Marlboro was having a problem maintaining his composure. "Who are you sending the RFQ's to?"

"I can't give you the names, because I honestly don't know. We have approximately one hundred and fifty RFQ's in courier envelopes ready to go. I would assume that at least one of your divisions will receive a formal request, but that's not a guarantee. As well, I believe that we will be publishing bid notifications in a number of newspapers world-wide."

"With an order or orders this large, aren't you going to perform a pre-bid qualification?"

"No, we don't believe we have the time."

"When do you expect the RFQ's to be released?"

"Six to eight days from now."

The table was silent. Everyone was trying to absorb the information that I had just released.

Marlboro was fumbling around in his jacket pockets. Finally he found his business cards and reached over to hand me one. "Would it be untoward to ask you to add me to the list of people scheduled to receive the RFQs."

"Not at all."

I took his business card and put it in my shirt pocket.

The waiter was standing over my shoulder and asked if I would like some more port. I responded in the positive and so did Liz.

Ambassador Evans motioned to the lady who seemed to be the

affair organizer. She went over to him and he whispered something her ear. She smiled and nodded.

As soon as the waiter had made his rounds with the port, the rest of the people at the table, excluding spouses approached either Liz or I with their business cards asking to be added to the list of companies that would receive the RFQs if they weren't already on it. We graciously accepted them all.

Ambassador Evan's leaned towards me; "Did Ambassador Middleton mention the invitation from the Prime Minister for you and Elizabeth to have your honeymoon in the UK compliments of the British government?"

"She did Mr. Ambassador and we were both honored. I am sure you can understand however, that where we honeymoon hasn't been a top priority."

He smiled; "I understand, I really do understand."

Liz had been talking to Ambassador Middleton. Liz turned and squeezed my thigh to get my attention. She leaned over and whispered; "There's a place where we can have a cigarette."

I looked at Ambassador Evans and asked him to excuse us.

I stood up and helped Liz from her chair. Ambassador Middleton and her husband stood up as well. I grabbed my glass of port. Ambassador Middleton led the way through the dining room door and down a hall to a set of French doors; she opened them out onto a patio.

There were some chairs and small tables with ashtrays. We all sat down and lit cigarettes. I saw Liz shiver a bit, it was a pleasant evening 67°, but Liz had a bare back. I took my suit jacket off and put it over her shoulders.

Liz, port and a cigarette, if there was a heaven, this could be it; I thought to myself.

We sat their enjoying the night air and our cigarettes. No one said anything. We finished our cigarettes and went back to the dining room. More than half of the guests had left.

Ambassador Middleton asked if we were ready to go. It was 11:29 and I was definitely ready, Liz nodded her head.

We walked over to Ambassador Evans thanked him and his wife for a relaxing evening and a wonderful dinner, I added and the excellent port. He smiled, shook our hands, and we turned to leave. The fellow with white gloves who first greeted us at the door was standing there again holding Liz's shawl. He placed it over her shoulders, Liz adjusted it and we walked to the limo. Liz entered first, Ambassador Middleton next, I followed behind and Ambassador Middleton's husband entered last.

In a few seconds we were headed back to the hotel. I think the port was beginning to sneak up on me, I felt a little light headed.

When we pulled up in front of the hotel, Ambassador Middleton reached over the back of her seat and brought forth a plastic shopping bag. "Ambassador Evans wants you to have this; it's a couple of bottles of the port. It's to compensate you for having to deflect the questions from Marlboro. He has asked me to deeply apologize, everyone was told that it was a social evening and business was not to be discussed." I took the bag from her; "This really was not necessary. Thank the Ambassador for us; I know I will enjoy it."

We said our goodnights and Liz and I proceeded to our room.

As soon as we got into the room, Liz wrapped her arms around my back and kissed me passionately sticking her tongue in my mouth to tickle my tonsils. She broke the kiss; "That's because I love you." She kissed me again in the same manner and then broke the kiss; "That's because I love you very much." She kissed me again, this was even more passionate as she mashed her lips against mine and allowed our tongues to entwine together. When she broke the kiss, she looked at me with very sultry eyes; "That was for the earrings, and there will be more later . . . I need to undress."

I followed her into the bedroom and we both took our clothes off and hung them up. Liz very carefully took her new earrings off, stopped to give them a final look and placed them in the box. Liz reached up and with a few finger movements her hair fell to the sides of her head. She shook her head to adjust the position of the strands. I had gone into the bathroom to retrieve the bathrobes, I helped Liz into hers and we went into the sitting room and both very ungracefully sat down or should I say fell onto the loveseat. Liz curled up against my arm.

Liz squeezed my arm; "I'm wiped. I really like to listen to you talk business, you sound so knowledgeable, that guy Marlboro tried to get something concrete about the products from you and you foiled him at every step! I am very proud to be with you Mr. Dafoe. I think the port has gotten to me, I am feeling extremely mellow and I think I'm babbling."

A few minutes passed and I realized that Liz had fallen fast asleep. I really didn't want to disturb her, but I thought that the position she was in could lead to a very stiff neck. I removed my arm from her grip and stood her up; she had woken but was still half asleep. I picked her up in my arms and carried her into the bedroom and gently placed her on the bed. I pulled the covers over her and went back into the sitting room to turn off the lights.

When I returned, Liz's bathrobe was on the floor. I took my bathrobe off and climbed into bed. I lay next to her, as soon as she felt me in bed beside her, she rolled over; I could hardly hear her say; "Spoon position!" I curled up to her warm body, put my arm around her waist and my hand flat on her silky smooth tummy and fell fast asleep.

Chapter 8 – 267 days to alien arrival

I woke to find myself sleeping on my side facing away from Liz. It was early 6:11, but I was wide awake. I turned to look at Liz, she was still sound asleep; she had a very peaceful look about her. I pulled the covers over her shoulders and very slowly swung myself out of bed, I didn't want to disturb her.

I put my bathrobe on and went into the sitting room where I made a pot of coffee.

Marlboro had brought up a couple of points last night that I really didn't have answers for. The first was who would we be sending the RFQ documents to? The answer, that I had given Marlboro, was a pile of bull. However, when he said it, I wondered to myself how we would quickly create a list of qualified companies. The question had remained in my mind for the balance of the evening. The answer only came to me on the ride back to the hotel in the limo. I would ask the Security Council delegates to have their trade and commerce departments compile a list of potential companies. However for those government departments to come up with a list of qualified companies I would have to give them a list of the manufacturing skills that would be required to produce the items.

I have always enjoyed the smell of freshly brewed coffee. I poured myself a cup and sat down on the loveseat. I leaned back and closed my eyes and brought the manufacturing instructions for the solar collector system to the forefront of my mind.

I went through the information and created a list of the processes involved. The aliens had arranged a tour of one of the manufacturing facilities that made the solar systems and I played the tour in my mind and made another list of each of the processes.

I then compared and merged the two lists into one.

I realized that there may be two components of the solar system that would complicate and possibly negate the manufacture and assembly by just one company. A glass dome and an electronic assembly had to be produced. While the alien factory had machine shop and other metal bashing assets, they also produced the glass domes and the electronic assemblies. In my opinion it would be unusual for any single company on this planet to have all of the capabilities required to assemble the solar system and produce glass domes and electronic assemblies all under one roof.

I pondered the problem for a bit. I had two choices. I could make it the responsibility of the manufacture of the solar systems to find a source for the domes and electronic assemblies in the same manner as finding a source for the metal or I could send out a specific RFQs for the domes and a specific RFQ for the electronic assemblies and then supply them to the manufacture of the solar system. There were advantages and disadvantages to both choices.

I brought the specification of the dome to the forefront of my mind to see how complicated the domes were.

I read it over three times and the only thing that I truly understood was the title; *Specifications for Glass Dome*. The document was filled with terms and jargon that I could barely pronounce let alone understand. It had all sorts of tolerances with respect to the composition of the glass and its shape. I had no idea if these tolerances were within the capabilities of any glass dome manufacture or if it would take a highly specialized organization.

I had mentioned early on in the story that I had business acquaintances all over the world and as I read the document it struck me that I knew an expert in glass; Tina Williamson! Tina was the chief engineer for a glass company in the Netherlands.

I went over to my laptop and formatted an email.

Hi Tina,

Hope all is well.
I need a favor. I have attached a document that lays out the specification for a glass dome. I would appreciate it if you could read it

over and tell me if this is a highly complex and very tight tolerance dome requiring advanced manufacturing techniques or if any manufacture of glass domes would have the capabilities to produce it.

Thanks

Will

I quickly typed the specification that was stored in my brain and added it as an attachment to the email and hit send.

When I hit send, my email handler started to download a stack of emails. I hadn't checked my email since before I left to visit the aliens. I was used to receiving forty to fifty emails a day, ninety percent of them were junk or spam. I watched the inbox and junk mail box numbers grow. When it had finished I had downloaded 3,217 emails into my inbox, 987 emails into my junk box and my anti-virus software had blocked 19 emails.

I had two email addresses, one for business and one for personal. I opened my inbox and quickly realized that in my haste to prepare for the voyage to the extraterrestrials that I had forgotten to forward or put an out-of-office auto responder on my business email address; my stomach churned. What an idiot I thought to myself.

I immediately created three new inbox folders; *Business emails to be forwarded, FORHUM, Later* and began to sort the new unread emails into one of three new folders plus the delete folder. Even with my new found mental efficiencies, it was a very slow process.

I made a mental note to buy the domain names *FORHUM.org* and *For-Humanity.org*.

It was 8:04 when I finally finished sorting the emails. I knew that I would have to contact Steve at the office very soon. I couldn't let those emails just sit in my inbox, but the instant I forwarded them to Elli or Adam, they would know I was back and wonder why I wasn't contacting them.

I was just about to pour myself a fresh cup a coffee when Liz poked her head around the bedroom door; she had a devious look on her face. In a very stern voice; "We have some unfinished business to take care of! Get in here."

She disappeared and I went into the bedroom. Liz was standing there in her birthday suit, her nipples were extended. "Drop your bathrobe and lie down."

I did as I was told. Liz climbed on top of me her face was inches from mine. Her voice was soft and sultry. "Good morning love of my life. Thank you for a wonderful evening and those extraordinary earrings." She put her lips against mine and we made slow tender passionate love.

It was 10:37 in the morning when we walked out of the bedroom, freshly showered and dressed. On instructions from Liz I put on the grey suit. Liz had picked out a matching shirt and tie for me to wear. I had told Liz that I needed to prepare a document for the meeting and then we could have something to eat before we went over to the UN complex. Liz said she would continue to work on the logo. We both went to our respective laptops.

Liz raised her head; "I received the site documents from Major Phelps. Do you want to look at them now?"

I thought about it for a minute. "Copy the file to a flash drive and we will get the UN to print us a couple of copies. I think it will be easier to review them in hard copy rather than on the computer." I retrieved a flash drive for Liz and handed it to her.

I had left my email handler open. It was set to auto download new messages every fifteen minutes. I looked at the inbox, three new messages. Two were spam which I quickly deleted and one was a response from Tina.

I opened Tina's email:

Hi Will,

Nice to hear from you, it's been awhile. Do you have any plans to come to the Netherlands in the near future? I have received a promotion, I am now a Vice-President.

I read over the specifications that you sent. I wouldn't say that just any glass manufacture could meet all of the requirements, but any mid to high quality company would have little problem. We could do it here if you need some made, let me know the quantity and delivery schedule and I will have the sales department prepare a quotation for you.

Have a good day and give me a call next time you're in the Netherlands.

Best

Tina

I decided that I would provide the domes at no charge to the solar system manufacture.

I quickly typed four documents each containing a list of the skills required for each assembly; the solar system, the glass dome, the electronic assemblies and the marker.

I copied the documents to my last flash drive.

Liz was in a state of deep concentration. "How's the logo coming?"

"I put the logo aside. I was reading the site documents that Major Phelps sent. There is a lot of information about each site and he included at least ten pictures with each one. He also listed the advantages and disadvantages from his perspective as he put it. They all have third party environmental studies; some of the results of the studies are downright scary. This one has buried, unexploded munitions scattered all over the property."

"We will have to come up with a method of comparison. Are you ready for something to eat, its 11:42 and we have to at the UN at 1:30. I would like to get there a few minutes early so that I can have the documents printed? We should consider buying a printer, one of those three in one units; printer, fax, scanners; a complete home office, there not expensive."

Liz nodded her agreement with the idea.

I heard a low level ping come from Liz's computer.

"I finally received an email with an attachment from the Ministry of Transport. I'll copy it to the flash drive and we can review it later. Yes, I'm hungry, let's eat! But, I need a kiss first. I'm beginning to suffer from kiss withdrawal." Liz had a big grin on her face.

She stood up and came over to me and kissed me hard. "That's better." She giggled.

We grabbed the flash drives and headed to the lobby for something to eat in the coffee shop. We were seated promptly and placed our order.

"Liz we didn't call Barbara yesterday!" there was a level of remorse in my voice.

"It's okay I called her when I was having my pedicure."

I was relieved and sighed; "Thank you."

Liz had a big smile on her face; "Don't thank me, I had to call her to discuss what type of dress to buy."

I broke out laughing.

Laughing is contagious and Liz started to laugh with me.

Still laughing; "The fund raiser was last night, you know the one Mom and Dad were attending with the President and Vice-President. I wonder how it went.

"Do you think they asked the Vice-President about Wilbur the Saint Bernard?" She broke out laughing again.

She could hardly catch her breath; "I'm sure, I'm one hundred percent positive they did; Mr. Vice-President how is Wilbur? I understand he has been ill." Liz could hardly sit up straight she was laughing so hard. "I'm surprised I didn't get a phone call last night. Maybe they have disowned me. I bet they are just beside themselves. Woof, woof."

Our food arrived. Liz took the napkin and wiped the tears from her eyes, she was desperately trying to compose herself. "Will, I have never laughed like that in my entire life! Everybody in the restaurant is looking at me and I don't care."

"They're looking at you because you're so very beautiful."

Liz gave me a big smile.

Our meals arrived and between bites we smiled at each other. We finished and the table was cleared, but it was only 1:03 in the afternoon too early to go to the UN building.

"Liz, do you think it would be inappropriate to ask Vice-President Almont if we could have access to an aircraft and flight crew?"

Liz didn't hesitate; "No. Do you want me to ask him?"

"If I'm not asking too much of you."

Liz gave me one of her devious smiles; "Too much as your wife or too much as your subordinate?"

I chuckled; "As my subordinate."

"I can see how beneficial it would be if we can fly when we want, rather than having to live with commercial airline schedules. I know that NASA has two aircraft that they are not using. If we need to fly overseas, I would much prefer to be in an aircraft that has NASA on its sides rather than United States Air Force. I'll speak to him privately before or after the meeting. If I ask him in front of the others he may think that I am backing him into an untenable situation if he wants to say no and I don't think it's in our best interests to do that."

I gave her a nod. Liz was sharp, I thought to myself.

We left the hotel hand-in-hand and walked over to the UN building to the back entrance. We stopped at the patio for a cigarette. We had only been standing there a few seconds when Ambassador Marino arrived. We went through the usual hand shaking ritual. Ambassador Marino pulled two red passports from his pocket, looked inside one and handed it to Liz, he then handed the other one to me. In his broken English and a big smile on his face; "Italia diplomatic passport for you and your lady. Italia bureaucracy very big, very slow."

I had forgotten that the Ambassador had said he would supply me with a diplomatic passport. I was impressed with his thoughtfulness in providing one for Liz as well. Liz and I both thanked the Ambassador. I held up a flash drive and motioned to him that we had to go inside. He nodded as he lit his cigarette.

We entered the meeting room and stood by the door for a moment. Only half of the delegates were present. Vice-President Almont was sitting at the table on his own. Liz nudged my arm and started to walk towards him. He immediately stood up and walked towards her.

I turned and went over to the four commissionaires sitting in a corner. As soon as they saw me walking towards them they stood up. I handed one of them the flash drives and ask them to make me copies of the skills documents for all the delegates and two copies of the air force base and municipal airport information for me. The girl asked me if I wanted the skill documents translated. I hadn't considered that. I thought about it for a second and said no. The delegates could get the documents translated by their own people I thought, it would save time. With a purpose the girl immediately left the room.

I walked away. I didn't want to interrupt Liz's conversation with the Vice-President. I glanced over though at the two of them to make sure everything seemed to be okay; they were smiling, chuckling and talking. A good sign I thought to myself. I knew Liz could handle herself. That lady made me proud.

I noticed a thick pamphlet sitting on an empty chair, sat down beside it and started to look at it. I didn't want the Vice-President to see me standing off to the side watching him and Liz, even though that was exactly what I was doing.

It was 1:25 and more delegates had arrived. Liz and the Vice-President finished their conversation and shook hands. The Vice-

President walked back to his seat at the table and Liz walked towards me. Facing me, her voice very low; "No problem, I'll explain later."

I stood up and we went to the table to take our seats. Just as we sat down the commissionaire girl returned from her mission with a stack of collated documents and a manila envelope. She walked over to me and put them on the table in front of me, she reached into her pocket and pulled out the flash drives; "I brought back the flash drive that you gave the Prime Minister a few days ago." I thanked her and she abruptly turned and headed for her chair.

Prime Minister Harmon entered the room and stood behind his chair, he gave a slight nod to Liz and I, he looked warn out and very tired. Everyone else went to their chairs and sat down. It was only when everyone was comfortably seated that the Prime Minister pulled out his chair and sat down. "I call this meeting to order. Ms. Montgomery, Mr. Dafoe thank you for coming. I am pleased to be able to tell you that we are on schedule, actually a number of hours ahead, thanks to the two of you. Providing us with the document hours ahead of schedule allowed us to commence translation earlier than expected. You have my personal gratitude for your efforts in this matter. Is there anything you would like to present or discuss with us?"

"Thank you Prime Minister. Yes there is! I need the help of all the delegates here. Once we have the meeting with the General Assembly and then inform the population the next critical stage will be getting the solar systems and markers manufactured. My current plan is to send out RFQs to a number of companies and to place notices in a number of international newspapers and on the Internet. However, I would like to be able to send the RFQs out to qualified companies immediately after the population is made aware. I could probably think of some companies to send the RFQs to, but it would not be a broad list."

I paused and looked at the delegates; their facial expressions seemed to indicate that they supported what I had said so far.

"I have created four documents that each itemizes the skill set necessary for each item. Without boring you with the details, I have decided to split the solar systems into three RFQs, which is why there are three documents. I am asking that each delegate pass the skill list documents to their appropriate government departments and ask them to create a list of companies that should receive the RFQs. I apologize but I was unable to get them translated in advance of the meeting. If you could have your government department email me the list of companies, their address and contact information as soon as possible, we would save a lot of time and effort. Thank you."

Liz handed the batch of skill documents to the person on her right, who took one off the top and passed the balance to the person on their right. It didn't take long for everyone to have a set of documents.

The Prime Minister had his head down reading the document and didn't notice that the Ambassador from Morocco had his hand in the air because he wanted to ask a question.

He finally put his arm down and spoke; "Mr. Dafoe, first I would like to commend you on your foresight and initiatives. I am sorry to say that our bureaucracy is far from efficient and it will take some time to compile the list of companies."

"Mr. Ambassador, if I may offer a suggestion. Pass the skills lists to one or more of your commercial attaches at a foreign embassy. I have found, from personal experience that these individuals are quite knowledgeable about what specific companies can do in their countries."

"That's an excellent idea, thank you Mr. Dafoe."

The Prime Minister raised his head after finishing reading the documents. "Thank you for the documents, Ms. Montgomery, Mr. Dafoe. Do you have anything additional?"

"A question, Mr. Prime Minister; "Has there been any consideration with regard to who will speak to the General Assembly?"

The Prime Minister looked embarrassed by the question; "None whatsoever. I guess the primary speech will come from me, in my role as President of the UN Security Council. I will have to give it some consideration and discuss it with the other delegates. Thank you for bringing it to my, our, attention. Anything else, Mr. Dafoe, Ms. Montgomery?"

"Nothing at this time Mr. Prime Minister."

The Prime Minister looked around the room there was a level of anxiety in his voice; "Do any of the delegates have anything to bring forward?"

There was silence in the room.

The Prime Minister continued; "I would like to suggest a later start tomorrow, 1:30 p.m., does that suit everyone."

There was no break in the silence.

"Thank you all, I call this meeting adjourned until tomorrow at 1:30 p.m."

The Prime Minister quickly rose, as did everyone else, I picked up the manila envelope that contained the copies of the air force base documents and headed for the door with Liz. The Prime Minister managed to intercept Liz and I before we made it to the door.

"William, Elizabeth; May I have a moment?"

"Yes, Mr. Prime Minister."

He reached into his coat pocket and removed an envelope. His voice was low; "This is the money that was committed. There is a check for you personally for one hundred thousand dollars US and checks for capitalizing FORHUM in the amount of 22.5 million dollars US. The balance of 2.5 million dollars is supposed to be here tomorrow. The Minister of Finance will be providing you with a letter confirming that the one hundred thousand dollars and that your monthly fee is tax free."

I took the envelope from his hand. "Thank you Mr. Prime Minister."

"Are you getting the support you require from the contacts that I supplied to you?"

"Yes we are, Mr. Prime Minister."

"If you have any problems whatsoever, you contact me immediately."

It made me wonder if trouble was brewing on the political front back in Canada. It was only idle curiosity.

Thank you Mr. Prime Minister, if we experience any difficulties we will contact you immediately."

He shook our hands and then briskly left the room.

Liz and I stopped at the patio for a cigarette; it was early 3:49. I looked around to make sure that no one was close enough to hear our conversation; we were alone on the patio. "Liz, what did the Vip say?"

"There is no problem in getting a NASA Learjet placed at our disposal." Liz looked over both her shoulders. She had that devious grin on her face, she leaned towards me and in a very low voice; "It probably won't be equipped with a bedroom." I laughed. Liz stood upright and continued; "It will have navy flight crews, apparently NASA doesn't have any of their own flight crews!" She shook her head in wonderment. "I told him that it would be perfect if it could be wherever we are. We would like to have it in New York. He will confirm the arrangements with me tomorrow."

"Great!"

"We resolved that in less than a couple of minutes. The rest of the conversation was about Mom and Dad at the fund raiser last night. Will, you have to picture this in your mind. The Vice-President and his wife were standing beside President Wycliffe and the First Lady; they were all schmoozing two deep pocketed supporters. My Mom and Dad entered the room. They were always a bit late in order to make a noticeable entrance. They saw the group that the VP was with and headed straight for them. Mom who has aspirations of being the next Secretary of State, another Hilary, looked at the VP apparently with a very somber expression on her face and asked him how Wilbur was and told him how bad she felt knowing that he had been ill. He said that she must be confusing him with someone else, because he didn't know any Wilbur. Apparently the Pres and First Lady were honed into the conversation as were the two supporters. My mother said your Saint Bernard, apparently that caught the Pres off guard and he started to laugh out loud. The VP asked her who told her that he had a Saint Bernard called Wilbur and she said that it was me. Everybody around Mom and Dad were laughing. The VP said he told her that I was having her on, and that he didn't have a dog, let alone a Saint Bernard called Wilbur. Apparently Mom and Dad sulked away and the VP said he didn't see either of them for the rest of the evening, he thinks they left right after the conversation, but he couldn't be positive about that.

That's so perfect, in front of the President and the First Lady." Liz was chuckling, her eyes were glowing.

We finished our cigarettes and I suggested that we go back to the hotel and put the checks in the room safe.

On returning to the room, I went to the room safe that was in the bedroom closet. When I went to open it, it was locked. Liz saw my frustration and pushed me aside; she keyed in a code and opened the safe.

"I put my earrings and the diplomatic passports in there this morning."

"Smart girl!"

I placed the envelope in the safe along with our two Italian diplomatic passports and closed the door and checked the latch to make sure it was locked.

I looked at Liz, she was just radiant. Her face was more beautiful every time I looked at it. I took her in my arms and kissed her; we fell on the bed and undressed each other. Liz seemed to have an unyielding sexual appetite. I wondered how long it would last.

After an exhausting hour and a half, we showered and dressed. It was 5:13. I wanted to peruse the potential facility locations. Liz was going to work on the logo. First I wanted to call Barbara. When I told Liz that I was going to call Barbara, she handed me her phone; "I'll talk to her after your finished."

I spoke to Barbara for a couple of minutes before she asked to speak to Liz. I passed Liz the phone and walked away feeling somewhat dejected.

I took the package of site synopsis documents out, found an open area on the sitting room floor, plunged myself down and started to read them. I thought I would start by making three piles – good, fair and don't bother. I knew that there was little sense in having an excellent pile.

The first three I perused ended up in the "don't bother" pile. Not a good sign I thought to myself.

The next one was a good, and the next two were fair. I wasn't sure if they were actually better than the first three or if I had lowered my standards. But I carried on. The next site was CFB Downsview, I had grown up within walking distance of that air base and yet with everything going on I had forgotten all about it. I read the summary that had been prepared:

Following World War II, the Department of National Defense was in need of property for stationing Royal Canadian Air Force squadrons to protect the concentration of industry and population in southern Ontario. In 1947, the federal government acquired and consolidated 270 properties in Downsview surrounding the De Havilland manufacturing plant. This large tract was developed in the ensuing years as RCAF Station Downsview and became part of the Canadian military's front-line defense of the region.

In 1995 the "Downsview Framework Plan" was released and the Canada Lands Company was directed to manage the planning and development process for the property.

The base closed on April 1, 1996.

In 1998, Canada Lands Company incorporated a subsidiary named Downsview Park to assume responsibility for managing the development of the former military base. Public consultations and a design initiative took place through the late 1990s and early 2000s.

Parts of the property are currently undergoing development, while the airfield is being managed as the Toronto/Downsview Airport and is still in use by the successor to de Havilland Canada, Bombardier Aerospace.

Downsview Park still houses some Canadian Forces regular and reserve units and is home to the Canadian Air and Space Museum. Numerous buildings have been demolished, especially on the west-side of the former base.

Reading about CFB Downsview brought back fond memories. From the age of seven through to seventeen, I lived close enough to the base that my boy friends and I would often walk to the chain link fence that surrounded the facility and watch the CF-104 jets landing and taking off. I remember when a CF-104, on a dark and extremely foggy night, landed on a road that was fifty yards south of the runway, but parallel to it. A few days later all of the street lights that had been used to illuminate the road were removed.

I need an "excellent" pile after all, I thought. I put this document on the seat of the desk chair.

I finished sorting the southern Ontario sites from the Department of Defense. I had put the central Ontario air fields to one side and started on the ones from the Ministry of Transport.

Liz had just finished her lengthy conversation with Barbara when the room phone rang. I managed to standup, my legs were stiff from sitting on the floor and answer it before the forth ring.

"William, this is Prime Minister Harmon, I hope I'm not disturbing you."

He didn't wait for me to respond.

"I have been discussing the meeting with the General Assembly and a question has come up. Would you be prepared to address the members?"

The question really didn't catch me off guard. I was wondering if they would ask, suggest or even take it for granted that I would speak. I didn't want to speak; public speaking has never been one of my fortes. But I knew that I really didn't have an alternative. "Mr. Prime Minister I will speak to the membership if requested."

"Thank you William, I knew I could count on you. I will advise the members of the Security Council."

With that the call abruptly ended. I had wanted to ask him what he would want me to speak about. He probably didn't know yet, I thought. I'll bring it up at tomorrow's meeting.

Liz called me over to see the logo on her laptop. Describing a picture is not easy but I will do my best. In the centre of the picture is a globe of our planet, a deep blue Atlantic Ocean on the right and the European and African continents on the left. There is light emanating from behind the globe. The globe is surrounded by four cupped hands. The hands are not touching the globe, it appears to be floating in the center of them and the light from behind the globe is shining on the palms of the hands.

I gave Liz a smile; "That is excellent, you are very creative."

Her face told me that she was proud of what she had accomplished and she had every right to be proud. "It's not quite finished, if you really like it, we should send it to a professional graphic designer to have it enhanced. I'm not very good with shadows."

I bent over and gave her kiss.

Liz immediately went back to work on the logo and I went back to the airport synopsis documents. Every time I reviewed a site, my mind automatically compared it to the Downsview site and the Downsview site always appeared to be better.

I finished perusing all of the sites. There was only one other site that peaked my interest. Niagara District Airport it was a joint municipal airport under the jurisdiction of Niagara Falls, St. Catharines, and the town of Niagara-on-the-Lake. There were no commercial flights, and it appeared that there were only a few business jets using the facility. It provided pilot training and served as a recreational air field.

From a personal point of view I liked the thought of living with Liz in Niagara-on-the-Lake much more than Toronto.

I placed the Niagara District Airport in the "excellent" pile. Two excellent and four good, actually better than I had expected. I stacked the good, fair and don't bother piles on top of one another, with the good on top and placed them back in the manila envelope.

I picked up the synopsis of CFB Downsview and read the entire document. Then I read the entire synopsis of the Niagara District Airport. Both appeared to have most of what we would require in a facility.

Liz walked over to me; "Any luck?"

"One decommissioned former air force base and one Municipal

airport stand out. The air force base is actually within Toronto city limits. The Municipal airport is near Niagara Falls, it would be a lovely place for us to live, I would prefer to live there than Toronto."

Liz didn't respond to my comments; "Are you getting hungry?"

It was 7:42. "Yes, any suggestions?"

With looked at each other and both said "Bistro" at the same time. Liz leaned over and gave me a kiss; "Was that your telepathy working?"

I didn't think that I had read Liz's mind; "No, we are just in tune with one another!"

We took our jackets and had just opened the room door when Liz's cell phone rang. She looked at the screen and with a very big smirk; "It's Dad!"

We backed into the room and closed the door. Liz positioned the phone, in front and below her mouth and motioned me to listen. I stood beside her our bodies touching.

Liz was grinning; "Hi Dad, how are you and Mom?"

The voice that came back was stern and angry; "Elizabeth, your mother and I didn't find your buffoonery funny. You embarrassed us in front of the President, First Lady, Vice President and a number of other important individuals! We are both disgusted with your recent antics."

"Elizabeth, this is your mother." If voices could kill, I thought. "I want you to call Vice President Almont tomorrow and apologize to him. I am sure he was very embarrassed."

I thought Liz was going to break out laughing; "I really don't understand. I spoke to the Vice President earlier today and he told me that everyone thought it was hilarious, even the President and First Lady laughed. Dad, you and Mom need to get your sense of humor realigned. You need to lighten up."

In a very questioning voice, Liz's father butted in; "You spoke to the Vice-President today?"

"Will and I met with the Vice President for a few hours this afternoon."

Liz's father was obviously perplexed; "Elizabeth what are you meeting with the Vice President about and don't tell me its cemetery plots for his dog?"

That was the trigger, Liz broke out laughing very hard, she tried to talk, but only laughter emerged from her mouth, she couldn't stand still, she couldn't stand up straight as she put her hands on her stomach.

I took the phone from her hand.

"Mr. and Mrs. Montgomery this is William. Elizabeth is unable to speak at the moment." I'm sure they could hear Liz laughing in the background.

Her father's voice was stern and demanding; "Mr. Dafoe, with all due respect, I would like to know what you and my daughter are up to."

Now, I'm a salesman. I am able to diffuse tense situations. However, in this case I decided to fan the flames. "Mr. Montgomery, with all the respect that is warranted, it's none of your business!"

Liz had stopped laughing and was intently listening to the conversation. I looked at her to make sure she wasn't getting upset with me, my tone and specifically what and how I was communicating with her parents. She was smiling, a smile that said carryon, tell them what lousy parents they have been.

Liz's Mom broke into the conversation, her voice was as stern and demanding as her father's; "Elizabeth is our daughter we have a right to know what she is doing."

"Elizabeth is a grown woman. I realize that may come as a shock to you. She doesn't have to report to you, obtain your permission to do anything or follow your bidding."

I paused to allow that to sink in. I can be quite vicious when provoked. "Elizabeth loves you both very much, personally I don't understand why. But, I won't allow you to control her every thought and movement any longer and I definitely will not allow you to use her as a pawn in your political games and aspirations."

Liz's mother broke in; "How dare you!"

"I dare because I am deeply in love with your daughter. I will protect her with my life if necessary."

"Wait until she has another one of her bouts of depression, we'll see how much you love her; we'll see if you stand by her side then."

I'm sure, by the tone in Liz's mothers voice that telling me about the depression was supposed to come as a surprise to me, a revelation, it was to inform me that Liz was keeping secrets from me and that she wasn't the woman I thought she was.

"I have seen your daughter enter a bout of depression and it was obvious that you and her father were the triggers. She called you a few days ago to tell you that she was engaged, one of the happiest days of any girls life, she wanted to share her happiness with you, her parents. But the two of you are so totally consumed with your own wants; you

226

didn't even hear her. Elizabeth is finally standing up to you and you can't handle it. I suggest that the two of you open a bottle of wine and decide whether or not you can accept the new Elizabeth and whether or not you want to be part of her life."

I switched to my pleasing salesman's voice; "Liz and I are just heading out the door for dinner. Have a great evening." I disconnected the line before they had a chance to respond.

Liz came over to me there were tears in her eyes. She put her arms around my neck. "Thank you darling; thank you for loving me; thank you for standing up for me; thank you for protecting me. I love you so much!" The thank you kiss that followed was extremely warm and tender.

Once in the elevator, I looked at Liz; "I hope I haven't ended your relationship with your parents."

Liz smiled; "If you have, so-be-it. But I doubt it. Old habits die hard and they know we are politically connected at the highest levels. They will want to take advantage of those connections and they will also be concerned that if they break the relationship it will have negative repercussions on them politically."

On the walk to the Bistro we didn't talk, but Liz had a tighter grip than usual on my hand.

We ate our dinner and talked about the potential of CFB Downsview and Niagara District Airport, my potential speech to the members of the General Assembly and what we needed to accomplish tomorrow before our meeting with the Security Council. Liz seemed very relaxed. I don't think she was suffering any ill effects from the conversation with her parents.

When we left the bistro we stopped at our wine store and picked up three more bottles of wine.

When we got back to the hotel, Liz grabbed her note pad and started to write reminders to herself of things to do tomorrow. "Will, this is my list of things to accomplish tomorrow morning. I haven't prioritized them yet.

"One; call Major Phelps and see if there is any additional information about CFB Downsview. Also ask him if he could find out if the Air Force would be open to moving out of the facility.

"Two; call the lady at the bank and ask her to open an account in the name of "For Humanity" and the acronym "FORHUM"; if she needs an address I am to use your home address. She's bound to ask who the signing officers are."

I thought about it for a second. "You and me for the time being, one or the other, both aren't necessary."

Liz made a note.

"Three; send your check to your bank. I'll need an address and contact name."

I gave her the pertinent information, which she noted on her pad.

Four; order printer; all-in-one office from Amazon. I'll do that this evening."

Liz and I had discussed the printer over dinner. The printers are relatively heavy and bulky and I didn't want to have to carry one back from a local computer store even with a taxi. I thought that the best approach was to order a machine, that was in stock at Amazon.com and have them deliver it to the hotel.

"I'm going to order a few office supplies as well."

"Liz, add 50 flash drives to the order please."

Liz made a note on her pad. "Five; make love to Will."

"You need a note to remember to do that?"

Liz laughed.

"Five; create some stationary and six; start creating a list of companies that we will send the RFQs to. That's my list. Anything else boss?"

"I think you have it covered. I think we should take the rest of the night off; drink some wine and cuddle."

Liz had a big smile on her face; "Sounds very good to me. But I want to order the office stuff first."

Liz took a minute to organize some papers. I sat beside her while she read the specifications of a few all-in-one office printers. She had picked the one she thought was best, described the features to me and asked for my opinion. I told her to order it. With a click she added to her shopping cart.

While Liz was adding some office supplies and the 50 flash drives to the order, I opened up a bottle of Bordeaux. By the time I had popped the cork and filled two wine glasses Liz had completed her order. It will definitely be here the day after tomorrow, with a little luck possibly tomorrow.

I handed Liz the remote control and she found our music station, I turned off all but the desk lamp and we sat on the loveseat listening to the music and sipping the wine all curdled up against each other.

We talked about everything and nothing. I told Liz about the offer from the UK to have us honeymoon there as the guests of British government and I told her that I didn't know what to say to Steve at my office. Liz told me about a few crazy incidents that happened when she was a member of the President's cabinet and a few funny stories about her parents and their political adventures. I suggested that they would make a good reality TV show; Liz agreed; she came up with a title; "*Political Suck-ups.*"

We talked about who we would invite to the wedding. Liz said she had a few relatives that she hadn't seen or spoken to in years and she would like to invite them. Liz didn't put her parents on the list. I wasn't sure if she felt that it was assumed they would be on the list or if she didn't want them there. I didn't ask. She told me how her parents had estranged all of their relatives. I told her that I would like to invite Daniel, his wife and their two kids and their spouses and Joël and his girlfriend.

Liz brought up our astrological signs, made me worry a bit because I don't believe in astrology in any manner whatsoever, but after listening to Liz for a few seconds I knew this was just idle chit chat. Liz knew my birthday, October 7th; I'm not sure if she found out from Barbara or by snooping and it didn't matter. I knew Liz's birthday from snooping, September 28th. Liz pointed out that two Libras were an excellent match.

We finished two bottles of wine and headed off to bed. We kissed and cuddled a bit, Liz put her head on my shoulder and we went to sleep.

Chapter 9 – 266 days to alien arrival

At 5:02, Liz and I were awakened by a clap of thunder that lifted me off the bed. I immediately noticed that the clock on the night table was not working. "We've lost power."

Liz moaned a little and put her head back on my shoulder and snuggled into me. I lay there with my eyes wide open; the shot of adrenalin that I received from the clap of thunder had me wide awake. Liz was sound asleep; I just lay there and enjoyed the feel of her soft skin against me. Eventually I dozed back off to sleep.

I think I woke because of the numbers from the clock flashing in my face. It was 1:18 a.m. according to the flashing clock, but I knew it was 6:55 a.m. I bent my head a bit, an awkward position and kissed Liz on the head.

She stirred; "Time to get up?"

"You can lie there a few more minutes if you'd like." She wiggled her body against mine. "Is it raining out?"

I tuned my ears to the sounds coming from outside. "I think raining may be an understatement. It sounds like it's coming down in torrents."

Liz wriggled some more; "Let's just stay in bed all day and make love."

"If we only could! But we have things to do: places to go, and people to see."

Liz's voice was so very soft and alluring; "You're a party poop!" She moved her hand down from my shoulder where it was lying, across my tummy and gently clasped her hand around me.

It didn't take long for me to react, Liz's sounded excited. "Maybe you are fun!"

Around eight we showered together, I'm not sure if I remember how to wash myself anymore, got dressed and went into the sitting room. Liz picked up her phone and announced; "I'm going to make some phone calls. Why don't you order us breakfast?" She picked up her note pad and went back into the bedroom, so as not to be disturbed by my room service order. I called room service and ordered us breakfast.

I was thinking about the speech that I would have to make in front of the General Assembly. I wanted to start to write it, but without knowing what topics I was supposed to cover, it was next to impossible.

I could hear Liz in the other room talking to someone. She was being very polite but firm.

There was a knock at the door, I expected to see a waiter with the room service cart for breakfast, but instead it was a bellhop with a luggage cart. I let him in and he unloaded two boxes, I gave him a tip and he left. I looked at the labels on the boxes and couldn't believe it, they were from Amazon.

There was another knock on the door, this time it was room service. He set up the table; I stuck my head into the bedroom. Liz was doing her usual pacing and talking to someone. I caught her eye and mouthed "breakfast". Liz nodded.

Liz came out of the bedroom, smiling. "Everything is under control." What's in the boxes?"

"It's the stuff you ordered from Amazon last night."

"You're kidding!" Liz shook her head in disbelief.

I sat Liz at the table and we started breakfast. Liz told me about her conversations as she ate. She told me that Major Phelps was very non committal and somewhat wishy washy when she asked if the Air Force would be willing to leave the facility. I said that we would take it up with Prime Minister Harmon.

Liz quickly finished her breakfast she was anxious to setup her new toy and get her hands on the office supplies.

The printer box had some rain drops on it, it made me think that the walk to the UN was going to be a real joy. I helped her open the printer box and we pulled it from its packing. It presented a challenge, where to put it. After looking around the room, we took one of the table lamps off a side table next to the loveseat and after putting a piece of packing on the table to protect it, put the printer on the table top.

Liz looked at the unit perched on the table; "That will work just fine."

She proceeded to open the second box and went through it to make sure everything she ordered had been delivered; she moved the box with the office supplies to a corner of the room.

"Liz, I think we should save the boxes and packing material, they may come in handy. I'll put them in the closet."

Liz nodded her approval and I proceeded to collect all the packing material, put it in the printer box and place it on the floor in the coat closet.

Liz was typing on the laptop. She printed off two letters and went into the bedroom with two manila envelopes.

I decided to perform some additional research on the CFB Downsview and the Niagara District Airport. I sat down at the desk and started to Google. I typed in a search for Niagara District Airport; in a few more clicks I had a map of the airports location. I wanted to know what was around the airport. I zoomed out and looked at where it was situated relative to the cities and towns in the area, highways, and hydro corridors. The map showed a large vacant parcel of land directly south of the airport. It backed on to the airport property. I zoomed in so that I could read the printing on the parcel. *"Ontario Government – Employment Lands."* The description meant nothing to me. More searching and I found a specific real estate prospectus for the property. Reading through the prospectus I discovered that the property was owned by the Ontario Government and was available for purchase. It was seventy-seven hectares, basically farm land; it was being leased out as farm land on a month to month basis. This might be the perfect opportunity. Very convenient for the Federal government to purchase and turn into an international zone, runway access from the adjacent Niagara District Airport, good highway access and close to where I would like to live. I should call Prime Minister Harmon and have him get the ball rolling.

Then I thought that Liz and I really should see the property before we get the Prime Minister involved. Maybe we can scoot up there tomorrow. We'll see if we have the NASA aircraft available. Too many ifs ands or buts and so little time.

Liz was returning from the bedroom with the two manila envelopes, when her cell phone rang. I heard her say Vice-President

Almont, I didn't tune into the conversation, I was thinking about the property next to the Niagara District Airport.

Liz came over to the desk where I was in deep thought, and bent over and gave me a kiss; "That was Vice-President Almont. The NASA Learjet will station itself at Newark airport; it should arrive here around 1:00 p.m. today. It will be at our disposal 24/7. When we want to fly somewhere we just call a number at least one hour before departure. It has a Navy flight crew; pilot and copilot, no flight attendant. There is one small problem, if you can actually call it a problem; they cannot provide any kind of food service, if we want to stock the galley we will have to make the arrangements ourselves."

"You've done well Tonto!"

Liz had a big smile on her face; "Thank you Kemosahbee."

I told Liz about the property that I had identified and my loosely conceived plan to go see it tomorrow. I showed Liz the prospectus and specifically a map of the property on my laptop screen and asked her to print a copy.

Liz had a small look of frustration; "Move over."

She sat down at my laptop and her fingers danced on the keyboard. In a couple of minutes, with an air of confidence; "You can print it yourself. The printer is wireless and I have set it up as your default printer."

I bent over and gave her a big kiss.

I printed a copy of the prospectus. I would take it to the meeting. If the opportunity presented itself I would present it to Prime Minister Harmon.

It was 11:04, far too early to go to the UN. I was anxious. I wanted to do something, to get things underway.

I thought that the delegates might like to see a few pictures of the extraterrestrials and their planets. I quickly ran the pictures through my mind and picked out twenty that were of reasonable quality. I went to my suitcase found the appropriate memory cards and proceeded to copy the pictures to my laptop and add captions. I then printed sixteen copies. The printer that we choose was not a "picture quality" unit. I decided to copy them to fourteen flash drives so that the delegates could print quality copies at their leisure. I would only provide the pictures to the delegates if the discussions made it appropriate to do so.

Once I had the picture task accomplished, I relaxed at the desk and lit a cigarette.

While I was pondering my navel, and humming Aquarius, a thought entered my mind. Why am I planning on manufacturing the solar systems in one location and shipping them around the world? The basic solar collector system is made up of three components, the Xanfor module, glass dome, electronics assembly and a metal stand. The metal stand would be extremely heavy and quite large, why not build it right at the generating plant. There is nothing fancy about the stand, it only has two basic functions; keep the Xanfor module level and provide a mounting area for the lugs to connect the outgoing power wires.

It would make much more sense and cost a lot less money to ship the utility a component kit comprising a dome, electronic assembly, Xanfor module and instructions on how to build the stand. I am so brilliant, I thought to myself.

I pondered the advantages and disadvantages to operating in this fashion. There were a few serious advantages: We could control the quality of the key components. Keeping an inventory of modules would allow us to respond to orders quickly and provide spare modules if necessary. It should also make the solar collector system less expensive and provide additional economic benefit.

The only disadvantages that I could think of were related to logistics. We would require a receiving department to inspect the components and a shipping department that could package the kits that we would be shipping to hundreds of different locations around the world. More space would be required and we would need more material handling equipment. We could contract out the design of the packaging material for the kits and make the packaging material another RFQ, more to keep track of, which might equate to a larger finance department.

I would have to start to consider the new organizations staffing requirements.

My brain was running at full steam, I had to focus. Another couple of thoughts entered my mind. I didn't want Liz to become my administrative assistant. She was far too intelligent and creative to be working on basic administrative duties.

"Liz, are you in the middle of something?"

"No darling, I'm just refining the logo."

"I want to talk to you about a few things."

Liz's face had a foreboding look.

"Liz, I don't want you to become my de facto administrative assistant. You are the Deputy Managing Director. I was very impressed with Cheryl, what do you think about offering her the position of administrative assistant?"

"Cheryl would probably jump at it. When I met with her a couple of months ago she wasn't happy at the Whitehouse since I had left, she had little work to do and the work she was given was usually a make work project, I doubt if things have changed. She is extremely efficient and cares about any assignment she is given, she thinks and is not afraid to stand up and say something doesn't make any sense. She has a good personality, is single and as far as I know she has no ties to Washington, she has only been there for two or three years, her family is in Idaho, I think."

"When you have a moment, why don't you call her and feel her out. I don't want to offer her anything formally until the meeting with the General Assembly is finished and out of the way."

Liz seemed to really like the idea; "I'll do it this evening, I have her home number."

"The next item is your apartment in Washington. Have you given any consideration to getting rid of it?

"It has crossed my mind a few times, but there have been so many important issues to deal with that I haven't really thought about it in detail. I don't need it or want it; I expect to be living with you for the rest of my life. As soon as I have a place to send my belongings to I will cancel the lease. The landlord won't mind, it's a very popular building and he has a waiting list of potential tenants."

"Do you have a lot of stuff?"

"I don't have any furniture worth shipping. I'll donate it all to Goodwill or the Salvation Army. I have a lot of clothes, a computer which I can't give away unless I fully erase or destroy the disc drive, a jewelry box, six collectable china figurines, a painting and a couple of picture albums. It could all be packed in boxes and shipped anywhere."

It was 12:55. "We should probably get ready to leave."

Liz gave me a wet kiss on her way to the bedroom. She came out a few minutes later looking as scrumptious as ever. I glanced out the window, it was still raining, but it was more of a drizzle than the downpour we had all morning.

"We have a few minutes before we have to leave. Let's have our cigarettes here, I don't want to stand on the patio in the rain."

The turmoil of thoughts that had been clogging my brain had subsided quite a bit. I was more concerned about getting Liz to the UN building without her getting soaked.

At the appropriate time we put our jackets on, I grabbed the umbrella. Liz pushed "2" on the elevator floor panel and looked at me. I guess I had a questioning look on my face. "We need to stop at the hotel's business facility to send the checks out for FORHUM and your personal account. In the business facility Liz took two courier envelopes, wrote out waybills and deposited them in the courier box. We then proceeded to the hotel lobby and headed off to the UN building.

We managed to avoid the puddles and the torrents of water being directed onto the sidewalk from passing vehicles.

It was 1:27 when we entered the meeting room. I hung our jackets on the coat rack and we proceeded to our chairs. A few delegates and Prime Minister Harmon had still not arrived. By 1:33 everyone had arrived with the exception of Ambassador Balabanov. The Prime Minister looked at his watch: We'll give Ambassador Balabanov a few more minutes before we start."

A few of the delegates rose from their chairs and walked around the table to where Liz and I were seated. They passed us lists of companies that should receive the RFQ documents. We thanked them and they returned to their seats.

Just then Ambassador Balabanov walked into the room. He looked really upset; "I apologize to everyone for my tardiness. The hotel elevator power failed with me in it!"

The Prime Minister was shaking his head in disbelief.

Ambassador Balabanov took his chair.

Prime Minister Harmon tapped his pen on the table to get everyone's attention. "I call this meeting to order. Thank you all for coming. Everything is going as planned. All of the notices for the meeting have been sent out. I have already received numerous phone calls asking me what the meeting agenda is. Some countries are very upset that we have called the meeting on such short notice without an agenda. I am guessing that I am not the only one who has received these types of communications."

About two thirds of the delegates raised their hands.

The Prime Minister continued; "I had a call from the French Ambassador to the United States. He informed me that France would not be attending the emergency meeting of the General Assembly. He also informed me that France was considering leaving the UN Security Council and the UN altogether."

Some of the delegates were shaking their heads in disbelief.

Vice President Almont interjected; "The President informed me this morning that he had received a telephone call from the President of France, imparting the same information. The President apparently questioned their resolve in exiting the UN and was lambasted with questions pertaining to our intelligence in believing any of this."

Ambassador Zhang Wei leapt to his feet, knocking the back of his chair to the floor behind him, he was irate; "Does anyone really care what the French think or do? The People's Republic of China does not. The French have always been backwards in their thinking and prefer to take the opposite stance to the prevailing theory no matter what the evidence is to the contrary. If it's raining they will say it's snowing! Mr. Prime Minister, fellow delegates, I think we should ignore the French and move on to important matters."

With that he turned around picked his chair up and dropped back into it.

Everyone started to applaud.

It was obvious that Ambassador Zhang Wei said what most everyone else was thinking.

Once the applause subsided Prime Minister Harmon brought the meeting back to order. "Mr. Dafoe, do you have anything you would like to discuss?"

"Yes, Mr. Prime Minister, I do."

"Please continue."

"Will FORHUM, be able to use the translation services of the UN? The RFQs can be sent out in English, as I am reasonably confident that most companies receive RFQs in English no matter where they reside. However, the manufacturing, assembly and installation instructions are a different matter. I would like to be able to provide the assembly and installation instructions in the language of the country placing the order. I'm in the midst of creating a budget for the new organization in order to set the selling prices for the products. Translation services could be a major expense. FORHUM, while not a true subsidiary of the UN has a very close relationship, especially considering that the Board of Directors of FORHUM is defined by the members of the Security Council."

The Prime Minister looked around the room at the delegates to see if anyone had an answer to the question. No one responded.

"Mr. Dafoe, I don't have the answer to your question. I will have to find out. However, as this would appear to be a unique situation for the UN, getting a definitive yes or no could take a long time. I would suggest that you budget on the basis of sourcing translation services from a commercial entity."

Liz made a note on her pad. *Translation services.*

"Please continue Mr. Dafoe."

"There are one hundred and one containers sitting on Roosevelt Island. They are going to have to be moved. I would think that the City of New York would like them moved as soon as possible. I hope to have a location in Southern Ontario identified very soon. That being said, the containers will have to be transported from the island to the new location in Canada."

I looked over at Vice-President Almont and then back to the Prime Minister.

"I would respectfully suggest the use of the US Army Transport Command to move the containers. However, if that is acceptable to the US government, would Canada be prepared to allow the US military to cross the border?"

Vice-President Almont jumped in; "I can make arrangements for the US Army Transport Command to undertake the transportation of the containers, subject to Canada allowing them to cross the border. We will provide security to the border. Mr. Prime Minister."

The Prime Minister without hesitation and with a confident voice; "There will not be a problem at the border. We will undertake security from the border to the final destination."

Vice-President Almont spoke again; "I will contact the US Army Transport Command and have them prepare to move one hundred and one cargo containers from the Roosevelt Island location to somewhere in southern Ontario. I will also provide you and Ms. Montgomery a contact name and number at USTRANSCOM that will be waiting for final instructions and a definitive destination."

"Thank you Mr. Vice President. Thank you Mr. Prime Minister."

The Prime Minister spoke; "Mr. Dafoe, I will provide you with a contact name and number at the Canada Border Services Agency and another for the army, who will provide security. You will only have to advise them of dates and the actual border crossing location. I will ensure that the convoy of containers is not impeded in any manner."

"Mr. Prime Minister; will you be able to provide security for a period of time at the drop-off location in southern Ontario?"

"I will make security arrangements that include security at the site in southern Ontario."

"Thank you Mr. Prime Minister."

Liz was writing copious notes on her pad.

"Please continue Mr. Dafoe."

"I have nothing more at this time, Mr. Prime Minister."

The Prime Minister scanned the delegates; "Does anyone have any questions or comments?

No one spoke.

"Mr. Dafoe, some of the delegates and I have been discussing the meeting of the General Assembly and who will be speaking and what topics they will cover. We have some ideas, but they involve you and we would appreciate having your input before we make any final decisions."

The Prime Minister paused to gather his thoughts and glanced down at a pad of paper in front of him, he was, for all intent purposes, reading from his notes. "The meeting would start with the Secretary General of the United Nations; Chitundu Owusu calling the meeting to order. I would be the first speaker in my role as President of the Security Council. I would cover the following topics: When and how the message that was received from the aliens; the contents of the message; why the Security Council believed it to be legitimate and tell them that human race would not be annihilated. I would then introduce you."

He paused and took a sip of water, his voice sounded nervous; "You would discuss the outcome of the meeting with the extraterrestrials; what was behind their concerns; the agreements, compromises and commitments you made, specifically what a country had to do to avoid annihilation of its people; and all the benefits that humanity would obtain.

After you have completed your speech, the President of the Russian Federation has asked to speak and that would be followed by a speech from the President of the People's Republic of China.

The Secretary General would then close the meeting.

The hurdles or challenges that we haven't resolved are in the details. How do we give the members enough information so that they can go home and start to do something? As an example, who do they communicate with to get some advance planning information before they order solar collector systems and markers? Who can they ask questions of with regard to the agreements and compromises? Who can they ask questions of pertaining to your visit with the aliens? We would expect to be deluged with requests for information from the press."

"Mr. Prime Minister may we take a twenty minute recess while Liz and I ponder what you have outlined?"

The Prime Minister glanced at his watch. "We will recess until 3:15."

The challenges the Prime Minister had outlined definitely required a cigarette. I stood-up and Liz followed, we put our jackets on, I took our umbrella from the rack and we headed for the patio at a brisk pace. We stopped at the glass door and perused the situation; it wasn't raining at the moment although the patio was laden with puddles.

I looked at Liz and she nodded her okay with a smile and we ventured forth onto the patio carefully trying to avoid stepping into puddles.

"Any brilliant thoughts?"

Liz looked into my eyes with that sultry expression that she knew turned me on; "other than going back to the hotel and making love for the rest of the afternoon, no!"

We lit our cigarettes, we didn't speak. We were holding hands. The Prime Minister was correct in his thinking. It was important to send the delegates home with some assignments. We would also need someone to field questions from the press and someone else to field questions from the leaders of the countries.

"Liz, what do you think of hiring a PR firm to handle the press attacks that we will face? We can give them a briefing and allow them to be at the forefront of responding to enquiries from the press. I don't want to give interviews to the press or appear on any news shows, I don't know about you?

Liz pondered what I had said for a few seconds."I don't want to talk to the press and I especially don't want to appear on any news shows. I think that you have a good concept, but I think we should use a crisis management firm and let them decide if we need a PR company."

I must admit I hadn't considered a crisis management firm but I agreed with Liz, it was the right approach. "Do you know any crisis management firm that could handle it?"

With a smile on her face; "I do! Davis, Malthus and Associates. I am acquainted with Sarah Malthus; we went to Harvard Law together. I know the firm has handled some of the biggest crisis management exercises in the US.

"You can present it to the delegates!"

I wanted one more cigarette but I felt Liz shiver, it wasn't that cold, but it was very damp and the sun was hidden behind thick dark cloud formations.

I tugged on Liz's hand; "Let's go back in.

We sat down in our chairs, the Prime Minister saw we were back and walked over to us. He reached into his jacket pocket and took out an envelope, he had a frustrated expression on his face; "The remaining two and a half million dollars." Liz took the envelope from him and put it in her purse.

We still had a few minutes before the meeting was set to come to order. "Mr. Prime Minister I know that you are severely overloaded but I would like to take a moment to discuss a potential site." He nodded. I told him about the site adjacent to Niagara District Airport and outlined what I would like to happen, if after Liz and I viewed the site tomorrow we were still in agreement that it was a good choice for the facility. I thought that the best way to proceed would be to have Public Works Canada purchase the property from the Ontario Government. Then in whatever manner necessary declare the property as an International Zone. FORHUM would then lease the property from Public Works Canada. I handed him the real estate prospectus. He said that he would put the Minister of Public Works on standby and that we should call him as soon as we know if we want him to proceed with the purchase of the property.

The Prime Minister leaned into me and with a whisper: "I want to unofficially thank you for choosing Canada as the location for FORHUM. It will mean a lot to Canada."

By this time it was 3:15 and all the delegates had returned and were seated. The Prime Minister went back to his seat and called the meeting back to order.

I looked around the table at the delegates and then focused on the Prime Minister; "Mr. Prime Minister, Ms. Montgomery and I have a couple of thoughts that we would like to present."

Liz had her hand under the table and squeezed my thigh.

"The first point is the speech to the General Assembly. I will speak. However, you should be aware that I'm not a good public speaker; I don't deal well with large audiences. But, I will do my very best, that's all I can promise."

The Prime Minister interjected. "The members of the Security Council have complete faith and confidence in you Mr. Dafoe and I am sure that you will do an excellent job."

"I thank the members of the Security Council for their faith in me." I paused made a phony chuckle and smiled at the group; "I hope that you all feel the same way after my speech!

"Mr. Prime Minister; with regard to the second point; we can prepare a "To Do" document that provides a list of things that each country should do and how they should go about doing them. In the document we will provide an email address and fax number that can be used for questions about the markers and solar system collectors. I would also suggest that we ask each country to designate an individual as their prime contact with FORHUM. The challenge will be getting the document translated in time for the meeting of the General Assembly. I can prepare it this evening and deliver it to the translation department tomorrow morning."

The Prime Minister had a small smile on his face; "That would be excellent Mr. Dafoe. If you call this number, they will come to your hotel and pick it up as soon as it is ready they are available 24/7." He opened his address book and quickly wrote a number on the bottom of his pad; tore it off and handed it to Liz.

"Please continue Mr. Dafoe."

"Mr. Prime Minister, we have always said that the benefits derived from the aliens would be shared with all of humanity not just members of the United Nations. Is there a list of non-member countries, with contact information?

The Prime Minister shook his head no. He asked if any of the delegates were aware of a list of non-member countries. They all responded in the negative.

"Mr. Prime Minister; May I speak?"

"Please do Ambassador Chopra."

"The Indian Department of State has a list of all the countries in the world and their leaders. It is kept very current. I don't believe that it would take much effort to cross reference the list of UN members and create a list of countries that are not UN members. I would be pleased to arrange for the creation of such a list."

"Thank you for your assistance in this matter Ambassador, could you arrange to have it emailed to Mr. Dafoe or Ms. Montgomery?"

"Mr. Prime Minister, please consider it done."

"Mr. Prime Minister; Ms. Montgomery and I will ensure that all of the non-member countries also receive a copy of the "Overview" Document and the "To Do" document."

"Thank you Mr. Dafoe."

Liz was panting at the bit to speak, and stood up; "Mr. Prime Minister; the other matter that you referred to was, how to deal with the press and other enquires that really don't have anything to do with preparing for the arrival of the aliens in 266 days. It is a question of public relations on a global scale. However because of the shear volume of enquiries I believe we would all be best served by a proactive rather than a reactionary posture. We deliver the press and countries reams of information on a continuous basis and offer no additional information until we believe its release is justified. In that vane I suggest we contract with a crisis management firm to maintain control of the public's view towards you as the Security Council and us as FORHUM. I know of a crisis management group; Davis, Malthus and Associates, that I believe would handle this matter extremely well, they have a lot of experience protecting the images of governments and large corporations, while disseminating information, some that the public may not appreciate. FORHUM would be the contracting party.

I should also point out that neither Mr. Dafoe nor I have any intention of being directly interviewed by the press nor do we have any intention of appearing on any talk or news shows."

"Ms. Montgomery, I for one think that contracting with a crisis management organization to handle the interface between the public and us; the Security Council and FORHUM is a brilliant idea."

Liz sat down and maintained her outward composure. She grabbed my thigh and buried her long pointed finger nails into it. Obviously internally Liz wasn't quite as composed.

The Prime Minister continued; his face seemed even more relieved. "As FORHUM will contract the crisis management company the decision on whether or not to proceed is completely up to Mr. Dafoe. However, I am sure that Mr. Dafoe and Ms. Montgomery would like to know if any of the delegates are against FORHUM hiring a crisis management organization. Are there any comments or questions?"

"Ambassador Middleton."

"I would like to express my concurrence with Prime Minister Harmon. I also believe that hiring a crisis management organization is an excellent idea."

There were a lot of "Here Here" and table slapping in agreement.

The Prime Minister spoke; "Mr. Dafoe, Ms. Montgomery, it would appear that you have the unanimous support of the members of the Security Council. Is there anything else anyone would like to say or bring forward? "

I glanced around the room, no raised their hand or spoke.

"Mr. Prime Minister as there doesn't appear to be any critical business to discuss. I wondered if the delegates would like to spend a few minutes of there time viewing a few of the pictures that I took on my trip."

The Prime Minister surveyed the table, everyone was smiling and nodding. "I would enjoy seeing some of the pictures from your trip Mr. Dafoe."

Liz reached into her purse and pulled out a manila envelope containing the printed pictures and the flash drives and circulated them in a similar manner as all other documents; she passed them all to her right.

Once all the delegates had the papers with the pictures and a flash drive, I continued. "First allow me to apologize for the poor picture quality I didn't have access to a picture quality printer. I placed the same photos on the flash drive so that you can have them properly printed or processed."

I looked around the table and smiled at the delegates. "The second problem is that I am the world's worst photographer! Please let me amend my last statement; I am the worst photographer in the galaxy! And, no amount of processing can correct that I'm sorry to say."

A few of the delegates chuckled with their heads down scrutinizing each picture intently.

There were only a few questions about the pictures which I answered. I had expected the delegates to ask a lot more.

A little while went past as the delegates talked amongst themselves, pointing at pictures and making comments to someone beside them.

The Prime Minister interjected into the peace and tranquillity of the room. "Ladies and Gentlemen the day after tomorrow we will be in front of the General Assembly. Everything is in motion and there is little more that we can do at this time that will have any serious impact on the meeting. I respectfully suggest that we don't meet tomorrow. I think we all need some time away from this room. However, I do think we should meet the morning of the meeting just in case there are some last minute items or suggestions. You all have my telephone number; please don't hesitate to use it. I have the ability to make contact with Mr. Dafoe and Ms. Montgomery if we need to involve them in any matters. Are there any objections to adjourning this meeting and returning at 9:00 a.m. the day after tomorrow, the day of the meeting with the General Assembly?

No one spoke at the table, but the delegates were collecting their papers and obviously getting ready to leave.

"Before I adjourn the meeting, I would like to thank all of the delegates for their invaluable support over the last week and I would especially like to thank Mr. Dafoe and Ms. Montgomery for their tireless efforts and their excellent council."

All of the delegates including the Prime Minister stood and applauded Liz and I. As the applause began to subside the Prime Minister raised his voice above the clapping noise; "I call this meeting adjourned."

Liz and I stood up and tried to walk to the coat rack. Each delegate stopped us and shook our hands. The Prime Minister had stood back and was the last to approach us. "If you need anything at all call me, at any time." He shook my hand with a very tight grip; "you make me very proud to be a Canadian." He gave Liz a big smile and reached for her hand; "Have you given any thought to becoming a Canadian once you're married? I would be honoured to personally swear you in as a citizen of Canada."

Liz's face turned a bright pink, she was blushing, "Thank you Mr. Prime Minister."

Liz and I retrieved our jackets and the umbrella from the coat rack. We headed towards the exit door and the Prime Minister headed in the opposite direction.

When we got outside it was raining again. I opened the umbrella to shield Liz and we walked as fast as we could back to the hotel. We didn't manage to miss all the puddles and a taxi hit a pothole full of water just as we walked past; luckily my legs took the brunt of the cascading water and protected Liz from getting saturated.

Once in the hotel room I gave Liz a big hug and kiss which was reciprocated. I have to get out of these clothes, my pants are soaked. Liz looked down at my pants, and started to laugh; "Poor boy, did you have an accident?"

Liz and I both changed. Liz put our suits, a couple of blouses and a couple of my shirts in a laundry bag and called the concierge to have them picked up for dry cleaning.

"Liz, I need you to do a few things." Liz took her notepad and sat down by the desk. I was pacing the floor. "Call the crew of the NASA jet and tell them we will be flying to Niagara District Airport tomorrow; departure time 10:30 a.m. You can tell them we won't be there for more than a couple of hours and then we will be returning to New York.

You will also have to call the airport in Ontario and find out what we have to do to arrange for immigration and customs clearance. Make a note that we need to take our passports, it would probably wise to take our diplomatic ones.

I noticed that there was a helicopter service out of the Niagara District Airport. Call them and see what advance arrangements have to be made to use their services. I would like to have a helicopter tour of the potential property."

"Put a package together of the information we have on the Niagara airport and the adjacent property, including the maps that we can take with us tomorrow."

"You might as well call Barbara, because if I call her she will only ask to speak to you anyway."

Liz laughed.

"Just a reminder, you were going to call Cheryl.

Please call your friend at Davis, Malthus and Associates and see if she can meet with us in New York tomorrow evening?

We should send the check that the Prime Minister gave you to the bank.

We need to order some expense account forms.

Can you come over here and give me a kiss?"

Liz looked at me with a glow in her eyes and softness in her voice; "I think this could be construed as sexual harassment, but I do want to keep my job!"

She stood up and slowly walked towards me, a very provocative walk; her hips moving gracefully side to side, her big brown eyes were focused on mine, she didn't blink. She gently put her arms around me and placed her lips against mine. I felt very warm inside, a feeling of utter bliss; I didn't want her to ever stop.

We were in each other's arms for a few minutes. Liz slowly moved her lips from mine, still hugging me. "Do I get to keep my job boss?"

I smiled back at her; "At least for a couple of hours."

Liz chuckled and walked back to the desk and picked up her pad and a pen again.

I carried on; "Have you ever registered a domain name?"

"That's a new one for me."

"Make a note that we have to register domain names and I'll show you how it's done. We will also require a hosting company."

"Liz, I need an hour or so of uninterrupted concentration to write the "To Do" document. Can you start working on the other items?"

"I'll go into the bedroom so as not to disturb you."

"I think it makes more sense for me to go into the bedroom, that way you can use your laptop and the printer if necessary."

Liz smiled and nodded. I went into the bedroom, on the way I couldn't resist giving Liz a kiss, shut the door leaving it slightly ajar; lay on my back on the bed. I shut my eyes and started to format and write the "To Do" document in my mind.

It took me exactly 47 minutes to create a 45 page "To Do" document, slightly over a minute per page. My brain processing power and memory access seemed to be getting faster the more I used it.

I could hear Liz on the phone in the other room. I thought I would take advantage of this alone time and start to work on my speech. This was going to be a lot harder than the "To Do" document, because I didn't have a mental outline of the points I wanted to cover.

I started to make a list of the points, but I kept going around in circles. It was time to take a break and give it another try later.

I got up from the bed and walked into the sitting room. Liz was sitting on the loveseat talking on her cell phone and using the computer simultaneously. She glanced up and gave me a smile; I sat down on the loveseat, and let her continue without interruption. I just watched her in action. She spoke with an air of confidence, reformatted and delivered the same idea or concept in different words when she realized that she was not being understood. Liz impressed me and listening to her conversation gave me an overwhelming sense of pride.

Liz said thanks and disconnected the line with whomever she was speaking with. She sighed and took a big gulp of air and a drink from a bottle of water she had taken from the room bar. She gave me a big smile and squeezed her hand against my thigh; "Some people in this world are definitely brain dead!

"Problems?"

"No, it's just the necessity of having to say the same thing ten times before it sinks in! Would you like an update?"

"I'll take an update in a few minutes. Let me show you how to register the domain names and buy a hosting package." I needed the domain name registered in order to publish an email address in the "To Do" document. Without an email address I couldn't complete the document.

I sat beside Liz; she had her computer on her lap. I gave her the URL for a site I had used in the past to register domain names. Once on the site I instructed her on the registration process. She registered ForHumanity and FORHUM as a .org, .com and .net; for a five year period. We spent a few moments discussing whether to use ForHumanity.org or FORHUM.org as the primary URL. Liz thought that we should use ForHumanity.org as the primary and redirect all the other domain names to it. I registered the .com and .net just to protect the name.

I then provided Liz with a URL for a website hosting company that Elli had found a few years ago. They provided excellent support, down time was minimal and their fees were competitive. We placed an order for hosting services.

We also signed up for a service that provides an incoming fax number, but delivers the faxes by email. I also needed that fax number to add to the "To Do" document.

Liz gave me her puppy dog look; "Are you planning on feeding me?"

It was 7:18; "What would you like to do for dinner?"

"Let's order a nice dinner from room service. I don't want to go out again in the rain and dampness. Then I'll fill you in"

I took the room service menu from the desk and passed it to Liz. I brought up a copy in my mind. Liz made her selection and I called room service and placed the order.

I sat back down on the loveseat, up against her; "What's happening?"

Liz grabbed her note pad; "I spoke to Barbara, she's fine she has been invited to a wedding and needs to buy a new outfit. I told her we would go shopping together."

Visions of a thousand dollar bill for a new outfit flashed through my head! I kept my mouth shut.

"The flight to the Niagara District Airport is scheduled. The airport will make arrangements for customs and immigration clearance.

The helicopter company doesn't have any bookings tomorrow, so they are available at our convenience.

I spoke to Cheryl and she is very excited about having a new job. She wants to be able to offer the Whitehouse two weeks' notice. She thinks that they will ask her to leave immediately. I told her I would get back to her in a few days to confirm."

"Does Cheryl know that the job is in southern Ontario and that she would have to relocate?"

"Yes. Apparently she has just ended a relationship and it wasn't pleasant. A guy she had been dating hid the fact that he was married. She needs a fresh start away from Washington and as I mentioned before she is not happy with her job at the Whitehouse, nothing has changed she still doesn't have any work to do and they are not planning on replacing me."

I pondered for a moment; "Call Cheryl back and offer her the position of administrative assistant. In the beginning it will be a do everything position, until we hire more staff. She may think that some of the assignments are well below her abilities."

"Starting when? What salary? And will we pay her relocation expenses?"

"She can start as soon as she can make herself available. If they ask her to leave, she can start the next day, if they accept the two weeks' notice, then we will wait the two weeks. I hope they ask her to leave immediately. Do you know what she is earning now?"

"I believe it is forty-two thousand dollars."

"What do you think – forty-seven five? A benefit package yet to be defined; overtime pay; hours could be long and there will definitely be a requirement for weekend work especially in the beginning."

"Cheryl is used to long hours and weekend work. I think she would come to work for us for a lot less than that, but I don't want to take advantage of the situation either. But forty-seven five with a benefit package would be more than fair."

"Relocation expenses?"

"Definitely!"

Liz made some notes on her pad.

"I will call Cheryl back later. We have never discussed my remuneration."

"You want to get paid? I thought that just being with me would be sufficient remuneration, not to mention having your hair washed and brushed and then there are the love making sessions, which I get no enjoyment from."

Liz was laughing very hard and could hardly catch her breath; "Well you thought wrong big boy! I want money, cold hard cash. What do you mean you get no enjoyment from our love making sessions?"

I broke out laughing. Laughing is contagious and the harder Liz laughed the harder I laughed and the harder I laughed the harder Liz laughed. Finally we had no more laugh left in either of us.

Liz took a drink of water and tried to compose herself. After a minute or so she continued on with her briefing. "I had to leave a message for Sarah Malthus; she was in a meeting and couldn't be disturbed. I asked them to make sure she called me tonight and they said they would.

"I have prepared an envelope to send to the bank with the check and letter inside; and I have prepared a package of information on the Niagara Airport and the adjacent land.

"I haven't ordered the expense account forms. We need to have a few more items or we will pay a lot for shipping.

"And, I gave you a kiss!"

"It's time for another one."

Liz leaned over and kissed me sticking her tongue down my throat and tickling my tonsils.

"Anything else boss? Oh, there is one more piece of information to impart; I received a message from my Dad to call home when it's convenient. He and Mom want to speak to me!"

I looked at her eyes, she didn't flinch, no sign of any sullenness, she wasn't pale. The great depression was definitely a thing of the past.

Very nonchalantly and with a grin on her face; "I'll call them, probably not tonight, maybe tomorrow."

"Liz. I need to type the "To Do" document so that the translators can start working on it."

"I'll go into the bedroom and call Cheryl before room service arrives. Sarah is bound to callback in the middle of dinner!"

Liz went into the bedroom and I sat in front of my laptop. I brought the "To Do" document up in my mind and proceeded to type it at high speed. I had placed some drawings in the document; these were two dimensional drawings that helped to explain the considerations that should be undertaken when choosing a site for vaporization.

I was always quite good at creating two dimensional drawings. I had actually taken architectural and mechanical drafting classes at the trade high school I went to. It was three dimensional drawings that I had problems with and I couldn't draw anything that required curvy lines and shadowing such as animals and people.

The drawings did slow me down substantially, not as slow as my former speed, but not as fast as I could type words. Overall I was making excellent progress. Liz came out of the bedroom and gave me a thumbs up; "Cheryl has accepted the position. I told her I would put it in writing and email it to her. She said she trusted me and wouldn't wait for the formal offer and would submit her resignation with two weeks' notice in the morning and let me know how they responded." Liz paused to collect her thoughts. "Will, how would you feel about dropping the formality of Cheryl calling me Ms. Montgomery and you Mr. Dafoe?"

"I would prefer to drop the formality, as you put it. I have no problem in Cheryl calling us by our first names."

We were interrupted by a knock at the door, which startled me. My first thought, was who the hell would that be? I had forgotten about the room service order. Liz checked the peephole and then opened the door. It was our dinner; Liz let the waiter in with the food service cart.

While he was pulling out the side leaves, I opened a bottle of very expensive Swiss Burgundy, vintage 2000 that we had purchased the night before.

The waiter left and I seated Liz at the table and poured us each a glass of wine.

Liz raised her wine glass; "To very happy days and better ones yet to come."

For some reason that toast made me smile from ear to ear. It made me feel so good that Liz was happy. "To the most beautiful woman in the world."

Liz blushed as our glasses touched.

We started into our dinners.

"Liz, do you happen to know how the navy flight crew that is at our disposal is compensated for expenses?"

Liz finished chewing on a shrimp and gently dabbed her lips with the napkin. "None."

"I would like to find out. I want them to be properly compensated while they are on call for us. What I'm really saying is that I don't want this to be a hardship assignment for them."

Liz looked up from eating; "That's one of the reasons I love you so much, you are always thinking about others."

At the end of the meal, I topped up our wine glasses. Liz was leaning back in her chair and I could tell from the expression on her face that she was unwinding, when her cell phone rang. Liz looked at me, "it's either Sarah or my parents."

She picked up her phone from beside her side plate and glanced at the screen; "It's Sarah!"

She stood up, picked up her wine glass and headed for the bedroom, I could hear her say; "I know; it's been ages."

I went back to my laptop. I wanted to complete the "To Do" document.

I was just typing the last page, when Liz appeared from the bedroom. I quickly motioned to her to give me a few seconds. She half filled her glass of wine and in so doing emptied the bottle. She took another bottle of the same wine and opened it and topped off her glass; went over to the loveseat and ungraciously plopped herself down. She looked exhausted.

I finished the document; copied it to a flash drive; picked up the room phone and called the UN translation department and told them I had a document to be picked up. I topped up my wine glass and went and sat down next to Liz. Her head was tilted back on the loveseat and her eyes were closed. When I sat down she opened them and smiled at me. "We were reminiscing! She brought back some good and not so good memories."

"Are you okay?"

Liz grabbed my hand. "I'm more okay than I have ever been in my entire life thanks to you! Will, it's not the pill, although that definitely cleared my brain. It's the way you care about me, look after me, talk to me, respect me and most importantly the way you express your love for me with your eyes."

"I could feel my cheeks turn pink and there was a warmth

travelling through my body. "You deserve it all and more!"

Liz gave me a smile that made me melt inside; "Sarah wanted to know a lot of details, but I danced her questions and really told her nothing more than this could be the assignment of her life. It was global and involved a lot of countries, senior government officials and a high percentage of the world's population. She was definitely intrigued. We are meeting her at her club for dinner tomorrow night at eight. She is booking a very small dining room so that we will have complete privacy. I have the address; it's about a twenty minute taxi ride. Have you considered what we are going to tell her?"

"I think we have to tell her everything. She can't really be of any assistance if she doesn't know the whole truth. We will just have her swear to confidentiality until after the meeting of the General Assembly. I thought that we would give her the overview document that I prepared for the Security Council. Could you please remember to print a copy of it tomorrow?"

Liz nodded; she was too mentally exhausted to respond. We sat there for a few minutes, holding hands and not saying anything. There was another knock at the door. I looked through the peephole. It was a girl dressed in a heavy yellow raincoat with a hood and carrying a closed umbrella. I opened the door and the poor girl stood there dripping water all over the carpet. "I'm so sorry that you had to come out in this weather."

The girl looked at me; rain water was dripping from her nose and her eye make-up was smeared. "It's not a problem sir."

"Can I get you a towel?"

"Thank you but it's not necessary."

I handed her the flash drive. She took it and put in a pocket under the raincoat said goodnight and turned towards the elevator.

I really felt bad for her. I shut and bolted the door, turned and looked over at Liz who had been watching me. "Hey boss, can we take the rest of the night off?"

"Sounds like an excellent plan to me."

I put the dishes in the center of the food table, dropped the leaves and wheeled into the hall and sat down beside Liz. Liz leaned over and rested her head against my shoulder, her hand on my thigh. I had been wondering if Liz's earlier comment about remuneration had a note of reality about it and if my inadvertent neglect in approaching the subject was bothering her. "Liz, we will discuss your remuneration tomorrow."

"I was just teasing you. If the truth be known, being with you is all the remuneration I want or need."

"It may be all you want or need, but you deserve to receive a pay check like everyone else."

"Whatever you decide will suit me just fine. Just make sure that any remuneration package you conceive has the benefits of being kissed by you, showering with you, having my hair washed and brushed by you, being spooned by you and a very substantial amount of sexual activity with you. Oh, and one other thing I want unimpeded access to your daughter."

She chuckled. "I can't wait to see how you write it up!" I put my arm around her and pulled her against me. We sat like that for a long time.

It was 10:52; "Liz I think it's time for bed." I took her by the hand and led her into the bedroom turning lights off as we went.

Once in the bedroom Liz sat on the edge of the bed. "I'm too exhausted to even get undressed."

I stood in front of her and undid the buttons on her blouse and took it off her shoulders. "You'll have to stand up." I took her hands in mine and helped her to stand. She wobbled as she stood, half asleep, her eyes barely open. I undid the buttons on her skirt and it dropped to the floor. I turned her around and undid the clasp on her bra and slid it off her arms. I reached around and cupped her firm breasts in my hands, trapping her nipples between my fingers, squeezing them ever so gently. A small uncontrolled moan escaped her lips. I positioned myself on my knees in front of her; I placed my fingers in the band of her panties and pulled her panties down her legs. Then I carefully lowered her silk stockings to the tops of her feet. I lifted one foot slightly so that I could remove her undergarments completely, then the other foot.

Stark naked, I picked her up, she put her arms around my neck and I placed her on the bed, I pulled the covers out from under her and tucked her in giving her a kiss on her forehead. Her eyes were closed but she gave me a smile.

I got undressed, pulled the covers back and climbed in beside her. She was lying on her side facing away from me sound asleep. I put my arm around her waist and was asleep myself in a few minutes.

Chapter 10 – 265 days to alien arrival

I was awoken to the feel of small kisses being delivered all over my face. I opened my eyes. It was 5:13 and still pitch black outside. Liz was leaning over me looking exceptionally radiant. "Your fiancée is incredibly horny! Would you mind very much taking care of her desires?"

I smiled and pulled her towards me. Yah, I minded. I minded having a extremely beautiful lady with a fantastic figure in my arms; I minded the feel of her intoxicating lips against mine, the sensation and taste of her tongue in my mouth; I minded feeling the warmth of her naked body against mine; I minded feeling her hard nipples piercing my chest: I definitely minded the feeling in my loins as I penetrated her and I hated feeling her body quiver against me as we came in unison.

It took us almost two hours to completely satisfy our lust for one another. It's a good thing we started early I thought to myself, we have a busy day ahead.

We performed our usual morning shower ritual, dressed casual; picked up the papers we needed to take with us, checked to make sure we had out passports, took our jackets and went downstairs to the hotel coffee shop for breakfast.

On the way to the coffee shop, I hit the ATM machine for a cash withdrawal.

We had a quick breakfast and had the doorman hail us a taxi and headed off to Newark Airport. When we were reasonably close to the airport Liz gave the taxi driver explicit instructions on where we needed to go. The NASA aircraft was parked on the tarmac at one of the air charter companies that operated out of the airport.

We walked into the reception area and saw two men in Navy uniforms standing close to an exit door. We approached them and introduced ourselves. They led us out to the aircraft, we boarded; one of the pilots closed the door and went into the cockpit to join the other pilot. He didn't shut the door to the cockpit. The individual flying as co-pilot looked over his shoulder and asked if we were ready to go. We replied in the affirmative. He reminded us to fasten our seat belts and a few moments later we were taxing. It took thirteen minutes for us to reach the end of the runway, a few seconds later we were airborne.

Liz and I weren't talking; we were just sitting holding hands. Liz's phone rang. Liz, looked at me, it's Cheryl and then hit the talk button. After some polite hellos and Liz listening for a minute she said "One second, let me ask Will." Liz pushed the mute button on her phone and looked at me; "Cheryl submitted her notice and they asked her to leave immediately, they will pay her for the next two weeks. When do we want her to start?"

"Ask her to pack a bag and head to New York and get a room at our hotel. Make sure she can afford the upfront cost of the air ticket."

Liz went back on the phone and with a little embellishment repeated what I had said to Cheryl. I heard Liz say; "That's perfect, we'll look forward to seeing you and by the way, we're not a government organization, it's not to be Ms. Montgomery and Mr. Dafoe; it's Will and Liz. See you later, Bye."

Liz disconnected and looked back at me. She will try to arrive this evening, but if not tomorrow. She has a credit card that has very little on it, so the flight and hotel won't be a problem."

"That's great."

Liz's phone rang again; "It's Dad. Hi Dad how are you? How's Mom?"

I tuned into the call.

The voice sounded forlorn; "We're both fine, Mom is on the line with me."

"Hi Mom"

The tone of her Mom's voice sure wouldn't have made you feel warm and wooly inside; "Hello Elizabeth; where are you?"

Liz had a smirk on her face; "I'm with Will aboard a NASA jet headed for Ontario, Canada."

Liz's father's voice hadn't changed; "Liz why won't you tell us what is going on. Are you in some sort of trouble?"

The smirk had left Liz's face; "I'm very sorry, but I am involved in a classified project, I can't tell you anything, I've been sworn to secrecy. I promise that by tomorrow afternoon it will all be made very clear to the both of you. I hope once you know what is going on that you will forgive my antics, I was given little choice."

Liz's mother was going to try to obtain some information; "Are you really engaged to a William Dafoe?"

"Yes mother, that part was the whole truth. I am deeply in love with Will and I know he is deeply in love with me and we are engaged to be married. We met on account of this project that we are both involved in."

Liz's father interjected; "Liz your mother and I are sorry for everything, the way we treated you and we will try to be better parents. Whether you believe it or not we have always loved you and still do. Maybe we didn't show it properly, we are both very sorry for that. We can't go backwards and undo what we did, but we want to move forward together with you . . . and Mr. Dafoe. Will you let us remain in your life Elizabeth? I could sense the remorse in his voice and I thought I detected that he was crying.

Liz started to cry; "I only ever wanted you to love me, nothing more and nothing less."

Liz couldn't speak anymore and handed me the phone. "Mr. and Mrs. Montgomery this is Will. Liz can't speak at the moment. We are hoping, pending the demands of this project, to be with you on the 15th and 16th as a family."

I could hear some sniffling from Liz's father, Liz's mother was more composed and her intonation in her voice was compassion, something I hadn't heard in her before; "We are both looking forward to meeting you Mr. Dafoe and to see our daughter again, it has been a long time, too long."

The co-pilot was motioning that we were beginning our descent into Niagara District Airport.

"Mr. and Mrs. Montgomery, I have to disconnect now, we have just been advised that we are starting our descent. Bye for now." I disconnected the phone.

I pulled Liz towards me; it wasn't easy because there were two armrests between us. I gave her the best hug I could under the circumstances and a kiss. "Are you okay?"

Liz had pretty much composed herself; "Yes, I'm fine. Do you know that I don't remember my father or mother ever using the L word before?"

"I think you may have the start of a new relationship with your parents."

"Do you think so, Will; is it possible?"

The planes wheels hit the runway and it took less than two minutes to taxi up to a building that for lack of a better description was the airport terminal.

There was a black sedan with the Canadian Border Agency decal on its door and a young uniformed agent standing next to it.

Liz and I disembarked the aircraft. It was a pleasant day the sun was shining with very few clouds. We were questioned by the agent. We showed her our diplomatic passports and she immediately dropped the third degree. Welcome to Canada; "May I ask how long you intend to stay."

"A couple of hours at most, we're here to look at a piece of property." I pointed in a direction that was obviously wrong. Liz laughed and pointed at a big sign that said property available.

The agent chuckled a little and smiled; "Don't get lost!" Thanked us, got in her car and drove off. I was a little surprised that she didn't want to see any identification from the pilot and co-pilot.

It was 11:42. The pilot and co-pilot disembarked the aircraft and looked around. There was no place for them to get any food or a drink, other than a soda machine. I went over to them; "We will be a couple of hours, can you be back here by two?" I reached into my pocket and pulled out ten - twenty dollar bills that was part of the funds I withdrew earlier from the ATM machine. I stuck my hand out with the cash aimed at the co-pilot. "That's not necessary sir."

"I know it's not necessary, take the money and catch a taxi to a decent place where you can get some lunch. We'll see you back here in a couple of hours." I reached down, grabbed the co-pilots hand and shoved the money into it.

They looked at each other and then at me and together said "Thank you very much sir. First we'll check-in with the airport manager."

I looked around the airport, it was at best rundown. There were a dozen single engine and two twin engine aircraft tied down; they were vintage flying machines.

"Liz, let's walk over to the sign and see what we can see from the ground."

There wasn't much to see, it was a vacant field. It had been plowed under in the fall and it had a lot of ruts from the tractor tires. The ground looked very fertile. A shame to turn it commercial I thought to myself.

I took Liz's hand in mine; "Fancy a ride in a helicopter."

Liz squeezed my hand. We turned and looked at the buildings that made up the airport. We walked back towards the terminal. There was a trailer with a sign offering helicopter rides over Niagara Falls and parked in front of the trailer was an Eco-Star helicopter.

We went up a few steps and inside the trailer. Liz explained that she had spoken to someone yesterday about booking some time on the helicopter to view some property and pointed in the direction of the property sign.

Liz filled out some forms, pulled out her credit card for processing and then we followed the man outside. He asked what we wanted to see and I told him I wanted to view the property from above and take a look at the properties logistics, the roads primarily. He opened the door and Liz and I got in, Liz sat on the far right side and I sat on the far left side. In a few minutes we were floating about 500 feet off the property. The pilot started a narration, he pointed to the access road for the property, told us that it was single lane, paved, no curbs, ditches on both sides, half load weights in the spring and fall. He flew us along the road and showed us how it interfaced to the QEW, the main highway artery in the Niagara Region. Our trailers with the cargo containers would be coming up that highway. He informed me that the trailers would have an easy time at the highway on and off ramps. It was maneuvering into the property that could be difficult. He flew a little higher and pointed out Niagara Falls to Liz.

Liz stared at the falls; "They're magnificent. I've only seen pictures and pictures do not do it justice."

It hadn't entered my head that Liz wouldn't have been to Niagara Falls, that was very neglectful of me and I kicked myself.

I gave Liz some time to absorb the wonderment that only Niagara Falls can deliver. "Where is Niagara-on-the-Lake from here?"

The helicopter pilot repositioned the aircraft and headed south and over the highway. In a minute or two we were flying a circle around it. "Liz, this is the area that I would like us to live in. There are some very stately Victorian style homes."

Liz studied it from above; "Looks lovely."

The pilot circled the town two more times. "Anything else you'd like to see?"

I looked at Liz and she shook her head no and returned to peer out the window.

"No, that's fine, back to the airport."

The helicopter pilot aimed straight for the airport, we were on the ground three minutes later.

The pilot helped Liz out of the aircraft; "If you need to see anything else, just let me know. Are we going to be neighbors?"

"There is a high probability."

He smiled and went back into his trailer.

Liz and I climbed up the stairs of the NASA jet and sat down. It was only 1:37 and the pilots hadn't returned as of yet.

Liz looked at me; "What do you think?"

"I like it. I think it would work very well for us. What do you think?"

Liz pondered and collected her thoughts; "I like the location, but it doesn't have any buildings, which means we will have to construct some ASAP and there isn't any security fencing, two things we were looking for when we talked about an airport property."

Liz was correct, not surprisingly. I originally wanted to look at an airport property because of the buildings and the security. I pondered the situation. I knew I liked the property because of its location. But, on the other hand, all of the decommissioned air bases were dilapidated or environmental disasters. Using a municipal airport would create problems in zoning it as an International area.

I squeezed Liz's hand. "You are right as usual. However, I think, after looking at the alternatives that this property would require less construction then the decommissioned air bases. Secondarily this property doesn't come with a legacy of environmental issues. It would also be ultra convenient for the Federal Government to buy and declare it an International area or zone."

"Liz leaned over and gave me a kiss on the cheek; "You should know that I consider one of my responsibilities, as second in command, to be the devil's advocate. I just wanted to make sure that you could defend your decision to yourself. I happen to agree with your decision."

"Liz, could you call the Prime Minister and tell him that we have viewed the Ontario Government's property that is adjacent to the

Niagara District Airport and we would like him to proceed with its purchase."

"Liz winked at me; "Shall do boss." She took her cell phone from her purse and called the Prime Minister and informed him of our decision. When she disconnected she told me that he had already spoken to the Minister of Public Works and had him standing by. He would call him and tell him to purchase the property ASAP. He also said that he still hadn't figured out how to declare it an International Zone, but he had people working on it. He would keep us abreast of all developments.

"Liz, does Cheryl own a car?"

"She has a BMW 750. She won it in some sort of lottery. It is her pride and joy. Why are you asking?"

"I'm rethinking how we can best use Cheryl. I am considering having her come up here to handle the conversion of the property into an operational facility. What do you think? Can she handle it, under our guidance?"

Liz had an excited tone to her voice; "Cheryl would be the perfect choice."

"This is my thinking. I want to know if you concur. We brief Cheryl in New York and send her back to Washington to get her clothes and other small items, pack them in her car and come up here. She can live in a hotel until she finds suitable accommodation. Once she finds somewhere to live here, she can fly back down to Washington and make arrangements to ship the rest of her belongs and furniture. What do you think?"

"I think she told me that all her furniture is rented from one of those rent-to-own joints. She may be able to get rid of her apartment before she makes her first trip here, avoiding the need to fly back and forth. Will she need a work visa?

"I'm not sure to be honest with you. She will be working for a company in an International Zone, but living in Canada. I think we should get the Prime Minister involved. Let's not say anything to him about Cheryl until after the meeting with the General Assembly. I'll leave that in your hands."

Liz retrieved a small pad from her purse and made a couple of notes.

Just then our two pilots came up the stairs of the aircraft. "Ma'am, Sir"

"Did you find a descent place to have something to eat?"

"Yes Sir we did; thank you again." He went to pass me the money they didn't spend. "Hang on to it until the next time we fly up here, which I believe will be in the next day or so."

"Yes Sir; thank you Sir; Sir have you been listening to the news at all?

"No, why?"

"There is going to be an emergency meeting at the UN tomorrow and they won't say what it's about. It's been called by the Security Council. Every TV channel was interrupting their scheduled programming to announce it. There's all sort of speculation on what it's about. I don't like the sound of it personally, nothing good ever comes out of those meetings."

"Always think the best, is my motto. There is no sense in worrying about something that is completely out of your control."

I squeezed Liz's hand and she squeezed back. These boys were going to be very surprised when they find out our involvement in the UN emergency meeting.

"Yes sir, that's good advice. Are you and the lady ready to return to New York?"

"We are."

The steps were pulled up, door closed and the co-pilot took his seat. In a few minutes we were in the air and headed southeast.

"Liz, do you have a car?"

"My car was stolen from my apartment parking lot about two months after I arrived in Washington and I never replaced it. Public transit is quite good in Washington and the traffic on the roads is dismal at the best of times. The Whitehouse had a group of pool cars that I could use during work. If I needed a car for personal excursions, which was very seldom, I rented one."

Before we knew it we were back on the ground at Newark Liberty airport.

I went to the cockpit to speak with the flight crew. "We will not require your services tomorrow. If you want to go home please do. We will give you at least twelve hours notice of our next flight." They were pleased.

We caught a taxi and went back to the hotel.

It was 4:09 in the afternoon when we opened the door to our hotel room.

I looked at Liz and gave her a crafty smile. "Someone woke me up very early this morning; I don't seem to remember why." She grinned and punched me in the shoulder. "We are going to be up late with Sarah, I suggest we take a nap."

We went into the bedroom, didn't bother to remove our clothes and lay on the bed. We snuggled up against each other, a couple of kisses later we were sleeping.

I had set my mental alarm clock for 6:00 but I was up a few minutes earlier than that. I gave Liz a kiss on the forehead to wake her. I received a smile and kiss on the lips in return. We showered and dressed; business attire for both of us.

At 7:30 we made our way to the lobby and had the hotel doorman hail us a taxi. Liz gave the driver the address for the club.

Liz and I held hands in the back of the taxi. "I would like you to take the lead with Sarah. I don't want you playing the role of administrative assistant. Are you agreeable to that?"

She gave my hand a squeeze and even in the dim lighting in the backseat of a taxi at night, I could see that she was beaming and blushing.

"I would really like to take the lead. I truly appreciate your confidence in me. I'll try not to let you down."

I gave her a kiss on the cheek. "There's no possible way that you could ever let me down!"

We arrived at our destination at 7:57. A doorman greeted us and we entered the club. It was very quiet inside and as I looked around I realized that the place was empty, maybe three people in total. Liz introduced herself to the hostess, who immediately led us down a hall to a ten foot square room.

The room was very tastefully decorated, a flair of the Victorian era. It was decorated with red patterned velvet wallpaper with walnut trim around the doors, there wasn't a window. The ceiling had a crystal chandelier dangling in the center of it. The chandelier provided the only light in the room which was set to dim. There were four brass wall sconces but they were not illuminated. In the center of the room there was a round dining table, with an embossed linen table cloth. The table was set formally. Three high back Victorian style chairs were placed around the table at equal intervals. It was the perfect room if one had a mistress and needed a place for a clandestine rendezvous.

As soon as we entered the room, a woman seated facing the door rose; she quickly walked around the table with outstretched arms; "Elizabeth Montgomery, it is so good to see you."

In my opinion the greeting lacked sincerity. They had a quick hug.

"Sarah I would like you to meet Will Dafoe. Mr. Dafoe this is Sarah Malthus."

We shook hands; "It's a pleasure to meet you Will." Sarah's handshake was much firmer and more robust than you would receive from most men.

She pulled out a business card from I don't know where and handed it to me. I passed it to Liz. I could tell that Sarah didn't like that move. "Do you have a card Will?"

"No, I don't."

Sarah stood five feet, nine and a quarter inches, but was wearing shoes with one and three quarter inch heels. She looked older than Liz; I would have said mid to late forties. It didn't make a lot of sense if they went to school together. Sarah had auburn hair that hung just below her ears. She had a stocky build, with large hips and heavy legs protruded below her skirt. Her clothes were expensive, but she didn't have near the fashion sense Liz had. Her facial features were pleasant but she wore far too much make-up. She was adorned in expensive jewelry. I noted that she wasn't wearing a wedding ring.

Sarah had a big phony smile on her face; "Please have a seat!" She pointed at the chairs."

"Would you like a drink? Elizabeth, I seem to recall you're a Martini girl.

Liz responded with a stern tone to her voice; "Wine will be fine."

"Will what would you like?"

"Wine; thank you Sarah"

Sarah leaned from her chair and pushed a small white button that was on the wall. A moment later a waiter in a tux opened the door. He looked directly at Sarah. "Please bring us a bottle of Châteauneuf-du-Pape." The waiter nodded.

I was a little surprised; first, Châteauneuf-du-Pape is an overrated wine and consumed by people who have little knowledge of wines and buy based on price. Second, to order a bottle of wine without mentioning the vintner or asking about the vintage is a sign that you don't have a clue about wine.

So far, I wasn't impressed with Sarah. But I had a lot of faith and trust in Liz, and I wasn't planning on hiring Sarah as a sommelier.

Liz, glanced at me and then leaned forward in her chair, placing her forearms on the table; "Sarah, can you tell us more about your organization; its size, the type of assignments you have undertaken and your current work load."

I could tell that Sarah was taken aback somewhat by Liz's direct approach. Sarah glanced at me as if to say; why am I talking to Liz and not to you. When she looked back at Liz, her eyes caught site of Liz's engagement ring. Sarah caught herself staring at it and quickly looked at Liz.

Sarah started her canned organization presentation; she delivered it with high level of confidence.

We were interrupted by the waiter who opened and poured the wine. He didn't decant it nor did he provide a sample to Sarah before he poured the three glasses. This place might look good, but it really has no class I thought.

Once the waiter left the room Sarah continued her narration. She covered each of the partners and their backgrounds and named a few big assignments for each of them. She also highlighted a few big projects that she had worked on as the lead. She went into great detail about their methodology on handling assignments. She offered to provide us with references if we desired to verify what she had said.

When Sarah spoke she looked at me more than Liz, she wanted to judge my reaction to the information she was imparting. I tried to keep a nondescript expression, almost to the level of looking completely disinterested and bored. I wanted her to see Liz as the lead.

She paused at that point and looked at her watch. "Would you like to order dinner?

Liz responded in a matter of fact tone; "I don't see why not."

Sarah reached over and pushed the white button again. The waiter appeared almost instantaneously.

Sarah looked at him as he entered the room; "We like to order dinner."

The waiter started a dissertation of the menu, which apparently wasn't in print. He gave us a choice of three appetizers, two salads, two soups and three entries in quick succession. Once he had finished, he looked at Liz. Liz rattled off her choices. He then looked at me; I said that I would have the same. He looked at Sarah and she gave him her order. He didn't take any notes.

Sarah topped up our wine glasses.

"Where was I?" Sarah voiced out loud. "Oh, yes. Our business is crisis oriented, it's feast or famine and while we do have a few clients that consult us on an ongoing basis, most of our assignments emanate from some disaster that has happened or is about to occur. At this time we are not working any major assignments. I would also like to point out that the nature of the beast, crisis management, does not provide us with prep time. We are thrown into the pool to either sink or swim."

Sarah paused when the waiter appeared with our appetizers. As soon as he left, Sarah looked at me; "Any questions?"

I had no intention of responding, but I wanted Liz to ask a question, even if it was mundane in order to direct Sarah to Liz and away from me.

Liz knew what was going on, as I have said before, she is a very bright lady; "Sarah, what if any experience have you had with governments and the UN?"

Damn good question I thought.

Liz and I both started eating our appetizers as Sarah began her answer; "I want to tell you that for some reason, unbeknown to us, we have been branded a Republican organization. It happened years ago and we have not been able to shake it. It makes no sense to us, as we have an equal representation of Democrats and Republicans amongst the partners."

Sarah paused to take a bite of her appetizer.

"We have undertaken assignments for five state governments, all in respect to new legislation aimed at reducing the powers of unions in the civil service. A number of years ago we did some work for the US Department of Energy with respect to a new pipeline that the public was up in arms over. That was the only US Federal project that we have done. We undertook an assignment with the Government of Panama when they announced that they would be widening the Panama Canal. We have never undertaken any assignments from the UN."

Sarah paused for another bit of appetizer. Liz and I had finished ours.

Sarah put a smile on her face; "With what's going on at the UN right now, they could use some crisis management! Every news show and paper is headlining the emergency meeting and trying desperately to provide information that apparently they don't have. From a business point of view, I find the media's quest for sensationalism quite intriguing."

Sarah was just putting the last piece of appetizer in her mouth when the waiter showed up with our entries. He placed them in front of us and cleared the appetizer dishes.

There was silence as we all started eating our entries. The food was nothing special, but I was hungry and ate it. Sarah ate about half of hers, placed her knife and fork across her plate and pushed it slightly away from the edge of the table.

Sarah looked at me; "How can we help you?"

Liz finished chewing and placed her knife and fork across her plate. She dabbed her lips with the napkin. Liz's voice was very firm and business like; "We are a very large part of what is happening at the UN."

Liz paused to see Sarah's reaction. Sarah's mouth was open and her eyes had bulged out of their sockets. Sarah reached for her glass of wine and gulped down what was in the glass, she was trying desperately to regain her composure.

Liz continued, maintaining the business tone; "I won't get into all the details at this time, as it would take us hours. Suffice to say that three months ago an alien civilization threatened to annihilate the human race because of the threat we posed to peace in the galaxy."

Sarah had her eyes glued to Liz's mouth and was listening intently.

"Mr. Dafoe met with the aliens and negotiated a nine month reprieve of sorts and I can tell you that the entire human race will not be annihilated. That being said Mr. Dafoe committed to some undertakings that countries must adhere to in order to avoid having their specific populations annihilated.

Liz stopped for a sip of water. "This compromise or reprieve has some very valuable and exciting benefits for the human race including being supplied with advanced technology and medications to treat some of the world's worst ailments. The UN Security Council has been in meetings with Mr. Dafoe and me since his return and will present the situation to all of the members of the United Nations General Assembly tomorrow at 1:00 p.m. In order to disseminate the technology and medicines to the human race, a non-profit organization has been set-up called "For Humanity". It will operate from a location to be designated as an International Zone in southern Ontario, Canada. Mr. Dafoe is For Humanity's Managing Director and I am the Deputy Managing Director."

Liz paused to collect her thoughts and to allow Sarah to absorb what she had said.

Liz continued; "As you can well imagine, For Humanity, Mr. Dafoe and I, are going to be inundated for requests for information from every media outlet around the globe. We have a lot of work to do over the next nine months, the aliens schedule is very tight and we will not have the time to interact with the media. As well, we expect some flack, from countries and individuals about our choice of Ontario, Canada and the fact that we didn't openly search for a location globally for our primary facility.

Sarah was still listening to Liz intently.

"We want to appoint a crisis management organization as the "go to" for any media information requests and to take a proactive defense of our choice of location and any other matters that may rear their ugly heads. Mr. Dafoe and I discussed the differences between a PR firm and a crisis management organization and we both agree that a PR firm doesn't have the inherent capabilities for this assignment. I thought of you, and we decided to approach you and see what your thoughts are and if this assignment might be of interest to you."

Sarah was noticeably shaken by what Liz had said, her head was down and she was staring at the table top. Sarah raised her head and looked directly at Liz; she had finally realized that Liz was not my secretary that she was a key player; "Elizabeth, thank you for thinking of me. I am still trying to grasp everything you said. It's not every day that someone tells you that civilization may cease to exist. I am very excited to think that I might be a small part of this historic event. I believe that Davis, Malthus and Associates are quite capable of undertaking this assignment and in doing so provide you with the media barrier you desire."

Sarah was a salesperson; "What happens next?"

We were interrupted by the waiter asking us if we wanted desert. We all declined. He picked up the entrée dishes and left the room.

Liz didn't even glance at me for a facial approval; "Mr. Dafoe and I would like to go for a walk. We won't be too long, would you mind waiting for us here?

"I can leave you alone here if you would like and go sit in the bar area, you can come and get me when you're ready."

"Actually we would prefer to go for a walk and get some fresh air."

Liz had read my mind, I wanted a cigarette too.

We stood-up and walked down the corridor to the front door and out on to the sidewalk, we walked a few paces from the front door and simultaneously reached for our cigarettes and lit up.

Liz bumped into my shoulder; "I enjoyed that; I think I took her pompous ass down a few notches!"

I laughed; "You certainly did."

Liz relaxed for a second; "What do you think Will?"

"I'd prefer to hear what you think."

Liz paused to collect her thoughts; "I think it's highly probably that her pompous ass makes her very good at what she does. I don't know how one determines which crisis management organization is better than another. I think they're qualified; they had a good rep with the Department of Commerce and I know they have taken on some significant corporate scandals."

Liz paused to take a puff of her cigarette.

"There is another advantage in using Sarah. She is aware of my background, my previous bouts of depression. The press is bound to find out and it won't come as a surprise to her. As well, she may want to take a proactive approach to it and it saves me from having to go through it with someone else. I also think we should tell her that we're engaged. My vote is that we give her the assignment."

"I agree, you can inform her of your decision. Tell her we would like to meet with her after the meeting with the General Assembly has been adjourned. We don't know what time that will be, so she will have to remain on standby at the hotel, but 3:00 p.m. would be the earliest we would be there. We will arrange for a small meeting room at the hotel under "For Humanity", she can bring others if she so desires.

Liz smiled and nodded.

I bumped her shoulder this time; "Let's walk around the block and make her think that the decision is a difficult one."

Liz gave me a big smile; "Let her sweat a little!" She bumped my shoulder again.

We walked down the street to a set of stop lights, crossed and walked back towards the club on the opposite side of the street and passed the club, crossed at another set of lights and walked back to the club, finishing another cigarette.

We were gone for 32 minutes.

Sarah was waiting for us in the bar; I could tell by the empty glasses and three tonic bottles that she was on her third hard liquor drink. I suspected it was gin and tonic. She immediately jumped up when she saw us enter. Sarah started to walk towards the dining room when Liz stopped her.

"Why don't we just sit over there for a minute?" Liz pointed to a small table with chairs; there was no one else in the bar, except for the bartender and we would be far enough away that he wouldn't be able to overhear our conversation.

Once we were seated Liz immediately went into action. Liz told Sarah that we would give her and her organization the assignment. She told her to meet us at the hotel in a meeting room that would be prearranged and gave her the time frame, and that she could bring additional staff. She handed Sarah a copy of the Overview Document that I had produced for the members of the Security Council and told her we would have additional documents tomorrow.

Sarah was trying to keep her business demeanor face, but it was obvious from her voice that she was really excited about this opportunity. "Thank you very much, I, we won't let you down."

It was 11:27 and it had been a long day. Liz started to slow down, I could tell she was getting tired; "Sarah, this must remain highly confidential until after the meeting with the UN General Assembly has taken place. You should also be aware that Mr. Dafoe and I are engaged to be married. The Security Council was made aware before I was named Deputy Managing Director of For Humanity."

Sarah looked at me and then at Liz. "Congratulations to the both of you." Her voice actually sounded genuine.

Liz as she began to stand looked at Sarah; "We have a very busy day ahead of us. We will see you tomorrow." Sarah stuck out her hand and I shook it. She hugged Liz. "Thank you again, I will be there tomorrow."

We went to the door and asked the doorman to hail us a taxi. I noticed that Sarah had gone to the bar and the bartender was making her another drink.

Chapter 11 – 264 days to alien arrival

It was 12:02 a.m. by the time we got back to the hotel room. Liz and I hadn't said a lot to each other in the taxi, we were both far too mentally fatigued to speak.

The message lamp on the phone was flashing. I looked at Liz; she pulled her cell phone from her purse. "Damn, I forgot to turn it on after the meeting with Sarah. I have a message from Cheryl."

"I wouldn't be surprised if she left us a message here as well."

Liz hit her message button at the same instant I hit the room phone message button. The room phone message system was louder: "Message received at 8:41 p.m." "Ms. Montgomery, sorry Liz, I'm in the hotel, room 1215; give me a call when you get the message."

The message on Liz's cell phone was very similar.

Liz gave me a questioning look; It's after twelve should I call her?

"I would, under the circumstances, I doubt if she is sleeping."

Liz went over to the room phone and hit 1, 2, 1, 5; on the keypad. There couldn't have been more than one ring in Cheryl's room when she answered. "Cheryl it's Liz; I'm so sorry for calling so late, I hope I didn't wake you. . . I understand. . . Will and I have a 9:00 a.m. meeting at the UN tomorrow and then we will be attending the meeting with the General Assembly. Can you meet us at 7:30 in the coffee shop for breakfast? . . . Try and get some sleep. . . Good Night."

Liz looked at me sheepishly; "I didn't want Cheryl to sit around all day without speaking with her."

"That's fine darling, I agree whole hardily. I need a glass of good wine, would you like some?"

"Yes please."

We drank the wine relatively quickly and headed for the bedroom where we got undressed and climbed into bed, I set my mental alarm clock for 6:00. I pulled Liz against me in spoon fashion; "We will have to get up in a few hours." Liz pulled my hand up from around her waist and brought it tight around her, the side of my hand was tucked up against her breast. She pushed her back against me and snuggled up against me as if I was a duvet. We were both fast asleep in a couple of minutes.

My mental alarm clock went off preciously at 6:00. I was surprised when I realized Liz wasn't in bed, I tilted my head up and saw her wearing one of the bathrobes looking at my suits, shirts and ties. When she saw I was awake, she came to the edge of the bed; "Good morning my love." And then gave me a very sweat kiss.

"You showered without me!"

Liz walked back to the closet. "Yes, we have time constraints this morning. I'll make it up to you later. I'm picking your wardrobe out for today. Go shower darling."

This was the first time since my return that I would be showering without Liz, what a bummer, I thought. I hoped this wasn't a sign of how the rest of the day would go.

I did as I was instructed and went into the bathroom and showered. When I came out of the shower stall Liz was standing there, she had a towel in her hand and started drying me, when she was finished she handed me the other bathrobe. "Sit down at the vanity!"

I sat down in the chair that Liz usually occupied. Liz took the comb from the vanity countertop and combed my hair. She then picked up a pair of scissors. She caught my questioning look in the reflection in the mirror. "I'm going to trim your hair."

Liz didn't wait for a reply or comments. She commenced trimming my side burns and some long hair that was covering the tops of my ears. Comb scissors, scissors, comb. She would look in the mirror and trim a little more.

"Turn and look at me." Liz studied her handiwork. "That's much better." She had a sense of pride in her voice, a job well done.

"Where did you learn to do that?"

Liz had a big smile on her face; "I've never done it before, trim a man's hair. I wouldn't want to try to give you a complete haircut, but I only trimmed a few hairs that were out of place or too long."

"Come here and I'll give you a tip for your excellent work." Liz bent over and I kissed her long and hard.

"Go get dressed while I put on my make-up."

It was 7:03. My clothes were laid out neatly on the bed; suit, shirt, tie, underwear, socks, cufflinks, belt.

I let my bathrobe drop to the floor and had just put my underwear on when the phone rang. I went to the extension on the night table and answered.

"Hello!"

"Mr. Dafoe?"

"Speaking"

"My name is Kyle Armstrong; I'm head of security for the UN. There's a media frenzy underway in front of the UN facility that extends way past your hotel. Prime Minister Harmon called me a little while ago. He is concerned for your safety as well as Ms. Montgomery."

I wasn't at all concerned about my safety; I knew I was protected by the aliens. But Liz's safety was another matter.

"The hotel is secure; there are a number of New York police, FBI and Homeland Security agents there providing protection for foreign diplomats, you and Ms. Montgomery. The challenge is to get you and Ms. Montgomery from the hotel to the UN complex safely and unimpeded."

"We have faced media frenzies in the past, not quite at this level, but we have a method to move the two of you safely from the hotel to the UN complex. Known only to a few, there is a tunnel from the hotel to the UN complex. At 8:50 this morning, four of my top security people will come to your room to collect you and Ms. Montgomery. They will escort you through the tunnel and then to the Security Council meeting room. Is that acceptable to you Mr. Dafoe?"

"Thank you Mr. Armstrong, I appreciate your concern and actions. Ms. Montgomery and I will be waiting in the room for your security people at 8:50."

"Good!" the line was disconnected.

Liz, came out of the bathroom, she looked fantastic; "What's up?"

"Potential security problem, due to the media. It's under control, but we need to make a change to our planned meeting with Cheryl." I picked up the phone and dialled Cheryl's room and told her that there was a small change in plans, we would have breakfast together in our room."

I put my socks, pants and shirt on. There was something I had to do right now, that I should have done days ago.

I went to the suitcase I had retrieved from my container and reached into the side pocket. There was a small case, I opened it. Inside was a device about half the size of a cigarette box. There was a moulded side piece on one side that would fit preciously in my ear. I stood up and placed the ear piece in my ear. The device was extremely light weight.

Liz was standing by the bedroom door watching me. "What are you doing?"

I'm calling the aliens. I went and sat in the desk chair. I put a finger to my lips signalling Liz not to talk. I could only communicate with the aliens via mental telepathy. But I could only use my skills over short distances, about 50 feet under the best of circumstances. The device that I had placed in my ear was a brain wave amplifier and transmitter plus receiver. It would allow me to communicate with the aliens aboard the spacecraft that was circling earth. I closed my eyes and wrote the aliens a message in my brain. I concentrated on the message to the total exclusion of everything else.

I felt like I had been concentrating for hours, but it was only fifteen seconds when my brain heard; "Message received and implemented."

My head slumped forward, I was totally exhausted. Liz ran over to me, and held my head in her hands; "Are you okay darling?"

"Water please."

Liz literally ran to the bar fridge and grabbed a bottle of water, popped the cap and handed it to me. I put the top of the bottle in my mouth and chugalugged it all. I carefully removed the ear piece.

Liz was upset and scared; "Are you going to explain what just happened."

I reached over the desk and picked up my cigarettes, lit one and took a big drag. "Liz, don't be upset I'm fine, just mentally drained. I will explain the details later. For now you should be aware that there is an alien spacecraft circling earth. It has been there since I arrived. Its only mandate is to protect me. It took action when I landed when some hot head with Homeland security took a shot at me. Before I started my journey home the extraterrestrials provided me with a device that would allow me to communicate with the aliens aboard the spacecraft. I was told that if I required anything I was to contact them. I required something so I contacted them. I should have arranged it before I arrived back."

"What did you require, that was so god awful important?"

"I requested that you and Barbara are provided the same protection that they are providing me. They immediately acknowledged that they would."

Liz bent over me and gave me a tender kiss, she backed away and in a very stern voice; "Don't you ever scare me like that again!"

I sat there for a couple of minutes and finished my cigarette. Liz had already gone into the bedroom to finish dressing. I went to the bedroom and put my tie and suit jacket on.

At preciously 7:30 there was a knock on the door. A little paranoid after the conversation with Armstrong, I looked through the peephole. However, as expected it was Cheryl.

I opened the door; Cheryl had a huge smile on her face. Cheryl extended her hand; Good morning Mr... Will, old habits die hard!

Cheryl was dressed business casual; dark blue pants, flowery blouse, low healed light blue shoes and no noticeable makeup.

"Come in and have a seat. What would you like for breakfast? I passed her the room service menu. She didn't even open it. "I'm not a big breakfast eater. I'll just have orange juice, toast and coffee."

I picked up the room phone and called room service and placed a breakfast order.

Liz popped out of the bedroom; "Good morning Cheryl, I hope you slept well?"

"Good Morning Liz, I did, but I got up early and was going to go for a run, but when I got to the lobby I realized that I was in the midst of utter mayhem so I went to the gym on the second floor instead."

"Liz, why don't you tell Cheryl what's going on and what her first assignment will be."

Liz motioned Cheryl over to the loveseat and pulled up an occasional chair in front of her. Liz lit a cigarette, I sat by the desk with half an ear tuned to Liz but primarily thinking about the speech, I would have to make in a few hours. I lit another cigarette.

I glanced over to Liz and Cheryl, Liz was talking and Cheryl was totally engrossed in what she was saying.

It was 7:50 when room service arrived. Liz and Cheryl walked over to the table. Cheryl's orange juice and toast were at the end of the table. It wasn't an overly comfortable spot, so she picked them up and placed them on the desk and turned her chair so she could face the table.

I had ordered the usual from room service Eggs Benedick for Liz and me. I looked at Liz; "Did you mention the meeting room to Cheryl?"

Cheryl had a bit of rye toast in her mouth, but managed to say; "I'll take care of it as soon as you leave."

Liz interjected, with some food in her mouth; "I asked Cheryl to be at the meeting with Sarah."

I nodded my concurrence.

"Will, Liz I wants you to know that I have some experience with construction projects. My first job was as an assistant, well if truth be known a gofer, for a construction company superintendent. I can read a set of building plans. I am familiar with RFQs, bidding, scheduling trades, time lines, work permits, inspections, working with architects and most importantly getting coffee."

Cheryl chuckled at her own joke.

"We've lucked out."

"I take it you don't have any major problems in relocating to Canada?"

"None at all, I am actually looking forward to the peacefulness of small town living again. I grew up in a small town in Idaho; population was about three thousand people. My father is a farmer and he is the son of a farmer."

"I'm sorry that we are going to have to leave you alone for the morning."

"Liz has given me a stack of information to read and I'll go online and see what accommodation I can find in the area."

Cheryl paused to collect her thoughts; "Liz, Will I want to thank you so much for giving me this awesome opportunity and for believing in me. I promise that I will give you one hundred and ten percent." Her voice was choking up.

I mentally checked the time it was 8:45. Our escorts would be here in five minutes. I finished my coffee. I looked at Liz; "Are you ready?"

"As ready as I'll ever be."

There was a knock at the door. I checked the peephole; I could see the faces of two individuals in grey police style uniforms.

I opened the door.

"Mr. Dafoe, we're here to escort you to the UN." They had

handguns in holsters on their waists. I held the door open for Liz and followed her out the door, leaving Cheryl behind. Once I could see down the corridor, I saw another security officer standing at the far end of the hall just below an exit sign, and a forth officer standing about two thirds of the way down the hall. The second two officers not only had handguns but they had assault rifles as well.

One officer at the door told Liz and I to follow him, the other officer was behind us. We walked briskly toward the officer that was two thirds of the way down the corridor. I glanced behind me, and the officer who was previously at the exit sign had moved in beside the officer who was behind us. We reached the officer in the corridor and he opened a corridor door, the sign on the door read; "Hotel Staff Only" he went in followed by the first officer, Liz and I and the two officers behind us. We were led to a freight elevator. One of the officers pushed B2 and the elevator started its decent. The door opened and I could tell we were in the bowels of the hotel. We were guided along another corridor with cinder block walls and bare light bulbs in porcelain ceiling fixtures. At the end of that corridor we made a left and walked some more. We came to the end of that corridor; there was a door with a keypad mounted on the wall. The lead officer keyed in a code and opened the door. The six of us were soon walking in a tunnel with a curved roof and relatively low lighting. We walked two hundred and seventy six yards and came to another door with keypad security access. It was opened for us, and there was a small foyer with a set of stairs going up. We went up the stairs, through a couple of doors and ended up in a hallway which I immediately recognized as the hallway Liz and I walked to get to the patio. It was only twenty feet from the entrance to the Security Council meeting room.

I turned and thanked the officers. They turned and hurried off. Liz and I walked into the meeting room. It was 8.59.

Liz and I looked around only half of the delegates had arrived. Liz bumped my shoulder to get my attention; "I'm going to go speak with Ambassador Middleton."

I decided to sit at the table and work a little more on my speech.

It was 9:31 when Prime Minister Harmon, entered the room. Those who weren't already seated took their places. "I apologize for being late. My meeting with the Secretary General to bring him up to speed took substantially longer than I expected.

"You should be aware that Secretary General Owusu was very

angry that we did not advise him and involve him in our deliberations with the crisis when it originated. I expect that he will make formal complaints to our governments.

"I would like to call the meeting to order.

"It would appear that every news network in the world has sent at least one crew and some have sent three and four and there must be at least a hundred independent paparazzi snapping photos of everyone and everything.

"I want to keep this meeting very informal. If you have anything to present, please do so, there is no real agenda for today's meeting.

"Are there any items that anyone wishes to cover?"

Liz looked at me then at the Prime Minister; "Mr. Prime Minister we have contracted with a crisis management firm. Anyone in this room is more than welcome to utilize their services. We are going to use them specifically to keep the media from assailing us and for providing overall public relations. The company is Davis, Malthus and Associates; the lead partner is Sarah Malthus. I have made copies of her business card for each delegate and will pass them around." Liz reached into her purse and pulled out a stack of half sheets of paper and passed them to Ambassador Lucus, representing South Africa, who was seated to her right, he took the top copy and passed the stack of copies along.

"We are meeting with Davis, Malthus and Associates this afternoon to give them the details of the situation, so they won't be ready to respond to the media until late this afternoon or early evening."

Prime Minister Harmon responded; "Thank you Ms. Montgomery."

Ambassador Kaddur the Moroccan representative spoke; "Mr. Dafoe will you be providing us with more pictures from your trip? I think everyone would like to see more of what the extraterrestrial world's look like."

"Definitely Ambassador! I took more than 6,500 pictures. Due to my lack of photography skills, duplicates and pictures of my finger; I would guess there are 5,000 or so reasonable quality pictures. I will be releasing them all. However, I must put captions on them or they have little if any meaning. That will take some time. I will release them in yet to be defined batches."

Some of the delegates chuckled.

Ambassador Middleton interjected. "What about the story of your visit?"

"I am hoping to write a number of books, with the help of a ghost writer, the proceeds of which would go to FORHUM, detailing my exploits. There is of course the account of the meetings that took place to negotiate with the aliens. I was there for three years and during that time there were incidents that were humorous, others that were very serious and others that I believe are heartwarming. I also believe that it's important to provide a chronicle of the alien societies. But most important of all is a story that relates to our history, the history of civilization on earth as we know it today. It played an important role in the negotiations, one that I had not expected.

Mr. Prime Minister, if we have time now, I would like to speak about it."

The Prime Minister glanced at his watch, it was 10:17. "I believe we have the time, does anyone object?"

None of the representatives voiced an objection.

"Please carry on Mr. Dafoe."

"Mr. Prime Minister, delegates; I believe that this information should be treated as highly confidential at this time; not to be released until after we have complied with the terms of the agreement.

"Approximately eighteen thousand years ago, the governments of fourteen planets came together to form the Group of Inhabited Planets. The initial mandate of the group was to expand trade, including tourism between the fourteen planets, to share technologies and to jointly explore the galaxy. It is basically the same scenario that we have as countries here on earth. We are constantly trying to enhance trade and tourism between countries, sell our technologies to each other and with the international space station as an example, jointly explore outer space.

"Three thousand years after the initial formation of the Group of Inhabited Planets it had grown to twenty-six planets. At that time, crime levels on the planets were very similar to what we currently experience here on earth. Jails were full and all of the planets were experiencing major incarceration funding problems. As well, they realized that more than eighty percent of all crime was committed by those who had criminal records.

"In their wisdom and I say that facetiously they decided to jointly find a planet that they could use as a penal colony; in the same manner

281

that the United Kingdom created a penal colony on Australia in the eighteenth century.

"To make a long story short they chose earth to become the penal colony for the members of the Group of Inhabited Planets. Over a period of three hundred and fifty years, the twenty-six planets transported over thirty million hardened criminals, men and women to planet earth. Each criminal that was sent to the penal colony on earth was provided six months of food, plant seeds, live stock and some primitive hunting weapons and some basic hand tools.

"Each of the twenty-six planets was assigned a different location on earth for their penal colony."

I paused and poured myself some water.

"That is the basis for the different characteristics of humans on this planet in different regions of the globe.

All of the delegates started to talk amongst themselves, some shaking their heads in disbelief.

I paused for another drink of water and then carried on; talking above the delegate chatter. "The transportation of criminals to a penal colony was stopped when the Group of Inhabited Planets developed methods and techniques to truly rehabilitate 99.99 percent of criminals so that they would not offend again. They had also developed techniques to detect the potential of criminal behavior in someone and correct it before crimes were committed.

"Crime on any of the Group of Inhabited Planets today is negligible. One group of aliens actually apologized to me because their crime rate had increased last year. This planet has a population of sixteen billion beings and they were apologizing because last year they had eight murders, fifteen assaults, and twenty-three robberies.

"I'm sorry I digressed. I learned about the penal colonies from an alien friend that I made on the transport ship that took me to the planet where the Council meets. I managed to bring it up during the negotiations and quickly realized that The Council of the Group of Inhabited Planets believed that they were somewhat responsible for the current human experience; that populating the planet with beings that had a predisposition or mindset for criminal activity may be one of the key factors in our overwhelming desire to dominate others. As part of my negotiations I was able to key into this guilt and leverage it to our benefit."

"After a minute or so, the Prime Minister spoke, I could tell by the sound of his voice that he was shaken by what I had just articulated. "Mr. Dafoe, what you have just told us changes human history dramatically. I think you are right when you suggest that we don't mention it until after we have complied with the terms of the agreement. It is the type of news that could cause great civil unrest. I think this is a good time for a break."

The Prime Minister glanced at his watch. "Its 10:20 let's reconvene at 10:35.

The delegates immediately started chattering with one another.

Liz and I decided to see if the patio was available for a cigarette. As we walked to the door Prime Minister Harmon intercepted us. We shook hands, then he shook Liz's hand, he looked at me with wonderment; "I didn't expect that."

He paused to collect his thoughts; "I spoke to the Minister of Public Works, he has spoken to someone in the Ontario government and they have concluded a verbal agreement for the Federal Government to purchase the land adjacent to the Niagara District Airport. Appropriate paperwork must be done and he informed me that it could take two to three weeks to complete it. He has made it a priority and apparently the Ontario government wants to get rid of the property sooner than later so they have agreed to make it a priority. The Minister advised me that there is no reason you cannot consider the property to be yours and may proceed with any enhancements it may require for your purposes. Once Public Works has ownership they will work out a formal lease agreement with you.

Secondarily, declaring it an International Zone is handled by Public Works, it's only a property designation with some tax implications. I am supposed to receive the name of someone in the government who will be able to advise you on the implications of being in an International Zone. I will forward it to you as soon as I receive it."

"Thank you Prime Minister; "I hate to bring up another matter that I need some help with."

The Prime Minister smiled, "I am here to serve!"

Liz chuckled.

"Mr. Prime Minister; we will need some immigration council. I am a bit confused about the employment status within an International Zone as it relates to visas. Does Liz need a work visa or some other document so that she can go back and forth across the border without being challenged? I'm also pretty confident that we will be hiring other foreigners to work for FORHUM and I need to know what immigration problems I may face or what paperwork needs to be filled out."

"I don't know the answer to that question off the top of my head, but I will get you a contact in immigration, after our meeting today. Should you run into any roadblocks, please contact me and I will have them removed."

"Thank you Mr. Prime Minister."

The Prime Minister smiled and walked away, Liz and I made a beeline to the door and walked down the hall towards the patio. There were two well armed security officers at the door.

I looked at one of them with a pleading expression on my face; "Can we go out for a cigarette?"

"The patio is secure at this time. Please stand relatively close to the door, just in case."

He opened the door and let us out; we both pulled out our cigarettes and lit up.

Liz looked at me. I thought she looked upset; "There is a lot you haven't shared with me."

"Liz, please forgive me, there is so much I want to tell you, it has just been a lack of time."

"I know that darling, I'm just being difficult." Her face had a smile on it and she leaned into me and gave me a smoky kiss."

We put our cigarettes out and went back into the meeting room and sat down.

Prime Minister Harmon called the meeting back to order. "Ambassador Dardaza would like to ask a question."

"Mr. Dafoe can you tell us anything about the religious beliefs of the extraterrestrials?"

"Mr. Ambassador, I can only really speak for four of the fifty-seven planets. I am a salesman and one of the first things you learn is that you never discuss religion. What I am about to impart, is based on what I believe to be the case, primarily through osmosis, on the four planets that I visited. I do believe it applies to all fifty-seven planets, but I don't have concrete evidence to support that.

The extraterrestrials don't have formal religions as we do on earth. They believe in what I'm calling a dormant deity. Let me try to explain what I mean. They have no scientific justification for the elements that originally created the universe. Scientifically they have evidence to support the big-bang theory, whereby the universe originated seventeen billion years ago from the cataclysmic explosion of a small volume of matter at extremely high density and temperature. The problem is that they have no explanation for where this small volume of matter came from.

Their belief is that a deity created the small volume of high density matter, but that is where their belief in a deity ends. They believe in the scientific evidence that everything else came to be by chance or evolution, that no deity had any involvement; hence my terminology of a dormant deity. They don't worship anything in the religious sense and they don't pray. The only way I can describe their beliefs and how they are practiced is to liken it to Buddhism and Zen meditation although there is no formal religion nor is the meditation done in groups or at special locations, a family may meditate at the same time and if you go to a park you may see numerous people meditating, but they are not meditating together; if that makes any sense. The extraterrestrials are very much at piece with themselves."

"Thank you Mr. Dafoe, I believe I understand their beliefs even if I don't agree with them."

That response made the hair on the back of my neck standup and I wasn't going to let this arrogant, self-important civil servant get away with it. "With all due respect Mr. Ambassador, that is one of the biggest problems with the human race. We need to provide an opinion on the beliefs of others. There is absolutely no need for you or anybody else to agree of disagree with their beliefs. Why can't you just respect that those are their beliefs? The instant you voiced an opinion you are creating a conflict; a totally unnecessary conflict.

Can't you see that you are confirming exactly what the aliens have implied since first contacting us? We want conflict; we knowingly create it without any thought."

Everyone was looking at me. It was only the second time that I had raised my voice in any of the meetings with the Security Council. Liz squeezed my thigh indicating that I needed to simmer down. The first time I apologized, I had no intentions of apologizing this time.

I looked around the delegates and caught the eyes of Ambassador Balabanov, he had a big smile on his face and gave me a small nod. Apparently he for one appreciated my response to the Pakistani Ambassador.

Ambassador Zhang Wei interjected; "Mr. Dafoe, are there other technologies available from the aliens?"

"The simple answer is yes. However, I believe we have to be very cautious on the technologies that we take primarily for global economic reasons. The aliens offered to supply me with technology that would completely negate the use of carbon based fuels in vehicles of any size, ships and trains. It would be based on the technology that we will be using to replace our nuclear generators. On vehicles, a small solar panel approximately ten inches by six inches would be mounted on the trunk lid, roof or hood of the vehicle."

I looked over at Ambassador Middleton with a grin; "That's boot and bonnet for those of us from across the pond!"

Ambassador Middleton laughed.

"These solar systems would supply and store more than sufficient energy to drive an electric motor. The vehicle would never need fuel. The problem as I see it is, if we announced today that there was no longer any need for fossil fuel as an energy source, it would create a global economic crisis the likes we have never experienced before. The aliens wanted me to take the technology in order to help keep our atmosphere free from the contaminants generated by burning fossil fuels, especially since they will be cleaning the atmosphere for us.

The same technology could be used to directly provide unlimited electrical energy to homes, factories and commercial buildings. Utilities around the globe would be out of business in a few years. Unemployment would skyrocket.

If the members of the Security Council disagree with my evaluation of the economics of this new technology; I would be pleased to reverse my decision and request that the aliens provide us with the technology."

Ambassador Zhang Wei responded as soon as I finished speaking; "Mr. Dafoe I agree with your evaluation of the economic calamity that this new technology would have on the economy of earth. I do believe however that we should try to find a way to implement this technology without creating an economic crisis.

Mr. Prime Minister may I respectfully suggest that a committee of senior economic advisors representing the industrialized and oil producing nations be formed to see if they can find a solution to this dilemma?"

Before the Prime Minister could respond Vice President Almont took the floor; "Mr. Prime Minister, I agree with Mr. Dafoe's evaluation of the situation and I agree with Ambassador Zhang Wei that we must find a way to utilize this technology without creating a global economic crisis."

Ambassador Middleton spoke; "Mr. Prime Minister, I support the formation of a committee!"

I glanced around the table and everyone was nodding their accord.

After some contemplation the Prime Minister responded. "I said at the beginning of this meeting that we should keep it informal and I believe that all of us here, because of what we have been through over the last 100 days or so have developed a close working relationship and a bond that allows us to speak freely without concern for diplomacy."

The Prime Minister paused and took a drink of water.

"Please bear that in mind when I say that I hate committees. They have meetings to set the place and date for another meeting. The politics and personal agendas of the individuals involved in the committee overshadow the need to find a solution and when they do finally issue a report it so full of ifs ands or buts that it is impossible to actually implement any of the couched in "it's not our fault" rhetoric.

Please don't misunderstand; I agree with Mr. Dafoe's evaluation and judgment, there is no doubt in my mind that accepting the technology without being prepared for its impact would create economic disaster around the world. Just at this table alone, Canada and the Russian Federation would lose tens if not hundreds of thousands of jobs, literally overnight.

I'm sorry to say that I don't have an answer, but I don't believe a committee will help."

I thought entered my mind; "Mr. Prime Minister I may have a solution."

The Prime Minister had a very frustrated look; "Mr. Dafoe, please proceed."

"Let me first say, that I am sorry I didn't think of this when I was with the extraterrestrials and while I have a concept in my mind, I don't have all the details worked out. Although we have never discussed it, there will be some economic impact when the nuclear generators are replaced with the solar collector systems. My feeling is that a percentage of the workers will be redeployed by their utilities. But I am reasonably confident that some layoffs will occur, probably in the mining industry and in industries that support nuclear power plants. However, I don't believe that it will create a huge bump in unemployment statistics.

The impact of any new technology is relevant to how quick it is implemented. Let me try to be more definitive. If we were to announce that all vehicles, ships, houses, factories and commercial buildings would no longer require any type of fossil fuel or require any connection to the electrical grid or natural gas lines, it would create a global economic meltdown. However, if we were to release the technology slowly in bits and pieces I don't believe the impact would be evident. As an example, if we said a year from now, that we would be able to equip all commercial ships with the new technology the impact would only be to manufactures of ship board fossil fuel engines. However that would be offset by the requirement for new electrics, installation facilities, repair and maintenance, even colleges would have to supply courses on the new technology. Please bear with me. Then a year or two after that, depending on the economic impact that occurred with the ships, we release a unit that is for trains and a couple of years later we release a unit for large commercial buildings and factories. In other words, we feed the technology into the market place at a slow controlled rate, a rate that the economy can absorb. We have faced changes in technology in the past. Thousands of clerical positions were eliminated by computers, but the first ones were at large corporations that used main frames. Then came mini-computers and medium size companies could utilize them and more clerical positions were lost. Now every company has a computer. The same situation has occurred with cell phones, they are slowly eliminating the infrastructure necessary to support land line communications. Years ago cloth was weaved by hand and glass was hand blown. In other words, we introduce smaller solutions over an extended period of time."

Ambassador Balabanov interrupted; "Please excuse my interruption, I understand what you are saying, but what would prevent a private company from releasing all of the solutions at the same time?"

"Mr. Ambassador, we, being FORHAM, control the key material for the solar units, the element Xanfor, the solar systems cannot be produced without it."

"My apologizes Mr. Dafoe, It had slipped my mind."

The Prime Minister had lost the frustrated looked and actually appeared rejuvenated. "Does anyone have any other comments or questions?

Ambassador Zhang Wei stood; "I think Mr. Dafoe has come-up with an excellent concept, I am continued to be impressed with his wisdom and sharp mind across many subjects, now he appears to be an expert in global economics." He gave Liz a big smile. "Of course I fully realize that behind every great man is an even greater woman!" I looked at Liz, she was blushing.

Ambassador Zhang Wei continued to stand and then he started applauding; the rest of the delegates, including the Prime Minister stood and started to applaud. I was pretty sure that the applause was for me, but I thought I owed Liz one. So I stood up and looked at Liz and started applauding. When I did, the applause doubled in loudness. Liz had turned beat red.

The delegates began to sit, the applauding ended. I sat down and felt five sharp nails dig into my thigh.

Ambassador Zhang Wei remained standing; "Mr. Prime Minister may I suggest that we accept Mr. Dafoe's concept and allow him to proceed with an implementation plan. He can present the plan to the Board of Directors whenever he is ready. Should we disagree with the timing, as the Board of Directors of For Humanity, we can revisit the situation at that time."

The Prime Minister didn't hesitate; "All in favor?"

I scanned the table; all but one of the hands was raised; Ambassador Dardaza from Pakistan.

"All opposed?"

Ambassador Dardaza raised his hand. Ambassador Zhang Wei looked at Ambassador Dardaza and shook his head in disbelief.

"The motion is carried thirteen votes for - one against. Mr. Dafoe, please prepare an action plan for presentation to the Board of Directors of FORHUM at your convenience. Are there any other questions or comments?"

I had one other point; "Mr. Prime Minister we haven't discussed the medications or vaccines that the aliens have provided us. It is our plan to go out for tender for the supply and delivery of each medication and vaccine. FORHUM will buy them from the manufacturers and distribute them. In this manner we will have some control over the end price, hopefully making them affordable to all individuals. I would however like to point out that there will be some economic fallout when we introduce these medications and vaccines.

The Prime Minister looked at his watch; it was 11:57. "It's almost noon and I would like to adjourn the meeting. Lunch is in the room next door. I need some quiet time before I have to speak.

"Does anyone see a need to continue to meet every day? I would think that we all need a few weeks break at least. I know I do. May I suggest we call a meeting for May 3rd at 10:00 a.m. It will be a regular Security Council meeting, but perhaps Mr. Dafoe and Ms. Montgomery could attend and give us an update as to what if any progress is being made with respect to the alien visit. We would put you at the top of the agenda and then you can go about your business."

"We will attend Mr. Prime Minister."

"I would also like to relinquish my role as the President of the Security Council at that meeting. I think we should go back to our monthly rotation. If there is no further business," The Prime Minister surveyed the table. "I call this meeting adjourned. I almost forgot; please meet in the room next door at 12:45 to be escorted to your seats in the General Assembly hall. Thank you"

The delegates all started standing and collecting their papers.

The Prime Minister looked over at Liz and I and mouthed "A word please."

We walked to a corner of the room. "I have made arrangements for Elizabeth to sit with the other members of the Security Council. William, you will be on stage with me. After the meeting, Elizabeth, please remain in your seat. UN security will take you to a location where you and William will be escorted back to the hotel. Under no circumstance is either one of you to attempt to get back to the hotel on your own. What are your plans for tonight and tomorrow?"

Liz responded. "We are supposed to have a meeting at the hotel with the crisis management group this afternoon."

"Believe me; that's not going to happen, they won't let those people in. The hotel is literally in lockdown mode right now and will remain that way until the media dissipates. I would suggest that you stay in the hotel and have a conference call with them. I would also suggest that you make arrangements to fly up to Niagara or Toronto tomorrow. You have spoken to the UN Head of Security Kyle Armstrong?"

"Yes, he made arrangements to get us from the hotel to here underground."

"He will make arrangements to get you safely from the hotel to the airport. Just let him know your plans." He pulled out a business card and handed it to Liz. "This is his contact information."

"How do I get to the General Assemble meeting room?

"I'll meet you back here at 12:45. Elizabeth you meet the rest of the Security Council next door at the same time."

"Thank you Mr. Prime Minister."

The Prime Minister had a smile on his face; "I wished that all of my team performed half as well as the two of you do!"

He turned and went to speak with Ambassador Dardaza.

I looked at Liz, "Are you hungry?"

She shook her head no.

"Cigarette?"

Liz gave me a big nod yes.

We went out and stood on the patio near the door again. Liz gave me two quick jabs to my shoulder. I looked at her questioningly. Liz had a big smile on her face. "That's for standing and applauding."

"My applause was sincere."

I received a kiss for that statement.

"Will, I'm a bit scared. I don't like all this security mumbo jumbo."

"Don't be scared. Believe me when I tell you nothing can happen to us and it's not UN security that will save our butts, it's the aliens. I have complete and utter confidence in them.

We do have to change some of our plans though. Call Cheryl and have her cancel the meeting room; Have Cheryl call Sarah and explain that the hotel is in lockdown and we will have to make it a conference call at 4:00. Then call the navy pilots and see if they can be here for a flight to Washington at 11:00, we'll take Cheryl home and then they can fly us up to Niagara, where hopefully we can hide for awhile. Once you have confirmation from the pilots, call Armstrong and tell him we will need to get to Newark airport by 11:00 or whatever time you agree with the pilots.

Please call Barbara and let her know what's happening. I need to put my mind into relax mode before the speech. Let's go back in."

It was 12:29. Liz and I went into the Security Council meeting room; there was no one else there. Liz sat down on one of the chairs that lined the wall and started calling people. I sat at the table, dropped my head and just tried to clear my mind.

I felt Liz's hand on mine and looked up. "Hi Darling, everything is arranged. Barbara is fine."

I checked my mental time clock it was 12:42; "You better go next door."

"Not before I get a kiss."

I leaned over and kissed her passionately.

Liz stood up and walked towards the door, she turned and gave me a smile; "I love you, give them hell." She left the room. A couple of minutes later the Prime Minister was at the door, I stood and walked towards him. He gave me a nervous look; "Ready?"

"I think so, I hope so."

I walked beside him although he was leading the way; we went up a flight of stairs, across a hallway and down two flights of stairs and walked along a corridor. A security officer was standing by the door. He keyed in a security code and opened the door for us. There was another security officer on that side of the door. We appeared to be back stage of a theater. A young lady in a light blue commissionaires outfit walked us out and onto the stage and pointed to two occasional type chairs that didn't go at all with the decor. I followed the Prime Minister and sat.

The noise from the 1,800 plus delegates was deafening. I glanced out over the crowd. There were twenty-seven video TV cameras most on tripods, but a few were being held on the shoulders of operators.

It was 12:59, a minute to go I thought.

Secretary-General Owusu entered from the side of the stage and went to a large podium towards the back of the stage. At preciously 1:00 p.m. his gavel came down three times. He paused for a couple of seconds to see if the noise would abate, it didn't. He hit the gavel another three times and things began to quite down. He introduced Prime Minister Harmon in his role as the current President of the UN Security Council not as the Prime Minister of Canada. The Prime Minister rose from his seat and walked slowly but with confidence towards the podium.

Prime Minister Harmon had reached the podium and began speaking. "On behalf of the United Nations' Security Council I would like to thank you all for coming especially on such short notice. As the current President of the Security Council it falls upon me, on behalf of all the members of Security Council, to inform you of a global crisis. I would like you to bear with me as I explain, from the beginning, an imminent situation which surpasses any other crises the human race has ever faced, not by a small margin, but at a scale that most would have never in their wildest dreams imagined."

Silence truly gripped the auditorium, even the few groups who had been talking amongst themselves were riveted to the Prime Minister.

The Prime Minister stopped for a few seconds and scanned the delegates which allowed the translators to catch-up and to ensure that everyone was truly paying attention.

"On January 1st of this year at preciously 12:00:000:000 a.m. Greenwich Mean Time or Coordinated Universal Time a message was received by five of the world's radio telescopes. It is important that you understand that by preciously I mean just that. These radio telescopes are connected to atomic clocks which are accurate to 2 nanoseconds per day."

A chart showing the locations of the radio telescopes positioned on a flat map of the world was displayed on a screen which had been lowered just to the right of the Prime Minister.

The Prime Minister continued; "You should note, that each of the five radio telescopes contacted belong to one of the five permanent members of the Security Council. Whether or not this is meaningful piece of information, we don't know at this time. The Security Council's investigations concluded that the technology does not exist that would allow anyone on this planet or from a satellite to deliver a message to multiple targets all over the world at preciously the same instant."

The Prime Minister paused for a moment and then continued; "As you can see on the slide to my right, each radio telescope, that received the message, is located on a different continent. As well, each of the radio telescopes was searching a different quadrant of the galaxy. None of the quadrants had any similarity as too their distance from earth and the frequencies being scanned varied dramatically."

The Prime Minister carried on; "I would also point out that radio telescopes that were in relatively close proximity to radio telescopes that received the message, did not receive the message".

The chatter between delegates increased to a point where it required a couple of bangs of the gavel by the Secretary General to bring silence back to the room.

The Prime Minister continued; "There are many interesting technical points about the message we have received which I will discuss with you later. At this time I believe that you should hear the message, but before it is played I want you to know that there is a positive outcome to the message. Please keep that in the back of your mind while you are listening. As I previously said, the message will be played over the general assembly sound system. Each delegate will be given a copy of the message so there is no need to transcribe what you hear or to take notes.

Before it's played I am going to raise my arm and ask you to remove your headphones and disconnect yourselves from the translators. I know that this request is unusual and probably unprecedented, but I would ask that you bear with me as the reason for this will become evident when you hear the message. When I lower my arm I would ask that you replace the headphones so that you are connected with the translators again."

The Prime Minister slowly raised his arm and as he did so I glanced over my shoulder and watched the delegates removed their headphones. Some did it quickly while others seemed to do it with trepidation, as if removing their headphones would somehow place them in jeopardy. After what felt like a lengthy period of time all of the headphones were finally removed and placed on the tables in front of each delegate. The Prime Minister then nodded to a technician in the sound control booth and the message was played over the sound system.

"To the people of the planet they call earth. This notification comes to you from the Council of Inhabited Planets – the governing body representing fifty seven inhabited planets and over ten trillion sentient beings.

You are hereby advised that due to your technical capabilities of sending objects into space to explore the galaxy, combined with your history and psychological mind-set towards war, power, greed, corruption and the genocide of groups of individuals who do not hold to your ideologies, compounded with your continuous development of weapons of mass destruction; it has been deemed necessary to take immediate action and a motion has been unanimously approved; All human life on the planet earth must be sacrificed to protect the lives of all sentient beings in the galaxy. This motion shall be carried out in precisely one hundred days.

Under the governing rules of the Council of Inhabited Planets you have the right to present a defense and argument with respect to this motion. To present a defense and argument, the Council has agreed to sanction one human from the planet earth an audience in front of the entire Council. Your chosen emissary must be at coordinates of

40.7675573972 latitude and -73.9456279843 longitude at preciously 12:00 p.m. on January 3rd. He or she will be transported by a shuttlecraft to our planet. Your emissary will be returned to the same location at 12:00 p.m. on April 5th; a trip duration of precisely ninety-three of your days. If you do not send an emissary the motion will be implemented without further notice."

The Prime Minister lowered his arm and motioned to the delegates to replace their headsets. A few minutes went by while the delegates talked to their associates and to delegates at adjacent tables.

The Secretary General banged the gavel a couple of times and most of the delegates came to order, a few conversations continued and a couple of bangs from a gavel were not going to stop them.

The Prime Minister started to speak again; "Ladies and gentlemen may I please have your attention". He paused for a moment, until the table conversations had abated.

"As I previously stated, the situation is under control although not fully resolved. We, being the members of the Security Council chose an individual to present a defense and argument against the motion generated by the Council of Inhabited Planets. That individual returned on April 5th and will present you with the current situation momentarily."

That was my cue to standby. I would be called to the podium in a few minutes, I wondered what type of reception I would receive, but, surprisingly my hands were still dry and I wasn't nervous. I might actually get through this without my normal level of hysteria!

"However, before I call him to the podium, I had previously mentioned that there were a few very interesting technical points about the message that we received and you have just heard and I would like to take a moment to highlight a couple of them.

If I may ask the President of Brazil what language was the message in?"

The President of Brazil hesitated for a moment, looked at his colleagues at the table, he had a perplexed expression, as if the Prime Minister was asking a trick question; "Portuguese of course!"

Prime Minister Harmon then asked the Prime Minister of Japan; "What language was the message in". The Japanese Prime Minister responded without hesitation; "Japanese!"

Prime Minister Harmon asked the Prime Minister of the Ukraine;

"Mr. Prime Minister what language was the message in?" The Ukrainian Prime Minister responded with a deep and forceful voice; "Ukrainian!"

All of the delegates started chattering to their colleagues and others close by and only by raising his voice could the Prime Minister bring the audience back under some control.

"Yes", he said with a very load voice, trying desperately to maintain a level of domination over the delegates; "The message has the unique ability to be heard in the first language of the individual listening to it. We have given copies of the message to senior audio scientists around the world and no one can explain this phenomenon."

He peered out at the delegates "if anyone in the auditorium did not hear the message in their first language please raise your hand."

I quickly scanning the delegates, from where I was sitting not one hand was raised. I wasn't at all surprised.

The Prime Minister continued; "Another interesting point about the message is that it can be copied to any media in analog or digital format, but once it has been copied to that media, it cannot be erased or written over and even when copied it retains its ability to be heard in the first language of the individual listening to the message. The message's language even changes subtly for different dialects of the same language.

"The third unique item that we have found is that there is no evidence that a message or any analog or digital data is on the media. Scientists have spent days trying to identify the format of the recorded message. Yet with all our technology we have been unable to see anything on any media. With our technology all of the media we have looked at that contains the message appears to be blank.

"Feel free to have your own scientists investigate the technology within the message and the media."

After pausing for a few minutes to allow all of the message's technology to sink in and be discussed amongst the delegates the Prime Minister spoke; "I would now like to introduce Mr. William Defoe, the individual who was chosen to be the emissary of the human race and meet with the Council of Inhabited Planets.

I stood, inhaled deeply and began walking towards the podium. As the Prime Minister and I crossed paths we stopped and shook hands, I'm not sure why, it just seemed like the appropriate thing to do. My legs weren't quaking underneath me, which was unusual. I reached the podium and placed one hand on each side of the slanted top and gripped it as if I was going to pick it up. I slowly scanned the delegates from right to left.

I pulled up my speech into the forefront of my brain and looked out over the delegates. There was very little chatter in the background.

I wasn't going to waste time with salutations. I put my forceful voice into play mode; "The Prime Minister of Canada has used the words "positive outcome" and "under control" to describe the current state of affairs with regard to the message received from the extraterrestrials.

"With all due respect to the Prime Minister, what has been negotiated with the extraterrestrials far exceeds the words "positive outcome" and "under control". The extraterrestrials have provided us with technology that will be of benefit to every man, woman and child not only now, but for millennia to come.

"Medical technology that will cure and prevent some of the worst diseases currently facing mankind: They have provided us with the formula for a vaccine that will immunize us from all known viruses, including the common cold.

"They have provided us with the formula for a medication that will regenerate our immune systems. It is a complete cure for AIDS as well as other immune deficiencies.

"They have provided us with the formulas for medications that will cure not just control glaucoma, clogged arteries, acne, migraine headaches and diabetes.

"And although a number of diseases will be eradicated by the use of the immunization vaccine; that won't help anyone who has contracted the disease prior to immunization. The aliens have provided us with formulas for medications that will cure Poliomyelitis, Influenza, Ebola virus, Systemic lupus erythematosus and Creutzfeldt-jakob."

I paused. I wanted all of this to sink in.

"Ladies and gentlemen; the gifts from the extraterrestrials don't end with vaccines and medications.

"They will be cleaning our atmosphere of all contaminants.

"They will be cleaning all of our oceans, seas, lakes, rivers and streams of pollutants.

"They will be collecting the more than 100 million pieces of manmade space debris currently in orbit around our planet.

"They will bring back the Ozone layer to its thickness in the year 1,500."

I paused again and scanned the delegates.

"We will be able to replace all of our nuclear generating stations with solar power in less than nine months. This solar power is a highly advanced technology that is relatively inexpensive to install and has a 25 year life with negligible operating costs.

"And we have been provided with technology that will allow us to predict earthquakes and volcanic eruptions eight weeks before they occur."

I paused again.

"I am sure that you are thinking to yourselves, what do the extraterrestrials want in return for all of these gifts?

"What they want in return can easily be described as another gift from the extraterrestrials, in my opinion the most important gift of all. They want us to destroy our stockpiles of weapons of mass destruction: nuclear, chemical and biological; something that we should have done a long time ago. They want us to stop developing new weapons of mass destruction and they want us to stop using nuclear power to generate electricity or for anything else. How many of you, whose countries operate nuclear power stations, are waiting for an accident to occur? How many accidents have to occur before we come to the realization that nuclear power can and will kill thousands or have we forgotten Chernobyl, Three Mile Island, and Tokaimura!

"The aliens realize that in many instances we lack the technology to destroy our weapons of mass destruction as well as the radioactive elements in nuclear generating systems. They will be providing us with a convenient and inexpensive method to dispose of all of those hazardous materials."

I paused to allow the delegates to absorb what I had said to this point. I looked out over the podium at the delegates. Most seemed engrossed by what I was saying; a few seemed to be oblivious to what I was saying.

"This is what is going to happen. Each country will define, using technology provided by the aliens, areas where they have placed nuclear material and weapons of mass destruction. In 264 days alien spacecraft will circle the globe and using advanced technology, vaporize the materials and weapons that have been placed in the defined areas. There is no residue left or toxins created from the vaporization, it is completely harmless as long as you are not physically in the defined area.

"What could be simpler? Detailed written instructions will be provided to all countries.

"We all want to live on a planet that is not held hostage by weapons of mass destruction or the fear of a nuclear generating station meltdown. The aliens are providing each country with an enormous incentive to comply.

"When the aliens arrive to vaporize the weapons of mass destruction and the nuclear materials they will be scanning every square inch of the planet to a depth of over 100 kilometers. If they find that a country has hidden any weapons of mass destruction: nuclear, chemical or biological; or nuclear material outside of the defined areas the entire country will be vaporized. There will be no second chances or notification."

That brought the delegates to life, chatter amongst all the delegates, shouts at me and the Secretary General, hand waving, pounding on desks. It was like being in a classroom with disruptive eight year olds. The Secretary General banged his gavel a few times to no avail. After more than five minutes the noise began to subside.

"From your irrational outburst of displeasure I can only assume that you want to have weapons of mass destruction, you want to have the potential of a nuclear holocaust."

I paused, there was little background chatter.

"There may be some concern that during the process of collecting the weapons of mass destruction that some countries may become vulnerable and open to an attack by another country. To protect against a country taking advantage of the disarming period, the aliens have sent spacecraft which are now circling earth. They will be monitoring the planet. Any missiles, rockets or other projectile fired during the collection period will be vaporized as soon as it leaves the ground. If it is a conventional weapon a two hundred square yard area surrounding the point of the firing will be vaporized. If it is a mass destruction warhead the country that fired it will be vaporized.

"Ladies and gentlemen, the days when countries can hold other countries hostage are going to come to an end.

"This is an unbelievable and unprecedented opportunity for all countries to make peace with their neighbors; an opportunity to end aggression everywhere."

I paused; there was a table behind me with a pitcher of water and some glasses. I turned and poured a glass and gulped it down. I had Gobi dessert syndrome, I was parched. I thought about my speech up to this point I thought it was actually going quite well. I had expected the outburst of displeasure amongst the delegates.

I returned to the podium.

"The technologies, medications and vaccines will be made available through a not-for-profit organization that is called "For Humanity", the acronym is FORHUM. It will be headquartered at an International Zone in Canada. The Board of Directors of the organization are the representatives of the nations that make up the UN Security Council. I will be the organizations Managing Director.

"Ladies and gentleman, many of you may be thinking; our country doesn't have any weapons of mass destruction or nuclear power plants, this has no relevance to us. You are incorrect. While the primary goal is to eliminate weapons of mass destruction and nuclear materials, the aliens are prepared to vaporize anything placed in a defined area. If you have disposal problems with any materials such as medical waste, used oil or landfills that are overflowing with garbage you can define those areas for vaporization. If you have areas that are laden with landmines you can define those areas for vaporization, if you have derelict buildings, dams anything that you would like removed you can designate the area for vaporization.

"You will also have the opportunity to benefit from the new solar collector systems. While we must first deliver the solar systems as replacements for the nuclear generating stations, once that commitment is fulfilled, the technology will be available to every country, inexpensive and reliable electrical energy for everyone on the planet. This technology surpasses cold fusion which has been an unattainable dream for decades."

That basically ended what I had to say. I did want to mention the documents again.

"Ladies and gentlemen, as I previously mentioned you will be receiving a package of documents at the end of the session. I understand that the package will also include a digital and analogue copy of the message that was received from the extraterrestrials. One document is an overview of what I have said to you today and the other is a "To Do" document which will inform you on the actions that you need to take, it also provides you with a contact email and fax number that you may use should you require any clarifications. I must personally apologize as I understand that the translators did not have sufficient time to translate the "To Do" document into all of the languages represented at this meeting today. The translators are not to blame. I was tardy in delivering the original to them.

"Additional information will be forthcoming as and when it's produced and will appear on the For Humanity website; forhumanity.org.

I paused and looked at the delegates. They had simmered down and most seemed to have accepted the situation. There were a few that I could tell were still irate.

"Mr. Secretary General I relinquish the floor."

I turned and headed back to my seat beside Prime Minister Harmon.

The Secretary General had introduced the President of the Russian Federation, Viktor Masmekhov; he had been waiting in the wings. As he walked he had to pass Prime Minister Harmon, the Prime Minister stood and they shook hands. He turned towards the podium and met me as I was returning. He stopped, so I did the same, he put his hand out and shook my hand placing his other hand over mine. He had a huge smile on his hardened face, President Masmekhov was a tall man, five feet, eleven and three quarter inches; he had a well proportioned physique, thinning black hair with a high hair line. He was wearing a black suit that didn't fit that well.

We broke the handshake and I continued to walk towards the Prime Minister. As I came up to him, he stood and held out his hand with a relaxed smile on his face; "An excellent speech Mr. Dafoe." I shook his hand: "Thank you Mr. Prime Minister."

President Masmekhov was just reaching the podium. The Prime Minister and I did not have access to any translation earphones. I thought that I would try to read Masmekhov's brain waves, but I was concerned as there was a lot of ambient brain wave activity in the room.

I shut my eyes and tried to focus on President Masmekhov's brain waves to the elimination of all else.

I missed his opening salutation; I was having problems separating Masmekhov's brain waves from that of Prime Minister Harmon's, who was sitting right next to me. But I managed to hone in during his first sentence.

". . .a great opportunity for all of us. This is a defining juncture for the human race. We can continue up the road of war and self annihilation or we can take the fork in the road that leads to peace and well being for everyone. We must put our jealousies, our hatred for others, our fears and aggressions to one side.

"The Russian Federation supports and defends the agreement made with the extraterrestrials. We will destroy all of our weapons of mass destruction; we will close and dispose of all of our nuclear power plants and convert them to the solar energy systems graciously supplied by the aliens.

"The Russian Federation holds out an olive branch to any and every country. We will no longer interfere in the internal workings of any country; we will promote peace and goodwill amongst all nations; we will respect the views, ideas and ideologies of others.

"As a sign of good faith and goodwill we are hereby relinquishing our claims to the Kurile Islands and returning jurisdiction back to Japan. We will be promoting free elections in Chechnya within the next 120 days to allow the population to decide if they wish to be separated from the Russian Federation. Should they vote to be an independent country the Russian Federation will honor their wishes without any interference or question. We will also support their membership in the United Nations as an independent body.

"We will be dramatically reducing our military capabilities. We will be eliminating all but two of our aircraft carriers. Those two will be reconfigured into hospital ships able to provide humanitarian aid to all countries. The balance of our navy will be reduced; large warships will be dismantled, with the exception of four which will be converted to unarmed disaster support vessels, it is our intent to place them in strategic points around the globe so that they can respond to support requirements needed after natural disasters; smaller ships will be converted to rolls in coast guard search and rescue and scientific research. Our submarine fleet will be decommissioned with the exception of two submarines that will be converted for scientific research of our oceans.

"Our air force bomber, fighter and helicopter squadrons will be decommissioned although some of the aircraft and pilots will be transferred to scientific research and search and rescue duties.

"Our army will be downsized to twenty percent of its current operational force and be reconfigured to provide internal security and border patrol for the Russian Federation.

"Our overall educational system will be enhanced to provide better and more accessible education in the sciences, arts and other humanitarian purposes.

"We challenge all nations to join with us. This is a new era for humanity, let's close the book on past differences and join together so that all the peoples of this planet can live in peace and prosperity."

My concentration was interrupted by the sound of applause which was growing louder and louder. I opened my eyes to witness ninety percent of the delegates on their feet applauding and banging their flat hands on the table tops.

Prime Minister Harmon had risen and was applauding, I thought it best if I followed suit. I glanced over to Secretary General Owusu he had come out from behind his throne and was applauding with the rest.

The applause went on for over four minutes, that is an unbelievable amount of time for people to clap and then slowly started to subside. I went back to concentrating on Masmekhov's brain waves.

President Masmekhov continued; "We have one man and one man only that we must thank for this golden opportunity, a man who put his life on the line for all of humanity and brought us gracefully into a new era, a remarkable new era; "Mr. William Dafoe!"

The President turned and looked at me and started to applaud and motioned me to come up to the podium. I rose and started walking back to the podium, I was feeling very embarrassed. The Prime Minister rose and joined in applauding within seconds most of the delegates were on their feet applauding and banging desks.

When I reached the podium the President broke his applause long enough to shake my hand.

The applause subsided; "Mr. Dafoe, on behalf of the people of the Russian Federation we wish to present you with our highest honor; Hero of the Russian Federation."

President Masmekhov removed a small blue velvet covered box from his jacket pocket. He opened the box and removed a gold star on a blue silk lanyard and placed it over my head. He shook my hand with a tight grip, everyone start applauding again.

I looked out at the delegates and raised my hand as a signal to stop applauding. The applause slowly subsided. When it had stopped I moved towards the podium, President Masmekhov backed away a bit to give me room.

I wasn't prepared for this. I didn't have a speech prepared in my mind to read. My penchant for nervousness when speaking to a large audience reared its ugly head. Focus, focus, focus I thought to myself. I tried desperately to relax and focus. Can't speak to a large audience then speak to one individual, I brought up a picture of Liz in my brain. I would talk to Liz, not a crowd of 1,800 people.

I focused on the picture of Liz in my brain; "President Masmekhov it is with great honor and humility that I wear this medal."

I decided that it was time for a bit of humor, after all that is a big part of me, the salesman.

"And with all due respect Mr. President, when I was saving humanity from annihilation from the aliens, I was saving my ass as well!"

There was silence for a second that felt like an eternity; poor joke, bad timing, poor delivery, was I going to receive a gong, a hook from the side of the stage would be coming out to hall me off the stage.

Then, out of nowhere someone amongst the delegates broke out laughing, followed instantly by the President, and before long laughter permeated the building.

I backed away from the podium and motioned for the President to take my place. He shook my hand again, he was still laughing. I walked back to my seat at the side of the stage where the Prime Minister was standing in front of his chair. It was obvious that he had laughed. He shook my hand and we both sat.

I wasn't honed in on President Masmekhov's brain waves. He said a few words and from his actions I assume he turned the floor back to the Secretary General. He walked past the Prime Minister and me and smiled at us both and then disappeared off the stage.

The Secretary General banged his gavel again. The delegates quieted down almost immediately.

"The President of the People's Republic of China, Liang Kang Hou wishes to address the delegates."

President Liang Kang Hou appeared from the stage wing, he is a short five foot, six inch stocky man with grey hair that appeared to be uncombed. He was wearing a dark blue suit, with pant legs that were dragging on the floor. As he passed the Prime Minister and me we rose and shook his hand. He had a perturbed expression on his face.

He quickly walked up to the podium.

I had been to China many times and I liked dealing with the

Chinese. I had dealt with individuals of Chinese origin in many other countries, as well. In my opinion, the Chinese don't have a sense of humor. They take everything you say very seriously and to heart. I had to be very careful to keep my joke repertoire well concealed when I dealt with them.

President Liang Kang Hou immediately started to speak. I had managed to sync with his brain waves when he shook my hand on his way to the podium.

He started with a very long and winded salutation to the members and then got directly down to what he wanted to say. His voice was firm; "The People's Republic of China also supports the compromise agreement negotiated by Mr. Dafoe in its entirety."

He paused

"President Masmekhov is a very hard man to follow. The People's Republic of China accepts the challenge presented by the leader of the Russian Federation. In response we will dramatically reduce all of our armed forces. We want all nations to know that the People's Republic of China wants world peace and have a desire that we all live together in harmony. We would like to show our commitment to this end and in a gesture of goodwill. We hereby acknowledge the existence of and recognize the fully independent country of Taiwan and wish to set up an exchange of Ambassadors as soon as possible.

"We are also relinquishing our control over Tibet. This morning the Chinese military had already commenced to disengage itself from the area, although it may take a few weeks to complete the removal of all troops and equipment. We will return the state of Tibet to its inhabitants, the Dalai Lama is encouraged and welcome to return, his safety is guaranteed. We will maintain a minimal police force presence in the area until a new Tibetan government can be formed and take over day-to-day internal security matters. All other Chinese government offices will be removed from the Tibetan state. Once they have formed a new government, the People's Republic of China would like to exchange Ambassadors with the country of Tibet. The People's Republic of China will also support the membership of both Taiwan and Tibet into the United Nations."

There was silence amongst the delegates. I think they were all in a state of disbelief. I stood up and started to applaud as loudly as I could. Prime Minister Harmon joined me and before long most of the delegates were standing and applauding. For China to relinquish control of Tibet and recognize Taiwan as an independent country surpassed even my wildest expectations.

I heard footsteps from my left and turned my head; President Masmekhov had appeared from behind the stage wing and was literally running towards President Liang Kang Hou. He grabbed the President's hand and shook it wildly. They exchange a few words, which I was unable to hone in on.

President Masmekhov stood in front of the podium and leaned in towards the microphone; "All of the Russian Federation military bases equipment and manpower currently stationed on the border with the People's Republic of China will be removed."

President Masmekhov went to the side of the podium.

President Liang Kang Hou placed his mouth up to the microphone; "The People's Republic of China will also remove its entire military presence on the borders with the Russian Federation."

The applause grew louder with the announcements.

President Masmekhov had turned and was about to walk away from the podium when Prime Minister Harmon started walking towards it. Prime Minister Harmon placed his hand on President Masmekhov shoulder and directed him back to the podium. The Prime Minister shook President Liang Kang Hou hand and then placed himself at the podium; "Canada will remove all of its northern military installations, including those of its allies that border on the Russian Federation."

This was becoming a "who can out do who" contest. The removal of bases of allies, there was only one ally in this case, the United States of Aggression, whops I meant the United States of America. It would be interesting to see their reaction. President Wycliffe wasn't even scheduled to speak to the delegates. The question of course is would they follow through. At this time it didn't matter, even the gestures were valuable.

President Masmekhov and the Prime Minister shook hands and President Masmekhov took control of the podium. "We will remove all of our northern military installations that border Canada."

The applause was continuous.

Prime Minister Harmon leaned into the microphone. He was beaming from ear to ear. "Mr. Dafoe, you are responsible for all this world peace, I hope you're happy?"

The Prime Minister and both President's looked in my direction and applauded for a few seconds.

The applause began to die down and Prime Minister Harmon and President Masmekhov took their leave of the podium.

Everyone began to sit, silence was returning to the room. President Liang Kang Hou said a few more words, but I don't know what they were as I wasn't honed in to his brain waves at the time, I was too busy humming Aquarius, something I did often. It was probably little more than returning the floor to the Secretary General as he walked away from the podium after speaking.

The Secretary General banged his gavel three times and called the meeting adjourned.

It was 2:47, the meeting went on longer than I had expected. Prime Minister Harmon jumped up from his chair and looked at me; "Quick!" I followed him as we walked briskly to the wing off the stage. There were a six security officers there, very well armed, as soon as we were off the visible portion of the stage one of the security officers, that had protected me previously told the Prime Minister to go with two of the officers and for me to come with him.

We walked around the back of the stage; Secretary General Chitundu Owusu was walking in the opposite direction with two officers. He smiled at me as we quickly passed one another. On the far side of the stage we walked through a door and along a corridor until we came to a small meeting room which we entered. The security officer spoke into his shoulder mike and then looked at me; Ms. Montgomery will be here in a couple of minutes. Sure enough, a couple of minutes later Liz walked into the room with two security officers. The instant she saw me she gave me a smile of relief; grabbed my face between her hands and kissed me.

The lead security officer asked us to follow him. I took Liz's hand in mine and held it very tight and we briskly walked along a number of corridors and up and down a few staircases. I quickly realized that we were back at the door leading to the tunnel connecting the hotel with the UN complex. We scurried along the tunnel, two officers in front and two behind us. In a few minutes we were back in the bowels of the hotel and rushed into the freight elevator; seconds later we were standing in front of our hotel room door. Liz pulled her keycard from her purse, opened the door and stepped inside. I looked at the lead officer and thanked him and his partners. He said that the arrangements for our trip to Newark airport were still being resolved and that someone would be in contact with us before eight this evening to give us the details. He suggested that we stay in our room and order room service for dinner. I thanked him again and went into the room, I closed the door and made sure the deadbolt engaged.

Liz stood facing me, her hands at her side. I grabbed her hands and pushed them behind her back forcing her torso hard against me. Our lips met and felt her tongue slide deeply into my mouth. I held her tight and reciprocated. For me it was the perfect release of the pent up energy and stress.

I took my jacket off and hung it over a chair, loosened my tie and looked at Liz; she was radiant as ever; "Wine?"

"Please!"

I opened a bottle of wine and poured us each a glass. Liz was sitting on the loveseat and I joined her. She immediately grabbed my hand, she looked into my eyes she had a look of wonderment about her; "I love you so very much, my darling! You were fantastic, brilliant at the podium!" she was squeezing my hand very tight. "I sat there on the edge of my seat watching and listening to you and all the time I kept thinking that incredible man loves me and we are going to be married. I am so proud of you Will, so proud that you want me. I cried when they gave you the standing ovation."

Liz was choking up; she stopped for a second and took a gulp of wine.

"Vice President Almont and I had a chance for a private conversation before the General Assembly meeting was called to order. He told me what happened when you landed, it made me shiver. He said that he hoped that he could consider us friends, I said he definitely could, I like him Will and he was always fair to me when we worked together at the Whitehouse, I hope that's okay?"

Liz didn't wait for an answer.

"I asked him why Wycliffe wasn't there. He asked if I wanted the official party line or the truth. The official line is that he has a very bad cold and the doctor didn't want him to fly. The truth is; he has no balls, pardon me; he didn't want to speak to the assembly, because he didn't know what to say."

"Why am I not surprised? I hope the press eats him alive. He is going to have to respond in kind to the gestures made by China and Russia or the USA is going to be admonished by every other nation. I would think that the press is attacking at this very moment."

"According to Almont there is a press conference scheduled for

3:30. Do you want to watch it?"

"I really don't want to, but I think we should."

I stood up and opened the armoire and passed the remote control to Liz. As I did the room phone rang. I walked to the desk and picked it up.

"Hello"

"Mr. Dafoe, my name is Kelly Stevens, I am a producer with RNN; we would like to interview you on a live TV feed."

"All press and media enquiries are being handled by Sarah Malthus at Davis, Malthus and Associates. Her telephone number is"

Before I could finish Stevens interrupted; "Mr. Dafoe the world is very interested in hearing about your meetings with the aliens; you owe it to them. We are willing to pay you a substantial sum for your time."

I was being pleasant, however the offer of money, angered me. He wasn't interested in knowing about my meetings with the aliens, he wanted ratings, advertisers and to make a name for himself. I calmed myself; "Thank you for calling. Have a great day." I disconnected the phone. I didn't have a chance to put the phone in its cradle when it rang again.

"Hello"

"May I speak with Mr. Dafoe please?"

"Speaking"

"Mr. Dafoe my name is Vivian Hallsworth I am with WNN and I would very much appreciate some of your time. I am sure you have a very busy schedule, but you are the man of the hour, possibly the man of the century. Can you spare me some of your valuable time?

"Ms. Hallsworth, I am not going to provide any interviews now or in the future and please don't try to offer me money, it won't change my mind.

"Please call me Viv. Mr. Dafoe how is the world to honor you if you won't talk to them, make yourself available?"

"Ms. Hallsworth, I don't want to be honored. I am not the messiah returning from the mount. I'm a simple guy who wants to get on with his life. The real story is with China and Russia and what President Wycliffe will say in a few minutes. Do you realize Ms. Hallsworth that we, our children and grandchildren are facing the real possibility of global peace and prosperity."

"Mr. Dafoe I was told by Vice-President Almont that you were a remarkable individual, the likes that he had never met before. That you undertook the mission without any compensation of any type or in any manner; you asked for nothing more than security for your daughter in the event you didn't return.

You may not want to be honored Mr. Dafoe, but I will tell you that I personally hold you in great esteem. I will respect your request for privacy. If you should change your mind in the future, please don't hesitate to contact me. I thank you for your time and I thank you for what you did."

"Thank you Ms. Hallsworth, I appreciate it." I disconnected the line.

Liz interjected; "I called Cheryl and asked her to come to our room. She can field the phone calls."

"Not just another beautiful face! I wish we had the time to get under the covers, I would really like to ravish you, for hours."

"I would like to be ravished for hours by you!"

There was a knock at our door, I checked the peephole it was Cheryl. I opened the deadbolt and opened the door, let her in and closed the deadbolt behind her.

Liz immediately told Cheryl she was to answer our room phone and if it was anyone from the press she was to put them onto Sarah Malthus at Davis, Malthus and Associates. She also told her to pour herself a glass of wine. Cheryl didn't.

Liz turned up the volume on the TV, the press conference was about to start. I sat on the loveseat beside Liz and took her hand in mine. Cheryl sat at the desk close to the phone, but adjusted her chair so that she could watch the news conference.

"Ladies and Gentlemen the President of the United States"

"Good afternoon everyone, thank you all for coming"

The President looked horrible, either he had a bad cold or a good makeup artist, I wasn't sure which. His voice sounded fine, which made me lean towards a good makeup artist.

"A lot has happened today. It was the start of the culmination of events that started over one hundred days ago, at midnight on December 31st. I have personally been involved from the outset, from the moment that I was made aware of the transmission from the aliens. I was an integral part of the process that resulted in the selection of Mr. William Dafoe as the world's emissary. It is obvious that we chose the right man.

I stand behind the agreement that Mr. Dafoe negotiated with the extraterrestrials. I will be presenting legislation to congress that will provide for the destruction of our nuclear arsenal and other weapons as required by the aliens. I will also ask congress to pass legislation that will provide for the closure of all our nuclear generating stations and other nuclear storage facilities."

Interesting! He is not committing to destroying weapons of mass destruction and converting nuclear generating stations to solar, he is only committing to present appropriate legislation to congress. He is also implying that he is not doing it because eliminating weapons of mass destruction and closing nuclear power plants are the right things to do for all of humanity. He is doing it because the aliens require it. If he's not very careful, the United States will end up as one of the countries vaporized. Liz was right, he has no balls.

"I am forming a committee to investigate the potential of reducing our military and what that would mean to our commitments for the security of other nations and our commitments to NATO."

"I sure hope that the American people don't buy into this crap. They should riot in the streets and burn the Whitehouse to the ground. Actually he should be impeached."

"Are there any questions?"

Almost every hand went up. The President looked at the press seated in front of him; "Andy"

"Thank you Mr. President. Both the Russian and Chinese Presidents made some very broad commitments today, especially with respect to very major reductions in their militaries and their military capabilities. We don't appear to be responding in kind with gestures of goodwill and good faith. Why are we not jumping on the opportunity to make this a safer world?

"We must stand by our security commitments to other nations and to NATO." While the words spoken by President Masmekhov and President Liang Kang Hou were encouraging, we believe that we must hold fast until we see their actions."

The President turned his eyes off Andy and solicited another question.

"Katrina"

"Mr. President as a citizen of the United States of America, a country that I believed to be interested in promoting peace and prosperity to all, I find your rhetoric to be reprehensible and totally unacceptable."

The rest of the press core looked at Katrina and started to applaud. The President turned and walked away from the podium and out of the room. The Whitehouse press secretary went up to the podium and tried to speak, but the applause was overbearing. All of the cameras were focused on the press core and their applause for Katrina.

Finally the group settled down and the Press Secretary started to speak, her voice had a tone of complete embarrassment. "Ladies and gentl—"

She didn't get the word gentlemen out of her mouth when someone in the back of the room stood up; "Katrina said what we are all thinking and feeling and I think she represents the majority of the citizens of this country. I suggest that our President reevaluate his response and change his attitude or I can see the citizens of this great nation revolting in the streets.

The Press Secretary finally managed to speak her tone was harsh; "This press conference is over!" The cameras stayed focused on the empty podium and then went back to the news anchor of whatever station we were watching.

It was 3:37. The press conference was over in less than five minutes. Liz and Cheryl were both glued to the TV screen. I on the other hand needed another glass of wine.

The news anchor didn't know what to say. He smiled at the cameras and then said; "Greg Jefferies is speaking with Senator Mackie the head of the Republican caucus. Greg are you there?

The picture changed to a man with a microphone, obviously Greg Jefferies and a man next to him who must be Senator Mackie. Greg raised the microphone to his mouth and looked at the camera; "Senator Mackie, this has been quite a day!"

"Yes it has Greg."

"I am sure, Senator Mackie that you watched the UN General Assembly meeting that took place earlier today, do you have any comments?"

"Well Greg, these are definitely interesting times. I think people are forgetting that we only have Mr. Dafoe's story; we have no hard evidence that the aliens don't want us to get rid of our weapons of mass destruction so that they can attack us. Maybe the only thing that is preventing an attack is that we currently have weapons that could repel them.

"Are you saying the Mr. Dafoe is lying?"

"I'm saying that he may have been brain washed, or he may be an unwilling pawn in a conspiracy with the aliens."

"You're kidding, right?"

Greg was shaking his head in disbelief.

"No Greg I'm not kidding. I have never trusted the governments of Russia or China; it's possible they are part of or even behind the conspiracy. It is also possible that Russia and China may be falling into a cunningly set trap and the United States must be careful before it makes any commitment to disarm. The Congress and Senate will review all of the pertinent information and in conjunction with our military advisors we will decide what if any actions to take."

"What about the time element Senator?"

"Greg, there is ample time for due process."

"Thank you Senator, back to Eric Mondale at news central"

Eric Mondale was shaking his head in disbelief. "Thank you Greg. I don't know what to say other than I think I will pack my family up and move to Fiji.

Cheryl interjected. "It's almost four, should I call Sarah?"

Liz nodded; "I think so." She turned the TV off with the remote control.

Cheryl removed her notepad from her purse and dialed a number. "Do you know, sometimes you can wait three of four minutes before you get dial tone. The press must be overloading the telephone system."

"Hello, Sarah?"

Hi, Sarah, this is Cheryl; I have Ms. Montgomery and Mr. Dafoe with me, I'll put you on speaker phone."

Liz and I both said "HI Sarah" simultaneously.

Sarah had her business voice on; "Mr. Dafoe, Ms. Montgomery I have a number of people with me, including one of my senior partners Tom Davis."

A voice said; "Hi"

Liz sat down near the desk. "Sarah I assume you and your staff watched the speeches from the General Assembly this afternoon."

"We did"

"The speeches, especially the speech by Prime Minister Harmon and Mr. Dafoe should have given you ample insight into what has occurred and what is going to occur."

"We recorded it. I want to be able to show it to my grandchildren, in the unlikely event I have some."

Liz ignored the feeble attempt at humor from Sarah. "We have already had two phone calls from the press wanting to interview Will. He declined both of them. We are sure that he will be inundated with requests for interviews, now more than ever. Did you happen to see the President's press conference and the interview with Senator Mackie?"

"We saw the President's press conference and recorded it. I didn't see Senator Mackie, but Tom did. Tom and I have had preliminary discussions about what Mackie said. At first I thought that we should defend Mr. Dafoe, but Tom believes that Mackie was not credible, and the reactions by the interviewer and by Eric Mondale, who is a very well respected news anchor, reduced his credibility close to zero. I now agree with Tom that at this time we should just ignore it."

"This is Tom; Will, are you sure you don't want to be interviewed. We could have a great deal of control. We could demand that the interview be taped and that it couldn't be aired without our permission. I'm not sure I understand why you don't want to face the press."

"The primary reason is that I don't want this exercise, situation, call it what you may, to be about me and I believe that the more exposure I have the less exposure will be given to the primary message, that message will be diluted. It's about peace and prosperity for the human race, even more so after the speeches by the President's of Russia and China. It's not about me in any manner whatsoever."

"Tom again, I understand your feelings. Are you watching RNN, if your not you should turn it on."

Cheryl picked up the TV remote control and after pushing a few buttons had RNN on the screen. A big banner was displaced across the screen "Breaking News" below it were the words "Rebellion in the Whitehouse".

A few moments later Eric Mondale appeared on the screen. "Good afternoon. The President is experiencing an unprecedented dissension in the ranks of his cabinet! RNN has learned, from very reliable sources, that minutes after his press conference the President has received letters of resignation from six key members of his cabinet. Secretary of State Danielle Furlong; Chief of Staff Barry Fitzwater, a long time personal friend of the Presidents; Secretary of Defense Leonard Millhaven; Ambassador to the United Nations Donna Salazar; Attorney General Jessie Colfax and the Secretary of Energy Graham Foster. We have also been told that further resignations are imminent."

Mondale paused and read a piece of paper that had just been placed on his desk. "Sources at the Pentagon have advised us that General Stewart Adams the Chairman of the Joint Chiefs of Staff has submitted a request for early retirement."

A hand appeared on the right corner of the screen and dropped another piece of paper on his desk, Mondale read it; "Apparently 43 Republican members of Congress have advised their party caucuses that they will be sitting as independents effective immediately."

I motioned Cheryl to mute the sound. "Sarah, Tom this is going to go on all night. I suggest that we move forward. From my standpoint, this dissension in the government is good for us. It's providing the press with the fodder they need to create sensationalism and maybe they will back off us for awhile."

Liz took the reins again. "We want you to do three things. Be the contact for any press enquires and requests for information. Requests for general information or interviews are to be shelved. Requests for specific clarifications such as; "What is the date of the arrival of the aliens?" should be responded to. Most if not all of the answers to specific questions should be in the documents that we will email you right after this meeting. If you do not have the answer please send a request through to Cheryl by email. We want you to prepare a plan that is proactive to feed the press information. We will be producing additional information as quick as we can. Captioned pictures of the alien planets are an example of what will be forthcoming. We will also provide you with information that pertains to the operation of FORHUM such as new senior positions filled, contracts awarded, order fulfillment. FORHAM is to be as transparent as absolutely possible. We would like you to tell us the type of information we should prepare and in what order. Let me clarify what I said, we do not want to vet this plan. The plan is for your benefit not ours. All communications should be funneled through Cheryl. If it is urgent and you cannot reach Cheryl you can contact me. Contacting Will directly should only be as a measure of last resort. At no time should you give out direct contact information for any of us.

The final item is a website. We have registered ForHumanity.org as our primary domain name; we have registered others that will auto forward to that one. We have only registered the English version of the name. Now that the Internet is allowing foreign language domain names we would like to register ForHumanity.org in as many languages as possible, for a five year period."

That statement really surprised me. Liz and I had never discussed or even mentioned domain names in other languages. I was impressed.

"We have already contracted for the website hosting, Cheryl will send you the name of the hosting company, but we don't have a website. I have created a logo that should be polished by a graphics designer, which Cheryl will send you. I don't know if you have the capability to create websites in house. I don't really care. I want you to undertake the overall responsibility of designing one for us or having one designed for us. The primary key, besides a highly professional appearance will be its availability in many languages. We would like suggestions on which languages to concentrate on first. It's our plan to upload all documents that are generated so that they are available to everyone.

We have already started referring the press to you. Sarah we have been using your name. If you want to designate someone else in your organization let Cheryl know."

Liz paused to collect her thoughts. "I don't have anything else. Do you have any questions?"

Sarah responded; "I think we understand what you want from us. How long will you be in New York?"

"We will be leaving tomorrow morning."

"Have a safe trip and thank you again for believing in us. We won't let you down. Bye!"

"Bye!" Liz disconnected the phone line.

"Liz looked at me, she seemed a bit frenzied. "I need a wine refill! Cheryl, are you sure you wouldn't like a glass of wine?"

Cheryl looked at me, "Okay, but just half a glass."

We just sat there for a few minutes not saying anything, sipping our wine. Liz and I had lit cigarettes.

"Cheryl I have a number of assignments for you."

Cheryl retrieved a pen and pad of paper from her laptop case and gave me a smile and a look of "proceed". So I did. "I will let you set your own order and priorities.

Finding accommodation for yourself is very important; I don't want you living out of suitcases. If you should run tight on funds talk to Liz or me. We will be reimbursing you for all of your expenses in relocating, including costs of gas, hotels and all meals until you find an apartment, please save all of your receipts. I expect you to eat well, and I don't want you staying in a dump motel. Liz and I will come up with a flat monthly car allowance that we will give you."

Cheryl had a big grin on her face.

"I want you to check your cell phone costs. If the roaming charges are high for its use in Canada, I would like you to get another cell phone in Canada. We will pay your cell phone bill as an expense.

Will you require a moving van to bring your personal effects from Washington to Niagara?

"No, I will be able to put everything in my car, if necessary I will ship a few items by ground courier to a Niagara location. My furniture is rented."

"Great! We will need to find an architect, hopefully relatively local. He should have expertise in commercial, industrial and warehousing. The facility will be in an International Zone, we will not require building permits from the municipality. We should however, make contact with the locals and keep them informed on what we are doing. I want the facility to be environmentally friendly, have trees and look very prestigious and ultramodern.

I want you to arrange to rent some trailers preconfigured as office space, a meeting room and kitchen lunch room and an independent trailer configured as a security office.

We will need to buy a very large Quonset hut and have it installed on a concrete pad. It needs to be heated and have lighting.

We will need to buy a forklift that can easily lift cargo containers for outdoor and indoor use.

We will need a concrete pad for the cargo containers; a temporary electrical hook-up, it's my plan to eventually install one of our solar collector systems to provide us with all the energy we require. We will need water and sewage to the property.

We will require a high security chain link fence, barb wire, around the property with appropriate gating; security cameras and other security devices. See if you can identify a security consultant in the area.

Arrange for six phone lines from bell and a high speed Internet hookup.

I would like For Humanity signs put-up to replace the Ontario Government for sale signs.

Find out from the post office what our mailing address is and arrange for a secure mailbox on the corner of the lot. Then arrange for business cards for the three of us.

See if you can identify a competent head hunter in the area. I realize we may have to go to Toronto, but I would prefer not to have to go that far."

I looked at Cheryl and smiled; "That should keep you busy for at least a day."

Cheryl smiled back; "Only if I take a few coffee breaks."

We all laughed.

"There is one more thing. For the next nine months we are going to be extremely busy, it will require a lot of hours, nights, early mornings and weekends, which you will be paid for, so please keep track of your hours. However, your welfare, the welfare of all the employees, is paramount to us. If we should start to work you past your level of fatigue, you are to tell us! If you need a weekend off to relax and unwind, tell us! No one will think any less of you. I can guarantee you that Liz and I will be taking mental health breaks."

Cheryl's eyes had moistened, she tilted her head down and inhaled a big gulp of air, she then raised her head and looked at Liz then at me and then back to Liz; I hadn't said anything to my parents about a new job. I knew they would ask a lot of questions that I couldn't answer until after the meeting with the UN General Assembly. After the meeting I called them. They asked if I had watched the meeting. They were so energized; my mother and father never show any type of excitement. It's the dawn of a new era for civilization and then my father said; "that William Dafoe is quite the man". I seized the opportunity and told them that I had resigned from the Whitehouse to take a job with For Humanity. That I would be working for Liz, who I had told them all about previously and for you.

You have to understand something; my mother and father have never been more than two hundred miles from the farm. They have always said that anything they could possibly need or want is right here. They have never stayed in a hotel or travelled on a bus, train or airplane.

My father was thrilled for me and all he wanted to know was when they could come and visit me in Ontario, Canada! Believe me when I tell you that they wouldn't be coming to see me!

Will, Liz, you are both such wonderful people. I wake up in the morning and pinch myself to make sure this isn't just a dream. I don't know how to thank you!"

Cheryl had tears in her eyes. Liz went to her and gave her a sisterly hug.

Cheryl looked up at me, tears were slowly moving down her cheeks. "Can I have some more wine please?"

I topped up our glasses.

Liz and I sat down on the loveseat. I grabbed her hand and announced; "I am mentally exhausted, totally spent, I don't have one grey cell still functioning!"

Cheryl chuckled; "You're a Hercule Poirot fan?"

"I'm proud to admit I am."

"I enjoy reading all of the Agatha Christie books. Her characters are so well defined and her mysteries are original. I wish I could write."

Just then the room phone rang; "Here we go again!"

Cheryl answered it.

"Hello"

"May I ask whose calling?"

Cheryl muted the phone and looked at Liz and I; "It's UN security."

Liz rose from the loveseat. I could tell she was tired; she didn't have the usual Liz bounce in her steps. "This is Elizabeth Montgomery"

"I understand, thank you very much, Bye"

Liz turned and looked at me. "They have arranged for a coast guard helicopter to take us to Newark airport tomorrow. Security will come and get us at 10:30 and escort us, apparently there is a helipad on the top of the hotel."

Cheryl's eyes were glowing; "Wow, I've never been on a helicopter."

Cheryl looked at Liz, "I should be going. I'm sure you two would like some alone time."

Liz responded; "Please have dinner with us."

"Are you sure?"

"Yes, we're both sure."

"Thank you, I will."

Liz passed Cheryl the room service menu and returned to sit beside me.

Cheryl took our dinner orders, called room service and placed the orders. I chuckled when I heard her say "make sure the room service table can seat three!"

We had muted the audio on the TV but the video was still playing.

I saw an inset picture of the Prime Minister of England Jeremy Coxwald on the upper right side of the screen. I picked up the remote control and released the mute.

"….. Minister has called a press conference for tomorrow morning at 9:00 a.m. British time which would be 2:00 p.m. eastern standard time here in the US. Prime Minister Coxwald was unable to attend the meeting of the United Nations General Assembly as he is recovering from gallbladder surgery."

A map of the South China Sea and the Sea of Japan appeared in the top right hand corner of the screen. There were red circles around two groups of islands. "Earlier today Japanese Prime Minister Kazuhiro Miura announced a goodwill gesture to its neighbors. Japan was giving up all claims to the Senkaku Islands and the Dokdo volcanic islets. The Senkaku Islands have been claimed by both China and Taiwan and the Dokdo volcanic islets have been claimed by South Korea.

"Not every nation is celebrating the agreement with the aliens." The picture changed to President of Iran, Mahmoud Ahmadi. "Iranian President Ahmadi announced on Iranian TV that Iran would not remove or stand down any of its weapons in order to give the Zionists and opportunity to attack.

Back at home" The picture changed to President Wycliffe. "The number of resignations from the President's cabinet now stands at eight with the latest people to defect being; the Press Secretary Pauline Smith and the Secretary of the Interior Jose Ramirez. The number of elected Republicans that have become independent now stands at 62.

Impromptu crowds have formed in front of Federal buildings in major cities across the nation. Signs call for President Wycliffe to resign, others want him impeached.

Meantime there has been silence from the Whitehouse.

This is RNN keeping you up to date."

I clicked the "OFF" button. I had had more than enough news. But at least they weren't talking about me.

There was a knock at the door. Cheryl stood up and checked the peephole, opened the door, it was our dinner. This food service cart was a little longer than the one we had in the morning and had a leaf at one end as well as the sides. I opened a new bottle of wine. I picked up the three glasses and went into the washroom, rinsed them out and dried them. I poured three glasses; I didn't bother to ask Cheryl. I placed the glasses on the table, and helped Liz into her chair, put her napkin across her lap and sat down myself. Liz and I were across from one another and Cheryl was comfortably seated at the end.

We were quiet, a little too quiet. Liz broke the silence. "Cheryl, is there anything you will miss in Washington?"

"Possibly a girl friend, but nothing much else. But Niagara isn't that far from Washington, we could visit on the odd long weekend. But you know how those types of friendships are, when you're not in the same city they often wane. I had a couple of very close friends in Idaho and when I accepted the job in Washington, we promised to call each other at least once a week and to visit. We called weekly for the first four or five weeks and then it was every two weeks and that became a month and I haven't heard from either of them in at least six months. I have tried to call, but I have only ever gotten their voice mail and they haven't returned my messages."

Her face turned into a big grin; "Wait until they find out who I'm working for now!"

Liz and I smiled at each other.

We finished our appetizers and I pulled the entrees out of the warming box and placed them in front of the girls and topped up the wine glasses.

Cheryl looked at Liz; "Is there anything you miss?"

"There are a number of excellent restaurants in Washington; I wouldn't say I will miss them because I'm sure Will knows of excellent replacements. There are some people that I miss a bit, I actually missed you Cheryl, and I mean that. I know we weren't really friend friends, we didn't socialize outside of the Whitehouse, but we had some interesting girl talk over coffee at times and a few good laughs at the expense of our colleagues and I could always count on you to keep me informed on the office gossip, especially who was sleeping with who."

Liz caught me lift my head when she said who is sleeping with who. "Will, you wouldn't believe what went on at the Whitehouse. Any intern, male or female was considered fair game and in the eyes of many, it was their duty to service their mentor and the women were as bad if not worse than the men."

Cheryl started to laugh; "Last year at the Christmas Party"

Liz butted in; "I wasn't there, I was with my parents. Sorry Cheryl, please tell Will what happened."

Cheryl was trying to compose herself; "That's okay. The Secretary of State, Danielle Furlong was caught in a Ménage à Trois with two of her male interns in the Lincoln Bedroom by the Secret Service. There is an emergency silent alarm button in every room of the Whitehouse. If the button is pushed the Secret Service respond with guns drawn. Somehow in their sexual frenzy the button got pushed. Seconds later the Secret Service arrived, they heard a woman screaming inside the room so they burst the door open. They found Furlong on the bed, lying on top of one of the interns, inside her and the other intern was poking her butt from behind, Furlong was screaming deeper, deeper. These boys, and that is what they were boys, couldn't have been older than seventeen. Furlong is at least fifty-five. The two interns were dismissed a few days later and Furlong walked away scot free. I am sure that the interns were coerced into the bedroom."

Liz and I were laughing.

"There are so many stories of sex in closets, offices, the lawn and the Whitehouse guest bedrooms. Do you remember a number of years ago one of our President's was caught in the Oval office with his female intern on her hands and knees under her desk?"

I nodded, I was still laughing too hard to speak.

"You may remember that the First Lady stood by his side. I wasn't at the Whitehouse at the time, but gossip has it that one of the male interns had been bonking her for months."

Liz and I finally composed ourselves.

Liz and I lit cigarettes after dinner and the three of us just sat there chatting about nothing. It was 8:03 when Cheryl stood up and announced she was tired and going to her room. Liz told her to be here at 10:25 in the morning with her suitcases and to call down to the front desk and inform them that she was checking out.

Cheryl said goodnight and Liz and I were alone.

"Liz, would you like to join me for a bubble bath in the whirlpool tub?"

"Sounds wonderful!"

Just as we got up from the loveseat, Liz's phone rang, she smiled when she looked at the screen; "It's Mom, go start the bath, I'll be with you shortly."

I left the sitting room and started running the water into the tub. The tub had a widespread Roman waterfall spout. I stood there for a second and watched the waterfall. It was quite impressive. I found the small bottle of complimentary bubble bath and spilled into the tub just below the spout. Instantly bubbles started to appear. This was a big tub and filling it was going to take some time. I went back into the bedroom and undressed, hanging up my clothes. As I did, I realized that I didn't have a suitcase; the one I brought back from my trip with the aliens was filled with memory cards and other small items. I remembered that there was a luggage shop in the lobby. I would call down in the morning and have them bring me one. I wasn't in the mood to head downstairs now.

I went back to the bathroom the water was only about three inches deep. I put on a bathrobe and went back to the sitting room. Liz was sitting on the loveseat, a smile on her face, still talking to her Mom.

I drained the wine bottle into my glass and went and sat beside her. She grabbed my hand and gave it a hard squeeze. I was too mentally tired to hone into the conversation.

Every now and then Liz would say; "yes", or "uhha".

"Mom, Dad, I don't want to be rude, but Will and I are exhausted we were up quite early this morning for an early meeting with the Security Council prior to the meeting with the General Assembly."

There was a pause.

"Yes, I was there, I was sitting with the members of the Security Council."

Pause.

"We were just going to have a bubble bath and relax. We have a big whirlpool tub in the bathroom."

Pause

"Goodnight" Liz disconnected.

"Liz, would you call Barbara and just make sure everything is okay."

Liz immediately brought Barbara's name up on her smart phone screen and hit connect. "Hi Barbara it's Liz, your father and I just want to make sure your okay."

Pause

"Okay, yes we're fine. We'll be in Niagara tomorrow; I'll give you a call from there when we are settled."

"Love you too, I'll tell him. Bye." Liz disconnected. "She's fine, she hasn't received any calls and no one appears to know she exists. I'm to tell you that she is very, very proud of you and loves you very much."

Liz glanced down at her phone, I have a text message. She brought it up on the screen. "It's from Prime Minister Harmon; he has given us a contact name with the Canadian Department of Immigration."

I took Liz by the hand and led her into the bedroom. I had her stand in front of me and I slowly undressed her. I allowed my hands to touch every square inch of her soft skin as I removed her clothes, I cupped her firm silken breasts in my hands from behind her, she was enjoying every minute of my caressing. I kissed her lightly on the neck. Once she was naked I put my arm around her waist, walked her into the bathroom and helped her climb into the tub; I dropped my bathrobe on the bathroom floor and climbed in after her, the hot water was very soothing and I could feel it relaxing my muscles. I sat so that my body was stretched out as far as I could while still keeping my head above the water, reached over and slid Liz on top of me so that I could feel her breasts against my chest, her thighs against mine, she put her arms around my neck and rested her head on my shoulder, I pulled her against me, shut my eyes and just allowed my brain to drain.

I opened my eyes with a start. I had fallen asleep and Liz was sound asleep on top of me, her arms draped lightly around my neck. The water had cooled down dramatically and was no longer providing a soothing effect. I tightened my arms around Liz which had the desired effect she began to stir and wakeup. She moved her body against mine and kissed my neck. Liz murmured in my ear; "Hmmmm, that was very nice." I wasn't sure if she was talking about the kiss or her nap.

I squeezed her tight; "The water's getting cold, it's time to get out." Liz wriggled her body off mine. I climbed out of the tub and retrieved a bathrobe for her; helped her step over the tub sidewall and into the robe. I took a towel and wiped the tips of her hair; most of her hair had remained out of the water and was dry. I took another towel and dried her legs. The bathrobe had taken care of drying the rest of her. I used her towel to dry my legs and torso, Liz took the towel from me and dried my back. I led her into the bedroom; she dropped her bathrobe from her shoulders in a very provocative move. I picked her up in my arms and placed her on the bed with my arms around her. She looked into my eyes, her eyes were sultry, warm and alluring all at the same time, her face was radiant and beautiful; "Make love to me Will, very slowly, all night!" Her lips met mine and we made love for hours until our physical exhaustion matched our mental exhaustion, we fell asleep in a tangled web of arms and legs.

Chapter 12 – 263 days to alien arrival

I opened my eyes; it was 6:37 a.m. I felt rejuvenated and full of energy. Liz had her head on a pillow with her arm across my chest and her leg over mine. She was still sleeping, it was early and there was no need to wake her. I just laid back and enjoyed the feel of her leg and arm around me. It was 7:02 when Liz began to stir. She opened her eyes and saw me watching her. Her face beamed; "Good morning darling!" She raised her head and gave me a passionate kiss. I loved the feel of her tongue in my mouth and Liz knew it.

She pulled back with a big grin on her face; "We'll finish this later, let's shower."

We did our usual morning shower routine and no, it wasn't becoming mundane.

We dressed casual, at least I was casual, Liz's idea of casual was still very fashion conscious.

I called down and ordered us breakfast from room service. Then I called the luggage store in the lobby, a recorded message told me it didn't open until 9:30, it was only 8:10. 9:30 would still give me plenty of time to pack. I went into the bedroom, Liz had her suitcase on the bed and was packing; she had opened the safe and removed her earrings and the passports and placed them in her purse. She said that all of our clothes wouldn't fit into her suitcase. I informed her of my plan to buy a new suitcase.

Liz looked at me; "What are we going to do with the printer?"

I pondered for a moment."We can pack it up. We saved the box and packing material and send it up to Ontario by courier ground."

Then I realized I was being dumb. "Liz, shipping the printer will cost more than it's worth. We can buy a new one for less."

"Stick a note on it and tell housekeeper that she can have it!"

Liz nodded her approval.

"Liz, you didn't tell me what your Mom wanted when she called last night."

Liz continued to pack while she gave me the lowdown.

"The conversation centered around two things. How lucky I am to have you; that you could have any girl in the world; how I must do everything and anything to hang on to you; I'm not to show you what I turn into when I get depressed; how pleased they are that you will be joining the family and so on and so on. I told you that they would come sniveling on their hands and knees once they knew that you are the "Chosen one"."

Liz looked at me and snickered; "The other item, of course, was what was happening at the Whitehouse and congress. They are having doubts about Wycliffe's ability to lead the nation; they are attending a meeting this evening to discuss how the party should respond to the situation; all a pile of goobledegook. Oh, and they want to know if we are still coming on April 15th; I told them that we would have to let them know."

There was a knock at the door; "Breakfast I hope!" I went to the door, checked the peephole and opened it. The waiter wheeled in the food service cart. I signed the bill and he left. "Liz, breakfast" I called out.

Liz walked into the sitting room and I seated her at the table. "Will, are you going to treat me like a Princess forever; pulling my chair out, placing my napkin on my lap, opening doors for me, washing and brushing my hair?"

"No, longer than forever. Are you complaining?"

Liz smiled; "Not at all. My parents won't know how to react when they see you treating me like a Princess. You know, I don't deserve you?"

"It's the other way around my love. It's I who doesn't deserve you."

I removed the metal covers from our breakfast plates and sat down.

Liz looked at the meal in front of her. "Eggs Florentine; looks yummy"

"I thought we needed a change from Eggs Benedict."

Liz and I started eating our breakfasts.

"There was one other thing. When Mom called Dad wasn't on the extension yet. She told me that she is a little concerned. Apparently he went to the doctor last week and didn't tell her he was going and hasn't said anything about it since. She wanted to talk to me about it, I think, but Dad picked up the phone and she immediately changed the subject."

"Is it like your father to hide bad things from your mother?"

"I'm really not sure. I know they care about each other in a weird fashion. At times it's more like a business partnership than a marriage."

"It could be a male problem, prostate, how old is your father?"

"Sixty-eight"

"It's possible. I will talk to him and try to find out what's going on. It could be a problem that I have a medication for in my cargo container."

Liz smiled; "I like knowing that I can count on you. Thank you darling."

After breakfast Liz finished packing. She took all of the packing material and the box for the printer and put it on the floor in front of the printer. She then hand wrote a sign:

Dear Housekeeper, We are unable to take this printer with us. Please take it home or give it to someone else that can use it. It's brand new and shouldn't be trashed.

It was 9:31. I called the luggage shop in the lobby and told them I needed a suitcase. I gave them a loose description, two wheels; pull out handle; large enough for three suits, six shirts and assorted socks and underwear. They said they would be pleased to send one up to the room.

When I finished with the room phone, Liz called down to reception and informed them that we would be vacating the room by the eleven o'clock check-out time.

A few minutes later the luggage shop arrived with my suitcase. It was bigger than required, but I took it. The fellow who brought it had a handheld credit card reader and took my card for payment.

I took the suitcase into the room and started to pack. The room phone rang. I answered expecting it to be the press. I was wrong, it was Vice-President Almont. He wanted to give me a heads up that it looked as if President Wycliffe would be resigning this evening and if he did, he would become President. He wanted to ensure us that if things unfolded the way they appeared to be that Liz and I would have his unconditional support. I thanked him and he hung up.

I told Liz about the conversation. She gave me one of her intellectual looks; "Almont will make a much better President than Wycliffe. The problem that Almont has is that he doesn't have the public speaking finesse that Wycliffe and other Presidential candidates have. If he can gain the position of President due to the resignation of Wycliffe, he will have a chance to prove his abilities and hopefully be elected next time based on his actions rather than his public speaking ability."

Smart lady I thought.

Liz had started to pack my suitcase while I was on the phone with Vice-President Almont. She was folding each garment carefully and making sure that creases were kept to a bare minimum.

Once she had completed her task and was satisfied with her workmanship, she checked the closet, bathroom, drawers and safe to make sure she hadn't missed anything.

I zipped up my suitcase and took Liz's and mine into the sitting room. Liz took my laptop from the desk and put it in its case along with some papers. She then opened my suitcase on the floor and carefully put my laptop case in and then laid her laptop beside it. She took the remaining office supplies and put them on top of the laptops. She stood back and looked at her handiwork. "We need something to fill the suitcase; everything is going to shift."

"Use my jacket" I went to the closet and took my leather jacket out.

Liz folded it and laid it carefully on top. "Will, get my jacket as well."

I handed Liz her jacket and she folded it and put it on top of mine. "That's perfect"

I zipped up the bag; I had to push down a little to get the zipper sides to meet, nothing was going to shift. I stood my suitcase beside hers and brought my suitcase with the memory cards over. I unzipped it, I went into the bathroom and took two bath towels and brought them back into the sitting room and carefully wrapped the four remaining bottles of wine that we hadn't yet consumed in one and the two bottles of port that we had received from Ambassador Evans in the other. I placed the packages gently in the suitcase and zipped it up.

I looked at Liz "I think we're ready" It was only 10:12. Liz and I had another coffee and a cigarette together.

At 10:22 there was a knock on the door. Cheryl had arrived.

Liz and Cheryl chitchatted and it wasn't long after that another very strong knock occurred. Liz and Cheryl stood up and walked towards the door before I even opened it. There were two UN security officers, lightly armed at the door. I caught the eye of one of the officers. "Have things quieted down a bit?"

"Quite a bit sir, most of the senior foreign dignitaries left New York yesterday afternoon, right after the meeting a number of others in the evening. But, a lot of press is still hovering around especially after the demonstrations last night."

I grabbed the handles of my two suitcases and Liz and Cheryl grabbed theirs. We walked towards the elevator, definitely with less concern and trepidation that occurred yesterday. Once on the elevator, one of the officers pushed the button for the 46th floor, the highest floor in the building.

The elevator door opened and we walked down the corridor to an exit door. Through the door, there was a staircase going up. One security officer took Liz's bag and the other took Cheryl's bag. Cheryl then grabbed the suitcase from me that had the memory cards, it was heavier than she expected, she wasn't aware of the four bottles of wine and the two bottles of port. I went up the steps dragging the suitcase the one with the two laptops and two jackets.

At the top landing there was an exit door. One of the security officers pulled a set of keys from his pocket and tried a couple of them until he found one that opened the door. He stuck his head outside, turned around and told us to remain inside for a minute.

He went out on to the rooftop.

A few minutes later we heard the sound of a helicopter approaching. The officer opened the door and informed us that the pilot would not be turning off the rotors. He grabbed Liz's suitcase which he had left on the landing and we followed him out onto the rooftop. The wind from the rotors was unbelievable it was worse than a hurricane. The officers went ahead of us and loaded the two suitcases that they were carrying into the helicopter, then ran back to get the other two suitcases that Cheryl and I were carrying. We finally fought the wind storm and climbed in the helicopter, sat down and buckled ourselves in. The officers closed the doors behind us and we took off. The seats were nothing like those in the VH-71 helicopters that were assigned to the President. This was a coast guard search and rescue helicopter, it had no comforts; it was equipped for real life work. If one needed a comparison, the President flew in a limo; we were flying in the back of a dump truck.

There was no sense in any of us trying to communicate with one another the ambient noise from the helicopter's rotors was far too loud to talk over.

What probably would have taken an hour by car took less than five minutes by helicopter. Before I had even settled in my seat we were on the ground about 25 yards away from our NASA jet. The co-pilot of the helicopter; came around his seat to open the sliding door from the inside. He glanced at me and then did a double take. "You're William Dafoe!" He tapped the pilot on the shoulder, he turned his head. The co-pilot, was beside himself; "Geoff, we have just flown William Dafoe." The pilot swiveled out of his seat and came to the inside of the cabin, stuck out his hand; "Mr. Dafoe it is an honor to make your acquaintance." I shook his hand. I thought he was going to wrench my arm out of its socket. The co-pilot shook my hand after the pilot had finished, then in a deep southern accent. "Mr. Dafoe, you're a true hero. I'll be able to tell my grandchildren that I had the honor of flying William Dafoe the "Chosen One"." The pilot interjected quickly; "Aaron, you gotta get married before you can have grandchildren."

The pilot jumped out of the helicopter; "Let us help you with those bags sir." The co-pilot passed the suitcases to the pilot. Then the pilot helped Cheryl, then Liz and finally me out of the helicopter. They each grabbed two suitcases and lead us towards the NASA jet. Our NASA pilots had come out of the aircraft and were standing at the bottom of the steps. They put the suitcases in front of the steps. They both stood to attention and saluted me. "Thanks fellas, fly safely." They turned and headed back to the helicopter, each turning and looking over their shoulders at us as they walked.

Our NASA pilots took our suitcases aboard the aircraft. We climbed the steps into the aircraft and sat; Liz beside me and Cheryl across the aisle. Before he went into the cockpit, the pilot turned to me; "It's an honor to be your pilots, sir!" He didn't wait for a reply; turned and went into the cockpit.

We fastened our seatbelts and the crew started up the engines. We taxied for about five minutes in order to get into position at the end of the runway. In a few minutes we were making our assent.

Once we were airborne, I leaned over and whispered in Liz's ear; "I am concerned about Cheryl's cash flow. She wasn't making a lot of money and I don't want her to get caught short; no pun intended."

Liz chuckled.

"I have three hundred dollars in cash and I can get more when we land in Niagara. But I don't think Cheryl will take it from me, do you think she'll take it from you."

Liz smiled at me and in low voice so Cheryl wouldn't hear; "Give me the money." I glanced over to see if Cheryl was watching us. She had moved to the window seat and was staring out the window. I cautiously put my hand into my pants pocket and pulled out the folded three hundred dollars and slipped it into Liz's hand. Liz fumbled around in her purse and dropped the money into it. She undid her seat belt and sat down beside Cheryl. Liz and Cheryl were talking about something, but I didn't want to ease drop, but I was watching out of the corner of my eye. Then I saw Liz reach into her purse and pull out the money and quickly hand it to Cheryl. Cheryl immediately palmed it, to ensure that I couldn't see what was happening. They talked for a few more minutes and then Liz returned to her seat. She took my hand and squeezed it, saying nothing.

In 53 minutes we were making our descent into Reagan National Airport. We taxied for a few minutes and ended up at a corporate jet service facility. The co-pilot came out from the cockpit, opened the door and lowered the steps. Cheryl stood, elevated the handle of her suitcase and started to exit, as she did she walked in front of Liz and I; "I'll see you in Niagara in a couple of days." The co-pilot grabbed Cheryl's bag and placed it at the bottom of the steps. Cheryl exited the door, and then stuck her head back around the corner, she had a wonderful smile on her face; "Thanks for the money Will!" Liz squeezed my hand and looked at me; "I didn't tell her, honest." The co-pilot was pointing Cheryl in the right direction, in less than a minute she was inside the terminal building.

The pilot came out of the cockpit. "I'm very sorry Sir, Ma'am; we have to wait 35 minutes before we can depart. Would you like a coffee, tea, water?" Liz asked for a bottle of water and I said make it two. The pilot ran down the steps and into the terminal building. The co-pilot came back into the aircraft. "Sir I couldn't help but notice your package of cigarettes; feel free to smoke." I looked at him; "Thank you" Liz took her cigarettes out of her purse and I took mine out of my shirt pocket. The smoke felt good as I inhaled.

The pilot returned and handed us each a bottle of water, he had brought coffees for him and the co-pilot. "Sir, Ma'am; if you have a moment I have a cute story I would like to share with you." As we didn't object, he proceeded. "Yesterday a group of pilots and their wives or girlfriends went to the local base bar to watch the meeting at the UN General Assembly. When we saw you, we both pointed and said to our wives; "That's the guy we flew to Canada the other day". Then we told them that we would be flying you back there today."

He paused and took a sip of his coffee and then continued.

"Whenever a pilot has to fly and be away overnight their wives or girlfriends go through a leaving ritual, which includes being bitchy, I don't want you to go, I'm here all by myself, I've got nothing to do. It's all designed to make us feel guilty and it usually does. Well, this morning things were very different for the both of us. Our wives woke us early, pressed our uniforms, gave us big breakfasts, kisses at the door and literally pushed us out 45 minutes before we needed to leave saying; "You take care of Mr. Dafoe, take him anywhere he wants to go, if it means being gone for a week or two we'll understand. So, we have decided that we will be your pilots forever, even if we're not, do you get my drift?"

Liz and I both started laughing.

"Sir; could we impose? Would you autograph a picture? One for each of our wives"

"Sure, not a problem"

He reached into his flight bag and pulled out two copies of the front page of a Tampa Tribune newspaper. There was a six inch by eight inch picture of me with a big caption *The Chosen One*. "I'm not sure what to write." I pondered for a second; "Is your wife a Star Wars fan? "Yes Sir." "What's your wife's first name? "Jackie, Sir" The co-pilot handed me a book to support the newspaper and I wrote in the bottom right hand side of the picture; *To Jackie, may the force be with you, William Dafoe*

Liz, was watching me write; "That's very good and appropriate."

"Thank you, sir"

I looked up at the pilot, "What about your wife?"

"She's not a Star Wars fan. She likes nonsensical movies like Airplane, Men In Black"

"Does she like Spaceballs with Mel Brooks and John Candy?"

"I'm embarrassed to say, but she has the DVD and watches it often."

"What's her name?"

"Cathy, Sir; with a C"

I took the second newspaper and wrote: *To Cathy, may the schwartz be with you, William Dafoe*

Liz watched me write; "I don't understand."

"That's because you're not a Mel Brooks fan. I'll explain it to you later."

Liz stuck her tongue out at me. Then gave me a kiss on the cheek; "You're my Chosen One"

The pilot, touched the co-pilot on the shoulder; "Time to go"

The co-pilot pulled up the stairs shut the door and went into the cockpit. Liz and I buckled up and held hands.

We each had another cigarette and talked, mostly about her concern for her father.

Before we knew we were on final approach to Niagara District Airport. A few moments later the wheels touched down and we taxied to the terminal.

The co-pilot and pilot both left the cockpit and helped us with our suitcases. They thanked me again and asked if they should standby here. Liz told them to go home and she would let them know our flight plans as soon as we knew them.

Liz and I walked into the terminal building with our suitcases in tow. A wall phone provided an instant dial to a taxi service. There was an ATM machine next to the phone, so I availed myself of some cash. We walked outside to the front of the terminal and waited for the taxi to arrive. It was a beautiful day, 72°F, no wind and just a few soft fluffy white clouds resting on a perfect blue background. I lit another cigarette, lighting a cigarette always makes a taxi come quicker! It worked! The taxi appeared before I was able to finish the cigarette. We had the driver take us to the closest car rental facility, where we rented a basic sedan. I put Liz on as an additional driver, without asking, that really seemed to please her.

I actually knew where I was. I opened the passenger door for Liz and walked to the driver's side and we headed off to one of the better hotels at Niagara-on-the-Lake. It took about twenty minutes to get there, we didn't talk; Liz had her hand on my thigh and was taking in the sights as we drove. We arrived at the hotel, I asked for their best suite. A do it all concierge placed our suitcases on a cart and we followed him to the room. He was full of idle chitchat; is this your first time here; are you here for the Shaw festival; we should see him for tickets for everything; he told us about the restaurants, the park and provided us with a host of other trivial information. I gave him a tip and he finally left us alone.

"Liz, did you notice that nobody recognized me. I was sure that when I showed my driver's license at the car rental place or when I checked in here with the credit card, someone would have recognized the name. It's great we can hide here out in the open."

The furnishings in the room were inexpensive, not near as nice as the furnishings we had at the Century UN Plaza Hotel in New York, but the suite was substantially larger. We had a balcony with a couple of chairs and a small table that looked out over a harbor where at least thirty sailboats were moored. The windows ran the length of one wall, with the drapes open the room was bright and alive. In the sitting room there was a large sofa, a coffee table, three occasional chairs, a desk with a chair, two side tables each with a table lamp, a floor lamp in the corner and an armoire.

Liz was sitting on the sofa, she chuckled; "I thought he'd never leave. Mr. Dafoe, I am in dire need of a kiss."

I sat down beside her and pulled her against me and gave her the type of passionate kiss that she delivers to me. I stuck my tongue in her mouth and tried to tickle her tonsils. I sucked the air out of her lungs and made her breath through my mouth, to take air from my lungs, her nose was trapped against the side of mine. I wouldn't let her break the kiss; I had placed one hand behind her head and the other between her thighs, I slipped my fingers under her panties and started to play. Her body began to writhe against my hand, she thrashed, I felt every muscle tighten and then she went limp in my arms. Liz's breathing was heavy, I could feel her heart pounding like a jack hammer against my chest; she couldn't catch her breath and she was like a rag doll in my arms. I put her head against my shoulder and just held her against me. It took a couple of minutes for her heart to stop racing and her breathing to sound normal. She placed her hand on my cheek, and looked up at me with bedroom eyes; "in case you aren't aware, I just had an unbelievable orgasm, I have never felt anything like that before; I thought that the heights you brought me to previously were fantastic, but they were nothing like what I just experienced. When you drew the air out of my lungs, it is so hard to describe, Will, I felt like we had merged, our bodies were one. Oh Will, I can't even begin to explain the pleasure you give me."

Liz remained with her head against my shoulder for another seventeen minutes, barely moving. It was 3:02 and we hadn't really accomplished anything today. Liz stood up and looked around the room and started to investigate, there were four doors; one was the entry door into the suite; another was a small two piece washroom, beside it was a door that had a door behind it, Liz opened both of them to find a bedroom with its own washroom that hotel could rent our as a separate room and the last door was the primary bedroom that went with the suite. "This will work out fine. If Barbara or someone else comes to visit they can stay in the other bedroom." Liz took the handles of both suitcases and towed them into what would be our bedroom. I got up and followed her. In the room was a four poster bed, the top of the mattress was much higher than normal, thirty inches off the floor. Damn, I thought I'll need a ladder to climb into bed. Liz's suitcase was on the bed open, Liz had gone into the bathroom and shut the door; I heard water flowing into a sink. I placed my suitcase on the bed and started to unpack. I hung our jackets in the closet by the entry way into the room; the laptops and office supplies went on the desk in the sitting room.

When I returned Liz was just coming out of the bathroom, she had some clothes clenched in her hands; when she saw me, her face turned pink, she looked like a child who was just caught with their hand in the cookie jar; "I had to wash and change, I was so wet, it felt like I had an accident. We have a whirlpool tub, not as big as the one at the Century but definitely big enough for the two of us and a walk in shower for two." Liz placed her damp undies and silk stockings in a laundry bag. Liz started unpacking my suitcase. She carefully hung up all of the suits, ties and the shirts that had been opened and neatly placed the others and my underwear and socks in the drawers of a bureau that was against one of the walls. She then did the same with her clothes. Liz took our collection of passports and her earrings and put them in the safe in the closet.

I took the empty suitcases and placed them on the floor in the closet.

Liz put her arms around me and gave me a kiss. I suggested that we go for a drive around the area. Liz wanted to make a couple of phone calls first.

Liz went into the sitting room, sat on the sofa and started to place her calls. I stayed in the bedroom. It was time to talk to Steve at the office. For some reason I was more apprehensive about talking to Steve than I was facing the 1,800 plus delegates at the UN General Assembly. I felt that I had let him down and I didn't like that feeling at all.

I sat on the occasional chair in the bedroom that was next to the night stand with a room phone on. It was 4:17; Steve should still be in the office. I dialed Steve's private number, part of my brain was hoping I would get his voice mail so that I wouldn't have to face him, but I knew that it would only mean doing this again at another time.

After the third ring, there was a voice at the other end of the line.

Steve was always upbeat and his voice represented that; "Steve!"

I tried to put my happy salesman's voice into play; "Hi Steve it's, Will."

He had a jubilant tone in his voice; "Hey man, how the hell are you; we all saw you on TV yesterday, I set up a big screen in the office so that we wouldn't miss the UN meeting; you've had one hell of an adventure; you looked good!"

"I'm really sorry for leaving you in the lurch."

"At first, I thought you were being a real shit; then we all began to really worry about you. Look Will, I understand that you had to do what you had to do. There are absolutely no hard feelings or animosity, believe me." Steve's voice was sincere, relief consumed me. "I know you won't be coming back to work here and after yesterday I have been contemplating how to replace you."

"Steve, as always you are a gentleman and scholar."

Steve's voice changed to serious; "Will, I'm sure you have been getting a lot of accolades and you deserve them all. I want you to know that I am very proud to know the man who saved the human race. You have always been the ultimate consummate salesman; they couldn't have made a better choice for an emissary to represent humanity."

His voice became upbeat again; "Please keep in contact and if you're driving past drop in and say hello, I'd really like to shake your hand. Have you spoken to Elli or Adam yet?"

"No, I wanted to talk to you first."

"I'm not sure what I'm going to do at this point, it had been in the back of my mind that you would return and I wouldn't have to face the problem."

"Have sales been okay?"

"There fine for now, the problem as I see it is twofold. Currently we are living on the sales pipeline that you created and drove. When I look at sales forecasts that are nine and twelve months out, I don't see where the business is going to come from. We aren't implementing any new sales initiatives; we're resting on our laurels. When you were here, we did something different every couple of months to try and open new markets, some worked, some didn't but we never stopped being aggressive. Elli and Adam don't seem to have the creativity or insight to identify potential markets that we haven't infiltrated previously. They keep attacking the same markets and you well know that we can't have growth unless we find new customers."

"May I comment? I didn't wait for an answer. "Many of the ideas that I came up with came from discussions with Elli and Adam; seldom at formal meetings, just sitting around at lunch time or after hours and chatting. Elli is very bright, but she is not overly confident in her creativity and ingenuity. She will seldom fight for an idea, unless she is 100 percent confident that she can defend it. Sales are 75 percent gut instinct, it's impossible to defend gut instinct. I never asked you for permission to implement a new idea; I told you what I was going to do. More times than not, you would give me a look as if I had just lost it. If you asked me to defend the idea, I ignored you! If you give Elli your look, she will start to question herself and in the end, she will yield to what she thinks is your superior judgment in the situation. I know that you couldn't sell a bottle of water to a man dying of thirst."

Steve broke out laughing.

"Secondarily, Elli and Adam may have been doing what you were doing, expecting me to come back. I was their crutch in a manner of speaking. Adam is a good salesman, but he needs direction. I think Elli can drive Adam, I have actually seen her do it. Adam doesn't want any administrative function in the organization; he has no desire, at least at this time, to be a sales manager he just wants to be out selling, he loves it and he's good at it. I suggest you talk to them, informally. Give Elli the chance to implement sales and marketing initiatives that she is confident in and don't ask her to justify her ideas. Tell Adam that he now reports to Elli, and make Elli marketing manager. I have always told Adam that sales is a function of marketing. Just let Elli do her thing without micromanaging her; keep it informal. That's my two cents, for what it's worth."

"Sounds good, I'll try it on for size."

"I'm sure that Elli and Adam now realize that I won't be coming back, so it's a new ballgame for both of them. I'm not going to speak to either of them today, because I don't want to inadvertently say something that might affect or interfere with your plans. Please tell them I'm very busy, but that I will call them in a couple of weeks and if you want a laugh, look at Adam sternly and say; "Will wants to know when you plan on submitting last month's expense account. Steve, I wish you the best, please say hello to Evelyn for me. I will speak with you again. Bye for now."

"Take care of yourself Will, Bye!"

I placed the handset in the cradle, I felt so relieved.

Evelyn was Steve's wife and a very nice woman. After my wife passed away Evelyn tried her best to befriend Barbara, but for some reason Barbara ignored her advances. It may have been too soon after her death or it could have been that she tried to become her mother. Liz on the other hand never tried to replace my wife as Barbara's mother; they were just extremely close friends.

I went into the sitting room, Liz was still on the phone and she was taking notes. I lit up a cigarette and watched her. This lady had two completely different characters. On one hand she was the extremely confident and intelligent business woman, who could think on her feet, could give as well as take and knew how to drive people, without alienating them. She was comfortable speaking with anyone, excluding her parents, including heads of state and gave an air of self-assured independence. Then there was the Liz who wanted to be loved and cherished, wanted to be held and taken care of. Wanted to drop her shroud of strength and confidence and be a little girl in someone's arms.

Liz, finally got off the phone, she looked exhausted. "Barbara is fine. I told her we were here. I told her we would come to Toronto and take her out for her birthday on Wednesday night, I hope that's okay? How far is it?"

"That's perfect. We can be there in an hour, an hour and half at the most depending on traffic."

"Good! The last call was with the contact from the Department of Citizenship and Immigration Canada. He took a long time hemming and hawing about what was needed and asked a lot of dumb questions.

I was almost at the point of hanging up on him and contacting the Prime Minister to see if he could provide us the name of a bureaucrat with half a brain. Then out of nowhere, he stopped hemming and hawing and said he would set us up in the same manner as Foreign Embassies who have foreign staff. He actually did it while I was on the phone with him. He has processed cards for Cheryl and I and will courier them here to us at the hotel. He did give me the official line," Liz started talking with a baritone male voice; "that the work visas he will issue only allow us to work for "For Humanity" we cannot work for anyone else in Canada. Anytime we get a new foreign employee we are to call him and he will issue the work visa and if a foreign employee is terminated or quits, we are to collect their work visa and send it back to him.

I will text Cheryl and give her the work visa number in case she has any problems at the border.

I need a cigarette and a glass of wine!"

I retrieved a bottle of wine from the bath towel in my suitcase and poured us each a glass. We didn't have any wine glasses I was forced to use some glass tumblers which didn't enhance the wine in any manner.

"Liz, I have an idea. I'm really getting tired of packing and unpacking. Why don't we send the NASA jet to pick your parents up on Saturday morning, rather than us going to see them? The plane can take them back on Sunday evening. We'll rent them a room here, unless you are comfortable enough to have them stay in the room next door, the one that connects to this room?

Liz didn't have to think about the suggestion at all. "I think it's an excellent idea. That way we have deemed control. I don't see any problem with them staying in the room that attaches to our suite, but I will think about it a little more, we don't have to decide that now. I'm going to call Mom and Dad and tell them that if they want to see us they have to come here and that we will send our NASA jet to pick them up. That will make them feel like big wheels!

Liz grabbed her cell phone and called her Mom and told her the situation for the weekend and explained that we would take care of flying them here and back on our private NASA jet. She said that she would have the pilot call and give them a pick-up time and location.

When she disconnected the line she looked at me with a big smirk on her face. "Mom said that it was nice idea. She actually sounded excited when I said it was our NASA jet. I'm going to call the pilots and tell them the situation."

Liz picked up her phone to call the pilots. But before she could, I interjected. "Liz, tell the pilots to bring their wives here for the weekend. They can take them to Niagara Falls. We'll rent them a car for the two days and get them a couple of decent hotel rooms."

Liz looked at me with an expression of awe. "That's a great idea. You are so caring."

Liz called the pilot and told him that we had two missions for him. The first mission was to pick up her parents. He should figure out a flight plan and times that would get them here between ten and eleven on the Saturday morning and return them on Sunday so that they arrive back between nine and ten in the evening. The second mission was to bring their wives with them and stay the weekend. We would take care of the expenses; they could have a mini vacation at Niagara Falls. I heard Liz say, that wasn't a suggestion; it's a mission that you will undertake.

Liz was chuckling; "He told me that bringing their wives wasn't necessary. I told him that we required them to do it."

I took my laptop and said lets book them nice rooms at Niagara Falls. We did a Google and found a nice hotel, not to ritzy and booked two rooms complete with dinner and breakfast packages. We booked them under my name and paid for them. I then booked us another vehicle from the car rental agency, a Cadillac V series sedan. The pilots and their wives would take the car we currently had and we would take the Cadillac. I thought impressing the Montgomery's would be important to Liz.

Liz, we need to go shopping. We need some wine glasses and a printer; another office in one and I need to get more cigarettes. I also thought we might drive around a bit and look at houses and areas."

Liz finished her cigarette and wine; stood up and walked over to me, she put her hands on my shoulders; there was a glint in her eyes. "Mr. Dafoe you have to get your priorities straight. First kiss then shopping!" She moved her hands from my shoulders to my cheeks, pulled my face to hers and gave me a smooch, a big wet noisy smooch.

We went down to the lobby and asked the concierge where we might find a computer store. He suggested we go to St. Catherines. I knew where the office supply store was in St. Catherines so that worked out fine. Liz and I drove around the side streets of Niagara-on-the-Lake looking at houses. We saw a number that had for sale signs that were quite nice, but nothing jumped out and said buy me! We then headed off to St. Catherines; it was less than a fifteen minute drive. We drove to the mall where the office supply store was and went in. Liz checked out the office-in-one printers and chose what she wanted. She suggested that we pick up another machine for Cheryl. We then picked up some printer paper and office supplies and a pad of expense account forms. When we finished shopping we put the items in the car and went into the mall and purchased some inexpensive wine glasses; four champagne; four red and four white and cigarettes for the both of us.

It was 7:07. Liz said she was getting hungry. I knew a very nice little restaurant in the heart of Niagara-on-the-Lake, so we left St. Catherines and headed back. We had a nice quiet and relaxing dinner. We talked about the type of home we wanted. We were sitting there finishing our wine. I realized that there was a subject that we had never discussed; children.

" Liz, do you want children?"

She looked at me as if she was afraid of answering the question incorrectly. She drank some wine and looked down at the table before she answered. "Do you?"

"Didn't anyone ever tell you that it's not polite to answer a question with a question?"

Liz raised her head; "I'm afraid I'll lose you."

That annoyed me; "Liz Montgomery, there is nothing you can say or do that will ever make me want to leave you. Do you understand?"

Her voice was so soft I could barely hear her; "Yes"

I picked up my wind glass and took a sip.

Liz was still staring down at the table, very quickly she blurted out; "I don't want children; are you upset with me?"

"I love you with all my heart. I don't understand why you not wanting children would make me upset with you. In all honesty Liz, I really don't want to raise another child or group of children. I've been there and done that. I don't want you to have to share your love with anyone else. I'm very selfish when it comes to your love, I want it all! I want our time together to be ours."

Liz raised her head she had tears in her eyes. "You don't know how relieved I am, Will. I can't have children. I'm sorry I didn't tell you before."

Liz relaxed a lot, and we changed the conversation to her parents' upcoming visit; where we should take them and what things to talk about. There was a reasonably high class restaurant in our hotel and I suggested to Liz that we have dinner with them there on Saturday night.

All of a sudden Liz had a devious look on her face; "I would like Mom and Dad to stay in the adjoining room to our suite. When they go to bed I want you to make love to me on the couch. I want them to hear me scream with pleasure when you make me climax."

Liz started to giggle, obviously she could picture her mother and father in the room next to ours wondering what exactly was going on.

I looked at Liz with a forlorn expression; "I can only make you climax once?"

Liz was still giggling; "Absolutely not, the more the better."

The giggle became a laugh.

We finished our wine and went outside to the car. There was a park bench just off to one side and we sat and had a cigarette. There was a full moon and a clear sky filled with stars, it was quite a romantic setting. I put my arm around her shoulders and held her against me.

After our cigarettes we drove back to the hotel, it was 10:17, I was getting tired. On our arrival at the hotel I looked for the concierge but he was nowhere to be found. I took his luggage cart and loaded the printers on it plus the bags of other items we had purchased and Liz and I wheeled it up to the room. We offloaded our bounty and I took the luggage cart back down the corridor and parked it beside the elevator.

When I returned to the room Liz was busily setting up the all-in-one office printer. I sat down on the sofa and pondered what we should try to accomplish tomorrow. "Liz, did we get lists of companies to send the RFQ's to from all of the Security Council members?" Liz stopped what she was doing and picked up her laptop and sat down beside me, so that her thigh was touching mine. She powered up the computer, a few key strokes later she had the information in front of her; "Azerbaijan and Guatemala haven't sent any names."

"Can you send them emails to remind them?"

It only took Liz a couple of minutes to send off the emails.

"I didn't even look at the lists, how did the delegates format them?"

"They all gave us lists based on the skill sets that you identified. I have merged them together with common fields so that we can create mailing labels or courier waybills."

"Great, I would like to try to get the RFQ's out to the companies we have on the lists tomorrow."

"How many companies do we have?"

Liz looked at the list on her computer; "four hundred and twenty-seven, how are we going to send them?"

"Courier. In the morning we'll call them and see who will give us the best rate."

I heard a "ping" from Liz's laptop. "I have an email from Cheryl. She is on her way; she expects to be here around ten in the morning . . . I'd like to see the news."

I opened the armoire and passed the remote control to Liz, in a few seconds she had clicked her way to RNN. A female anchor was talking and there was a picture of Vice-President Almont in the right top corner of the screen.

".........Wycliffe resigned. At eight this evening; Vice-President Almont was sworn into office by Chief Justice Holandale. President Almont has scheduled a press conference for tomorrow morning at 10:30. It's our understanding that none of the cabinet resignations were actually accepted by former President Wycliffe which should mean that the current cabinet, at least for the meantime, will remain in place. There has been no word from General Adams as to whether or not he still wants early retirement.

In other news the police and the FBI are no closer to identifying the killer or killers who earlier today fatally shot Senator Mackie outside his home. They don't believe it was an act of foreign terrorism, however nothing has been ruled out at this time."

We both looked at each other and I said; "Tell me you're surprised?"

"No, not surprised, but it makes me wonder how we can call ourselves civilized."

"Millions of people across the US have taken to the streets to celebrate the resignation of former President Wycliffe.

Earlier today British Prime Minister Jeremy Coxwald held a press conference. We will be broadcasting the entire press conference tonight at 11:30. The highlights of the Prime Minister's press conference included the reduction of British military forces by sixty-eight percent, the decommissioning of the Navy's carriers and submarines in a similar manner to the China and Russia's UN commitment, whereby some will be converted to scientific and humanitarian aid ships. The entire British arsenal of missiles will be decommissioned and the air force will be reduced by eighty-two percent, with a primary role as search, rescue and humanitarian aid. The Prime Minister commended Mr. Dafoe and said that everyone on the planet should be holding him in their highest esteem."

My picture appeared in the right hand corner of the screen.

I looked at Liz, "I sure hope that doesn't reignite the press feeding frenzy on me."

"Ms. Montgomery, we have a busy day ahead of us, may I suggest we go to bed."

Liz smirked; "I concur, Mr. Dafoe and I am very pleased that you said go to bed, rather than go to sleep."

Liz turned off the TV and headed for the bedroom. I checked the room door dead bolt and turned off the lights and followed her. A few minutes later our bodies were tangled together as we expressed our unrelenting desire for one another.

Chapter 13 – 262 days to alien arrival

It was 6:47 when I opened my eyes. Liz was in a very unusual position, I was lying on my back and Liz was sound asleep with her head on my tummy facing my feet. One arm was folded over my chest and the other was outstretched and between my legs. Her hair lay strewn on my chest. She was in a fetal position with her knees pulled up towards her tummy. I could watch her head slowly go up and down as I breathed. Other than our feet and ankles we had no covers on. I tried to reach the edge of the cover so that I could pull it up and over Liz's naked body, but I couldn't without disturbing her. We had a lot to do today, but Liz was sleeping so soundly that I couldn't bring myself to wake her.

I decided that I wouldn't waste the precious time, so I continued to work on the RFQs for the items we needed to get manufactured. Every now and then I would open my eyes and gaze at Liz.

It was 7:16 when I felt Liz begin to stir. She rolled over and with her head still on my tummy but facing me and looking half asleep she smiled; "Good morning darling" She turned her head and kissed my tummy.

"Did you sleep well?"

"I have never slept as soundly as I do when I am curled into you. You make me feel safe and secure. I love you so much. Is it time to get up?"

"Yes, we have a lot to accomplish today."

Liz changed her position so that she could kiss me; then climbed out of bed. We went into the bathroom and playfully showered. I dried and brushed her hair, she had this very loving expression on her face that I could see in the reflection in the mirror.

We dressed and went into the sitting room. It was 8:21.

"Let's go down to the restaurant for breakfast. I think we will be in the room for most of the day working."

Liz nodded and we went downstairs for breakfast. Then we went for a walk, it was an absolutely beautiful day, hand-in-hand, down to where the sailboats were moored. Liz asked if I would like to have a sailboat. I said I preferred boats with engines and a crew. Sailboats looked like a lot of hard work, and if I wanted to work I would get a job. That made her giggle.

We sauntered back to the room. I was the recipient of a few tender kisses on the way.

Liz plunked herself on the sofa; "What would you like me to do first boss?"

"Please call the courier companies and see what arrangements you can make for sending out the RFQs. You might as well ask them to provide us with a quote for all our courier business under a one year contract. As an incentive you can offer to let them promote the fact that they are the official courier of For Humanity.

While you are doing that, I'm going to bite the bullet and call Daniel and Joël."

Liz gave me a big smile; "I'm going to sit on the balcony and make the calls." She took her laptop and opened the sliding glass door and screen; she didn't shut the door, only the screen. I watched her carefully position herself in one of the wicker chairs and place her laptop on the table. She lit a cigarette and started to Google.

I turned and went into the bedroom, so as not to disturb her conversations. Daniel and I got boisterous at times. I picked up the room phone and dialed Daniel's number. I was quite anxious. I didn't know what type of reception I would get. The phone rang five times and then I got Daniel's recorded message. Damn, I thought to myself, Daniel usually goes to visit one of his kids from Friday to Sunday. I left Daniel a quick message:

Hi Daniel; it's Will; as I'm sure you're aware I'm back, safe and sound. Sorry I missed you, I forgot this was Friday. I will call you on Monday. Take care, give my regards to everyone.

I hung up, I felt somewhat relieved that I got his voicemail. Joël is next!

I called Joël's number, it rang twice and I heard "Birchler". "Joël it's Will. How are you?"

"I'm good. I have been seeing your picture on TV and in all the newspapers; you are more famous than a movie star."

"I know; it's a pain in the ass!"

Joël and I chatted for awhile when it struck me that he would be a perfect IT guy. On top of which he was fluent in French and German and reasonably competent in Italian. Joël had been bouncing around from job to job over the last few years. He couldn't seem to find a position he really liked.

"Joël, would you be interested in coming to Canada and working for the new organization "For Humanity" as manager of IT services?

"Would I be working for you?"

"Yes"

"I am very interested, but I will have to talk to my girlfriend. Would she be able to come with me?"

"She can come with you, but she won't be able to work in Canada."

"I will talk to her this weekend. Can I let you know on Monday?"

"Not a problem."

We chatted for a few more minutes and then said our goodbyes."

It struck me that it made little sense to use a headhunter for positions that I could fill myself from my international connections. I thought that it was important to hire my senior staff from a variety of countries. The middle management and junior staff could be locals. I made a mental list of the key positions that I would need: I needed a strong financial person relatively quickly; I wanted an electrical engineer, preferably someone with utility and solar system experience; I would like to have an electronics engineer; an individual who can handle the shipping and material handling logistics; I would need someone in human resources, familiar with employee benefit plans, that would have to be a Canadian; I would need someone who knew the global pharmaceutical industry to head that area; I should have a senior buyer; and lastly I would require someone to take care of security.

I pondered the list of senior staff and compared it to the list of people I knew. I immediately knew that I would have to use a headhunter for the person to head the pharmaceutical unit. My contacts were negligible in the pharmaceutical industry.

I managed to put at least two names to each of the positions where foreigners could be accommodated. I put the list aside in my mind and thought I would review specific individuals for each position over the next day or two.

I went back into the sitting room. Liz was just coming in from the balcony. She was holding her pad in her hand. "How did your phone calls go with Daniel and Joël?"

"Daniel wasn't home, I left him a message. I spoke to Joël and offered him the position of IT Services Manager. How did you do?"

"They all wanted time to prepare a quote for us; one wanted two weeks. I told them we didn't have the luxury of waiting for quotes. Two of them gave me their best one year contract prices from a price list, based on an unknown volume. They both said that they could do better, but the request would have to be processed by their quotation departments. I did speak to the VP Sales for Orion. They are very aggressive, he asked me to give him five minutes, which I did. He came back with a very high percentage discount schedule based on the type of service. We have an account number that we can use right away and he is sending us 750 air envelopes today, to the hotel."

"I'm going to type the RFQs and put them on a flash drive. Why don't you start making the waybills? Then we can go back to the office supply store and have them print the RFQs, it would take forever for our small copier to get them all done. Please remind me when we go to the office supply store that I need to get a new cell phone.

"I need a kiss first and foremost."

Liz and I met halfway and she gave me a nice moist kiss, holding it for a few seconds.

I went to my laptop to type the RFQs and Liz went back out on the balcony to start making the waybills.

At 10:23, I heard Liz's cell phone ring. She had a quick conversation, got up and talked through the screen door. "Cheryl's downstairs, I told her to come up."

A minute later there was a knock on the door. I didn't even bother to check the peephole, I could recognize Cheryl's knock. I opened the door and Cheryl walked right in. She looked good, big smile on her face, cheery eyed, dressed in slacks and a blouse and her shoes had negligible heels. She was carrying her laptop bag. "Good morning everyone!"

Liz came in from the balcony. "Uneventful trip?"

"I drove straight through, I stopped for gas twice." Cheryl looked over at me; "Gas is expensive here!"

"Welcome to Canada!" I said smiling.

"I'm sorry I'm late, I rented an apartment in St. Catherines this morning. I found it online and it looked good and I told them that I would be here this morning and if it looked that good in real life, I would take it. It did, so I rented it there and then. It was vacant, so I have already put my stuff in it. I have to get some furniture today or I'm going to be sleeping on the floor." Cheryl's voice was full of excitement. "Liz, it's bigger than the apartment I had in Washington, in a much nicer neighborhood and it's two thirds of the price and I get a garage for my car."

Liz responded with a big smile; "That sounds great Cheryl."

Cheryl looked at me and then at Liz; "I have a lot of things on my "To Do" list, is there anything you want me to do first?"

"Yes, did you happen to notice a mall with an office supply store when you were driving?"

"I can walk to it from my apartment."

"I want you to take a flash drive there and have them print the RFQs. Print four hundred of each, speak to the manager and see if you can open account there under the name of "For Humanity". While they are printing the RFQ's there are a few furniture stores nearby, I want you to go shopping for your furniture. If you cannot arrange for a bed to sleep in this evening, I want you to stay here, we have a second bedroom. I don't want you sleeping on the floor in your apartment."

I went over and copied the RFQs to a flash drive and handed it to Cheryl.

"Can I leave my laptop here?"

Liz and I both nodded. "Liz will make arrangements for you to pick-up a keycard for the suite from reception, in case we're not here when you return. Please make yourself at home."

"Will do!" Cheryl turned and left the room.

"Will, it's almost 10:30 do you want to watch Almont's press conference, because I would like to." Liz didn't wait for me to answer, she picked up the remote control from the coffee table and a few seconds later we had RNN on.

The picture was of a vacant podium, but we could see the press in the foreground. It was 10:28. A narrator was making idle chitchat while we waited for President Almont's arrival. At preciously 10:30 the Press Secretary, Pauline Smith entered the room and walked up to the podium. "The President has prepared a speech and then will answer questions; Ladies and gentlemen; The President of the United States."

President Almont entered the room in the same manner as the Press Secretary and went straight to the podium. Someone started clapping and before long the entire press core was on their feet and applauding very loudly. President Almont had a big smile on his face and raised his hand to try to stop the applause, it very slowly subsided.

"Ladies and gentleman, the last couple of days have been fraught with turmoil in America, at a time when the rest of the world is celebrating. I hope we can put those days far behind us, and pretend that it was nothing more than a bad dream.

"Yesterday afternoon, an elected official was gunned down; assassinated for presenting his opinions. He made no threats and whether or not you agreed or disagreed with his opinions is irrelevant and this is not the first time that an elected official has been shot for having a point of view. Senator Mackie was a close friend. I and I hope all Americans are appalled by this senseless taking of a human life.

"We have created a society where parents are afraid to send their children to school for fear of getting shot, taking our children to movie theaters for fear of getting shot. We are now creating a society where people will be afraid to express their point of view for fear of being shot.

"I for one have had enough of the senseless gun violence in this country and I hope that the American people will stand behind me when I say that "guns do kill". We have hundreds of state and federal laws whose sole purpose is to protect others and yet we allow and in some cases encourage people to arm themselves. In the very near future I am going to present congress with an amendment to the constitution that seriously reduces the availability of guns of all types. Our forefathers did not expect or see a future where a citizen's right to bear arms would mean the countless murders of thousands of civilians each and every year."

The press core stood and applauded. As it subsided the President continued.

"The second item that I would like to address is the Whitehouse cabinet; my cabinet. There will be no immediate changes to the cabinet. All of the resignations made by cabinet members were rescinded. The cabinet members, at a meeting early this morning, have given me their full and unequivocal support. General Adams, the Chairman of the

Joint Chiefs of Staff has withdrawn his request for early retirement. I was also informed this morning that the ninety-six congressmen and women who had decided to sit as independents have returned to their respective Republican caucuses."

The President paused and took some water.

"One hundred and four days ago, a group of aliens informed us that because we were uncivilized they would have to annihilate us for the safety of all sentient beings in the galaxy.

"We are the greatest country in the world, but that statement should have made every American; every man, woman and child question our civility, our compassion, our caring for others. We have been kicked in the butt; we needed it and deserved it. Billions and billions of dollars are spent each and every year, with a single intent; to have the means to kill others. The United States alone spent 875 billion dollars last year on the military. That is over 2,800 dollars for each man, woman and child in the country. At the same time we spent ninety billion dollars on medical research mostly funded by pharmaceutical companies interested in profit rather than finding cures for diseases that affect all of humanity.

"The President of the Russian Federation, Viktor Masmekhov, stood up at the UN meeting of the General Assembly and pronounced a unilateral decrease in the Russian military and challenged other nations to follow suit. The President of the People's Republic of China, Liang Kang Hou, accepted the challenge and in an unprecedented show of good faith and goodwill announced large cuts in the Chinese military and acknowledged the rights of the people of Taiwan and Tibet. The Russian and Chinese Presidents agreed to remove the military along their common borders. The Prime Minister of Canada committed to removing defensive shields between Canada and Russia and The president of Russia committed to removing their defensive shields along their border with Canada This morning in the UK Prime Minister Coxwell announced deep cuts in the British military and its weapon arsenals.

"My grandfather was a poorly educated farmer who had a phrase for every situation, one of his favorites was "better late than never". Well, we may be late in accepting the challenge presented by President Masmekhov, but our response will not be never. I have issued Presidential orders to the department of defense to cut our military spending by 77 percent next year and 86 percent the following year.

We will decommission all but two of our aircraft carriers. Those two will be converted to humanitarian aid with one stationed in the Pacific and the other in the Atlantic. We will decommission our submarine fleet with the exception of a few submarines which will be reconfigured for scientific research. Our large warships will be decommissioned. Our four navy hospital ships will be used for humanitarian purposes. Some of the smaller navy ships will be transferred to the coast guard to beef up our front line drug smuggling defenses. We will decommission all of our missile systems worldwide. All foreign military bases will be closed and the armed forces personnel will be returned home. Sixty-nine percent of our air force aircraft will be decommissioned. We are going to greatly enhance the capabilities of FEMA with the use of what were military transport equipment, MASH units and personnel. We will place emergency teams and equipment in strategic locations around the US that will allow us to respond to any natural disaster within hours. I have also issued a Presidential Order to have all of our nuclear power plants converted to the solar energy technology provided by the aliens. We will of course eliminate all weapons of mass destruction under our control, including our nuclear stockpiles.

"I will also be declaring April 5th, the day Mr. Dafoe returned from the aliens, a national holiday – *Humanity Day*."

The President paused. Liz was right, he isn't a good speaker, but he might make an exceptional President if he follows through on what he has just said.

The press core rose again and gave him a standing ovation.

The President looked tired. He was probably up all night. "Before I take any questions I would like to broach one other topic." He had put his speech away; he was going to wing it.

"I had the privilege of being our nation's representative at the UN Security Council meetings over the seven days leading up to the meeting at the UN General Assembly. The members of the Security Council worked diligently and together, putting away personal animosities in order to resolve many issues the likes of, no one has ever faced before, they worked exceedingly long hours, both in and out of the meetings. Their efforts deserve to be recognized. However, there are two people who stood out at those meetings, as a red rose would stand out in a field of green grass. They worked tirelessly and accomplished tasks in time frames that were nothing less than amazing. Their enthusiasm, resolve and abilities to come up with simple solutions, carried the rest of the delegates through some of the most complex issues and trying times. I am speaking of Mr. William Dafoe and Ms. Elizabeth Montgomery. Some of you may remember Ms. Montgomery as a former member of President Wycliffe's cabinet. Ms. Montgomery was originally assigned as Mr. Dafoe's confidant and liaison, prior to his departure. She has now accepted the position of Deputy Managing Director of *For Humanity*.

"There are no words that can describe Mr. Dafoe properly and do him justice. He stands there and tells you that he is nothing more than a salesman "a damn good salesman" is usually how he puts it. But, I would like to quote Ambassador Zhang Wei, the Chinese representative to the UN Security Council when he stood up at one of our final meetings and said; "I am continued to be impressed with Mr. Dafoe's wisdom and sharp mind across many subjects."

The President paused for another drink. He speaks better when he wings it. There was a tremendous amount of sincerity in his voice.

"I am honored and humbled to be able to call Ms. Montgomery and Mr. Dafoe friends."

Liz's voice was sharp; I'm going to send him a thank you email from the both of us. Did you want to hear the press conference questions and answers?"

I shook my head no. Liz turned off the TV; "I'm going to continue making up the waybills". She got up and went back out to her laptop on the balcony.

It was 11:43. I lit a cigarette and went into my normal ponder mode, I was humming Aquarius and thinking about the list of people I required. I was looking at the list and remembered an excellent electrical engineer that I had met in Japan; Hiroshi Kobayashi. If I remembered correctly which was likely with my new memory, he had worked for Takewaki Electric Power Co., Inc. on the engineering of the power grid connections to nuclear power plants and then went to work for Yamabe a company moving into solar power panel design. His English was quite good and I believe he was also fluent in Spanish. I had a home phone number for him in my memory bank, but it was over five years old. The Japanese don't move homes that often I'll call him. I went to reach for the phone when I realized it was 1:47 Saturday morning in Japan, I didn't think he would appreciate my call. I would put it aside until 7:00 this evening.

I always found time zones to be a pain in the posterior. I'd get all psyched up to call a client only to realize they were sleeping; it took the wind out of my sails every time.

I just had another brain storm. I had originally planned to publish the RFQs in newspapers around the world, but that would take time, not only to get the ads placed, but we would have to have them translated. It would bog Cheryl down and there were more important things for her to do. Why not forward the RFQs to the commercial attaches at the embassies and let them forward them to the appropriate companies in their country. We could include the skill set documents so they would know who to send them to. If they failed to forward them on, it would take the heat off us. No company could complain to us that they didn't receive a copy of the relevant RFQs.

I went over to the screen door. "Liz, can I interrupt you?"

She continued typing for a moment, then turned with a grin on her face. "You sure can, did you want to get naughty?"

"I would love to get naughty, but we don't have the time."

Her face went sullen.

"Liz, do you happen to have a list of the commercial attaches in the foreign embassies in the US?"

"No, but I know where I can get one."

I told Liz my idea.

"I'll get a hold of the list as soon as I finish this section of waybills. If we don't have time to get naughty, do we have time for a kiss?"

I opened the screen door, and gave her a small kiss, she put her arms around my neck and stuck her tongue in my mouth and held me there. When she broke the kiss she gave me her sultry look; "That's just so you know a little of what you're missing by not having the time to get naughty."

I kissed her again and slid my hand inside her blouse, which was unbuttoned at the top and then worked my fingers into her bra. I cupped my hand over her breast, squeezing it gently. Liz looked at me with a smile; "Stop that or face the consequences of being raped right here on the balcony!"

I went back into the room, before I lost my self control.

I had just resumed my pondering when there was a knock at the door. It was the concierge; he had his luggage cart loaded with 15 cartons with Orion stamped on the side. We stacked the cartons in a corner of the room. I gave him a big tip as he left.

I remembered Tina's email that offered to provide me with a quotation. I went to my laptop and replied to her last email:

Hi Tina,

Congratulations on your promotion. No plans to visit the Netherlands in the near future, but when I do I'll be sure to call you. Hopefully we can have dinner together.

I would appreciate a quote for the production of the glass domes. Quantity 1,000; Delivery ASAP.

Thanks

Will

I would have felt like an idiot after asking for her help if I didn't give her the opportunity to provide a quote on the manufacture of the glass domes.

Liz came in from the balcony; "The waybills are finished, I asked for a copy of the embassy list, but haven't received it yet. I received an email from Sarah, she said that the press has been relatively quiet, but she expects it to pick-up now that the situation with former President Wycliffe has been resolved. She also said they have implemented a number of email addresses. She sent them all with the passwords. I forwarded a copy to you and Cheryl. We should decide who is going to get which emails. She sent my logo to a graphic artist for touch-up and she expects it back later today. She is having a high res image created as a master which she will send to us. I can't think of anything else to report. I'm going to take a few minute break. Liz plopped herself down on the couch and lit a cigarette."

It was 1:57 when we heard a keycard put into the slot in the door. I hadn't activated the dead bolt when the concierge left, allowing Cheryl to enter the room. She had the luggage cart filled with boxes containing the RFQ's and a suitcase with her.

She wheeled into the center of the room and closed the door behind her.

"How did it go?"

Cheryl was still very bubbly; "It went fine, we have an account at the office supply store and the manager said that they would deliver to us anywhere we want. They service the Niagara airport now. I bought a new cell phone because you were correct Will, the roaming charges in Canada for the one I have from the US would have been astronomical. I bought some furniture, enough to set up a home and feel comfortable, including a flat screen TV. I brought a suitcase with a change of clothes, because I need to stay here this evening, they can't deliver my furniture until tomorrow around ten."

I looked at Cheryl then at Liz. "Can we start printing the waybills and stuffing the courier envelopes?"

Liz went out on the balcony and retrieved her laptop. Took it over to the desk and loaded the printer with paper. A few minutes' later waybills were being printed.

"How does this work Liz."

"I'm printing the waybills for the RFQ for the glass globes first."

Cheryl interjected; "I marked the boxes with the name of the product."

I went and brought a box of courier envelopes to the middle of the sitting room floor. Cheryl had found a box of glass globe RFQs and placed it on the floor next to me. I sat on the floor and Cheryl followed suit. We started stuffing the RFQs in the envelopes. Liz went to the printer and removed the first batch of waybills and put them in the pouches on the courier envelope. We had a regular production line going. Liz went over to the laptop and yelled at Cheryl and I. "We only need fourteen more glass globe RFQs."

We finished those and repeated the exercise with the electronics for the solar systems and the markers.

It was 4:55, when we completed filling the RFQ recipient lists that we had. I asked Liz if it was too late for an Orion pick-up. She immediately picked-up her phone and called her new found buddy, the Sales Manager at Orion. They talked for a minute or two and then Liz disconnected. He will make special arrangements for a pick-up. He asked if we could take them downstairs to the hotel lobby. We straightened up the mess on the floor and loaded the boxes of stuffed envelopes on the luggage cart. I went to take it downstairs but Cheryl stopped me and said she would do it. She wheeled the luggage cart through the open door and closed it behind her.

I looked at Liz who had plopped herself back on the sofa. "Cheryl is a gem, I really like her."

It was 5:32 when there was a knock at the door. I opened it and it was Cheryl; "Sorry I forgot my keycard. The courier envelopes are on their way."

"Liz, let's get out of here and go to the office supply store so I can get a cell phone. Cheryl can show us her apartment. I need some fresh air."

Cheryl looked at Liz with a sullen expression; "I don't want to be a third wheel."

"Liz smiled, "Don't be silly."

Cheryl put the grin back on her face.

We went to office supply store and Liz picked smart phones for both of us. She made a quick decision when we were at the office supply store that she should return her government phone, because she wasn't a government employee any longer. On top of which she didn't like the thought that her calls could be tracked.

Cheryl gave us directions to her apartment. It was a relatively new building, twelve stories, maybe five years old. The outside of the property was very well looked after; manicured lawns and shrubs, clean windows and no pot holes in the parking lot. When we got out of the car, Cheryl looked up and pointed to a balcony on the tenth floor; "That's my place" We went in and found a pristine lobby, flower box and marble floors, I was impressed. We went up in one of the two elevators to Cheryl's apartment. Her suite was at the very far end of the hall. She let us in. It was painted an off white. The floors were parquet hardwood, except for the kitchen, bathroom and a small foyer that had ceramic tile. The kitchen wasn't large, but not as small as some I have seen. The appliances were white and spotless, not bottom of the rung quality. One inch mini-blinds were covering all the windows. The sitting room had a sliding glass door to a balcony that wrapped around the edge of the building. She had a panoramic West and South view. The four piece bathroom was small, but comfortable.

Cheryl told us that she was very pleased with the apartment and that it was at least twice as nice as her Washington apartment. She said it had a big bright laundry room on the lobby floor that she would use. She was afraid to use the one in her apartment in Washington.

Cheryl said she was wiped, she had driven all night, and that she would take a taxi back to the hotel. We told Cheryl that Liz's parents were arriving tomorrow so she would be on her own over the weekend. We should meet at 8:00 Monday morning for breakfast at our hotel.

Liz wanted to go back to the mall. Once there, she took me into a menswear store to get me some casual clothes. Liz did like to shop! Liz's concept of casual clothes was about ten levels up from what I considered to be casual. She picked out five pairs of slacks, ten matching shirts and socks. We stopped at one of the tailoring while you wait shops to have the pant legs shortened. We didn't hang around waiting for the pants to be altered. Liz said I needed some new shoes, three pairs apparently. We also picked up boots for both of us so that we could tromp around our new property.

During this shopping extravaganza, Liz took a call from the navy pilot. He said he would call her as soon as he picked up her parents and give us a reasonably firm arrival time.

We loaded up the car with my new wardrobe and headed back to our hotel. We stopped at a Chinese buffet restaurant for dinner. The concierge was nowhere to be found, as usual, so we borrowed his luggage cart for all the garments and other items that we had picked up. As we passed the hotel reception desk, we picked up a courier envelope addressed to Liz.

We were back in our room at the hotel at 10:17. I hung up and put away my new clothes while Liz opened the courier envelope. It was the work visas for her and Cheryl. She put hers in her wallet, wrote a message on the envelope and slid it under Cheryl's room door.

I opened a bottle of wine, poured us each a glass and suggested to Liz that we go sit on the balcony. We sat outside, star gazing, sipping wine, and holding hands.

Damn, I thought to myself, I didn't call Kobayashi in Japan. I did a time zone calculation; it was one in the afternoon, tomorrow in Japan. I'll give him a try. I went back into the room and picked up my new super duper smart phone and tried to make it work. Liz saw me pushing on the screen and doing everything I could, she started laughing; "Give it to me! Now watch carefully." Liz pushed on an icon on the screen, paused and looked at me, then explained slowly how to enter the number I wanted to dial. She asked me for the number and I watched her follow her previous set of instructions. She pushed another icon and in a second I had Japanese ring tone. She passed the phone back to me; she had a big grin on her face.

A female voice picked up the phone and said something in Japanese which I didn't understand.

Very slowly I said; "Mr. Hiroshi Kobayashi, please."

In a very heavy accent I heard; "minute". I could hear some talking far off in the background.

Then a strong powerful voice; "Kobayashi"

"Mr. Kobayashi, this is William Dafoe; I don't know if you remember me?"

"I remember you when I see you at meeting at the United Nations. You are now a great man!"

"No, I'm just a salesman. How are you?"

"I am very well. You are good?"

"Yes, I'm very good. You know that I have a new organization, "For Humanity".

"Yes, I heard at UN meeting and it is in the newspapers here."

"I would like to offer you a position with the new organization; Manager of Electrical Engineering. I need someone who has your knowledge and abilities. The position would be in southern Ontario, Canada."

"You honor me."

"Are you interested Mr. Kobayashi?"

"Yes, what is remuneration?"

"I will give you a ten percent increase in what you are currently earning. Plus benefits and pay all your relocation expenses. Are you married? Do you have children?"

"I currently earn eight hundred thousand yen per month. I am married, we have no children."

"I will pay you eight hundred and eighty thousand yen per month in Canadian dollars. There might be one problem; your wife will not be able to work in Canada. I would want you to start as soon as possible."

"I do not think that this will be a big problem. I must discuss it with my wife, parents and the company I work for now, before I can say yes."

"I understand, how much time do you need?"

"I must have until Tuesday is that okay?"

"That is acceptable."

I gave Kobayashi my contact information and we said goodbye.

I thought that I better start working on a budget. But I was too tired now and I needed some down time.

Liz looked over at me; "What are our plans for tomorrow?"

"When the pilot calls, we'll go pick-up the Cadillac from the rental agency. You'll take the Cadillac and I'll take this car and we'll drive to the airport. Then you and your parents in the Cadi and me with the pilots and their wives in our car will go back to the rental agency and have the pilots sign on as additional drivers on our car. Then you, me and your parents will do something – any ideas?"

Liz reached over and grabbed my hand and gave it a squeeze. "I suggest that we bring them back to the hotel, let them freshen up and then have lunch in the main dining room downstairs. After lunch I think we should go for a walk along the main street. Mom and I can shop and you and Dad can watch." Liz chuckled.

"Do you know Will; I think this is the first time in my entire life that I am actually looking forward to seeing Mom and Dad; is that horrible of me?"

I squeezed her hand; "No, it's understandable." I filled our wine glasses and lit a cigarette. "We will have to make sure we tell reception to make-up the room after Cheryl has left, otherwise it might not get made up until three. Would you like to take them to the theater on Sunday?"

"I think we should suggest it to them and see if they would be interested. Can we take them to the best restaurant in the area tonight?"

"Of course my love, I was planning on that."

"I'll put my hair up so that your earrings stand out!" Liz paused to finish her wine.

She stood up leaned over and gave me a kiss; "I'd like to go to bed now, the operative word being "bed"; she was grinning like a Cheshire cat.

She took me by the hand and led me into the bedroom. We spent the better part of the night making love.

Chapter 14 – 261 days to alien arrival

I am not going to give you a boring day by day narrative culminating with the alien arrival. It really is nothing more than the story of a business start-up. The initial days revolved around setting up a temporary facility using prefabricated office trailers. We had the cargo containers transported from New York to Niagara. Joël accepted the position as Manager of IT Services and left his girlfriend in Switzerland. Kobayashi took a one year leave of absence from the company he worked for and brought his wife to Niagara. Kobayashi installed the first working solar collector system at our facility. Over the first sixty days we hired forty-one people. By the time the facility was fully operational we had eighty-seven full time staff. We contracted the manufacture of all the parts of the solar systems, the volcano and earthquake warning systems and the production of the medications and then commenced distribution.

We couldn't find a company anywhere in the world that was willing to undertake the processing of the Corbolite into radioisotopes, so we built a facility on our site to handle it, which is one of the reasons our staffing was substantially higher than I had originally expected.

After President Wycliffe resigned and the dust had settled somewhat the press came at Liz and I hot and heavy for interviews. Sarah managed to keep everyone at bay although for the first six to eight weeks there were paparazzi everywhere we went. They even went after Barbara for awhile when she came to stay with us in the summer.

The stock market reacted instantly after the meeting with the UN General Assembly. Share prices in any company that was related to uranium mining and nuclear power plummeted. A number of pharmaceutical companies, especially those that had medications for diabetes, glaucoma, colds and migraines, saw their share prices drop by as much as fifty percent. Companies that supplied the military also took a beating. However, that was offset by large gains in insurance companies, hospitals, ship building, high ticket consumer goods, hotels, airlines, banks and other financial institutions. Overall, world-wide, in the first six months, there was a net loss of about 175 thousand jobs.

Liz and I had a number of enjoyable weekends with her parents.

We grew even closer together and surprisingly, at least to me, our intimate times were increasing in passion each and every time. We always went to sleep in each other's arms and we never stopped our morning shower rituals.

We bought a piece of land overlooking the lake and built a custom hexagon shaped home with a courtyard in the middle with a roof that could open. We also had a roof that opened over our master suite, which included a very large bathroom with a roman tub recessed into the floor, so that Liz and I could make love under the stars. We had a wine cellar that would hold five thousand bottles. Our home was powered by a small solar collector system, 100 kilowatts, that I brought back in my personal cargo container.

Another incident, which I am not even sure bears noting, occurred when I had taken a morning to apply captions to some of the pictures I had taken. I was going through my memory and came across a group of pictures I had taken at a beautiful park near the Council building. I pulled out the appropriate camera memory cards and realized that the pictures on the camera didn't quite match the pictures in my memory. The pictures on the memory card showed three female aliens; the female aliens were not in the pictures in my memory. I recognized one of the females as Licia the alien who escorted me to the shuttlecraft for my short trip home. I checked my brain memory and could not find anything about her or the other females. There was no doubt in my mind that the pictures from the camera were accurate hence I was having memory problems. I checked two hundred pictures on the memory cards and one or more of the females were in thirty-seven of them, but when I viewed the pictures in my memory they weren't there.

I sat back and thought about what was occurring and realized that many of the memories that I had about being with and doing things with Quanch my guide seemed distorted. It's hard to explain but it is as if she was put into my memories using a photo editing program. I also realized that over the three years I was away, and Quanch had been with me the entire time, that I didn't have one camera picture of her.

I also had some, what I would call unusual memories. I could remember the brain enhancement procedure, but there were no aliens in those memories. I could also remember having dinner alone, yet there was food on three other plates. I remember being introduced to an alcoholic beverage but there was no one else present. Little things that didn't seem to be correct were all over my memory.

I have no explanation of any of the discrepancies between the memory cards and my mind or the vacant chairs at dinner tables, but it only seemed to revolve around the three females and Quanch. All of my other memories appeared to be intact. It haunted me for a long time, but eventually I let it go.

I tried to teach Liz to cook, but as intelligent as she was, and she really tried, she was hopeless! We still hadn't found time to tie the knot officially.

Cheryl was fantastic and became a close friend as well as Facilities Manager. Liz taught Cheryl fashion and make-up. Cheryl met a great guy and it looked as if the relationship was getting serious. Cheryl's parents boarded an airplane for the first time in their lives and came up to Niagara to visit for a week.

We built the most awesome facility, ultra modern with the most advanced materials, most of them donated by manufacturers so that they could use the *For Humanity* facility in promotions. Even our material handling equipment was donated. The facility has a fully equipped kitchen and dining room which we required due to the number of visits from dignitaries. It had an exercise room, staffed daycare center and a meditation room. Cheryl found one of my alien clown outfits and put it on display in the lobby in our new main building.

NASA transferred the ownership of the Learjet to For Humanity and we had it painted with the For Humanity logo that Liz had designed. General Adams made arrangements for the Navy pilots to be assigned to us permanently and they moved with their wives to Niagara. It was actually Cathy's idea to open a daycare at the facility, it turned out that she had a bachelor's degree in early childhood development and was qualified to operate a daycare, so we hired her. Jackie ran the dining room on an as needed part time basis. When we had a dignitary arrive Jackie would make arrangements for one of the local chefs to cook.

Liz and I were the guests of the heads of state in a number of countries. I always felt so proud to have Liz on my arm. She was always the most attractive lady at any of the receptions. Of course she had to have a new outfit for each and everyone. Prime Minister Harmon and his wife Lucy became friends and we spent a number of weekends together. President Almont or the First Lady called Liz at least once every couple of weeks and we were invited to spend a weekend at Camp David with them.

We negotiated an agreement with Canada Post which allowed us to use "For Humanity" stamps for letters mailed from our facility.

On September 28th, Liz's birthday, I sent a message to the extraterrestrials requesting the procedure to commence trade talks. Within the next twenty-four hours I received messages back from the trade commissions' of all fifty-seven planets providing me with lists of the items that they had available for sale within the galaxy, including the solar collector systems for ships, trains and vehicles.

Although a lot of pictures of our new facility were taken from helicopters and through the front and rear gates we didn't allow any media inside until it was complete. I provided Vivian Hallsworth, from WNN, the first inside tour of the facility, because I appreciated her attitude when she called me for an interview after the first meeting with the UN General Assembly. Liz and I both met her but declined interviews. We had Cheryl, in her capacity as Facilities Manager give her and the WNN film crew the tour.

There were, however a few incidents that are worth bringing to your attention. On April 15th the day I met Liz's parents for the first time there was an incident on the Gaza strip.

Liz and I had just finished dressing for dinner with her parents. It was 7:56 p.m. and we were going to walk into the sitting room, when I received a ping inside my head. "Damn!"

"What's wrong darling."

"The extraterrestrials are trying to contact me."

"You're not going to have a session like you had a few days ago?"

"No, it's only when I want to send them a message, not when they are sending me a message. Go keep your parents company."

Liz wasn't thrilled, I could tell by the sullen expression on her face, but she did as I asked. I closed the bedroom door behind her and retrieved my alien communication device from the side pocket in my suitcase and quickly put it in my ear. A few seconds later I received a message.

"At precisely 12:55 a.m. GMT, April 16th, Two hundred and sixty-nine rockets with conventional warheads were fired from Gaza. All rockets were vaporized at liftoff; a 200 square yard area at the point of each launch, including 873 humans was vaporized."

That ought to make everyone stand up and take notice. I realized that I should be carrying the communication device with me at all times. I put it in my suit jacket pocket and went into the sitting room.

When I came out of the bedroom, Liz and her Mom and Dad were standing on the balcony. Liz turned her head and looked at me questioningly. I mouthed "everything's fine"

Chapter 15 – 260 days to alien arrival

I was sound asleep, when I heard the phone ring. It was 7:37 a.m., I reached for it, my voice sounded like I was half asleep, which I was; "Hello"

"William; It's Prime Minister Harmon, I hope I didn't wake you."

He didn't wait for an answer.

"I am calling about an incident that occurred yesterday in Gaza. More than 800 people were vaporized."

"I am aware Prime Minister"

"They are saying that there was no reason for these deaths and that the aliens have turned aggressive and are killing people for no reason."

"Mr. Prime Minister, those 873 people were in the midst of firing 269 rockets with conventional warheads. I take it they haven't bothered to relate that small piece of information?"

"I must admit William that I thought that might be the case."

"I would suggest you contact the Americans or the Russians I am sure that they both monitor rocket launches in that area. The launches would have occurred moments prior to 12:55 a.m. GMT, April 17th and would have been a very short duration, because the aliens vaporized the rockets as soon as they were fired."

"How is it that you're aware of exactly what happened?"

"The aliens have given me a receiver which allows them to send me messages. They sent me a message moments after the incident occurred."

The Prime Minister didn't push for any additional information on my ability to communicate with the aliens.

"How is everything else proceeding?"

"It's coming together, slower than I would like, I'm an impatient individual, but we are within time frames."

"I have complete faith in you and Elizabeth. Thank you for speaking with me. Goodbye"

"Goodbye Prime Minister"

I looked over at Liz who was awakened by the call; she was still only half awake. "It was Prime Minister Harmon asking about the Gaza incident. Go back to sleep, darling."

I heard a very sleepy; Okay" and she rolled over and went right out.

After the four of us had breakfast we were all in the car headed for Niagara Falls. We had been driving for seven minutes when Liz's cell phone rang. She pulled it from her purse and looked at the screen. It's the Whitehouse she announced.

"Elizabeth Montgomery"

A female voice at the other end; "Ms. Montgomery please hold for the President."

I pulled the car into an empty parking lot and shut off the engine. Liz was holding the phone so that I could hear the conversation, so could her parents in the back of the car.

"Elizabeth; I'm sorry to disturb you on a Sunday morning. I spoke with Prime Minister Harmon this morning, he told me what William had said and I had General Adams immediately review our satellite photos of the Gaza Strip. He identified the attempted rocket launches and he confirmed it with his Russian counterpart. I wanted to let you and William know that we are releasing the information through Davis, Malthus and Associates, as we speak."

"Thank you Mr. President."

"Elizabeth; thank you for your email. How are you and William fairing?"

"Personally, fantastic, Sir. For Humanity is coming along fine we will meet our targets."

"I knew you would Elizabeth."

"If there is anything I can do please don't hesitate to contact me. Have a good day."

"Thank you Mr. President." The phone line was disconnected.

When I glanced in the rearview mirror both of Liz's parents had their mouths open in awe. Their daughter just had a personal conversation with the President of the United States.

I relate this incident to show you the complete arrogance of mankind. This incident confirmed that the aliens did have the technology to vaporize anything they wanted and that they had the technology to monitor the firing of rockets and missiles and to determine the type of warhead, conventional or mass destruction. You would think that any country that doubted the sincerity or technical capabilities of the aliens would have immediately commenced to comply with the terms of the agreement that I negotiated.

I should also mention that I managed to get Liz's father alone and confronted him with the supposed secret visit to his doctor and explained that his wife was worried about him. He said that it was really nothing just a bit embarrassing because he felt that it was a sign that he was getting old. When pressured, he told me that he had a hearing problem that was caused by an infection called otitis media and that he shouldn't have ignored the problem for as long as he did because now he needs to get hearing aids. I did a mental search through the list of medications that I had brought back from the aliens and sure enough I had some pills that would cure the infection and bring his hearing back to normal. At least at the level it was before the infection. Once my personal cargo container arrived in Niagara; I couriered the two required pills to him and the instructions. His hearing was back to the way it was prior to the infection in less than eight hours.

Chapter 16 – 174 days to alien arrival

It was 10:07 in the morning when we received a frantic telephone call from the Ukraine one of their solar collectors had exploded and killed thirteen people and seriously injured another twenty-seven. We immediately dispatched Kobayashi and two of his senior engineers to the site.

We were aware of the potential danger of the solar collector, if the Xanfor was exposed to oxygen, it would create a major explosion. The Xanfor module was made by the aliens with a glass not available on earth. It was shatter and crack proof. The one weak spot, if you could call it that was the sealant used between the glass plate and the side material. That material would melt at 3,000 degrees Celsius. We knew that oxyacetylene torches could create a flame temperature of 3,480 degrees Celsius. However, there was no reason to have an oxyacetylene torch anywhere near the solar collector module. Even so, we did install warning labels in ten languages on all four sides of the unit. We had also placed warnings on the covers and within the installation and maintenance instruction manuals.

The Ukrainians were swearing that they did not have an oxyacetylene torch in the area. We had our doubts.

The story went out on the international wire services before our team was on site. The usual press sensationalism abounded.

With the full co-operation of the President of the Russian Federation, Kobayashi sent some suspicious fragments that he had found at the explosion site to the top research lab in Moscow. His suspicions were confirmed when they identified the fragments as pieces of oxygen, acetylene tanks and a welding nozzle. The Ukrainians had no explanation as to where the fragments came from.

I wasn't surprised that someone had tried to open the glass module. Humans are a very curious group of people, especially when you tell them not to do something.

We used Sarah at Davis, Malthus and Associates to quell the situation.

Chapter 17 – 147 days to alien arrival

Another interesting situation developed when the Dutch Drug Administration announced that it wouldn't release any of the new medicines until "For Humanity" did detailed clinical evaluations and drug trials.

We informed them that we were not planning to undertake any clinical evaluations or drug trials and that if they wanted to do them they would have to do them on their own.

A minor political uproar took place with their Ambassadors calling the representatives of the Security Council who were the Board of Directors of "For Humanity" and those Ambassadors calling Liz and I.

This went on for a couple of weeks, before the Dutch Drug Administration relented and put the drugs on the market, with a warning that there had been no clinical trials and that anyone taking them was doing so at their own risk.

Chapter 18 – 117 days to alien arrival

I happened to turn on the news after Liz and I had showered and we had our morning coffee. Liz was in the bedroom getting dressed. There was nothing overly exciting, but there was a story about a large asteroid, about the size of ten, two story houses that was going to pass by earth this afternoon and evening. Its trajectory would take it between the moon and our planet at a height of about seventy-five thousand miles and our gravity would sling shot it towards Venus. There was no worry about it hitting our planet, but it was likely it would hit Venus.

My interest in asteroids and other astronomical type news had increased since my visit to the other planets. I had gone so far as to invest in a reasonably sophisticated telescope, which I would peer into in the evenings. I wondered if I would be able to see it this evening through my telescope. I put it in the back of my mind when Liz came out of the bedroom and we headed off to the For Humanity facility.

Around noon, Cheryl stuck her head in my office and suggested that I might want to turn on the news. NASA had just announced that a piece of the asteroid, about the size of a house had broken away from the main body of the asteroid and that the piece was headed for us and was too big to burn up in the atmosphere; meaning that it would hit the planet causing enormous damage and loss of life.

The pictures from NASA were outlining the trajectory but they could not pin point the impact area yet. You could hear the panic in the voice of the NASA scientist as he explained what the outcome of the collision with earth might mean.

Then some wiseass pointed out that if the United States, China and

Russia had not destroyed or decommissioned its missiles that they could have been used to destroy the piece of the asteroid that was heading for earth and that maybe we should reconsider activating some of our missile banks, although they couldn't be put back in operation fast enough to destroy this fragment, they could be used in the future.

They had a telescope image of the piece as it was travelling through space and while we were watching it, it just disappeared. You could tell that NASA scientists were panicking in an effort to find out where the piece of asteroid had gone. The cameras were turned off and we were returned to a news commentator at some studio.

I was just about to buzz Liz and ask her to come into my office when I received a ping in my head.

Since the Gaza incident I was never without my alien communicator and I immediately plugged it into my ear;

"5:07:43 p.m. GMT. Asteroid on collision course with earth vaporized."

Short and sweat. The aliens had saved our asses. They don't expect accolades, a thank you or any recognition whatsoever and some people on this planet still believe that they are hostile or that we need missiles for self defense. That would lead to another arms buildup. Sometimes I really question our level of intelligence.

I called Cheryl into my office and asked her to call Sarah and tell her that the asteroid that was headed for earth was vaporized by the aliens on their own merit. Sarah should release the info ASAP. I gave Cheryl the precise time that the vaporization took place.

The afternoon brought numerous phone calls from heads of state, some thanking me. I did my utmost to convince them that I had nothing to do with it. The aliens wish us no harm.

Chapter 19 – 108 days to alien arrival

It wasn't all disasters. One of my most memorable experiences occurred when Liz and I were invited to attend a state dinner with the Prime Minister of Canada. Unusually, Liz and I were not the guests of honor; the Dalai Lama was visiting Canada as head of state of the newly formed independent country of Tibet.

I have never been one to have heroes. I have no interest in the exploits of athletes, professional or amateur; I think most of them are prima donnas and movie and TV celebrities were as phony as three dollar bills. There were some people that I did look up to: Stephen Hawking the British theoretical physicist; James Lovell, Jr. commander of the Apollo 13 mission and General George Patton, Jr. commander of the US Third Army in World War II. But the man who topped the list of people I admired was His Holiness the 14th Dalai Lama, spiritual leader of the Tibetan people.

I had read many of the Dalai Lama's books, more than once. I found his wisdom and compassion for humanity to be inspirational to say the very least. I'm not ashamed to admit that on more than one occasion, when I was alone with the aliens for three years, remembering his words gave me strength and comfort. It was hard for me to believe that I would have the opportunity to see this great man in person.

Under direct orders from Liz and under her detailed scrutiny, I had a new tux tailored for the occasion; she even ordered me a tailored frilly silk shirt and bought me a set of exquisite sapphire and diamond shirt studs and cufflinks. Liz had ordered a full length, three quarter sleeve white silk flowered Chinese dress with a high neck. She purchased a hair broach with diamonds and rubies that matched the earrings and the tennis bracelet that I had bought for her. She looked stunning and was by far the most elegant woman at the dinner.

There was a small reception prior to the dinner that Liz and I were invited to attend. At the reception Liz and I had the honor and privilege of actually talking to His Holiness for twelve minutes uninterrupted. He said the he was in awe over my accomplishments with the alien beings. I explained to His Holiness how I compared the alien beliefs and humanity to those of his and what I had read in his books. He said that he hoped that someday in the near future we could spend more time together, discussing the alien beliefs and philosophies.

It was an evening I will never forget. I'm sorry to say that at the time of writing this chronicle I have not had the opportunity to have another meeting with the Dalai Lama. I hope that I can arrange it after the arrival of the aliens.

Chapter 20 – 27 days to alien arrival

The last almost disaster occurred when we received orders for large quantities of markers. We had originally ordered ten thousand sets of markets which I thought at the time would be more than sufficient to meet the requirements of all of the countries. Not long after, due to demand, we had to order another ten thousand sets. With these last minute orders we cleaned ourselves out of inventory and had to scramble to have another five thousand sets made. We delivered the last of the orders with six days left prior to the alien arrival.

Chapter 21 – 1 day to alien arrival

That brings us back to the beginning of the story. The Prime Minister had given his speech, he had introduced me and I was now at the podium.

I had taken the time to prepare opening remarks, although I decided that I wouldn't follow the protocol of the salutations.

I looked at the delegates with a smile on my face.

"Ladies and gentlemen; it has been a trying and exciting year for all of humanity. I would like to spend a few minutes discussing what we have all accomplished.

"To my knowledge every nuclear power plant has been decommissioned and replaced with solar collector systems; a total of 743 - 512 megawatt solar collector systems have been delivered, replacing 433 nuclear power plants that were in operation and 65 that were under construction. 382,000 megawatts of power in total

"We have produced and distributed 238 million dosages of medication.

"Twenty-seven earthquake warning systems have been delivered and eight are operational.

"Sixteen volcano eruption warning systems have been delivered and four are operational.

"We have delivered 23,672 marker systems.

"I think that everyone in this meeting hall should have a huge sense of pride in what has been accomplished in such a short period of time.

"I would like to explain to you what is occurring above us at this time.

"Earlier today a segment of the spacecraft assigned to the 72nd Reconnaissance Armada of the Group of Inhabited Planets arrived and placed themselves in position over the planet. The spacecraft that are here include five Advance Science Vessels, each with a crew of 56; three Science Vessels, each with a crew of 127; one Senior Science vessel with 342 crew, one Hospital vessel with 270 crew; one Repair and Overhaul vessel with 98 crew; one Warehouse vessel with 45 crew; one Command and Control vessel with 92 crew and the Flag ship of the 72nd Reconnaissance Armada with a crew of 87."

I decided not to mention that I had met Admiral Purvo, the commander of the 72nd Reconnaissance Armanda, on a couple of occasions when I was with the extraterrestrials.

"The five Advance Science spacecraft will spread themselves over longitude twenty degrees and will fly west to east, they will be followed by the three Science spacecraft; those spacecraft will be followed by the Senior Science vessel.

"My understanding is that the Senior Science vessel will be replenishing our ozone layer and clearing the space debris. The three Science spacecraft will be cleaning the atmosphere, oceans, rivers and lakes. The five Advance Science spacecraft will be performing the vaporization of the areas within the markers as well as searching for weapons of mass destruction that have been hidden. Should they find hidden weapons they will relay the information to the Command and Control spacecraft. If the crew aboard that spacecraft concurs, after their own investigation, they will vaporize that country.

"It is estimated that it will take approximately eighteen hours to complete all the tasks. They will commence at preciously 12:00 a.m. GMT, that's twenty-three minutes from now.

"I have been provided with a device that will allow me to receive transmissions from the alien spacecraft during their mission."

I reached into my pocket and held up the communication device that the aliens had given me. I backed away from the podium to get a glass of water from a pitcher that was on a table behind the podium.

A man in a commissionaire's uniform came on to the stage and spoke to the Secretary General.

The Secretary General banged his gavel to get the attention of the delegates. "If I may interject? I have been advised that water, coffee, tea and sandwiches will be made available during the period we are here. Thank you. Sorry for the interruption Mr. Dafoe, please continue."

I finished my glass of water and walked back to the podium. I had sixteen minutes to kill before the spacecraft started their mission. I realized that this was a very serious time, but I thought that a little humor was needed to thin the air, as one might say.

"Ladies and gentlemen, I'm an old man and I hope that you don't expect me to stand at this podium for the next eighteen hours. I will be here, but it is my intention to sit!

There were a few chuckles from the delegates.

I walked over to where the Prime Minister was sitting, he had a big smile on his face, I smiled back. I went behind the chair I had been sitting on and pushed it towards the podium, it made horrific scratching sounds as the legs of the chair dug in to the hardwood flooring. I parked it beside the podium, retrieved my glass of water and sat down.

There were a few more laughs from the delegates.

Eleven minutes to go. I could get up and sing a song; with my voice I'd probably clear the hall.

I decided sitting there was the best I could do.

I was looking out at the delegates and caught the eye of Ambassador Evans and we waved at each other. He had called me once since our dinner together, because he had received a complaint from a British manufacturer that we weren't playing fair. I had investigated the matter and realized that "fair" was in the mind of the beholder. We had given a number of contracts to British manufacturers and although the company that he was calling about had the lower prices, I decided to give the order to a Spanish company in order to spread the benefits of the contracts to more countries. Ambassador Evans understood and told me not to concern myself about it. I never heard anymore.

As a note, when we went out for a quote, we always put in the RFQ that the lowest prices would not necessarily win the order. Items such as delivery, quality and geographic location played an important part in who we issued a purchase contract.

I started to daydream a bit, thought about Liz; she was somewhere in the building seated out of sight with President Almont and a few other senior dignitaries.

Chapter 22 – Alien arrival

I was startled out of my daydream by a ping in my brain. The aliens are calling I thought to myself. I stood up and took the communication device from my pocket and gently maneuvered in into my ear.

"Mission has commenced"

I went to the podium.

"Ladies and gentlemen, I have just received word that the mission has commenced."

I was sitting in the chair for twelve minutes, running through my wine collection, when someone touched me on the shoulder from behind. I turned and looked up it was Ambassador Balabanov.

I stood and we faced away from the delegates and shook hands.

"William, are you sure that the alien spacecraft are here? No one has them on their radars."

"I'm sure Ambassador. They are invisible to our radar systems."

He smiled at me, patted me on the shoulder and walked off the stage.

I sat back down. It was going to be a long eighteen hours.

An hour and twelve minutes into the mission I received a ping.

"Nuclear powered aircraft carrier and three nuclear powered submarines vaporized, 4,978 people."

I knew they must be French. I was sure that the all the other nations with nuclear powered ships had decommissioned the reactors some would be replaced with solar collector units. As France had not sent any delegates to the meeting I decided to hold back on informing the General Assembly.

Four hour and twenty-three minutes into the mission I received a ping. I got up and went to the podium:

"Marker group 5457, 3rd marker not responsive"

I went to my mental list of marker groups and found marker group 5457 it belonged to Argentina

I shouted; "Argentina", I looked around the room and identified a lady with her arm in the air.

"Your marker group number 5457 has a defective or misaligned marker. Please have it corrected immediately."

She immediately called someone on her cell phone.

With the installation instructions for the markers, we requested that someone with at least one spare marker be on standby at each location in case a problem was identified; after all these were electronic devices that could fail.

Eleven minutes later I received another ping.

"Marker group 5457, functional."

I looked at the representative for Argentina, she had her cell phone in her hand; it appeared she had an open line to someone. I raised my hand with my thumb up. She waived back, said something to whomever she was speaking with and put her cell phone back on the table.

Forty-two minutes later I received another ping. This was the message I was hoping that I wouldn't receive.

"Columbia, seventy-five thousand five hundred liters, bio weapons stored in mine shaft. Country vaporized, forty-six million people"

I slowly stood up and walked around my chair. There was a lot of chatter in the hall. I slammed my fist into the podium to get their attention. Everyone immediately stopped talking and looked at me. I know my voice was somber; "The aliens discovered seventy-five thousand five hundred liters of bio weapons stored in a mine shaft in Columbia."

I paused.

"The country has been vaporized along with its population of forty-six million people."

No one said a word, most sat down, a few were crying. The Columbian delegation, flopped into their chairs, they said nothing. Other delegates were staring at them.

Damn, I thought to myself and this is a country that had a

representative on the UN Security Council, they were privy to everything, how could they be so stupid.

Before I could get back to my chair, I received five pings in a row. The spacecraft were flying over the US and Canada. The US had more marker groups than anyone else. The messages were related to problems with marker groups four for the US and one for Canada. Before I could even finish advising the US about the problems I received seven more pings, five for the US; one for Mexico and one for Guatemala.

That went on for five hours until they finally reached longitude 137°. I was worn out. I went to the table and poured myself another glass of water. A young lady came out of the side wing with a tray of sandwiches and placed it on the table and gave me a smile. I took a couple of sandwich halves, some black olives, put them on a plate, picked up a napkin and went back to my chair.

I received two pings while the spacecraft were over the Pacific Ocean which I didn't report to the delegates.

"Two nuclear powered submarines vaporize; two hundred and thirty-four people."

"Nuclear powered submarine vaporized; one hundred and eighteen people."

Things settled down until the space craft arrived over New Zealand. They informed me of a marker problem that I later learned was a landfill. The problem couldn't be rectified because New Zealand didn't order any spare markers. The aliens moved on without vaporizing it.

There were a couple of marker group problems over Australia that had to be dealt with. Then I received a ping that I had been expecting.

"North Korea, nuclear, chemical, bio weapons; country vaporized; twenty-five million people"

I walked up to the podium, this time the delegates quieted down without me banging my fist on the podium.

"North Korea has been vaporized along with twenty-five million people."

That didn't seem to upset the delegates as much as Columbia did. It's possible that they all thought it would happen.

The spacecraft were now over the Russian Federation, China and India. All three had a lot of marker groups and based on my previous experience over the US I wasn't surprised to receive a multitude of marker group problems from the aliens. All were resolved successfully.

I received a ping.

"Kazakhstan, unmarked nuclear missile in silo, property not visited for twenty-one years, appears abandoned and forgotten, vaporizing site, no country vaporization"

This was a good message; it proved that the aliens weren't out to just annihilate populations. I went over the podium. "Kazakhstan"

Someone in the back of the room raised their hand.

"Apparently you have an abandoned silo housing a missile with a nuclear warhead."

I could see by the expression on the representative's face that this was news to him. I could also tell that he feared the worst.

The aliens believe that the government and people of Kazakhstan were unaware that this missile existed. They are going to vaporize the silo, missile and warhead, but they are not vaporizing the country.

There was relief on the representative face as he shook the hands of the people around him. There was some applause in the room.

I sat down in my chair and waited for the next ping and I didn't have to wait long and then there was another and another and another.

"Pakistan, nuclear and chemical weapons, country vaporized; one hundred and seventy-eight million people"

"Iran, nuclear, chemical and bio weapons, country vaporized; seventy-five million people"

"Ukraine, nuclear weapons, country vaporized; forty-six million people"

"Syria, bio weapons, country vaporized; twenty-one million people"

"Israel, nuclear, chemical and bio weapons, country vaporized; eight million people"

I rose from my chair and walked slowly to the podium.

"Ladies and gentlemen; "Five countries have been vaporized" I paused I was chocked up and needed to compose myself. "Pakistan, Iran, Ukraine, Syria and Israel; a total of three hundred and twenty-eight million people"

There was complete silence in the room. I walked back to the chair and just grabbed the back of it and hung on.

As the spacecraft continued over Africa and Europe there were a number of pings relating to marker groups, all but one was resolved.

Then I got the ping that I was expecting and I was reasonably sure everyone else was expecting as well.

"France, nuclear, chemical and bio weapons, country vaporized; sixty-six million people"

I went back to the podium, for some reason, maybe their overall attitude and response to the aliens or maybe because I knew it would happen; they hadn't ordered any markers or solar collector systems. I know that the leaders of many countries tried their utmost to convince the French to take the situation seriously to no avail. I wasn't choked up.

"France has been vaporized. Earlier the aliens had vaporized all of the French nuclear powered naval vessels in the Atlantic and Pacific Oceans. Population vaporized sixty-six million people."

I was really hoping that this was the end of the country vaporizations.

I received a few more pings with messages about marker groups which were handled.

It had been eighteen hours and forty-three minutes since the start of the alien mission, a little longer than they had approximated when I received another ping.

"Mission complete; space debris vaporized; all but two marker groups vaporized; all bodies of water cleaned and purified; atmosphere decontaminated; ozone layer thickened; eight countries and four hundred and sixty-five million people vaporized. Spacecraft returning to normal galaxy patrol. Two spacecraft will remain in orbit; one for you and your family's protection; one to monitor the potential creation of weapons of mass destruction."

As soon as that message was completed I received another ping.

"Message relayed from Council: Thank you William for your outstanding leadership. All of the inhabitants of the Group of Inhabited Planets consider you a close friend. We are always here if you need us. May you have peace and prosperity."

That message really got to me, maybe because I was totally exhausted, but tears started to roll down my cheeks and I wanted to break out crying. I fought desperately to compose myself, but I wasn't winning the fight.

I wondered to myself, how would history record me and this event? Would they say that William Dafoe was responsible for the deaths of almost half a billion people? Or would they say that William Dafoe saved humanity? I knew that the media would concentrate on the negative, the half a billion people dead and eight countries vaporized as that provided far more sensationalism.

I stood up from my chair. I was sure that the delegates were as exhausted as I was. As I went to walk to the podium I noticed an entourage coming out of the wing. It was the members of the Security Council, led by Prime Minister Harmon with Liz beside him, she had a big smile on her face, they were followed by President Almont, beside him was President Masmekhov from the Russian Federation; then I saw President Liang Kang Hou, with the Prime Minister of England Jeremy Coxwald; the only other person I recognized was the President of Azerbaijan. Four men and two women were close behind the others. I quickly counted the representatives, removing Liz from the computation. Twelve, less France, Columbia and Pakistan, that added up and made sense.

I just stood there with my back facing the General Assembly. Liz dropped out of the line and stood back as each Security Council representative walked past me and shook my hand and stepped back to stand in a line behind the podium. I saw President Almont motion Liz to stand beside me. She came over to me and grabbed my hand very tightly. With her hand in mine I turned and stood behind the podium. I was really chocked up and tears were rolling down my face.

Focus; focus; focus I said to myself. I looked out over the delegates and took a big gulp of air.

"Ladies and gentleman; I thank you for your patience and your attention.

The aliens have informed me that their mission is complete and that the spacecraft of the 72nd Reconnaissance Armada are leaving the area to resume their scheduled missions."

I decided that I would take some editorial freedom with the messages I received.

"The extraterrestrials thank the human race for their cooperation. They hope that this is a new beginning for us and the start of closer ties with them."

I paused and took another gulp of air.

"The world is now free from the threat of all weapons of mass destruction. We no longer live under the cloud of nuclear meltdown. All of our oceans, seas, lakes, rivers and streams have been cleaned and decontaminated. Our atmosphere has been completely purified and is truly safe to breath; the ozone layer has been thickened and holes have been filled. Sixteen billion tons of waste, a high percentage of it toxic or hazardous, has been eliminated.

It's January 1st, the start of a new year for many of the people on this glorious planet and a new sense of humanity with goodwill for all, whenever your new year may be.

I wish us all lasting peace and harmony, for our children and our children's children.

Liz squeezed my hand very hard and out of the corner of my eye I saw her look up at the control booth and nod her head. A moment later, there was background music that slowly increased in volume until it inundated the entire hall. It was Aquarius!

I started to applaud as loud as I could and started singing the lyrics and Liz followed. The leaders of the Security Council nations began applauding behind me. Liz put her arms around me and gave me a kiss and whispered; "Happy New Year My Darling." Tears flowed down my face as the rest of the delegates stood and started singing and applauding.

www.ingramcontent.com/pod-product-compliance
Lightning Source LLC
Chambersburg PA
CBHW050904250626
47155CB00001B/92